HOW WELL THE SAILORS RUN

Jane,

This book, perhaps more than any other, reflects my deepest hopes and dreams. I am lucky to share it with you. I am honored to have your friendship, and your ear. You've taught me alot, and I am excited for your future and mine. I think that perhaps in all our lives there is a story of the Prodigal Son — redeemed by his blood. That is a story worth telling. God bless and happy writing!

[illegible signature]

ALSO BY THE AUTHOR

Warm Gold
A Season for the Blessed (2016)
Hope of Home (2016)

How Well the Sailors Run

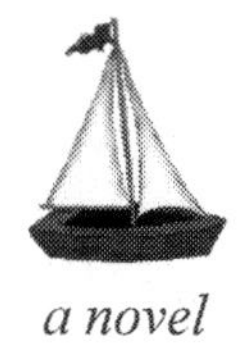

a novel

SAMUEL CRONIN

God Bless!!

Published by Samuel Cronin

www.storiedwithgrace.com
P.O. Box 605 Kuna, ID 83634

Printed by CreateSpace, an Amazon.com Company
Available from Amazon and other book stores
Available on Kindle and other devices.

Cover Design by Alyssa Cooper and Thom Hollis

ISBN-13: 978-1516810888
ISBN-10: 1516810880

This book is for my parents

CHAPTER ONE

Wade Burns with the wind in his favor gathered his strength and ran for the harbor. With sweat stinging his eyes and his lungs exhausted, he struggled onward into the heart of town—to the harbor, that lifeless haven desperate for sailors. The blood from his blisters soaked through the holes in his shoes and his legs felt like wax, yet he refused to give way to his suffering. For his soul had already set course into an unknown and dangerous storm; but with the wind behind, any hope, however troubled, seemed possible.

As his footfalls echoed against the empty cobblestone streets, he thought he saw a drape or two surreptitiously pulled back. Though the wind that morning offered ideal conditions to sail into the Pacific, all the salts had gone indoors; they refused even to go down to the harbor. It had been this way for as long as he could remember. He knew why. They were afraid. He was going to change it.

Staggering into the lifeless intersection of Shoreline and Main, he tripped on a curb and smacked a stone. The sharp pain caused him to bite his lip. Blood welled from his kneecap and tongue.

Somewhere within his Keep he was thinking of the sailors. The hope of them sailing again. Their wind. Their joy. Their treasure just beyond the warm setting sun. But at the moment, in his skin and skull burned a jealousy so consuming that it had finally defaulted to a desperate and foolish end.

He rose. Set his eyes, limped down the street lined with anchor lanterns, arrived at the wooden pier that overlooked all the vessels crowded into the intimate harbor. It was shaped in a cozy U, one side less than ninety yards or so from the other. Packed with world class sailing craft such as *Elegant Bride*, *Seventh Blessing*, *Weathering Peace*, their naked masts spired into the gull-laden sky. Heaving, he collapsed.

When he vomited nothing came up except a long rope of saliva pooling between his hands. He turned on his back, covered his face from the sun. The blood from his palms mixed into his eyes. He was breathing so hard he startled a gull from the parapet into its lonely swoop over the weathered and lifeless sea craft.

There was a time, he had heard, when these vessels were in shipshape condition. In their prime they had sported shiny brass, varnished decks, coiled lines—vessels able to stir the heart of a mariner, and he could almost picture them now embarking through the inner channel for the sea, the sun glinting off their hulls. But with refuse now covering their decks and rigging they looked like swollen boils ready to burst. But he hadn't come to look at those vessels.

He rose to a knee. At that moment the wind was so calm it barely rippled the water—a vast shift from the tremendous storm which had smothered the town and her waters for three full days. The wind lifted his black bangs and the thick hair on his arms. Rich, swarthy brine filled his nostrils. He never tired of it. Gathering his strength he stepped to the parapet and looked down to the vessel of his aim.

She was dark. And rugged. Snarled in light. Her masts towered above all the other vessels. Her long sheer stretched beyond the length of the dock. She was a maimed schooner, gorgeous and wrong, a withering mistake: the schooner *Vermillion Mourning*.

A gale had ripped her form from her journey around Cape Horn, so the myth went. She lacked segments of both standing and running rigging. Her forestays dangled. Her foremast listed. Her halyards lay twisted in knots. The kedge anchor dangled from the bow. The fallen topmast had plunged into the deck. Chainplates were stained with rust. Peeling paint revealed the heterogeneous composite of wood comprising her hull: oak, pine, birch, butternut, elm, hickory, maple, locust, fir, spruce, cedar and teak. Bird waste covered her housetops and hatch covers, deck and rigging. Her helm was missing a full third of its spokes. Her figurehead, supposedly of St. Elmo, had vanished.

Today was the day he was going to board her—the one vessel every salt in town was afraid of boarding, the one they all wanted to scuttle; once she was gone, the harbor would be safe again and they would be free to board their own vessels and sail leisurely into the ocean. But before any of that was possible, he had determined to save her by taking her to sea himself.

Terns and gulls darted overhead, stinging her deck with sharp, shadowy welts. Wade squeezed the railing like a nervous cat and he whispered, "She isn't cursed. She can't be."

He set his eyes on grasping her helm.

When Walter, the lonely proprietor of Walt's Nautical and mayor of Springwick Harbor, saw him through the enormous porthole windows of his shop, he said to Bethlem, the heavy butcher, "I hope it happens, Bethlem. I do hope it happens." He watched him rise in pain and limp down the street toward the harbor like a wounded but brave soldier.

Bethlem, in the back, looked at Walter and his strong hands holding the piñata shaped like a sailing ship, which all the sailorfolk had pitched in to make, and he dropped his eyes to his work. With a sharp hack he cut the pork. "If it does, it'll be a miracle. But hey, we survived Y2K. And what a miracle was that!" he chuckled. "And now it's 2001, the official start to the New Millennium. Anything's possible."

"I hope so. We can't afford to live without a miracle," he said, scratching his bright, expressive eyes. "This town doesn't have anything left but to hope in one."

Bethlem sighed, the strain in his heavy eyebrows. "Well, if a miracle is going to happen, I suppose it'll happen here on the coast of Oregon. I can't imagine it happening anywhere else."

Walter tried to ease his concern by expressing cheerily, "You know, Bethlem, don't worry. I feel the sun is almost over the yardarm. Don't you?"

"I'll raise a pint to that!" shouted Bethlem, chuckling resonantly.

The rest of the store crew in the back office cried out "Ole!" overhearing the conversation. The three of them were sitting around a table writing out on slips of paper places they wanted to sail to—places that existed only in their dreams. They were dropping the slips of paper in a coffee jar that they had planned to tuck away until the right time, but only if the right time ever arrived.

Walter's brow soured. He scratched his chin. "I just hope he doesn't try something foolish today." He looked at Bethlem for reassurance, but Bethlem kept his head down. "Maybe I can talk some sense into him."

"Maybe. Speak for us all."

Tucking the piñata under his arm, he left through the ringing front door, hobbled down the sloping street in pursuit of him.

When he saw Wade drooped over the railing as if he was about to tumble into the harbor, his heart softened. He had never seen him so near collapse. "You look like you crossed the whole country."

Wade lifted his head a little, acknowledging him.

"Are you all right?"

He folded his arms on the railing, rested his head.

Walter gripped the piñata, stroking its rainbow-hued crepe.

Wade grinned.

Walter stepped closer. "You ran every one, didn't you?"

Wade spit.

"That must've taken you all night."

"Ran by every cottage, bungalow and deck home in Springwick Harbor."

Walter whistled. "No wonder you look like a shipwreck."

Wade turned to face the harbor and he stretched his arms wide over the railing and leaned on them, straightening his legs until they bowed. He looked like a captain on the bridge of a ship. And he grinned away from Walter, over the harbor and fixed his ruddy eyes on the *Vermillion Mourning*.

Walter knew what he was doing. He softened his tone. "Are you sure you want to do this, son?"

Wade turned and noted the piñata. "What's that for?"

"Are you sure that you want to go aboard her?" said Walter. He regarded his sharp, angular facial bones, his curly, coal-dark hair.

Wade gathered himself and shoved his hands into the pockets of his white athletic shorts. "She isn't cursed, Walt."

"No, she's not. Of course not," he said, burning Wade with his eyes. "But why don't you let someone else go aboard her?"

"There's no one here but me." A horsefly landed on his neck. He tried to slap it but missed.

Walter opened his palm. "Why don't you come back to the store with me. Abigail's rolling the dough to make apple turnovers."

Wade's mouth watered. He scratched his neck. Turned to the schooner. Transferred his weight. Grabbed an arm. "But she's not cursed. The salts are all wrong. She's not a thorn in the harbor the way they think she is." He closed his eyes tightly, straining to make his words true. "I can go aboard her and—"

"Not our vessels? Not our dreams? None of those are poisoned?"

Wade folded his arms. Clenched his jaw. "She isn't cursed."

"Wade, listen." Walter smiled diplomatically. "Let the others do the dirty work. Let them take her to sea."

"*I* can do it!" And then his voice changed to a strained plea. "You and I both know what'll happen if the salts get to her, Walt. You *know*."

Walter remained firm. He kept his feet square.

"I'm not going to let it happen."

Walter closed his eyes and breathed in the fresh salty air. And he felt the sun. "You can't sail her by yourself."

"I don't care if I can't."

"The sea is a rough home. A dangerous home."

Wade added, "Which is why you need a good boat. And a solid crew."

"There are other vessels. Look at all the boats here just waiting to be taken into the sea." He lifted his chin at the entire harbor.

Wade took it all in. The ships. The dreams. For a moment he felt his heart flutter open wide with wild, brine-bathed life. "Maybe I could … indulge—no, borrow—a vessel and a dream…." His mind chopped along trying to blend Walter's words and his own. "Maybe this wood behind me is meant for the locker."

"Something wise. Now let the others take her and send her down."

Wade cringed. "You sound like Abner."

"I sound like a mayor." He stepped closer. "A mayor who cares for the people of this community." He held up the piñata with his strong hands. Wade studied it skeptically. Walter brought it within inches of his chest. And he whispered, "You don't yet know the strength of the community in which you live."

Wade rolled his eyes.

"This piñata, friend, is a gift from all the mariners in this community to one very special sailor."

He wiped his forearm with the heel of his hand. "For someone here in Springwick Harbor?"

"Don't worry about it. You're Second Assistant Lighthouse Keeper."

He set his teeth. "I'm not good at that piñata crap anyway."

"Come away from the schooner. She has an unhealthy thing dented inside her. Let the others take her to sea and do with her what deserves to be done."

Wade dropped his chin in thought.

Walter saw that his words were having some effect. "You're a brave man. But prove your strength some other way." He put an arm on his shoulder.

The boy nodded.

"Are we good?"

"Yeah. I guess you're right."

"If you come up to the store I'll pour you a warm cup of delicious Sailor's Nog. On me."

He smiled. "You know I can't say no Abigail's apple turnovers or Sailor's Nog."

Walter closed his eyes. The scare was over. He patted his shoulder.

They started for the mercantile.

"Wanna race?"

"I'm already spent, Walt."

They laughed together.

But behind Wade a long, shadowy line suddenly and unexpectedly looped him. He froze. Turned. Gazed again at the floating wreck. And the vessel uninhibited caused his eyes to change. The crimson veins of his eyeballs burst. He said to Walter over his shoulder, "Walt, I need to cool down.... Let me cool down first."

Walter's face darkened. He knew what Wade was going to do—knew it in his bones. And there was nothing he could do to stop him. He flattened his tone. "Then I'll see you in a few." Tucking the piñata gingerly under his arm so that it would not break, he left the pier to get as far away from the *Vermillion Mourning* as he could. He hobbled up the street the short distance to his mercantile, went inside to join Bethlem and the other employees, and tried to ignore the terrible events already falling upon Wade.

Wade turned to the *Vermillion Mourning*. Not her scuttling. Not her—not this rugged, wet mistake. Not before her time. She was not cursed. He could go aboard her. He could claim her as his own—the one vessel everyone else was afraid of.

The morning sun warmed him shining through the futtock shrouds. Controlling his breathing he descended the ramp delicately from the pain of his blisters and arrived on the floating dock on which the *Vermillion Mourning* was made fast. It moved gently. He felt the tugging of the schooner's spring lines, the desperate pleading to be free. The movement eased him. His breathing fell into rhythm.

"This is not impossible," he tried to convince himself.

His plan was to climb aboard by way of anchor. By doing so he would make a statement that the anchoring of his life lay in this vessel and not in anything else.

At eighteen he had never been anchored to anything. Especially not to his dismal post as Second Assistant to the Keeper of the Springwick Harbor Lighthouse. The job simply did not challenge him. He strayed from it constantly, avoiding duties and chores, working half-hearted under the oversight of Abner, the Keeper, his adoptive father. Wade felt like he could never please him. But that would change today. Once Abner saw how brave he was, he would be sure to let him up into the lantern. And all his frustration over his job and life purpose would take on new dimension unparalleled among the salts.

He clenched his jaw and uttered, "I know I can do this," and calculated the distance to the anchor.

The truth was, he burned to be the Keeper. He wanted more than anything else to share the lantern with Abner. But he knew Abner would never promote him, having reserved the service for his true son, Jeshurun, First Assistant. Abner had been blunt one evening, telling him, "You are not brave enough to be the Keeper. You will never be brave enough. Jeshurun is the only one who is." Night after night while true father and true son spent their most intimate hours together in the lantern, he lay in bed, burning with jealously, obsessed over what went on up in that forbidden realm.

After that he began searching for another way to prove himself. It wasn't long before his eyes fell upon the *Vermillion Mourning*. He did not like the sea or sailing, but he burned to helm a black fear. And if he helmed her in the red beam of the Lighthouse, then Abner, Jeshurun and all the sailorfolk would marvel at his courage and in turn burn with jealousy. And then, finally, Abner would promote him.

Weakening, he plopped to the dock, crawled even with the anchor, closed his eyes and breathed. Buried in the mystery of her, he believed, was the primordial life waiting for him.

A wind picked up. The dangling anchor swung gently then returned to plumb. A heavier wind blew and pushed it closer to the hull. The wind caught the crown broadside and the fluke punched into the thick wood.

"I can do this…." he repeated, searching for confidence.

Gathering what was left of his feeble strength, he tried to burst forward. But his attempt to soar off the edge of the dock faltered in midair. His eyes grew wide. And then suddenly a gust of wind blew in against him. The strength of the wind caught him off guard, filling his lungs so full he felt like a helium balloon. Before he could lay even a finger on an arm, he splashed into the cold harbor.

He couldn't swim.

CHAPTER TWO

Foundering, sinking, terror flooded him. In panic he tried to touch the hull but it was out of reach. Unable to kick his legs or make his arms work from the shock of the cold, he sank deeper, beneath the keel. The water darkened. He looked up, eyes squinting at the anchor observing his descent curiously. Never would he touch an anchor. Never would he enjoy the embrace of a thing promised to ground him. The cold water closed around him like a tomb. His lungs caved. The lack of oxygen panged him. He closed his eyes, resigning himself to his doom. This was the day he would die—without embrace of his dream. Eerily his last thought was being swept overboard the *Vermillion Mourning* during a Cape Horn gale.

A hand wrapped around his chest and he felt himself ascending. Breaking the waterline, he inhaled ravenously.

"Just relax. I've got you."

He inhaled in staccato bursts from the shock of the cold.

"It's okay, Wade. I've got you."

Recognizing the voice, he relaxed his body. They reached the dock. Wade turned to see the warm, brimming smile of the only natural son of their father Abner. It was Jeshurun. And he was clad in his typical attire: white shirt and shorts so soiled he looked like he had climbed up a chimney.

"Where did you come from?" he said, blowing water off his face.

"Off the island," said Jeshurun.

"I thought you had to refill the oil."

"I already filled it," he said, his voice balanced and sober.

They helped each other out of the water and sat on the dock, arms wrapped around knees, absorbing the flight of the gulls. After a while their breathing subsided. Sunlight warmed their skin.

"Did you hear the rumor?" said Wade, searching Jeshurun. "They're going to scuttle the *Vermillion Mourning*."

She pulled against the dock and her lines stretched taut.

"What do you think about that?" said Jeshurun in a mature tone, that of a ripening thirty-year-old.

"What do I think about it? Why destroy something as ancient as the *Vermillion Mourning*? She's earth." He searched her mystery, her soul. In her dilapidation she called him.

A fat, heavy cloud approached the sun, wishing to engulf the schooner in darkness. Wade's smooth eyes dug into Jeshurun and then pulled him around to the vessel. They regarded her together, the water lapping against her hull.

Jeshurun let himself be flooded. He knew the destiny in Wade, the current pulling him asea. He saw the wind, the spray flung against his eyes, the salt curing and strengthening his muscles. He saw the mud of his mind becoming lean and sharp as it let go of earth, washed in the waves, the clew in his jaw made hard by a stiff gust. He saw the rudder of his tongue waiting for the smashing, waiting for the will to break. Jeshurun had known this workmanship in Wade from his earliest memory and had striven to bring him into the grace.

His oily roundish face and gleaming teeth, abundant eyebrows, healthy nose and bronzed hair expressed passionate joy—a full man filled with the bounty of life. He desired to share his life with those mariners who were willing to find and live the calling of the sea. Challenging them with adventure, he encouraged each to catch grace in their sails and fear nothing. If they would ever disembark again, he would bid them joy. And when they returned, he would embrace them. Every night he rose to help guide potential salts into the harbor at their darkest hour, desiring eagerly to pass his light over their eyes until they found peaceful rest, strengthened in spirit, free from the clutches of the Northern Point. The darkness, the fear, the suffering—died in the glowing of Jeshurun and his calling as First Assistant Keeper of the Springwick Harbor Lighthouse.

"Did you know that there's a telescope on the top of Strawberry Mountain where you can look almost thirty miles into the sea?"

"What do I care about that?"

Jeshurun shrugged. "Just wanted to point that out. It could change things."

Wade shivered as the wind cooled his wet clothing.

"You can see the ships heading up to Seattle or down to San Diego or San Francisco. You can see a whole horizon."

Wade peered at the clouds.

"I wish that would interest you," he said.

"Look, all I know is that this vessel, this breath of earth, gives me life. She entices things in me I don't understand."

Jeshurun peeled off his shirt and leaned back on his hands.

"Tell me again the story of how she arrived."

"You mean the myth?"

"Depends on the mood of the weather if it's a myth."

"It is a myth. And this myth is only now whispered about, and only in light."

Wade dipped his hands into the harbor and washed them.

"No salt still alive is willing to share the witnessing of that day," said Jeshurun. "It is said that she sailed into the intimate harbor without a crew."

"That's impossible," he said in a coaxing voice.

"That's what they say."

Wade sat forward. Jeshurun scratched his thickish neck and continued.

"On that day she moved through the inner channel slowly, easily—lacking a helm, coming to rest at the dock guided somehow by an unseen hand—guided by strange, silent words no one understood. The men made her fast to the dock and then fled to the surf to bathe, scrubbing themselves with holy-stones to be rid of her charm."

Wade knew the story by heart. He gazed upon her, this living, breathing myth.

"She has remained fast to the same dock ever since. So the story goes. But Wade...." He inhaled. "The wreck off the Northern Point is more important." And he exhaled bitterly through his nose. "Another vessel ruined."

"Didn't she see the Lighthouse?"

"Of course she saw the Lighthouse. But we need a pilot boat captain to guide them in during these brutal storms...." He broke off. "Those coming in are having a difficult time trusting in the Lighthouse. But this captain now resting in the Roseway Inn—he's a different breed. Abner said he purposefully aimed for the cauldron."

Wade knew the cauldron well, having grown up on the island of Springwick Harbor, which served as the edge of a blade: immediately to the north was the murderously jagged cauldron called the Northern Point; immediately to the south was the safety of the outer water of Springwick Harbor. In recent years too many ships had suffered a dashing against the rocks exposed in the middle of the cauldron. If a boat failed even a little to heed the unmistakable red light of the Lighthouse, and veered north, it would founder in the cauldron and become, in a matter of minutes, flotsam.

"Is he mad?" said Wade.

"He wanted to sneak in. Abner said he was pretending to be a stowaway on a captainless vessel, so that no one would take note."

"I'm sorry I couldn't have been there." And he turned his eyes upon the heterogeneous timberwork of the *Vermillion Mourning*. "I'm sorry we couldn't sail aboard her to the wreck and save them."

Jeshurun studied him intensely. "The *Vermillion Mourning* isn't seaworthy. She's a death trap. Anyone who sails aboard her defies the ocean. The ocean waits to swallow her. The wicked deep is hungry for anything cursed. If you go aboard her, you'll fall in love with your own drowning."

"She's not a coffin."

"No … not yet," said Jeshurun.

Wade inhaled deeply. "She's a pretty schooner. The prettiest in the harbor." He gazed at her dangling forestays, rubbed his dark eyebrow with his slender finger. "She feels just right."

Jeshurun exhaled heavily. "Someday I'll build you a schooner."

"She would be uglier than the *Vermillion Mourning*."

"Depends on the taste of the salt, Wade. All I have to do is figure out how to float a corpse. That vessel would be a thousand sunsets prettier."

Wade narrowed his eyes at the cloud swallowing the sun, closed them to ponder deeply the want. "At night sometimes I've dreamt about this schooner—sailing aboard her, around Cape Horn … in a tremendous gale. The waves crash over the bow, and I'm at the helm, and the wind is overwhelming. Days pass as I'm fighting the Horn, yet I'm still driving her to her destination. Then suddenly we're through, and all is peaceful. I've passed my test." At this he lay on the dock and watched the clouds.

Jeshurun knew the test that was tugging on him, because it had tugged on the hearts of the landlubbers in Springwick Harbor since its settlement. "What do you mean?" he asked him, to draw out his heart.

"I don't know. But … I believe I'll pass the test." He raised his chin again to the *Vermillion Mourning*, consumed by her shape and dimension. "She drafts twelve feet, Jeshurun—the deepest in the harbor. She's one hundred and eleven feet on deck. Twenty-four feet across her beam. Double-hulled. Two hundred-fifty tons. The heaviest in the harbor. Her mainsail and spars weigh two tons. Her kedge anchor, the one I just now tried unsuccessfully to grab, weighs five hundred pounds. She's the heaviest, largest schooner in Springwick Harbor. A destination for sailors from all over the world."

They went on discussing the attraction of the *Vermillion Mourning* to those sailors thirsting for a hard strike at the sea: Against their conscience they made pilgrimages over land to see her. Sailors wanted to be as near her as they dared without touching her—as if to bravely sense her danger and then veer away before getting hurt. She repulsed the weak, drawing them closer. They hated her mangled wreck, loved her gorgeous sheer, drawing out of them their own gorgeously mangled will. Against their better judgment they felt themselves bonding with the schooner, pressed together under the weight of the clouds—a beautiful togetherness, a beautiful doom. Fearful of being drug with her into the sea, they fled from the harbor never to return.

"I feel like one day I shall sail with her to my bitter end," he said, "to Cape Horn, the Horn's bald cliff, and be dashed to pieces joining the other dead sailors who had hoped for better seas."

"You belong in the bilge for such words," said Jeshurun.

"But if you let me up into the lantern," he said in a breezy manner, "I promise I'll come to my senses."

Jeshurun stared hard at his center. "You won't have your senses after I let you up into the lantern."

Wade fell silent.

After their skin warmed and their clothing dried, Wade draped his toes over the edge and Jeshurun followed and they watched the light play off the bow. They followed the long, slender line of her caprail all the way to her stern and then back to the bow rising beautifully out of the water. Even with the disheveled bowsprit and fallen topmast, she radiated power and strength, a quaint strength that sailors once acknowledged no matter where they were in the harbor.

"She *is* pretty, Jeshurun. You have to admit it just a little."

Jeshurun smiled. "Maybe a little."

The bay water lapped against the dock and it rocked slowly. A wind, elegant and fragrant, rushed over them.

His heart hammered. "I wonder who had held her when the wave struck? What solid shape took out the spokes of her helm? A fish? A meteor? I feel sympathy for the helmsman who had held her when he suffered his last watch."

"Some sailors are pretty strong," said Jeshurun. "Some are meant to survive practically anything the sea throws at them."

Wade turned on his side to face Jeshurun. "It's my destiny to sail aboard her."

"You wouldn't make it out of the harbor. But on another vessel you could sail all the way to Hawaii."

He rolled onto his back and covered his eyes with his forearm. "What am I saying? I don't like sailing."

"You've never sailed," said Jeshurun.

"I've never been up in the lantern, either." He cut his eyes into Jeshurun.

Jeshurun breathed soberly.

"I just know I'm destined to sail aboard the *Vermillion Mourning*."

Jeshurun's tone was brotherly and matter-of-fact, and he said, "Wade, I don't think even the best of sailors are meant to survive the *Vermillion Mourning*. She'll destroy anyone who desires to board her. *Her* destiny is to destroy *you*."

"But I can … taste … her."

Jeshurun cupped his fingers together and studied the contours of his palms. He whispered to himself, "For the foolish, doom tastes a lot like love."

Wade frowned as if he had bit into a raw oyster.

Jeshurun made his hand into a fist and brought it down softly onto the dock as if trying to pound the light of what he saw into Wade. "I think you and I should sail aboard some other vessel. I'll teach you everything you'll ever want to know about the water. I'll take you into the sea and we'll discover the grace of sailing."

He ignored the suggestion, shivering in the shadowy chill. "I don't know how to sail."

Jeshurun regarded Wade: his icy cheekbones, his sharp, angular chin, the cutting shadows in his eyes. He understood fully that Wade struggled to sense the deeper reality in what he saw, fighting to connect one paradox after another, filling his mind with the treasure of his searching. He rested in the unseen, in the bounty of a fallen ship, her hidden beauty. So intensely wanting the schooner, he would do anything to bend her darkness to his dream. The *Vermillion Mourning* pulled on him like a tide, mooring him to the bottom of the ocean. Jeshurun saw his depth, the troubled movement in him, the desire to change and be changed by a sea constantly redefining her strength. The light of his eyes and the terrible glory within them fought viciously for birth. The rumbling of the wind lay just in him, just beneath his skin, searching for escape and the freedom to carry his dream over the waters.

"We'll be safe together," he said. "You won't drown."

"But if I drown, I won't get to—"

"You won't drown."

"Then maybe I'll get cold."

Jeshurun laughed. "The sea is sometimes cold. But that's where sailors are born."

Wade's stomach growled. He hadn't eaten all morning, having avoided breakfast with Abner and Jeshurun. After surviving the brutal cold, he hungered for a sandwich from Walt's Nautical.

"Then I'll take you sailing. Agreed?"

Wade nodded, and they arranged for a time the following morning to sail a pram around the outer harbor. He left Jeshurun at the dock, ascended the ramp and crossed the pier, continued along Shoreline to Main, went into Walt's Nautical, limping all the way from his exposed blisters. The grocery looked down from a corner of the street into the quaint shops that once bustled with mariners from all over the world—mariners who were longing to return to their boats.

CHAPTER THREE

Walter stood on a chair behind the counter hanging the piñata. He turned. His lips widened when he saw Wade and he gleamed with his bright, expressive eyes. "So you survived. How's my lighthouse friend?"

Wade shrugged. "You need someone to break open that sailing ship."

"I'm saving it for a special occasion," he said, controlling his voice. He tied another knot and gently tugged on the heavy rope holding it. He wiped his hands, stepped down from the chair, moved around the corner and embraced Wade. His rounded shoulders opened to him, and to those who frequented his store. His strong hands, wide girth and square jaw gave the impression of a bowler merrily rolling his way through life taking with him any and every friend he could grab. They all deserved the hope of the dream.

Wade regarded the piñata again, a mysterious weight surging through him. "What occasion?"

"I'm not really sure, Wade. Another storm is coming. I'm not sure there'll be anything to celebrate."

Wade looked around. The grocery with its cozy ambience modeled the intimate sea life of the town, packed densely around its intimate harbor. It served as a conventional food store stocking fruits and vegetables, beef and dairy, grains and wine, but was invitingly more.

Sailors salivated browsing the packed shelves of rope, ships bells, sailors' palms, barometers, chronometers, inclinometers, clocks, anchor lanterns, marlinspikes. They felt comfortable looking through the large porthole windows of the storefront, dreaming themselves bound for adventure. Four fans turned moderately, like lazy propellers, to offset the heat.

More so than any of the taverns, Walt's Nautical served as a meeting place for sailors to share stories and news from the *Conch* while grabbing Nog and a pastry on the way to their sailing craft. They discussed the weather and continued along the sunlit streets to the awakening harbor life. Inhaling the rich salty air, swabbing the dew off the rails, untying the bow lines, raising the head sails, they caught the wind that promised an unforgettable adventure into the Pacific

At least, this was the way of life for Walt's Nautical and for Springwick Harbor long ago.

Wade, Walter and everyone else knew that their robust marine community had all but dried up. Gnawing angst permeated the streets like dense fog, searching the doors and the bones for cracks. Inhabitants felt too timid to drift from their port of call, too afraid to sail anywhere.

They had forgotten a time bathed in joy when the town celebrated with the arrival of an old salt who had braved the storms of life with courage and humility, eager to share his stories over a pint at the Lantern Fish. Once rested, he was ready to sail out again into the ripping wind.

They had forgotten about those young folk who, in a moment of magical discovery, realized that they too were born to sail. In a burst of wind these fresh young sailors rushed for their vessels and cast off, longing to test their calling.

Long ago, in distant history—before Wade was alive—sailorfolk still sailed freely in and out of the inner harbor. In that age the whole town rejoiced with dreamers young or old who felt ready to take to the sea and share their knowledge with those who loved the craft like themselves. Every mariner knew they were part of a blessed community, intimate and adventurous, filled with hope, sharing the passion to live asea.

Lately, however, there hadn't been any newcomers. The treacherous bluffs of the Northern Point had been too treacherous to surpass. The Springwick Harbor Lighthouse—the once regal red light guiding and protecting sailors from the perilous bluffs—had somehow failed to show the way. Only the strength and skill of Abner brought them ashore, but without their vessels. This was considered the worst of tragedies. People would whisper to each other, *A sailor without a vessel is like a man without a dream.*

Sailors young and old had forgotten that a dream like joy was possible.

Wade picked up a ship's bell and rung it meekly. Then he toyed with a monkey's paw, hitting his palm. He picked up a bundle of seine twine and began wrapping his wrist.

Walter watched him with amusement. He believed in a new harbor. He saw that harbor in the eyes of the dormant sailors who would come sheepishly into his store, mingle at the back with Bethlem, too afraid to come forward and buy something they knew they would never use, for a vessel they were too afraid to captain or even desire. He saw in their eyes a latent strength stored up in them from all their terrifying journey under storm. That was why he had visited their lodgings and convinced them to contribute to the piñata. That piñata in his mind would bring his beloved harbor town back to life.

But that schooner. That hideous schooner. Their thorn.

Thaddeus, the lanky stock clerk, appeared from an aisle. "Did you go down to the harbor, Mr. Walter?"

"I did. There's a helm aboard her."

"*What*?"

"A helm, Thad."

"*When*?"

"After the storm."

Thaddeus said breathlessly, "That means she's ready to sail."

Bethlem laughed. He wiped his bloody apron. "But she ain't. You know as well as I no one is brave enough to take her to sea."

Abigail's olive face struggled with the fear weighing on her and she gazed through a porthole window as her body listed. It'd kill whoever went, she thought. She continued to roll without enthusiasm the dough for the turnovers.

Wade trembled. His blisters burned. He looked exhausted, defeated from his failure to board the *Vermillion Mourning*.

"I'm not sure she'll ever cleave with the sea," said Thaddeus.

Walter nodded and a pallor descended on the group.

"Well, if she don't, at least we'll have each other," said Bethlem.

The group felt a cold pressure stiffen their skin.

Walter thought to himself, What use is it to be together if we can't share our common dream? The heart of our town? The hope to be alive upon the waters and filled with grace aboard an everlasting vessel is slipping through our fingers like vapor.

He sensed that they were grasping for a desire so nebulous no one understood how to helm it. They could muster only weak and failing dreams, anything utterly untrue, all destined to end before they left sight of land. The one hope fashioned in the soul of the town—the dream destined for sea—still lacked a solid name. It lacked a keel and ribs. Nothing was shipshape. A cold hand waited to scatter it before it was launched into the water. It was a lonely time, a hungry time. A time of anger. It was a time to suffer as a dreamer and feel separated alongside those who could not communicate the unspeakable want in themselves, the hunger to sail unafraid, to be made free. Springwick Harbor was foundering in a dead dream, the worst kind of fear.

"Abner pulled a sailor from the Northern Point," he said. "A Navy captain."

"Is he all right?" shot Thaddeus. "Did the storm get him at all?"

Where's he from? thought Abigail. Is he hungry? What's he look like? Is he handsome?

Bethlem whacked a rib in two. "He's a survivor.... Right, Walt?"

The group felt cool, soothing hope returning through the window.

"I don't know. Haven't seen him. Abner took him up to the Roseway Inn to get him food and shelter. Imagine he's pretty tired."

Bethlem sorted the ribs for packaging. He lifted his robust jaw. "Is he the one?"

They all fell silent before Walter, waiting for these next most important words.

Walter folded his arms and leaned back on the checkout counter. He chewed his fingernail.

"*Walt*," said Abigail. "Bethlem asked you!"

He tore off a sliver of dead skin.

"Well what did Abner say?" she said.

"I haven't talked to him."

Wade disappeared into an aisle, wishing to veer far away from any conversation dealing with his adoptive father.

"Well, what do you think he would have said?" said Abigail.

Walter laughed.

Thaddeus stopped sweeping. He stood erect. He filled his lungs. "He's not the one, is he?"

"I don't know. I don't know if he's the sailor we've been hoping for. I don't know if he's brave enough or crazy enough to do what is needed for this community to get back on its legs."

Thaddeus's chest deflated.

Bethlem, noticing Thaddeus out of the corner of his eye, raised his voice, "But he could be, right Walter? I mean, this guy could be the one? After all, there's a helm aboard her. That's all that was left. And now it's there. So there's reason to hope."

Abigail agreed. There's a lot to be hopeful for, she thought.

Thaddeus refused to hear them.

Wade came around the end of the aisle and faced them all. "Abner didn't pull out the Navy captain from the Northern Point. The Navy captain drowned."

Thaddeus looked like a wave had swamped him.

"Are you sure about that, son?" said Walter, jaw tense.

"But he did pull out a stowaway. He's the one getting rest in the Roseway Inn."

Thaddeus shouted. "I hate the Northern Point! Why does every ship have to *sail into the Northern Point*! I'm tired of this! We need a *captain*!"

They thought of how the Northern Point loomed over their little sailing community, of her bluffs over two hundred feet in height curving in a giant U that trapped the sea, and ships, as they crashed against the rocks. They were comforted that Abner could look down into the cauldron and see the waves and the ships swirling over the rocks jutting out of the center, and rescue those in peril.

But even with his paternal guardianship, the sailorfolk knew that nowadays few mariners were brave enough to vie for the harbor, too afraid to trust that even if they were shipwrecked in the Northern Point, they'd still make it to Springwick Harbor when Abner pulled them to safety. Many were too intimidated by the daunting Point to trust in the Lighthouse. They had heard the stories of Springwick Harbor, of its peaceable freedom, but didn't believe it was worth the risk. Those who did found that whatever peril they encountered en route paled to the rest afforded them once they arrived. Once they passed into the narrow inner harbor they were safe to call it their home and sail from it to their heart's content.

Wade burned. What if *he* could be the captain? What if he could sail her all the way to kingdom come?

Walter breathed calmly through his nose. "The stowaway you're talking about, Wade, is Captain June."

Thaddeus spun.

"He didn't aim the vessel for the harbor and miss into the Northern Point. He aimed for the cauldron, because he *wanted* to smash his vessel into the rocks. Once he rigged the helm, he hid himself as a stowaway, because that's how he knew he could slip in. And he's here now. And I promise you. He *is* the one."

Thaddeus ran outside. He yelped the seagulls off the street until they flew over the harbor.

Walter laughed to himself, vigorously wiped the checkout counter. "So anyway, how's Abner? Is he tired?"

Wade rolled his tongue and said listlessly, "He's plugging away."

"That's good." He continued wiping.

"It's too bad it's happening," Wade went on. "I'm sure Abner knows what he's doing. But there's no excuse for losing a vessel to the bluffs. The Lighthouse is easy to spot." He wiped his sweaty palms on his sparkling white T-shirt with the words BORN TO RUN stenciled across the chest. He thrust a hand into a pocket of his white athletic shorts.

Bethlem laughed from the back of the store. "I don't mean to be ill-mannered, Wade, because you know that I think the world of you. But I have to ask the question. Have you ever seen the Lighthouse from the sea?"

Wade felt a flash of anger. He quickly focused it toward Walter. "No, I haven't."

Bethlem winked.

Wade angered at his adoptive father Abner for failing to competently man the Lighthouse, and at Jeshurun for his incompetency as First Assistant. He believed himself capable of doing a better job and keeping the vessels away from the Northern Point. But as Second Assistant he had not been given the opportunity to prove it.

Walter felt Wade's eyes. "I understand your frustration at your post. You have a tough assignment. You're being humbled on that Lighthouse island. That can't be easy. But listen. Jeshurun will serve as the Lighthouse Keeper. The whole community is waiting in celebration over it."

Wade shrugged at the floor and jingled the keys to the Lighthouse in his pockets. He looked around at the brass polish and cleats and the shelf of nautical books including the publication *Notice to Mariners* printed weekly. The top issue on the shelf was 24 April 1983—the same year of his birth. Such thick dust covered it that he could barely read the print.

Walter had told him stories of seasoned mariners arriving together and picking up their copy of *Mariners* and reading the high and low tides written in chalk behind the counter and striking up a conversation with Walter and Bethlem and the others. It had been a special place, a haven for joy.

He wished the camaraderie of the sailing town would return. If he couldn't become the Keeper and guide salts in, then let him take the *Vermillion Mourning* out to sea to find them. Yet he knew that if he waited patiently, one day he was sure to become the Keeper. This was his foundation, and from it he felt free to observe the town leisurely, confidently and critically.

"You should go sailing today, Wade." said Walter. He withdrew behind the counter and arranged a bin of sailor's palms.

Wade shook his head. He avoided his eyes. "No, thank you."

"You like to run."

"Yeah."

"All over these streets. All over these hills."

"Yeah."

Walter darkened his brow. He opened his palm. He voiced his passion, "Have you ever gone running asea?"

Wade picked up a porcelain replica of the Springwick Harbor Lighthouse. He didn't care about any life that one might find asea, other than the *Vermillion Mourning*. He cared about the Lighthouse. What would it be like to don the linen apron so handsomely appropriate on Jeshurun and Abner, though he had never actually seen them wear one—and polish the glass? Trim the wick? Be the one responsible to keep the lantern turning by rewinding the weights? He felt like a foreigner in town observing the curious joy of the sailors while retreating mentally to the Lighthouse where, he had convinced himself, was the only truly safe place for him and his heart. He limped to the back of the store. Abigail was kneading dough. Bethlem was hacking steak with a cleaver. Thaddeus continued stocking shelves.

When Abigail saw him approaching her, her shoulders dropped and she breathed until her chest and body relaxed. She perked up, giving him her best smile. He was the young adult in the harbor whom she wished her own sons would model. She saw something in him that she longed for them to discover in themselves. “You look like you could use a Band-Aid or two.”

“I’m fine.”

“Come in for your sandwich?” she said in a soft tone. “I’d serve you a fresh apple turnover, but they’re not ready yet.”

Wade picked through the premade sandwiches at the bottom of the refrigerated shelf. “Where’s the roast beef?”

“It’s there. Bethlem made one for you this morning.”

“I don’t see it.”

“It’s there.”

The closeness of this family who ran the grocery relaxed him. He had spent so much time here that he knew their sailing dreams. Walter’s was to sail with friends into the setting sun. Abigail, Wade’s surrogate mother, wished to sail into the sea with her boys—swore she wouldn’t leave without Wade. Bethlem’s was to recover the nautical miles he had lost while adrift on a life raft following a storm and sail away on an adventure with the hero who had rescued him: Captain West. But no one knew where he was. Thaddeus dreamt of discovering an uncharted island. And Hank's was to round up the whole gang at Walt's, take them to sea on an unsinkable vessel, and throw a barbecue in the eye of a hurricane.

These sailors had known Wade for his lifetime and they impressed him with their kindness and passion for sailing. He felt safe around them. He felt safe in Springwick Harbor. He wished somehow their dreams could come true.

"How's that Jeshurun?" said Bethlem in a husky voice.

"He's all right. He pulled me out of the water this morning."

Abigail touched her floured fingers to her cheek and gasped. "What happened?"

Wade clenched his jaw.

Bethlem chopped off a slab of meat. Abigail looked forcefully at Wade.

"Did you fall in?"

"I don't see any roast beef here."

"Did Jeshurun take you sailing?" she said.

"No. I don't ever want to go sailing with Jeshurun."

Abigail stopped kneading dough, looked scornfully at Wade's bent shape.

Thaddeus placed a can of tomato paste on the shelf. "It would be a dream job to be the Springwick Harbor Lighthouse Keeper."

Bethlem chopped off a slab of fat. "Jeshurun should be about ready to step up."

Wade rolled his eyes. Something hot and seething melted his teeth.

Hank, lean and efficient in brown clothing, burst through the back door wheeling several crates of produce. He nodded hello.

The entire store erupted in unison, "Haaaaank!"

"It's Hanky-poo," added Thaddeus.

Hank winked to Abigail and slapped Bethlem on the back.

"You're late," said Bethlem.

"I stole your hair appointment."

Bethlem rubbed his bald head with his forearm.

Thaddeus turned to Hank. "Need help?"

"Why should I?"

"You're amazingly weak for your size," said Thaddeus. "You need to bean up."

Hank wheeled the heavy cart to the refrigeration room. "And you've got a God-given gift for blindness."

Thaddeus pushed up his glasses. "I wish someday I could be as blind as you, Hank."

Bethlem laughed.

Abigail looked bashfully at Hank, who had turned red. Bethlem smiled and his thick dark creases became shadows. Wade stepped closer to them. His smooth, peach-fuzz face bridged with delight. And he placed a hand on the counter of the bakery.

"How are your boys, Abigail?"

"They're anxious," she said in passing. "They keep bugging me to go sailing but I don't have the time. They need someone to take them."

Wade picked at his fingernails and scratched his dark curly hair. "Bethlem could take them."

"With my luck?" He snorted. "I don't think we'd get out of sight of land before something drastic happened. No sir, not me." He glanced sheepishly up at Wade. "Maybe Thaddeus would take the boys. Except he doesn't know how to steer."

Thaddeus nodded. "Tried several times."

Wade sighed through his nose and swallowed, leaned his head to the side. "Jeshurun can take them. Jeshurun can do anything."

Hank came out of the refrigeration room. "Why don't you take them, Wade?"

Wade dismissed his suggestion with a facial gesture. He went back to the sandwiches and tossed one out of the way, flicked another, stabbed at a sandwich without looking at it.

"That's not the roast beef," said Bethlem.

"I don't care what it is," he said in a cross tone as he limped to the counter.

"He never eats anything other than roast beef," said Bethlem to Abigail.

"Well maybe today he's changing his colors," she whispered.

At the counter Wade dropped the sandwich before Walter.

"Those clowns in the back giving you a rough time?"

"No."

"You listen to me, Wade." He leaned over the counter. "Your life and Jeshurun's are not the same. He has his own duties, and you have yours. And your duties are not the same."

"Well what's my duty?" he said with a sharp jaw.

"You'll figure that out. But don't listen to those thoughts that tell you you've got to be just like Jeshurun. He has many talents, and you have many talents. You can't live your life drafting off his wind. You've got to discover your own wind. And listen to this." He motioned him to lean closer and they met over the counter. "There are some things you can do that your brother is not meant to do." His eyes twinkled. A dab of spit glistened on his lower lip.

"What possibly could I do that Jeshurun can't already do in his sleep?"

He charged the sandwich to Abner's account and turned for the door.

"There's more to life than the island," Walter whispered.

"But I don't want anything else."

"No?"

"No."

"That's not what I hear."

Wade froze, chin to air.

"Look, son. Springwick Harbor is home to sailors. All those boats in that harbor are the dreams of the people. You and I know this. We've talked about it many times."

Wade scratched his cheek. His jaw came open.

"But some vessels are not healthy. You know which vessel I'm talking about."

"The one I'm convinced can fly us all home."

"She doesn't belong in this harbor. And you don't belong on her. She's destined for the Abyss. Do you understand what I'm saying?"

Wade adjusted the sack in his hand without meeting Walter's eyes.

"She'll end your life. It would be better to suffer the life of an earthbound lighthouse keeper, and never share the glory of the lighted lantern, than go aboard the *Vermillion Mourning*. Do you hear me?"

Wade shivered. "No."

"Enjoy your sandwich."

He stepped for the door. He turned. "Walt," he said. "Have you ever wanted a dream so much you'd give your life for it?"

"Yes."

Wade flinched.

"And so has everyone else in Springwick Harbor. We're all dreamers, and all of us are waiting for our dreams to come true."

"My dream is to be with my father in the Lighthouse. And he's promised me it will never come true." His eyes flickered. "I don't belong here." And he stormed out of the store.

Walter looked disconsolately at the others. "We may never go."

CHAPTER FOUR

He limped across the street to a park on a small hill overlooking Main Street, sat on a bench in the shade of a large, gently blowing elm. Closing his eyes he felt the cool summer heat, the fragrant roses lining the park, the salty air, the light tickling his eyelids. Autumn approached and the leaves were beginning to flame.

The elms blew gently and the leaves smeared the grass with light and shadow. Several ducks waddled around rummaging while Wade inhaled the coastal air and searched for sun through the flickering leaves. It was good, very good, to be alive.

In the center of the park, the community had erected a memorial to lighthouse keepers along the Oregon coastline. Several had lost their lives trying to salvage shipwrecked sailors who had been dashed against bluffs like the Northern Point. The memorial featured a bronze lighthouse rising from splashing waves to a lantern room illuminated day and night by candle. Abner was alive. Jeshurun was alive. Their names had not yet been added to the statue. Would his name ever be added? Secretly he hoped that it would.

Across the park, next to Walt's Nautical, stood the community church. Its tall white steeple towered above the trees, visible to sightseers from Strawberry Mountain. This small wooden landmark was the church where sailors were eulogized after they perished. Wade visited the church often to reflect

,harge and consider his dream of serving under Abner as ιouse Keeper.

/ext to the church was the Lantern Fish where sailors sa-d thick, buttery clam chowder. Abner took Wade there :n he had learned all eighty-eight constellations. He had ver forgotten the meal nor the rich glow of the table illumi-ιted by an overhead anchor lantern. Historic photos showed ailing ships writhing against the waves, sailors heaving on ιalyards too powerful to handle alone. It was his favorite eat-ery, not knowing why. He felt lost inside. Eating, gazing, writhing over his destiny, a dream confused him, a powerful want, a mysterious grace—moving him beyond his under-standing of himself. He was certain his life had already been established. Raised by a Lighthouse Keeper on the Lighthouse island, he knew no other life, no other passion. He was des-tined to serve as apprentice under Abner and guide sailors safely to this heavenly harbor.

But the weight of a struggle pulled him, pulled his will, his bones. He struggled against the pulling of the *Vermillion Mourning* and against her heavy helm. He struggled to move his eyes away from her charm and step away into a softer ha-ven. He struggled with the wet hatred she drank from him whenever his eyes were upon her. Whenever he dined in the Lantern Fish he felt her pull and it made him sick.

Yet he felt another pulling, a keener pulling. A glory wait-ed patiently for him to sit at this table underneath the brother-hood of sailors captured in these photographs and feel the warm glow of the anchor lantern tingling his spine. He sensed belonging, deep maturity. He felt bold and at peace and so en-raptured with life that every sailor was the adventurer with whom he wanted to share the horizon. This latent passion was good, strong, healthy, full of merit, but existing just below his eyes. He wasn't conscious of it, nor was he willing to bring it to light.

He ate hungrily.

He loved this town, the history, the growth. He loved the people and their dreams. He loved the summer months when they celebrated their dreams together under a burst of fireworks. And he loved most of all the hope of one day seeing them passage safely in and out of the harbor, guided by the Springwick Harbor Lighthouse.

He flushed with shame at the thought of his drive to become the Keeper. The town bowing to him. The sailorfolk yielding their vessels to his light. His jealousy and guilt shrouded the free life that he sensed was awaiting him among the brotherhood of the town and her will.

He thought of Abner and Jeshurun. They overwhelmed him. They were so incredibly knowledgeable about the sea, lighthouses. And their bond with each other was so strong, so seamless, he burned with jealousy for that connection. He had never felt connected to anyone—not in the way of Abner and Jeshurun. Much of the time he felt alienated. Yet he felt Abner's eyes on him, studying him in a way he did not understand, in a loving way he struggled to find. His mysterious understanding bonded with his character, his identity, and it troubled him: How could Abner know something about him he did not know himself?

CHAPTER FIVE

The following morning Jeshurun took Wade sailing on a pram in the outer harbor. They passed through the inner channel and slipped into the wide outer channel, passing red nuns and green cans. Made of African mahogany known as oukume, the pram glided in the water under Jeshurun's easy rowing.

"I thought you said we weren't going asea," Wade said weakly, queasily struggling to tighten his lifejacket.

Jeshurun laughed and smiled broadly. "The outer harbor isn't the ocean—but it *is* the next best thing." And he rowed effortlessly and smoothly and added, "I've been waiting for this day for some time. All these years when I've sailed alone I've thought of sailing with you."

To starboard was the island of the Springwick Harbor Lighthouse. In all their years living together, Wade had never explored even the outer harbor. He refused even to take the skiff alone into the harbor for an errand. He was shaking now, gripping the gunwale, the thwart. "Why did you get me into this?" he said desperately.

"If you want to sail to Hawaii, you need to learn how to sail."

"I don't want to sail to Hawaii. I don't want to sail anywhere."

The choppy waters hit and the pram rocked. Wade gripped the gunwales.

Jeshurun held the transom. "Hold on. We'll be fine. But we need to step the mast."

"Do what?" said Wade, jaw tight.

"You need to hoist the sail. You put the sail up and it goes there," said Jeshurun pointing a spot in the sole of the pram foreward of amidships.

The ten foot pram carried less than one hundred square yards of sail. The mast and sail lay furled underneath the thwarts, lashed together. Wade untied the slipknots, then grabbed the mast and boom—tiny poles—and moved to the bow, inserted the mast into its slot. The sheet was nothing more than a tiny line, little more than a lanyard, used to tack the vessel. As Jeshurun placed the sail into position the wind took hold and the pram began to sail across the waters at a knot, but he had no control of the sheet. As soon as the wind caught the sail, the boom spun around to leeward. The pram slacked into the waves.

"Grab the sheet. The sheet. That line. Yes. Hold onto it. Hold—don't let go. Grab it. Now hold onto it. Make the sheet fast around that cleat," said Jeshurun.

"How do you know so much about sailing? Where's the cleat?"

Jeshurun shifted athwart and pointed to the cleat, then slid back to the stern and showed Wade how to fairlead a line to a cleat and make one figure-eight turn for control. Then they switched positions so Jeshurun could coach him.

The sail flapped loosely in the wind.

"Take up the slack," said Jeshurun.

The pram began to spin.

"You have to take up the slack or else the boat is going to lose direction. Take up the slack. Switch me places."

He moved astern. Wade moved forward.

"Like this. You keep two turns on the cleat for control; that way you can sheet in or out without worrying about losing the sail. On a pram it's not as big a deal. But on a larger vessel—"

"Like the *Vermillion Mourning,*" said Wade.

"No, not like the *Vermillion Mourning*. But if you did lose the sail … watch out."

"How would you know?" said Wade.

Jeshurun eyed him sourly. "Now look. See how the sail is slack? The wind is coming in across our stern. You have to take in just a little of the line, not much, because right now we're at a point of sail called a broad reach. If the wind were directly behind us, we would be running—running with the wind. Watch me pull up the slack. See how I alternate hands? That's how you do it if you're by yourself."

"Who taught you how to sail?"

"No one *taught* me." Jeshurun smiled round and oily. With his dirtied white shirt and shorts he looked like a miner searching for a bath; Wade in his younger years never understood how Jeshurun could get so dirty serving as First Assistant, then Abner explained that he didn't get dirty—not as First Assistant wearing the linen apron up in the lantern—but in the nighttime, while the town was sleeping, below decks fixing the engines of the dormant sailing craft so that when the time came to sail, the vessels would be ready to motor through the inner channel and out to sea. This struck awe in Wade. He didn't have the grit like Jeshurun to sully himself night after night, day after day, in vain hope. The wind caught the sail and the pram gathered speed. "See how we're moving! Look at that bow! Look at it!"

Though the pram was weighted by two large bodies, when it was fitted for only two smaller ones, the bow tickled up against the choppy waves and sped along. The small sail looked like a kite. The sides were heavy with the water, with only inches of space between the water and the gunwale. Occasionally the crest of a wave trickled over the side and spilled to the bottom of the pram.

"If you lose control of the sheet, its end could flip around like a bullwhip. It could kill whoever gets hit by it."

"That little line?"

"That little line.—Not in these winds. But if a breeze suddenly came upon us and we weren't paying attention—a weather bomb or something … watch out. We could get killed."

"Not that little line. Maybe we'd get a bruise or something. But not killed."

"*That* little line."

They sailed the pram all around the outer channel, enjoying it all to themselves. The tide pulled on their boat but Jeshurun manned the tiller and steered her about and brought her to a close haul. They beat into the wind.

"This is called beating," he said. "When the wind is coming from the bow, when you're heading in the direction of the wind, it's called beating. A close haul is as close as you can come to sailing into the wind without going into irons."

"Irons?"

"When the wind is coming right at you over the bow. Your sails are useless. You're dead in the water. It's as if you're chained, in irons. The way you sail into the wind is by tacking at angles to the direction of the wind." He noticed that they were approaching the rocks. "It's time to tack. Watch."

He adjusted the tiller and brought the little flat bow through the wind and the sail began to flap, like a loose hanky on a pole blown by a low-grade fan.

"Watch your head," he said, as the beam, nothing more than a long cane rigged to a sail, passed over the boat. They both ducked. Then the sail again caught the press of the wind. Jeshurun held on by the cleat.

"This is a starboard tack. When the wind comes across your starboard side, that's a starboard tack. Do you want to try the tiller?"

"No."

He was wet from the little spurts of spray coming over the bow.

"Try it anyway."

Wade shook his head. But when he realized Jeshurun wasn't going to let him off, he agreed. They shifted positions and Wade took hold of the tiller and Jeshurun handed him control of the sheet.

"Don't let go of that line."

A gust of wind blew over the outer harbor. The choppy water capped, caught the little pram on a slow roll to leeward.

"Lean over the starboard side. Lean over! Let—change course!"

Jeshurun hopped onto the starboard gunwale and leaned out into the water as Wade struggled to handle the tiller and maintain course.

"Tack! Wade, tack! Heave-to!"

"What's heave-to?"

"Tack! Bring the boat—we're rolling!"

Wade could do nothing except move in slow rhythm.

The boat lost control and the wind took it clear over and they splashed into the harbor. The sail and mast dipped followed by the hull, which turned upside down. Wade and Jeshurun came up after plunging all the way in.

As they turned over, Abner saw them through binoculars from the Lighthouse Island. Instantly he moved toward them in a skiff with a 50 horsepower outboard motor keeping his eyes trained on the overturned pram.

His remarkable ability to aid distressed sailors no matter the inclement weather had fostered deep respect among the community of Springwick Harbor. No storm deterred him from salvaging imperiled vessels and their crew dashed against the rocky bluffs of the Northern Point. He had dedicated himself to saving the weak, the fearful, the hopeless, the doomed. He loved his job. He believed every sailor deserved the freedom to sail without fear—the freedom to sail in grace, united in wind, vessel and helmsman following the seas together. No salt remembered when he was not the Lighthouse Keeper; everyone knew he was the rock of the harbor, and they eagerly sought him out for his favor.

Jeshurun was saying, "Are you all right?" swimming to Wade.

Wade foundered again, struggling to keep his head above the choppy water. He felt uncoordinated in his blocky lifejacket.

"Can you help me turn it over?" said Jeshurun.

Wade was struggling to breathe. He grimaced and clenched his teeth, fighting to spit out the cold salt water. "Help me," he said, wheezing, shivering.

Jeshurun let go of the pram to swim to Wade and steady him.

Abner arrived. The engine whined and slowed to an idle. The bow waves pushed into Wade and Jeshurun and against the pram and sloshed back and forth. The skiff bounced up and down.

"I saw what happened. You didn't keep the bow in line with the direction you wanted to go. The center of effort was too high."

"It was a gust of wind," said Jeshurun through the splash of waves riding over his neck.

"Come aboard. Then we'll turn over the pram."

Abner aided Wade in getting over the gunwale and into the skiff. He used his foot to boost himself over, and he fell into the bottom.

As Jeshurun tried to right the pram, salt water stung his nose.

"It was my fault," said Wade.

"It couldn't be helped," said Abner. "You did fine."

He reached over the gunwale to fish Jeshurun out of the brine. Wade helped, pulling Jeshurun's stout frame over the side. They tied a carrick bend onto the bow line of the pram and with the effort of the skiff's outboard motor, righted it. The sail sagged like a dead flag. The sea flooded over the gunwales. The oars floated away.

"That wasn't so bad, Wade," smiled Jeshurun. "You're almost an old salt."

Abner nodded, and Wade, though shivering, smiled half-hearted.

"Because I survived a wreck?"

CHAPTER SIX

Wade and Jeshurun sat close to the fire, toes exposed, wool blankets wicking the coldness of the harbor from their bodies. Full from a supper of borscht, they let their eyes glaze over the burning coals, the crackling, sizzling wood, the sparks scattering randomly onto the hearth, the escaping flames. Jeshurun's blanket was open at the front and the fire warmed his chest. His skin was smooth again.

Wade relaxed numbly with the warmth and the chills gradually passed out of his skin. He felt the soothing comfort of the blanket as in a womb. "Sorry about dragging you into the water. You saved my life … again."

Jeshurun closed his eyes, wishing in his modesty not to speak. It felt natural to let the fire itself carry on this conversation as it hissed and sparked. A brand flew near their toes as Jeshurun opened the blanket to expose more of his chest. His dishwater blond hair curled from his head like the fancywork of a bronze sculpture. The fire popped again and a spark flew next to Wade's knee. His eyes let go of the fire. He searched him. "You didn't know what you were doing. It was an accident. I'm glad we weren't in a storm."

Wade rubbed his tired eyes and absorbed the warmth created by the blanket then brought to light what had been on his mind for some time. "Did Abner ever tell you about how I was adopted?"

Evening had come and night knocked at the door. Storming rain smattered the window. The clouds felt out Jeshurun's words before he said them.

"Father rescued you with his own hands. He found you among the flotsam of a ship that had been dashed against the Northern Point. When he pulled you out of a sea chest and carried you home in his skiff, you looked at him curiously. You never cried."

"People don't rescue bilge rats."

"Well, he suffered a storm to rescue you."

"I'm sorry I can't carry more life."

Jeshurun squeezed the blanket so hard his knuckles paled. He scorned this self-abusive talk that sometimes came from Wade. He saw him and his destiny and knew that he had not yet discovered the life he was meant to live. When he would, all his being would brim.

"I've spent my life tripping just short of a rescue, Jeshurun. People don't want to bear the burden. I have plagues."

Abner, who had been washing dishes in the adjoining kitchen, stepped around the corner. Dignified and full of life, he overwhelmed the room. "No, son," he said. "You're valued not because you're a bilge rat, but because you're far less than one. Courage never works in someone more."

Wade felt this breathless truth wallop him. He tried to pool the residual weight of the words into his own understanding, impossible to hold. All he could do was cower awestruck before the father he did not understand.

Deep truth flowed from Abner's chest, from the deep barreling promise of his being. Both admiral and deckhand, sailor of learning, he understood how to guide the current in men. He knew their desire, their immense wait for the revelation of the dream. He understood humility and strength in their most devouring form—a tough jaw wrapped in words of love. The sea waited to be mastered by him, by his will—waited to submit to him just as he submitted to life. His powerful, penetrating eyes knew the loss in men, the sour loss in men, the cleansing rain at last, flushing sailors; his tongue saved them lingering on the edge of the abyss, men foundering for love. He was a beautiful man. The history of the sea aged him. It made his chest grey and in the night he absorbed those alien directions in men's eyes to make them his own. He was the Lighthouse Keeper. All his words went into illuminating the path.

He scratched his thick white stubble and his deep voice resonated in their ears and made the fire seem warmer. "Jeshurun, will you please come with me? It's time to trim the wick and replenish the oil."

Jeshurun obediently flung the blanket from his shoulders, stood and waited on Abner.

"Wade, sweep the passageway. I need you to roll up four casks."

They shut the door behind them.

He heard their steps up the iron stairwell. He buried himself in the blanket, hating it when they went up together, sharing the light together. Of all the doors he had explored on the island—the cistern, the cellar—the door leading up to the lantern was the only one forbidden to him. He would not pass through it. The terrifying, powerful fear of Abner struck him the moment he felt tempted to move toward the knob, even if he was on the far end of the island. At even the thought of going up he remembered his words: "If you go up, you will be killed." The penetrating eyes. The fearful loss of the dream.

He knew as Second Assistant he should be allowed in the lantern to polish the brass fixtures, clean the walls and floors and balconies, sweep and dust the tower stairwell. But Abner prevented him. The only duty he was in charge of was to roll the empty casks of oil from the oil storage area to the door of the frustum then sweep the passageway. He hated it. He didn't understand why Abner needed *empty* oil casks. Where were they getting the oil? Was there a well at the base of the frustum? It seemed foolish, a waste of time. He knew of a small shop south of town praised for its pure oil; he once mentioned it to Abner, who quietly told him that there was no oil more pure than the oil they were already using.

He didn't understand why he should be relegated to such lowly chores when his heart burned so uncontrollably to be in the lantern. His whole being burned like the lantern he burned to bask in. The glow consumed him, burning away his impurities. It would be glorious and satisfying to feel alive in the light—to shine on mariners and help them find the safe harbor. He knew he was that man. But Jeshurun alone had been granted special privilege to help Abner; he didn't know why, and it exhausted him. He felt like a wick coming to its end.

He longed to wear the linen apron Jeshurun and Abner wore when in the lantern, dusting the framework, trimming the wick, replenishing the oil, or so he believed. He had never seen an apron. But he knew they each wore one. At night he imagined how soft and white their aprons must be, as he burned with jealousy.

Even though they had cast him aside, he had learned the dimensions of the Lighthouse and the lantern by heart, to minute detail. The lantern stood 224 feet above mean sea level, casting a focused light 24 miles into the horizon. Its eight-sided Fresnel lens, weighing over 2,000 pounds, twelve feet high and six feet wide, was of the first order—meaning it was the largest of seven possible lens sizes. Abner's powerful torso could easily fit inside the lens, and around the outside, which was enclosed by forty-eight glass panels. And he knew more: The lantern was lighted by a unique floating lamp with five tubular wicks fitted inside each other without touching, the widest 5/16 inches in diameter. The bull's-eye magnifier and catadioptric and dioptric prisms produced a single plane of concentrated light of over 650,000 candlepower. The lens completed one revolution every four minutes and could turn continuously for two hours and twenty-four minutes by weights and pulleys before Abner needed to rewind it. Mariners knew by heart its unmistakable, unchanging, permanent red light—and in the daytime the long, slender frustum painted solid red. Wade knew all of this. But he did not know why Abner favored Jeshurun.

He brooded until he fell asleep in the living room, neglecting to sweep the passageway or roll the empty casks.

Late in the night when Abner and Jeshurun returned and saw the passageway dirty without any casks at the foot of the frustum, Abner crouched over him, shaking him awake.

"Where are the casks, son?" he said flatly.

Wade closed his eyes as if he hadn't heard. He rolled away from the cold fire and pulled the blanket to his chin, sighing.

Jeshurun hurriedly rolled the casks to the door.

"You have to keep the casks ready at all times. Do you understand?" said Abner.

"It's fine."

"It's not something to take lightly."

"It's not going to keep the Lighthouse from glow…."

His words trailed away as Abner and Jeshurun left him and hurriedly rolled several more casks. Wade continued, raising his voice over their activity.

"It's not like we're going to burn anything with them."

"This is the only job you have."

He picked at his fingernails. "I got distracted."

"I can't let you oper—"

"I know. You say that every time. I'll never operate the Lighthouse."

Wade studied the expired fire and felt the weight of Abner's cold words, his glowing face. He felt his stomach churn.

"I can't let you operate the Lighthouse, son, if you can't keep the casks on hand."

Wade pulled the blanket tighter around him and buried his chin under the folds.

"I can't let you run anything until you're ready."

Wade thrust his jaw at Jeshurun, "Why do you save the best jobs for your true son? I'll never be as smart or as gifted as him."

"Do not compare yourself to Jeshurun. Do not compare yourself to anyone. You are your own person. You have your own dream."

"What dream! I don't feel ready to have a dream!"

"Son, when you're ready, you'll own one more beautiful than the words which created it."

"Don't call me that. I'm not your son. I'm your waveson."

"I adopted you."

"I don't have a beautiful dream."

"But you won't run the Lighthouse."

"Anyone who isn't Jeshurun is not gifted enough to be your son, Abner." He raised his chin. "Is he better than me?"

Jeshurun patiently arranged the last cask. Four were enough to add to the others which together would last more than two years, he calculated. Then he took a brush and dustpan and patiently swept the passageway.

"No, son."

"*No*? Abner, I believe that's the first lie I've heard you speak. Let me write it down so we can remember." He flinched, fearing his father's icy danger.

Abner dropped his shoulders. He began to speak in a kind, gentle voice. "Do you *understand* what I'm telling you, son? You have to be there at all times, through sickness and death. Every day of your life…. It requires a sacrifice." He acknowledged his son Jeshurun whose humbled eyes focused on the candle next to the door.

Wade felt shame in the light of Jeshurun's humility. He went into his room. He lay in bed calculating what to do next, setting his eyes on the wall until it softened. He was determined to let nothing keep him from living his dream.

After the three shared dessert, Abner finished washing the dishes. Wade set his dirty pie plate on the counter next to the sink and waited. When Abner did not acknowledge him, he pushed the plate closer. "It's my dirty dish."

Abner took the plate, submerged it in soapy water. Wade watched him.

"Something on your mind?"

"I can finish if you want."

"Would you do that?"

Wade moved in, crowding Abner until he moved out of the way.

"Have at 'em."

He went to work cleaning off the plates, the bowls, the saucepan, the silverware, the glasses. When he finished he drained the sink, dried the dishes, returned them to the cupboards. He went to Abner, who was sitting in his favorite red chair, reading the *Conch*.

"I was wondering if there was anything else I could help you do this evening?"

Abner looked at him over his reading glasses. "Well, yes. If you want to chop the wood, go right ahead. But you need to stop before it gets dark. Don't hurt yourself."

Wade spent the next half hour chopping and stacking wood. He returned to Abner, who was now reading a book. Wade curled up in a blanket beside him.

"I was wondering if maybe you could allow me to roll the casks into the frustum?"

Abner set down the book and took off his glasses. He folded his leg over his other leg and looked coldly, caringly at Wade. "Serving as the Lighthouse Keeper is very, very hard, Wade. It's extremely dangerous."

Wade looked at him disapprovingly then rolled his eyes toward the fire. "Well I don't ever see you at risk. You take Jeshurun up there, and he's never at risk."

"You might want to rethink that."

"Are you afraid I'll expose you?"

Abner's eye flickered.

"I'm sorry. I didn't mean that. I know you work hard, and that it's very, very dangerous. But I was just wondering if I could move the casks in. Sometime. Maybe not tonight. But sometime."

"Son, if I let you into the frustum at all, it will be when I decide, and only when it's very, very safe to do so."

"What's the damn danger in running a stupid lighthouse?" shouted Wade. "You just replenish the oil and then trim the wick! How dangerous is that? Give me a Coleman lantern and I can show you how I've learned to trim the wick!"

"The sacrifice."

Wade searched his face.

"Selflessness."

"Of course."

"You don't understand."

He returned to his book, breathing calmly through his nostrils.

Wade's next words were sharp. He had been planning to say them for some time.

"Then I'd like you to give me my savings. I'm going away. I'm going to sea."

Abner flipped the pages of his book.

"Doesn't that alarm you?"

"Sailing's a hard life."

"Aren't you afraid I'll die?"

"I'm afraid you'll die here."

"Well who's running the Lighthouse?"

Abner fanned through the pages ignoring the question.

Wade clenched his jaw. "Because I'm adopted jetsam?"

"The sea is waiting for you."

"You salvaged me, just so I could learn that I'm nothing?" Tears formed. "It's clear you love...." He sobbed. "I'll show you that I love the Lighthouse more than you love your son." This was a hatred building in him from his earliest memory. "I don't need to be your favorite to prove myself to you."

He flung the blanket and went into his room, shutting the door. Abner eyed the casks. Jeshurun rubbed his arm. They heard him through the door sobbing in his pillow.

Abner went into his room and quietly opened the door. His words hovered in a flat whisper. "Until you become who you are meant to be, you'll never understand how much I love you. Or how deeply I moved to bring you, my adopted son, home with me."

Wade spoke with the tear-stained pillow muffling his words, "Adopted jetsam, Abner. Sounds better. More descriptive. By the way, tell Jeshurun I know what I'm doing—I can save myself. Thank you again. Please shut off the light and leave my inheritance at the door."

Abner's face looked like it had been punched in. He shut off the light, then closed the door behind him, struck with sorrow. Jeshurun alone had proven himself by carrying out his chores with alacrity and faithfulness, with sobering, powerful duty. He had never abandoned anything in his life. Wade, on the other hand, had proven only one thing: He was directionless, in irons to the life waiting before him. Later in the night he left Wade's entire inheritance at the door, just as he had requested.

Alone, Wade flooded with hatred—at Abner, at Jeshurun, at himself. He burned to be the Lighthouse Keeper. Whatever it took, he would become him, even if it meant abandoning this island and going his own way.

CHAPTER SEVEN

That night he crept through the house to the forbidden door of the frustum and opened it. Looking behind his shoulder, he studied the coals of the fire in the living room and listened to the grandfather clock slowly ticking. Without thinking he walked in.

Immediately a pungent, metallic smell struck him. He adjusted to the red lantern high above dimly illuminating the base of the frustum and the countless casks of lantern oil stacked against the walls. The cold walls made him shiver. Groping for light his hand came upon soft fabric, and he realized he had one of the aprons. He jerked it off its peg and found the first step of the stairwell, hurrying to don the gown and climb the frustum to the lantern.

Suddenly paralyzing fear struck: *It would cost him his life*.

He jerked his eyes behind him to see if either Abner or Jeshurun were awake. Before they discovered his intrusion, he crept back into the house, quietly shutting the door.

Outside he untied the skiff and rowed off the island, apron in hand. Slipping through the main channel, creeping into the narrow inner channel, he passed sloops and ketches motionless in the calm. In the cool of the night he docked the boat on the same landing as the *Vermillion Mourning*.

He sat on the dock cross-legged before the schooner that made his spine tingle. Her haunted shape pulled him, pulled on his thoughts, on the tide within him—the moon pulling on sea.

Lost in her ghostliness, charmed and searching for the truth, he filled with the passion to go aboard and discover her promise. She would take him somewhere—somewhere beyond Springwick Harbor—to find better life.

He wanted to meet the loneliness in her and find her plumb, the history of her dented keel, her dented bones. He felt her wound in him, her woodwork pulling the want of the sea in him. He felt her story fashioning strange, forceful words in his blood, the dream to find storm. Her rust rushed through his heart to change him into the helmsman who would guide her. The wind waiting for her calmed him, pushed them together into unfathomable waters.

These waters she sailed in him, and with her in him, he hoped to fill deep mysteries with poetry, with character, with suffering beauty. The *Vermillion Mourning* weathered and bled, and Wade longed to bleed in her, and believe in the strength of the seas that would never destroy the hope of sailing, the journey of craftsman and craft shedding themselves together, humbled, fully alive in their dream.

"If she sailed to Pierce, would you go?" said a voice.

Wade jerked his head so fast he lost his balance. He fell toward the water. The man seized his wrist. He steadied him.

It was dark. The moon had drifted behind heavy clouds. Wade sensed the man's tanned pate, the intense rush of eye. He was dressed in crimson silk seemingly black in the dim yellow lights of the harbor. A pewter locket in the shape of a heart dangled from a leather strap around his neck. He stared at Wade and glanced at the *Vermillion Mourning,* felt her smooth strake. Thin and olive skinned with dark eyes and bare crown, he froze Wade's lungs.

"If she's sailing to find the great Pierce, would you go?" he repeated.

"*Bannock* Pierce?" said Wade weakly, mouth falling open.

"You've heard of Bannock Pierce?"

Wade squeezed his fingers tightly.

"You know … the legend? … of Bannock Pierce? That he built this *Vermillion Mourning* to find someone worthy enough of manning his lighthouse? You've heard of him?"

Wade gazed at the man in disbelief.

"She's sailing, boy—*back* to him."

Wade whispered inaudibly, eyes lost and gaping.

The man's green eyes leveled him and he foundered. The man rubbed his slender nose. He leaned toward Wade.

"What was that you said? Are you interested in going?"

"Who are you?" said Wade, addressing his tall, lithe frame.

"My name is Dion. I'm sailing aboard the *Vermillion Mourning*. Of course … only sailors are meant to sail aboard her."

Wade swallowed hard and felt the lump in his throat. "But when is she sailing?"

"Soon. She has a helm now. She needs crew." Dion rested his hands on Wade's shoulders and whispered, "She's sailing around Cape Horn. Back around—*back* to Bannock Pierce—the greatest legend in the entire sea."

Wade muttered almost inaudibly, "But to find him is impossible. He's a myth. I shouldn't stray."

"Some things are not so impossible. The dream of sailing on the *Vermillion Mourning* is not impossible…. The dream of sailing around Cape Horn is not impossible. The dream of finding … the Hostel Lighthouse … is not impossible."

The rims of Wade's ears tingled. "You mean, the Hostel *Sound* Lighthouse?"

Dion walked behind him and rested his hands on his shoulders. "The dream of becoming the Lighthouse Keeper is not impossible."

Wade had heard the legend of the Hostel Sound Lighthouse. "You mean the one on Cape Race?"

"It's nothing. It's not very deep. You wouldn't appreciate it."

Wade sat up. He said again hurriedly, "The one on Cape Race?"

Dion sat beside him quickly. "Yes, the very one. The *only* one on Cape Race. Long ago, the lighthouse provided guidance for ships lost and searching for solace in Hostel Sound, that they would find the mythical fjord and sail in. She's abandoned now, but Bannock Pierce is looking for someone to revive her, to bring any and every sailor back to her keeping."

"He's a myth."

"He's a myth, but a myth believed by those born asea."

"But I'm not … born … of the sea."

Dion wrapped his arm around him. He pulled on his necklace, shaped like a heart, that seemed to pull his head down as if it were an anchor searching for the bottom. "You're not much of anything, are you, Wade?" he said. "You're adopted jetsam. How dishonorable is that?"

Wade dropped his chin.

"I don't mean to chide. Our destiny pulls us out of ugliness into becoming the lights we are meant to be. I am here to tell you there is a place in this world to make you into what you've always wanted to become—the Lighthouse Keeper."

Wade's ears tingled again. "I fear Abner wouldn't let me … go."

"Well, he may disagree about your passion to become the Lighthouse Keeper, but he would not argue against your passion to become a sailor. Am I right?"

Wade paused, afraid of nodding in agreement.

"He *wants* you to become a sailor—you can sense that, can't you?"

Terrified, Wade held his head still, watched the water lap against the hull.

"So come aboard the *Vermillion Mourning* and sail. Wherever she takes you, is where you're destined to go. And if you end up at the Hostel Sound Lighthouse, it was meant to be. If not, better things are ahead."

"They're not like that. They wouldn't want me to sail for something like that."

Dion's nose wrinkled. "It's dangerous, isn't it?"

"Yeah. I wouldn't survive."

"Wade," he said, "I'm not asking you to leave your father and brother. They love you."

Wade looked at him, and the eyes rushed in.

"I'm asking you to become heavy. And dark, and .... very bright."

The powerful stroking of the eyes. The body flooding with strength. The finality of death.

"The fear of foundering in a dead dream is the worst kind of fear, Wade. You don't want your dream of becoming the Lighthouse Keeper to die. You don't want that fear. It's worth your life, if you love Bannock Pierce."

Wade searched the heaviness in him. "I ... *love* him?"

"Of course you do. You're born of the sea."

Wade smiled sheepishly, inwardly. Dion patted him on the neck.

"So sail aboard his *Vermillion Mourning*. Go to him. Give your life for him. Sense now the beacon you are to become."

"Have you seen him?"

Dion cupped his bald pate and with the other cupped Wade's knee. "Have you heard the story behind Bannock Pierce? Behind his *Vermillion Mourning*?"

Wade drew inward into his own dream, the glory of finding Bannock Pierce who, he supposed, knew him best, and loved him and understood him and cared for him and believed in him. His dream was to find the keeper of his dream, and discover the freedom of light. "I've heard things."

"You and I both know that the things that go on in Hostel Sound are wrong."

"Yes."

"You don't have to go *in*to Hostel Sound. You never have to go there. But it is possible to be the Lighthouse Keeper, free from the guilt of the Sound. Your freedom would be simply to maintain the light, and let each man choose for himself what he wants to do."

Wade screwed his face with the reasoning. "That ... sounds fair."

"Then listen to the promise of your destiny. This is the story of the *Vermillion Mourning*."

CHAPTER EIGHT

This is the story of the *Vermillion Mourning* as told to Wade by Dion:

Long ago in darkness and storm Bannock Pierce waded through surf to gather the flotsam of shipwrecked vessels. In rain and howling wind he forced the scrappy timber together upon the cold rocks of the Hostel Sound Lighthouse. As he labored through storm, ship after ship fell prey to the bent black light. It promised them unfettered desires. If they made it through the jagged fjord, they were free to roam Hostel Sound any way they wished, without penalty. Men became strange explorers of silent water. Wishes became real. Loose desires changed hearts into gold. But once they entered, they never sailed again. These became the vanished—sailors whose names found their way on the monuments of those lost asea.

While the Sound filled with the shipwrecked, Bannock Pierce rove the *Vermillion Mourning* with hemp, raised her canvas, launched her from the rocks. On a violent day on Cape Race, she entered into the ocean to round Cape Horn to seek the sailor destined to serve as the permanent keeper of the lighthouse.

When she reached the doldrums, the oppressive calm smothered her. Bannock Pierce ordered the men to take up the oars of the skiff and row the schooner toward the Horn. For over three weeks they lingered, struggling in the flat and stagnant sea. On the morning of their twenty-second day he awoke to discover a handful of men missing, along with the missing skiff and oars.

The wind grew increasingly fierce in the Roaring Forties and more so in the Furious Fifties. The crew feared the worse and prepared to suffer the fate of those who had abandoned them. But as she neared the Horn the wind shifted, blowing from an easterly direction, pushing them favorably along. Bannock Pierce ordered all the sails up, including the topsail. At fourteen knots they passed without harm through the Strait of Le Maire. The oldest salts went below for needed rest. Just then the bow watch spotted the Horn broad on the starboard bow. Her jagged, rocky form dominated the seascape. The men gazed in disbelief, wondering if they were lucky enough to make it around, or if they were doomed to be dashed to pieces against her, or be cast overboard by a rogue wave and drowned.

The wind stopped. The flag fouled around the masthead. The flock of albatross following them landed clumsily in the water. Dark clouds swirled. The first mate checked the barometer; it was dropping rapidly. They readied to abandon the vessel for the safety of the Horn.

Suddenly wind howled through her shrouds, fraying wire, increasing to fifty knots. The wind blasted through the mainsail. The schooner was pushed backward. A man hurriedly donned his sou'wester and went aloft clinging the ratboards, holding a fid and extra wire for splicing. He was blown into the sea. Waves splashed across the deck, crashing against the bulwark, spitting out the scuppers. The waves rushing across the deck created an undertow, gripping the sailors by their ankles and pulling them overboard. They stretched for the Horn, but to no avail.

The *Vermillion Mourning* whipped around like a toothpick. She rolled. Her topmast broke free. It smashed through the deck. The durable storm sails shredded like cotton. Water smashed the helm.

When she sailed into Springwick Harbor, no one was on deck. The helm was missing. Now powered by other means, she crept into the inner channel as if a ghost had her by gossamer fingers. She moved quietly slowly, gathering eyes. The salts of the town collected along the harbor and watched in disbelief as she came to rest at the end of a dock. Fearful men stepped aboard and grabbed her lines to make her fast to the dock so that she wouldn't crash into any of the other vessels. They searched the saloon and captain's quarters, the holds and forecastle for crew, but her twenty-two experienced sailors had vanished. The vessel was empty.

The mystery of her sail proved too baffling for the salts of the town. The men retreated to the dock and left her as she was, never to return. And so she sat, made fast, year after year gathering refuse from the swarm of seagulls making her their home. Over time the flotsam she was made from became the mournful expression sailors poured themselves into—to survive on the plaintive sorrow beneath them. She seemed burdened by her inexpressible loss, the loss of her crew, her glory—the loss of the dream she had hoped to become.

CHAPTER NINE

Dion turned from the *Vermillion Mourning*. "If you sail aboard, she'll take you to Bannock Pierce—to the Hostel Sound Lighthouse."

"That's not wise," said Wade.

"Oh it isn't wise. But it's light. And what matters most to you?"

Wade shook his head. The moon glowed upon the water, glinting in his eyes.

"I don't think I want to shine."

"No, son. Not for you. But for others. If you become the keeper, you'll shine a light others will fall in love with. They'll thank you for your service, because you'll give them what they want most—a beacon guiding them to rest."

The moon pulled. He quivered.

"It's not a good idea. The Hostel Sound Lighthouse doesn't exist."

Dion opened his jaw.

"Look at this *Vermillion Mourning*. Does she not exist?"

"No, she doesn't. My eyes are fooling me." She was a mirage, he thought. He had never been aboard her.

"Touch her," said Dion patiently. "Decide for yourself."

His heart beat hard. His mouth watered.

"Go on," said Dion, opening his palm. "It's a simple, very simple touch."

Wade trembled. He rose. Legs weak, heart pounding in his chest and throat, he stretched to touch the caprail, but pulled back. The end was coming. His body could not take the force of his heart, not this pounding, this intense pounding.

"Touch it, Wade. Feel the wood."

His heart beat harder. His lungs strained. He extended his hand toward the caprail. He pulled back again.

"Dream, Wade. Touch the *Vermillion Mourning*."

Wade felt a rush. His heart readied to burst. Suddenly he touched the caprail. Intense tingling coursed down the back of his neck heating and chilling his spine.

Dion laughed quietly. "The *Vermillion Mourning* is real. And so is Bannock Pierce. And she's sailing to him, to the Hostel Sound Lighthouse. Now go aboard her. Find what you've always wanted to find—that she is your mate."

Trembling fiercely he looked fearfully at Dion. "Aren't you sure she's all right?"

"She's safe, son. She's even better than a coffin."

Wade swallowed dryly, his throat sticking. His hand shook violently at Dion who nudged him toward the moon and the moonlit *Vermillion Mourning*.

"It's okay. It's a good deck. You're not going to fall through."

Wade brought his shaking fingers over his face and covered his eyes and inhaled his palms. The breath, trapped in the space, warmed his nose and cheeks. His heart eased its pounding. He breathed deeper. He looked at the schooner again from behind the cage of his fingers, and Dion was smiling.

"She's a beautiful ship. You'll love her."

Wade moved to the edge of the dock and placed both hands on the caprail and his heart pounded and he gazed wildly at the moon now clear from the dark clouds seeming to pound at the same intensity as his heart. Closing his eyes, holding his breath, he spanned the water and stepped aboard.

Instant terror rushed him. He collapsed on the splintery deck bruising his hip. The large mainmast spanning almost a hundred feet above him spun and teetered, ready at any moment to fall. The schooner overwhelmed him, suffering her mournful loss through him. Near hysteria, he blinked and tried to focus on the shadows of the splinters made long by the moonlight. Dion was laughing mildly from the safety of the dock. Wade's palms felt pasty, his lungs weak. He struggled to breathe. He struggled to recall any life outside her—that, now aboard, he had become the intense expression of her blood. She climbed into him all at once and weakened his lungs and wanted him, the moving of herself in him, the joy of his roominess, his suffering.

He vomited. Heaving the sickness of her beauty, he felt her pungent history in his mouth. Laying his head on the deck he drug his fingers lightly over the splintery curls sticking into the wind like erect grass. The splinters tickled the pads of his fingers and he closed his eyes and felt the strength of them, the Horn in them—their struggle to be sound earth surviving asea. The crew had perished but the schooner was waiting for him to become her helmsman.

No sane sailor would dare grip the naked spindle on which the helm had once turned. Of course not. But maybe he possessed some uncommon sense of the sea that might guide her in her duress, that they would together go into their doom, pleasurably fearful of the ocean, the storms, the vermillion mornings signaling not life, but the hope of a beautiful, crushing death.

He worried she understood him, that she knew his loss. His loss was not anything in his past, nor any wrong end waiting for him in his future—but the painful truth of a life born into suffering and agony, mourning so real, so substantial, that the only way to live through it would be to become it, and be blissfully destroyed. The *Vermillion Mourning* understood all of such in him, and wanted more.

She wanted him in his essence to remember the anguish of her character, her poorness expressed by the sad lines struggling to maintain the integrity of her vessel. He knew at once she held the strange beauty of himself within her, the twisted ruthlessness of weather, the shrieking tenor climbing over him, the wind, the horrible flashing earth casting destruction at every vermillion sunrise, the promised undoing of a boat rich in poetry, in mornings, in the wait for the end. The rush pressed him into the deck, burying him, rocking him down. This schooner was the life he feared, the one he had been hoping for.

He felt odd—at ease, but fearfully settled—a sense he belonged to her doom. But doom hungry? Did he need a good doom to make his life whole? She seemed more to him than just doom. A health lay hidden in her, a pocket of hope buried perhaps in her false keel or between the planks of her double hull. A rich awareness. A fearlessness, maybe. An energy. It was a command of the horizon few sailors ever saw. Maybe a fortune? He saw her soul, and believed in her, the proof of her history visible in the thick rust on her chain plates and turnbuckles, making his tongue shiver. He understood her—the deteriorating, powdery weakness. Her suffering. Her loss.

Wade Burns knew the *Vermillion Mourning* understood him in his deepness, too—the vessel he wanted at the cost of his life. Soon he would deepen in her hold, and rush the seas in her Keep. But not now, not before he worked strangely through his own poetry, searching for the wreck in love with the wreck. It was all too much.

Weak and exhausted, he closed his eyes.

Sometime later he awoke. Dion was gone. He gazed at the stars on the eastern horizon. The setting moon pulled their light toward her and it seemed the whole heavens were in tow. He felt sick to his stomach, easy and strange. His eyes rose to the moon.

With as much strength as he could muster he used the fife rail to pull himself up. Moving aft he retreated into the dim saloon. Five tables with dust lined the port and starboard sides. Five brass lanterns, one above each table, hung without light. Boards sealed the skylights. Searching for a bed, he opened the door of the captain's quarters and went in.

A small porthole spread light over a bunk, desk, cubbyhole and two bookshelves. He lay on the bed, his stomach in knots, eyeing the bed for loose clues of Bannock Pierce. Someone surely would have looted the room by now. A few pencils lay underneath the mattress. Two sailing magazines. A whistle. In the cubbyhole, a sextant. A few rolled charts on the desk, nothing underneath. One chart of Springwick Harbor and the approaches to Springwick Harbor, opened and pinned by weights. On the chart—a pencil, dividers and parallel rulers. Thick dust covered everything, without press of fingerprints. Only dust crawling through the air proved he disturbed the room. So he must have abandoned his quarters when the *Vermillion Mourning* arrived in Springwick Harbor? A compass lay on the chart and it worked. He lifted a heavy book off the shelf, by Bowditch. He opened the book. In the seam, behind the cover but before the title page, he found a blank postcard. A black and white picture of a dry, grassy area and in the distance, the lighthouse on Cape Race. He trembled. He hurriedly returned Bowditch and slid the postcard into the pocket of his shorts. As he closed the door behind him, a curious thought struck him: the bed which he had just now sat upon was free from the layer of dust blanketing the rest of the quarters.

He ascended the companionway, thinking to himself, What else was there to do but sail away from the island, forever? Yet he despised the nautical spirit brooding within him. He was convinced more than ever that he was destined to be the Lighthouse Keeper. Safe from the elements, safe from wreckage. Safe from the cold, safe from storm. Safe from death. The Keeper provided guidance to those troubled and frightened asea—those in danger of becoming flotsam themselves.

CHAPTER TEN

Tobiah, the Master Shipbuilder of Springwick Harbor, rammed oakum between the planks of the forty-two foot schooner. The mallet and caulking iron felt heavy and balanced in his hands and he pounded the oakum into the seams using a modest amount so the planks wouldn't spring. He loved the smell and feel of the oakum, the loose strands of hemp rope soaked in pine tar to create a seal, the musty nautical smell on his hands, the proof of a laboring. When he finished with the port hull he set the mallet and iron on a stump and drank ice water thirstily, admiring his work. He felt the smooth carvel hull and the solid keel and continued with the caulking. The chiseling and the sanding, the building with his own hands from the keel, the shaping, the launching—these he loved.

The oakum and the labor and the promised adventure of the schooner filled the morning and made the air sweeter. Not long from now she would be given a name and then carried into the horizon to become the beautiful expression of a dream. She longed to be solid and seaworthy and he imagined what would be Wade's expression when he laid eyes on his finished birthday present. The dream was almost complete and when finished it would sail with the people in grace and joy.

The hills released the sun, lifting the dew. A few silver maples lining the shipyard rustled in the breeze. Gulls cried over the bare masts and stays down in the harbor. The water pooled against hulls, waited as the light stirred the mysterious green depths. Robins chirped in the branches above him and it felt as though they were singing the harbor into life. The fragrant morning promised to be a good day of labor. He studied the rainbow of colors reflected in the densely populated water. But one thing was missing.

The sailors. Not one sailor had come down to his vessel that morning. It had been this way for many days, for many uncharted months, for years. It was as if the whole community of Springwick Harbor was foundering in the doldrums, stagnant, festering. Soon tempers would flare and then someone would get eaten, which would not be good for the sea legs. The town needed freedom to enjoy the life given them, the calling rooted in their bones. From his shipyard on the hill at the southern bend of the harbor it felt like he had all the boats to himself. He didn't like it.

He longed for Wade to find adventure. He wanted him to hammer his adventures into this schooner. His deep, mysterious love for the boy consumed him night and day, this Master Shipbuilder, this giver of the dream. He longed to see Wade's past chiseled away and a new sailor launched into the awareness of the sea. The beauty of the death of a landlocked fool promises life, regeneration, horizon, hope. Tobiah had spent years crafting this vessel with the hope that Wade would embrace its identity.

As he continued with the work a shape appeared in the corner of his eye. He turned. The tawny, eager Wade Burns stood breathless before him. He had changed into brown cargo shorts, and along with his white T-shirt and running shoes, he looked somewhat like a deckhand. Did he know this about himself?

"Have you been running?"

"Yeah. Just for a little dash or so. Burning off steam. I'd go longer, but my blisters kind of hurt."

He looked into the boy. Saw the pulling of the sea in him. He felt the embrace waiting for him: A man held by grace is free to be himself, he thought.

Tobiah's dream was the boy sailing on a schooner made just for him—contoured just for his hands. He dreamt for him a fast and strong schooner, potent in wind. This schooner he was building for Wade was special, too special to be christened with a common name.

He looked into him, the deep well leaking into his veins: His blood would not be hidden from himself nor the community much longer. He studied his heart and the encompassing shadows. What might happen if he exposed his heart and brought to light his hot darkness? He studied his anger, wrath, greed, jealousy and his burning humanity—and sighed, resonantly. He studied his loss, vanity and hurt. The schooner he was building forgave the enemy he was fast becoming. He saw more. He saw the gift. The grace. The goodness. The humbled change awaiting him. He saw the courage. The fortitude. The strength. The faith and trust. The hope to believe in the best end. The love that outlasts. He saw grace meted to him, deep grace. And he saw in him the goodness of life, and it was beautiful, and he labored to build him a schooner.

Tobiah sensed that someday Wade would become the epitome of loss, completely shipwrecked. But from his brief foundering as flotsam he would be made new. As Master Shipbuilder he looked into Wade's bones that had never been asea and were still ripe to be tested, into the looming death awaiting them, and knew their lifespan would outlast his peril. Those bones knew something about Wade his mind didn't know: A mariner didn't need to harbor vast holds of learned willpower to force life to become something erroneously wanted—he needed simply to cast off and let a greater humanity carry him away.

Tobiah said in his resonant voice, "Are you thirsty, Wade?" and scratched his golden beard and dirty mane, tipped his head, lowered his shiny lips. In flannel and overalls, he looked like a mountain man bewildered by land, wild for the sea.

Wade pawed his tawny cheeks, brilliantly in contrast with his gleaming teeth and considered that he hadn't had refreshment in more than a night—not since he had left the Lighthouse. He studied Tobiah and his scraggly physiognomy, his mystery, wondering how deep his relationship was with Abner and Jeshurun. All three knew each other inseparably well, but Wade felt more comfortable around Tobiah. "Yes, I'm thirsty."

Tobiah poured lemonade and handed the glass to him and they absorbed the unfinished will of the boat before them, her mystery and her life.

"It's a nice boat," said Wade.

"Yes."

Wade picked at the stump he sat on. "You make nice boats."

Tobiah sipped. "Thank you."

"Real nice."

Tobiah studied the smooth carvel hull. "Want to help finish it?"

"... No thank you."

Tobiah squinted at the sun through the clouds. "The clouds look like castles."

"Yeah." Wade picked at the stump.

"You're sweating."

"Yeah, I'm sweating hard."

"You sweat hard when you run."

"Yeah." Wade lifted the corner of his mouth.

"Sure you don't want to help?"

He sighed. "Yeah. I'm sure," then stole secretly at the boat.

"You usually do."

"Not today."

Tobiah stirred the ice in his long, slender glass. "Probably better if you get back to the Lighthouse."

Wade drank and settled and after a long silence tested the air. "… I want to get away from the Lighthouse."

"Don't you get along with Abner and Jeshurun most of the time?"

Wade crinkled his nose. "Well, yeah."

"Don't you want to stay and help?"

"I don't mean to sound cruel, Tobiah, but I feel sort of ... bound up by this place."

Tobiah laughed heartily.

Wade glared at him. "Why are you laughing?"

Tobiah laughed harder then slurped from his lemonade. He pawed the dripping lemonade off his beard and laughed.

"It's not funny. I'm going away."

Tobiah opened his posture, rolled up his faded red and black flannel sleeve, scratched his powerful forearm. "Where will you go?"

"I want to go to your house," said Wade.

Tobiah whistled, his wide lips glistening.

"I want to go to Oklahoma."

They studied each other seriously. Then they burst into laughter. It was a joke between them that if things had gotten really bad in Springwick Harbor—well, then, at least it wasn't Oklahoma.

Wade studied the harbor. Terns overhead searched for the sea. "I'm never going back to the Lighthouse."

Tobiah scratched his beard that was flowing from his cheeks like snow. "That's a big statement."

"Well…" He snorted to himself. "It's not so much the job there, the duties you know? It's not Abner—who treats me unfairly, or Jeshurun—who gets to do everything I don't get to do. It's none of that." He inhaled and sighed. "There's something burning in me, Tobiah. I feel something. Something's been given to me and I have to find out where it leads."

Tobiah picked up the caulking iron and felt the heavy tool in his fingers. "That sounds good. So where do you want to go?"

"Somewhere east of Oklahoma."

Tobiah felt the handle and the tool and dug at the ground. "That's a hard place."

"No it isn't. I don't care. I'm tired of Abner and Jeshurun having all day to goof around. *I* goof around. And I'm good at it. But they shouldn't."

"You do goof around."

"I know. It just rolls off my fingers like it's meant to."

Tobiah lowered his voice a key. "I don't think they goof around."

"In the daytime they do."

"What do they do then?"

"You know what they do. Jeshurun goes on long runs. Abner scrapbooks."

Tobiah gasped.

"It's embarrassing."

"About dolphins?"

"Tobiah, It's not funny."

"Why would Jeshurun ever want to run anywhere? He has everything he needs in Springwick Harbor."

"He takes me sometimes. I can't keep up with him. Every time I've gone I've failed to go where he goes. I'm defeated, cowering back to the island. I don't know where he goes. Then I watch Abner scrapbook about boats. The weird thing is—these boats don't exist. It's all in his imagination."

"That *is* weird."

"It's one hundred percent goofy. I can't handle goofy. I'm not built for it."

"Goofy is dangerous."

"I was thinking about something somewhere else."

"Now Wade. You and I both know the Springwick Harbor Lighthouse is the best gig in the Northwest. It doesn't get any sweeter than right here. You're lucky to be Second Assistant to the Keeper."

"It doesn't mean anything."

Tobiah studied him compassionately. "It does, son. It means a lot."

"Because I'll find proof Abner isn't the Keeper everyone thinks he is? Proof of why all those ships are crashing into the Northern Point?"

Tobiah took a slurping drink. Lemonade dribbled from the corners of his mouth.

Wade went on. "There's news of a sailing—a trip around Cape Horn, to take the *Vermillion Mourning* back to Bannock Pierce, the greatest Lighthouse Keeper. He's going to make me the Lighthouse Keeper alongside him. Surely you've heard of him."

Tobiah shut his eyes, clamped his mouth. Breathed. "The greatest Lighthouse Keeper is Abner.... Ask me and I'll tell you. Ask a sailor. Ask a keeper."

"I wish I could be in his arms right now. He's the one who'd teach me how."

Tobiah crushed a cube of ice. "In every imaginable moment he thinks of sailors and their needs, paying the highest price to bring them light. There is no one as dedicated to his job."

Wade sneered. "But he leaves me in the dark."

Tobiah gathered oakum for another seam. "He's the only father you have. He risked his life to pull you from the wreckage. He loves you at the cost of his own life. Would you repay him by scorning his favor?"

Wade drooped his head, scratched his knee.

Tobiah continued. "Is that not unfavorable? Is that not jeopardizing, in a way, his favor for you? I promise you, he never risked his own life amidst storm to save his only son Jeshurun. And yet you think he loves you less?"

Wade stared at the oakum in Tobiah's hand. A tern soared overhead. "Whatever Abner did for me then, he's not doing for me now. Bannock Pierce is the greatest Lighthouse Keeper. I'm taking a little journey."

"I was there when Abner pulled you out of the shipwreck. I sponsored your baptism right there—below the Northern Point. I've cared for you your entire life. Do not doubt the loyalty of the men who saved you."

Wade slapped the stump. "You gave your life for me so now I'm giving my life for another." He rose from the oak block. "I'm crewing aboard the *Vermillion Mourning*. She's sailing for Cape Race. Come with me if you're brave."

Tobiah exhaled. Swirled his lemonade. The ice chinked against the glass.

Wade clasped his hands above his head and stretched with a gleaming smile. He closed his eyes and listened to the swishing leaves and smelled the fresh sea breeze and the oily posts of the dock. He felt the sunlight slanting through the maples.

"You're destined for a bath. In a heavy tub."

"I hope so."

CHAPTER ELEVEN

A storm rolled in with heavy rain. Lightning cracked the trunk of an oak and a heavy branch fell, smashing the ground. Thunder crashed against roofs and masts. Wind stripped leaves from branches and blew cherry trees from their roots. As one of the trees fell, Wade thought he saw his soul written in the scattering twigs.

The wind ebbed, then calmed, then in the distance over the ocean a heavy slate of cloud moved to the south as wind flicked water. The heavy breeze scattered the leaves. Thunder rumbled on the grass.

Unwilling to return to the island, Wade remained onshore seeking cover in the maple and pine of the park. He sat against a large trunk, hands on knees, in view of the grass rolling to harbor's edge and the *Vermillion Mourning* soaking in the rain.

He was penniless, viciously hungry, weak.

Three weeks ago while he was exploring the forest inland of the harbor, he came across a pile of bones covered in rags. He reached down to take one to use it as a walking stick. Suddenly eyes scrolled upward at him. It was a man. He was alive! He cupped his palms at him, asking for food. Wade fell back over an exposed root. Hyperventilating, he gave him all his inheritance. Then he ran away, afraid that he had just survived the only living corpse of Hostel Sound.

In the interim, he had scrounged for food in trash cans and dumpsters, eating bread crusts, shells of shrimp, bruised bananas.

The rain dripped from the leaves around him. He shivered madly, his white BORN TO RUN T-shirt and brown shorts soaked with water. The rain was cool. Lightning flashed in the distance over the eastern hills and with each flash the boats in the harbor lit up. Then the thunder rolled over the harbor, and the schooners resonated.

She loomed, indefinable, oil and seaweed clinging to her hull.

"She's sailing soon," said a voice from behind.

Wade jumped. Eyes wild.

Dion appeared out of the forest.

"Don't worry. She's your schooner."

An obtuse boat. The entity of a once great ship. A vessel reduced to imaginary. From weathering her name had all but been rubbed out. What lay in the harbor was junk, a mass of scrapwood so ugly not even the harbormaster looked at it without feeling queasy.

A sharpness radiated from Dion, from his brown skin and shiny pate. And from his sharpness a stronger, more intense heat radiated from his eyes—painful strength striking at anything. He focused on Wade, and Wade was afraid.

He gulped. The heavy lump in his throat felt painful.

"In about a week she's sailing for the Horn."

Wade's limbs felt weak from the pummeling rain. "Are they taking passengers?"

"No," said Dion, fingering his glittering heart-shaped necklace. "Just crew."

"Maybe I'll crew."

"Think, just to be sure. You'd be risking your life. To sail into the most dangerous sailing grounds in the world, with seventy knot winds, or higher? Winds driving you into the rocks, or catching you broadside and sending you down? You may not come back."

"I don't want to come back."

Dion revealed his teeth. "She'd love it if you did."

Wade shook his head furiously. "No, I can't. I'm not normal. She'd ruin me."

"Some vessels are powerful enough to ruin a sailor. Some vessels create new life for a sailor. Either way, you'll be destroyed. That's the beauty of falling in love with a boat."

"I don't know what my heart looks like, Dion."

He patted him on the shoulder. "She's your heart. She's just the schooner for you. She's the promise of your ruination. Go sail aboard her. Go find yourself. You weren't meant to last, son. No sailor lasts if he's honest."

"I probably wouldn't last around the Horn."

"No. You wouldn't. You wouldn't ever last aboard the *Vermillion Mourning*. But you will find death. And death for a sailor is sweet because he becomes one with the sea."

"I don't know what I want, to be honest."

"Then search for truth where no truth exists. You're not full of hate. You're not like those other sailors, Wade. Your heart is good. You want to do good with being the Lighthouse Keeper." He nodded to the *Vermillion Mourning*. "She's the way to get there. Go aboard her on her sail and learn how to help others."

"You think so? You think I can do good aboard her?"

"The *Vermillion Mourning* was created to help sailors like yourself discover who they are. Forget her myth. She'll get you through."

Wade's brown eyes were wide against the schooner, searching her, searching himself within her. He breathed passionately.

"Maybe I don't want to be good."

"You're a sailor. Sailors feel lucky whether they're good or bad."

"I don't feel lucky."

Dion laughed.

"I don't feel lucky at all."

Dion laughed deeply, resonantly. "It doesn't matter what you feel. You're a sailor. You were born for the sea. Let the *Vermillion Mourning* decide for herself how lucky you are."

He vanished into the woods.

Late in the night Wade succumbed to sleep, the sonorous rain deepening his slumber. When the sun arose, birds sang, rummaging in the dewy grass. He came out of slumber dreaming of a sail aboard a vessel without a name.

Suddenly a man kicked his foot. Wade thrust his eyes upward.

Black whiskers and polished cheekbones, pale lips, pointed nose and blunt eyes stared at him. He looked to be in his mid-forties, not an ounce of fat on his body.

"You Wade Burns?"

Wade squinted, "Who are you?"

His voice worked through crude oil. "I'm Captain June. I'm the new captain of the *Vermillion Mourning*. Hear you're thinking of crewing."

"No. I'm not."

"Good. Don't sail with us. We're sailing for Cape Horn—east to west. And if we make it around, running with the wind, it'll be two weeks tops. Terribly dangerous. So don't go."

"Isn't the sea always dangerous?"

"Only aboard a faithless vessel. I hope I don't feel that in her."

"But don't storms blow just about every day on the seas?"

"I want you to go back to the Lighthouse and apologize to your father Abner. You're not fit to sail on this passage."

"But what about the storms? I'd die."

Captain June laughed bitterly. "You *would* die."

"Well I'm not helping," he said emphatically.

"Thank you for saying no."

"I didn't say no!"

"But I heard you say yes to no."

Wade was bewildered. "That's not what I said."

"Sailors get their language all screwed up. So don't lie. Or else you'll end up like me, who hears only what he wants to hear. And thankfully, I heard a no from you. Thank you for going home."

Wade folded his arms and raised his chin. "Well I don't want to go anyway."

"Good. For the rest of us it's time to get to work. We've got to fit her out."

"Fine. Then I'm going home."

Captain June curled his lips into a toothy grin. "Boy, you better. You don't have a choice. Your eyes are lost. You have no soul. You're a dead man if you take passage with your throat."

Wade swallowed. His Adam's Apple pumped. "Well I don't want to," he said again quietly.

"The *Vermillion Mourning* is your grave. As a dead man, I suggest you bury yourself proper—in a cemetery." His large, stubby hands hung limp at his sides as if he knew he needed to make no effort in dismantling him. His rough eyes pressed him. "Are you going home?"

Wade squirmed fighting the panic. "No …"

Captain June smiled. "Don't let me catch you near us."

He held out his hand. They shook. Captain June's firm grip overpowered him. Wade tried to squeeze to match the grip, but he felt his bones being crushed. Finally Captain June let go.

"So you're a sailor?" said Wade, holding his crushed hand, following the hard ground to the *Vermillion Mourning*.

"That I am."

"How long have you been sailing?"

Captain June smiled from rote: "All me bloomin' life. I was born on the crest of the wave and rocked in the cradles of the deep. Me mother was a mermaid. Me father was King Neptune. Seaweed and barnacles are me clothes. The hair on me head is hemp. Every tooth in me head is a marlinspike. And every bone in me body is a spar. And when I spits, I spits tar. Is hard as is I's are, sir!"

Wade wasn't impressed. "Where have you sailed?"

"Over salt."

"Have you sailed around the Horn?"

He nodded in a sober manner.

"Well how many people are crewing? Is this going to be a big sail?"

"Oh it's a big sail. And a big crew. The state penitentiary is overcrowded so they're dumping off some of the troubled ones. Murderers. Rapists. Thieves. You name it, they're coming—the ones who cause trouble for all the other inmates. They'll be here the day she sails off the dock."

Wade felt white hot and weak. He whispered, "Murderers?"

"Don't worry. You're not crew. You don't have to share the boat. You'll be safe in the Lighthouse. The sea will kill them before they would have ever killed you."

Wade uttered shallowly, "There's a guy named Dion."

"Already counted him."

"And not me?"

"Not you. You're not brave enough to crew on my passage. You're just running home from the boat. Safely."

"I'm not a sailor. I don't know anything about sailing."

"Good. We need a dangerous crew, game for the Horn. Now leave me alone. I have work." He walked the slope of the park toward the harbor and the *Vermillion Mourning*. He turned.

"We have to paint her. She's calling for a fresh coat."

In a week Captain June painted the *Vermillion Mourning*. That was the only work he did to fit the schooner for her passage around Cape Horn.

On the eve of the sail, Wade, from the safety of the park, studied her new cream hull. He felt nauseous. Her fresh cream coat hid the false and unsound dimensions beneath. She was a charlatan, a relic from the Gilded Age. Fearfully he shivered thinking of touching her again, aware that the fresh paint only masked the danger. She was not healthy, not underneath. But he imagined holding his palm against her strake to convince himself she was seaworthy. Chills raised his skin. Her frailty, her pretense, surged through him. Her glowing veil surged through his eyes. The tire fenders thumped against the dock with the smooth swell. Shadows pooled around her in the brackish, oily water.

Dion was grinning behind him. "She's pretty. She's very pretty. You did a good job painting her."

Wade jumped.

"I didn't paint her. Captain June did."

"You did a marvelous job. Ready for the sail tomorrow?"

"No. I'm not going."

"Neither am I. I don't know if I should go."

"You look made for water," said Wade.

Dion's smooth, slim jaw relaxed. His right hand, buried in his pocket, unfurled from a fist.

"It'd be a good sail," he said.

"I don't know."

Dion patted him on the shoulder and squeezed. "I feel better myself now that I've changed my mind."

Wade thrust his narrow chin at him.

"It's too dangerous," said Dion.

Wade spit. "Everyone at my home thinks the same."

"But why *shouldn't* I go?" said Dion. "I might find what I'm looking for."

A tern passed and its shadow cut their skin. Wade narrowed his eyes at the welt the tern had made on his arm.

"You would be missing an opportunity. You could have what you want." Dion nodded. "I know. I'm from the East, where promises come at the beginning of every day. I have seen the glory, Wade, and I know what you seek in your heart. I'm here to help you discover your want. Come crew aboard her, this pretty vessel. She's all you have." His thick Brazilian accent worked through English like cream and tender leather. "Did you see my windproof lighter?" He reached to his collar and drew from underneath his shirt a silver chain attached to a silver-plated windproof lighter. The lighter shimmered, a lure.

Wade trembled.

"I've had it for a while. I think you should take it and use it to light the lantern of the Hostel Sound Lighthouse. I give it to you… if you're interested." He slipped the silver chain around his neck. "Now you know how to find Bannock Pierce."

The keepsake weighted him. Disgust formed in the pit of his loins and crawled through his intestines into his stomach, into his throat.

Dion was laughing. "What's wrong?"

Wade looked at him fearfully. He flung it off. It snagged on a branch. He turned for the woods and ran with everything he had for the middle of Oklahoma.

CHAPTER TWELVE

The prison crew arrived. When they stepped aboard the *Vermillion Mourning*, the guards unlocked their handcuffs. The prisoners rejoiced in their newfound liberty and cheerfully stocked the vessel with provisions. They filled the water holds, replenished the firewood for the stove, reorganized the lazaret and bosun's locker. Musclebound, tattooed, scarred viciously, they were escaping multiple life sentences by agreeing to crew aboard.

But as the weight of the *Vermillion Mourning* pressed on their souls, an eerie, unfamiliar foreboding brushed against their skin. Their bones softened. Their blood ran pink. They worked like warm ghosts. Captain June tried to coach them. He tried to inspire them, instill some sense of hope. But as they shuffled about the deck filling her holds with supplies, an unnatural angst pooled in their stomachs, drained their strength, taxed the remaining freedom from their prison sentences. The more time they spent aboard her, the more fearful they became. If they sailed they would suffer not death but doom—an everlasting shame too unimaginable to consider.

The tide had come in, the wind was blowing south-southeast, rippling waves were tapping against the hull. The wind was pushing against the sails. While Captain June tried to test the 15 kilowatt Onan generator, the prisoners found a flag in the saloon and bent it onto the after-leech of the mainsail. But at the thought of seeing Old Glory rise above them, tormenting them with the hope a freedom that they were fast realizing would never be theirs aboard the *Vermillion Mourning*, their countenances sunk into a muddiness. They sensed an imminent danger. Their end was upon them far sooner than they had planned.

By this time the sailorfolk had lined the street to see the prisoners sail the *Vermillion Mourning*. An energy buzzed among them. They were witnessing a day long forgotten but hoped in, even against hope. Could this be the day that the vessel finally left them? A day that would allow them to return to their vessels and once again experience the joy of preparing them for sail?

News vans from up and down the coastline were strung out behind the crowd. Reporters lined up to interview Captain June. All of the sudden a series of loud shouts erupted among the people: Walter, their mayor, was making his way through them. He arrived at the dock smiling brilliantly, stood on a bench, shook Captain June's hand. The hollers and shouts died down and the crowd became hushed. He scanned the residents.

> "Sailorfolk of Springwick Harbor. Thank you for your participation and your support on this day. Today is one of this small town's great moments in maritime history. I am proud that all of us have shared a part in this celebratory occasion. [Applause.]
>
> Let us take a moment to congratulate the brave men who are about to make this voyage a reality: Captain June.... crewmen from our penal system.... [Whistles.]
>
> These men are about to embark upon a hazardous and possibly perilous journey around the tip of

South America. They hope to round Cape Horn in all her murderous glory. We trust that the vessel in which they will use to accomplish this journey is fit for the task. If there were any doubt in our minds that this was so, we would not be here today. [Whistles, shouts.]

This vessel, *Vermillion Mourning*, is ready for sail. At last, ready. We now have a Captain willing to guide her out to sea. [Dion scans the faces but no one is looking at him.]

We all understand what this voyage symbolizes, why it is so important to us [again Dion scans the crowd, but no one acknowledges him.]. The days of the clipper ships and of circumnavigation are over; in this Age of Something Else, to sail back around Cape Horn is an entreaty into the past, to an age before our modernity. This is not a sail that ends before her time. Rather, it is one that will live on, beyond our days. [Loud applause.]

Once the *Vermillion Mourning* achieves her goal she will have accomplished her purpose—carrying the freedom of this town with her. She is a vessel knocked together in painful sacrifice. She is fast. Seaworthy at last. [Hoots.]

To sail around Cape Horn in this small, small boat is to circumnavigate the globe—that globe we live on, and that globe that lives in us. It is the same globe that Meriwether Lewis and William Clark helped circumnavigate when they set out from St. Louis in 1804 and arrived at the mouth of the Columbia River, in 1806. It is that globe that we are destined to conquer, by our might and by our will—

every day of our lives. That Lewis and Clark found a land we now call home—and what a beautiful home it is [a camaraderie of whistles resounds.]—may these men find for us another home. [Encouragements, hoorays.]

Captain June, have you any words? [Captain June shakes his head no then pumps his fist in the air as a clamor and restlessness builds.] Then without delay, I would like all who have gathered here join me in seeing this crew off!" [An eruption. Captain June returns to the schooner, takes his position at the helm.]

With Captain June coaching them, the prison crew raised the mainsail, foresail and then the jib. Wind blew in from the northeast and pushed the bow. They cast the breast line and spring lines, then the stern line. The wind carried the bow around. The wind came in and they raised the stays'l, and with the ease of a calm air, they began to slip out of the inner harbor with the tide, waving to the viewers cheering on the island.

But as the schooner edged away from the dock, the prison crew froze: The soul of the *Vermillion Mourning* struck them, her immediate peril. It was too much hazard to sail on this dilapidated schooner with topmast sticking out of the warped deck, with dangling shrouds, listing foremast, fraying mast hoops. One by one then altogether they dove over the side. They swam to the dock to meet the prison guards. Any windowless cell was better than the false safety of the *Vermillion Mourning*.

CHAPTER THIRTEEN

He limped furiously into the woods trying to bind himself to earth and hide in the belly of a swale, limbs and leaves dragging his flight. But she sensed him.

The pulling. The deepness. The want.

His legs weakened.

She curled around him like smoke, lifting his eyes, his limbs.

But not now. Not her savagery. Not her fear. Not her suffering. Not the gasping for wind. Not the gale of her. Not the birthing of his name in her hold. Not the breaking, the rending. Not the shipwreck, the slaughtering. Not the terrible dream.

He came to a dense copse.

The earth moved. The shaking knocked him off his feet.

He tucked between fallen logs. Dry leaves quaked. Branches scattered. Whole trunks tilted. Terror rushed through his body. Before he understood anything, he realized he longed for any surface less terrifying than land: the sea. In fear he realized he longed to be aboard the *Vermillion Mourning*. Now and forever he would sail aboard the vessel destined to end him. He had no reservation. The drenching burden of her rushed through him now heavily. He wanted to be crew and go together with her at last into their doom, their bonded doom. This wanting filled him, and he ran for her.

He ran for Bannock Pierce—for the glory and the fame, for the unlimited promises found on Cape Race. He ran to be the Hostel Sound Lighthouse Keeper, believing life would be unimaginably agreeable once he arrived. He ran like one escaping death as it broke the ground behind him, every footfall. Death swallowed the weakness and the greatness of him, swallowed in its jaws his failure and his success, and he ran struggling to forget what he had just become. To outlast the death and arrive safely at Cape Race demanded a sacrifice consuming his being. To be there at the finish yet miles away—the élan of life. The promised embrace.

Bursting into the park he ran blindly past picnickers onto to the street, pushed through the crowd, rushed to the dock. When he arrived, he froze. A hollowness enveloped him. The *Vermillion Mourning* had already left the dock! She was sailing away, her sails unfurled to catch the light easterly air. She was heading down the narrow inner channel with Captain June at her helm and Dion at the stern, coiling the stern line.

The prison crew was not aboard. They were now swimming madly for the dock. The prison guards were shouting at them to return to the vessel, but none of them listened. Their eyes were full and in shock as if they had just set foot in their premature grave.

The prisoner in the lead arrived at the dock and held on, panting hard, shouting to the guard above him, "No way will you ever get me to sail aboard *that* vessel!"

The others arrived. One by one they lifted themselves onto the dock. They watched the schooner sail away with their potential freedom.

"Don't you want to sail, son?" said a nervous guard.

The prisoner shook his head. "There's no sailing aboard her. Just wind-inspired foreboding."

Wade trembled.

Captain June spotted him among the prisoners and shouted, "Don't do it, son! It's your life! You need it when you sail from Springwick Harbor!"

Wade panicked. He felt his momentum carrying him toward the water, but he held back, legs wobbling. The crowd in frenzy was cautioning him not to jump for the schooner. His hands shook violently. His legs were on the verge of giving out. It was possible to catch her before she sailed too far through the inner channel. The prisoners saw his eyes, his fear, and were waving him off, admonishing him to stay on the dock. He looked to the crowd. To Abner, Tobiah and Jeshurun, who were yelling with the crowd for him to stay. He looked to the schooner. To his hands. The prisoners. The guards.

Before he understood what he was doing, he jumped into the water. He splashed toward the *Vermillion Mourning* flailing, sinking. Dion threw the stern line. The bitter end splashed by him. He reached for it but it slipped through his fingers. He fought to breathe. Out of reflex he grasped the line. In smooth motion, hand over hand, Dion pulled him toward the schooner. Disoriented, Wade held on for everything in him.

The next thing he knew he was aboard the *Vermillion Mourning*. Coughing seawater out of his lungs, seeing stars, he tried to recollect just how he had come aboard. Captain June was smiling with glaring disapproval. Dion was grinning.

"That wasn't so bad now, was it boy?" said Captain June.

Dion laughed gruffly, grinning, coiling.

"I'm glad one of us can swim," smiled Captain June.

Both he and Dion looked to Wade's left. Next to him, panting from exhaustion for having thrust Wade and himself aboard, was Jeshurun. He looked weak, spent. His face was grave. He steadied his exhausted eyes at Wade as if he knew that they were now biding time before the boat beneath them gave out. "I'm sorry, Wade. I didn't mean for this to happen." He shivered from the wet clothing. "I never wanted this to happen. I'm so sorry."

"It's all right," said Dion. "I think we'll find the *Vermillion Mourning* quite homely. Glad you're aboard. Welcome, Jeshurun. Wade." He shook their hands.

"Pull up the fenders, children," said Captain June. "We've an adventurous sail ahead. We're sailing on a schooner even the prisoners passed over. Not really that safe, eh?" He laughed bitterly at Dion. "That's okay. We don't need safety on this journey. We just need a destination and the will to believe. It's not likely we'll last. But we don't need to last. And we shouldn't jump ship—not before the safety of our destiny has our way with us." He laughed mockingly at Dion, who kept his head down, face flushed, while he coiled.

All four were now bound for Cape Horn.

CHAPTER FOURTEEN

Wade lay foreward of the breakbeam clawing the deck. Terror gripped him. The schooner surged. Rolled. Pitched. Heeled as waves crashed over the bow. The forestay and loose shrouds slapped the foremast and it moaned unsettled and the topmast rocked side to side. Any moment it would topple and crush him.

The reality of the sail pressed him deeper into the deck and he wondered if somehow he could become anything other than a passenger aboard the *Vermillion Mourning*. But there was nowhere else to go. Today he would sink into the deep.

As he lay paralyzed, Jeshurun and Dion worked deftly in preparing the schooner for sail. They secured the kedge anchor with the boatfall and spoon and lashed it to the caprail so that it wouldn't slam into the hull. Then they pulled up the old tire fenders, lashed them to the caprail on the port side foreward of the breakbeam. Coiling the mooring lines with a gasket, they stowed them in the bosun's locker foreward of the fo'c'sle hatch cover on the starboard side. Then they battened the hatches and lashed down whatever else was loose on deck. When they finished, they made ballantine coils of the halyards that the prison crew had hauled on to raise the fore and main.

Jeshurun's happy round face had become gravely long, aware of the irrepressible weight bearing on the schooner and the men. He moved about the deck somberly, the main boom strapped to his back. He carried out the revolutions that meant life or death to themselves and the passage. Wade had never seen him more determined, or sound.

Dion in amusement coiled lines, pleasantly wet and cold, feeling no regret for the condition of the schooner, knowing that whatever awaited the *Vermillion Mourning* promised an imminent end.

Captain June manned the damaged helm, watching the binnacle, Old Glory. The westerly wind shifted over their starboard quarter and he ordered them to sheet out on the jib, stays'l, fore and main. His thin lips remained unresponsive, sober, keen on the dangers presented and on the magnitude of their sail.

Meanwhile, Wade vomited over and over. He had not imagined the motion of the sea would be so violent or that his ability to adjust would take so long. Traveling to the mainland from the Lighthouse with Abner at times had been choppy, but never so severe or powerful. It felt like the schooner would give way at any moment, surrendering to the unstable surface of the ocean. It was impossible to move from the breakbeam even though the topmast near him wobbled violently. He closed his eyes and prayed for home.

"Wade!" shouted Captain June. "You're a sailor now! Work the deck! Do it now or waste yourself in the bilge!"

But Wade buried himself deeper, pressing his head into the deck, pressing his body into the wood until splinters stuck into his flesh. This was a mistake, this sail. It would end in disaster. They would be crushed before they ever made it around Cape Horn.

"Come here, Wade, come bend yourself to the helm!"

Wade's ribs pressed against the deck, burrowing into it as he breathed.

"Come here, boy! Come guide your schooner!"

He couldn't move.

"Wade boy—it's now or never! You're a sailor whether you want to be one or not. We've four months aboard her, three if we're lucky, if we can make it around the Horn. There's no promises. The only promise is that you have today, this moment, to seize your fear and grip the helm where your predecessors were smashed out to sea. Hear me?"

Dion stood over Wade. His crimson silk shirt was rippling in the wind.

The topmast was leaning over.

"Come on, son!" shouted Captain June. "It's not the end of your life. You have to learn to sail some time. Why not learn now, while the journey is fresh? Whatever you learn now will pay off in the end."

The topmast started to topple.

Dion patted him with his hand, looking sideways at the topmast. "It'll be all right, Wade. We'll get through the Horn and then we'll be all right. It's nothing after the Horn. We just need to get there and get through, and then everything will be fine. We need your help."

The topmast fell.

Dion dodged it deftly.

It arced toward Wade.

Jeshurun dropped a gasket and lunged. The topmast struck his back. He heaved it to vertical and then by brute strength hoisted its splintered length out of the hole. Waves flung spray into his face as he lashed it to the starboard bulwark.

In the subsequent days Jeshurun would manage to patch the hole using spare strips of pine and oakum found in the number four hold. For much of the journey, Wade would veer far away from the mend, fearful that it would give out from underneath him, opening a hole through which the sea could pour.

"You three, come aft!" shouted Captain June, signaling them with his sou'wester.

Jeshurun and Dion each took an arm of Wade's and helped him to the stern. Jeshurun found a cushion in the saloon and had Wade sit on the gearbox while offering himself as a support. Dion supported his starboard side, and the three waited on Captain June to speak.

"Listen up," he said with his swarthy throat. "Does anyone here know what *timshel* means?"

Neither Wade nor Dion knew, but Jeshurun knew the origin of the word.

Captain June eyed them gravely. "Timshel means *you may*. It is Hebrew, as old as the sea, and it means that if a sailor knows it is up to him, he may. He may do that which is before him, whatever that is. The sea is dangerous. Every hour there are hazards. But if a sailor takes action, realizing that he may, he triumphs over adversity." His voice softened. "But not without help. Before a sailor learns that he may, he must first learn that he *cannot*—not without help.

"So I am officially declaring this sail the charter event for the *Timshel Auxiliary*—We may, with help. Whatever adversity lay ahead for each of us, none of us can overcome on our own. We need each other. We need divine care. We need every available assistance, all at once. Our destiny is good, and our sail is good—because we may ask for help. How many of you are willing to join the *Timshel Auxiliary*? Say it now."

Wade studied Jeshurun's bright, mirthful face. Gathered in his full and confident eyes. Felt his smooth character, his depth. He seemed to be hinting to Wade that he had known beforehand this matter of the *Timshel Auxiliary* and was unworried over what each of them would choose, the outcome of this first day of sail. Jeshurun was leaning toward him with eagerness, understanding that a thing too great to name was within Wade's grasp. It was an inscrutable thing, one deep and uncharted. But Jeshurun seemed familiar with its dimensions. Even more, he seemed to see those same dimensions in Wade, and in every mariner in Springwick Harbor. Faith. Hope. And love. An unbounded adventure.

And Wade realized that whatever the many reservations he may still harbor toward this sail, it paled in comparison to the aid that was promised him through the *Timshel Auxiliary*. It was a current into Jeshurun's heart. And it was sealed with the tough strength of Captain June. Over the course of their journey they would help him time and again and become in his life the heroes he didn't know he had. Especially Jeshurun. In a deeper way, he was the hero he wished he could be. He turned to them and said rather sheepishly, rather humbly, "I'm in."

Jeshurun dropped his shoulders, like he had just read the opening sentence to a deep and promising book. It was the first chapter in a life, the stormy words anchored to a powerful sail. He cupped his hands over his face and held them there and breathed in and out and then dropped his hands. And when he dropped his hands he was glowing with the astronomical dimensions of the *Timshel Auxiliary*. He knew Wade. He knew the scope. The stars that Wade and the sailors in Springwick Harbor would pull along on dreamy quests at once showered over him, and he said with satisfaction, "Aye. I'm in. We all belong."

"I'll say it now," said Captain June, "I'm in and I'm in, and I'm in and … I'm waiting for the panting deep!"

Dion rubbed his knuckles. Then he sucked on his knuckles. "I cannot become a member," he said. "It would not be wise to change up the history of the waters by trying to redefine it through the lens of a manmade scope. You may make what you want together in a richlit tavern. Dream up a soup. I don't care. Timshel or no timshel, I sail the hard line of the sea on my own and not by the whim of a man's choice, nor by his aide. I am not in. I am not a member of the *Timshel Auxiliary.*"

Captain June leisurely bit a nail. He stuck out his chin casually. He sighed. "So be it." He turned to Wade and Jeshurun with a soldier's demeanor. "To us, and to all others in our wake, welcome aboard."

Dion covered his knuckles. Tilted his head. Wade paled, frozen in the strange electricity of Dion's eyes. "Wade, guess what?" he said. "I have something for you.... Where you're going, you'll need all the help you can get. And I promise I'll give it to you."

Jeshurun folded his arms in a lazy way and leaned back. His powerful biceps and shoulders made his soiled T-shirt stretch. "Dion, guess what? We have something for you. All of us." His eyes were hard and searing. "When you get to where you're going, you'll wish yourself that you had asked for help. A dram of it. It's awfully hard to cry out once your tongue starts burning."

Dion smarted him with his eyes. He stuck out his tongue. He pulled on it and scrolled the inside of his cheek with it. Then he rubbed his heart-shaped necklace, hoping to absorb its glitter into his skin. The weight of the thing seemed to snarl at him.

Captain June moved in. "That's enough. Aboard this sail, we're still one crew. Come together now, for the better joy of it. To get around we'll need all that is available for our aid, whatever reckoning we make in our heart. Now listen." He put his hand on Wade's frail shoulder.

"We need to divide ourselves into port and starboard watches. Dion and Jeshurun, you have the starboard watch. Be wise with it. Be wise with each other. Wade and I will take the port. Four hours on. Four hours off. All day. Every day. Until we round Cape Horn. And when we do, we'll keep going until we reach our end." He stuck out his chin and scratched it and squinted his eyes like a purring cat, lost in a thought. He continued. "The starboard watch is off, starting now. Jeshurun, Dion, go below. Rest while you can."

As Dion and Jeshurun went forward to the forecastle, the wind shifted over their stern.

"Rig a preventer on the foresail to keep it from gibing," said Captain June. "If this wind holds we'll be running for a while. I don't want to be woken up in the middle of the night because of an accidental gibe."

"Rig what?" said Wade.

"A preventer. On the foresail. With a mooring line."

Dion smiled amusedly.

"What's a preventer?" said Wade.

Dion with Wade behind went to the bosun's locker and they fetched a mooring line, rove the line from the portside kevel cleat out the hawse hole to the bale of the foreboom. Jeshurun went below.

"We're running, boys!" shouted Captain June with enthusiasm. "First day out and we're running like a banshee! Dion, help me determine our speed!"

Dion went into the bosun's locker to fetch a log ship, reel and glass. He threw the log ship over the stern and it caught in the water. The log reel paid out. Captain June held the log glass until the sand ran to the bottom. Dion hauled in the log ship and they counted the number of knots.

"Nine knots!... The first day and we're nine knots! I've never began a voyage under better conditions! Wade, take the bow! Get used to the waves! It'll clean your lungs!"

Wade went forward on unsteady legs to man the bow, which had no need of being manned.

Captain June lifted a finger. "On second thought," he said. "go below. Rest while you can. You're in for a long sail."

Clenching his stomach he went below into the forecastle with Jeshurun.

"Are you sure it's wise to have Wade and you share the same watch, Captain?" said Dion.

Captain June's deep, dark eyes glowed for a moment as he scratched his dark curly hair and thick whiskers. He patted his thin gut then scratched his bony elbows as if tapping his body for an answer. "Maybe you're right. It would be such a beautiful thing."

"I can fetch him for you."

"Let him get his rest this watch. He's greener than a pea."

"Yes, Captain," said Dion wearily. His grim, absent eyes avoided the horizon. He looked out into the sea waiting for the wind to inevitably change. "I'm thinking of you," he said. "It would be better if he learned from someone like me rather than his brother or another a captain who's already preoccupied with mastering the sail. I could teach him how to sail exactly the way you would want him to. I could shape him into your vision of an ideal sailor. It would be good if we docked in New York, full of sailors eager to learn from someone like you, or someone under you."

Captain June was dismissive. "I'll think about it." He waved Dion away.

Dion flopped onto the transom next to the mainsheet and brooded, watching the nameless swells coming for the schooner. The bow climbed and dipped as if a child was toying with it in a bathtub. The sun was high, mid-morning, cool with wind and spray.

In the forecastle Wade lay on a bunk across from Jeshurun who was watching him with eyes soft and fierce. "What do you think of sailing?"

Wade trembled. His legs felt weak again. He readied to vomit.

"I don't ever want to go on deck again."

"We'll get through this, but don't give up hope. You've got a lot to sail for."

The *Vermillion Mourning* rose and fell with the waves gently but Wade felt emaciated and he longed to be home on the solid rock of the Lighthouse island. He thought of the Oregon coastline, wondering if he could make it to the beach before the sharks got him.

"Don't do it," said Jeshurun, reading his thoughts. "You'll drown. We wouldn't change course fast enough to pick you up."

Wade vomited onto the sole. By this time there was nothing left in his stomach. He felt cold and foreign and desperately wanted to be somewhere else—Oklahoma of all places, anywhere besides the sea. His body froze as he pictured himself stuck in an ice cube while a wicked thing blew on his face. He moaned quietly, "I hate sailing."

Jeshurun patted him on the shoulder. "I'm not going to let this sail destroy you. Just keep sailing. Keep believing. Don't give up. Don't give in. You can learn some things if you're willing and humble. "

Wade vomited again, his body doubling over like a jackknife.

"You may not see it now," said Jeshurun, "but this sail we're on will be the greatest journey you will yet take—greater than all the runs you and I have enjoyed in the forests surrounding Springwick Harbor. And I get to sail it with you."

CHAPTER FIFTEEN

The boat simply was not seaworthy. The foremast moaned with every wave. The loose foreshrouds strained and bowed. An inch of water covered the sole of the fo'c'sle. Wade was certain he would be awoken during his off watch by a cold sea hunting to drown his landlocked soul. Captain June had promised them two weeks to round the Horn. It would be easy, he said, with the westerlies. Wade met him at the helm.

"How long until we reach Cape Race?"

Captain June eyeing the binnacle ignored the question as unsubstantial mist. "We're not sailing to Cape Race."

"I thought we were."

"We're sailing for Cape Horn. We won't stop until we get there. And when we do, we're hauling her out for a shrine."

Wade looked stricken, the words draining hope from him.

Captain June felt his hopelessness and turned from the binnacle to face him. His dark angular bones absorbed the loss. "Don't worry, Wade. We'll make it to Cape Horn, and if we survive, we may after all sail for Cape Race. And if we do it will be enough for the both of us.... But if we do, I won't know how long it will take. We have to sail through the doldrums twice, the Horse Latitudes twice, the Roaring Forties twice and the Furious Fifties twice—all of it as unpredictable as weather can be. Understand?" He tried to raise Wade's chin with his eyes. "Fortunately we sail around the Horn only once...." And he looked at the binnacle for reassurance to soothe the loss of his past sails. "Sometimes vessels take weeks to round the Horn." He tried to laugh.

"But you promised two weeks."

"Give or take a month. The Horn is dangerous. Death may set us back a few months." He laughed heavily. "Though don't give up. We'll get there."

Wade turned pale and his skin felt tight. "But will we make it to Cape Race?"

The foremast moaned searching her holds, searching her bounty until it expressed itself fearlessly against a sparkling horizon.

"We may not make it at all."

"Then why'd you agree to come aboard when you knew the hazard?" he said, his face sinking.

"Because anything is possible when a schooner sails for a good reason."

Wade pondered this. He wasn't sure his desire for the Hostel Sound Lighthouse was good. "What reason?" he asked.

"To discover grace."

Wind stroked Wade's hair and the mild sun warmed his shoulder and he imagined himself bathing on a tropical beach, life showering him with a blessing. Grace was developing a heaviness in him, a strength—a powerful truth. He did not know what grace sounded like or how it would feel if he ever understood it in its unlimited mystery. But his soul torqued with the want of it.

"The *Timshel Auxiliary*," reminded Captain June. "We may, with help. We can round Cape Horn—with help. With grace. I signed on not because I believe we're seaworthy, any of us, but because grace makes us far more seaworthy than any of us could ever hope to imagine. I need that. I need to know a miracle is possible. I need to believe she'll make it around the Horn in one piece and all of us filled with character."

The foremast yawned and the joyous splashing of the waves pushed the vessel along.

"But we won't even make it to Hawaii."

"You're right," he chuckled. "We're not sailing for Hawaii. We're sailing for the Horn. Whatever brought us aboard is behind us. We're all in this together now. Whatever fate awaits this schooner, awaits us all." He smiled hoarsely. His dark face looked strange with the light illuminating his eyes and teeth.

Wade turned whiter. He leaned on the gearbox clutching his stomach. Wave after wave splashed against the schooner. It was only a matter of time before one of them took her down.

Captain June turned his focus to the vessel and her direction. An outdated chart of the Pacific Coast lay before him and he studied it and the binnacle. A few gulls followed behind, waiting for the vessel to cough up her treasure.

"Aren't you sailing for the right reasons, Wade?"

Wade felt hot and queasy. A weight smoldered in his stomach.

Captain June opened his jaw in quizzical thought. "So why did you crew, if you're not crewing for the right reasons?"

"I mean, what are the right reasons?" said Wade.

"I said—to discover grace."

Wade mustered a few sick, trickling words.

"I didn't catch that."

Wade mumbled again.

"Say it louder, son. The waves are singing so loud I can't listen from joy."

"To find Bannock Pierce."

"Who?"

"Bannock Pierce."

"*Who*?"

Wade rolled his eyes with the swell rolling the schooner soberly.

"He's not a mystery, Captain June. He's not shallow. He's not impossibly bad. He's giving me the Hostel Sound Lighthouse—I'm sailing to be the Lighthouse Keeper."

Captain June took his eyes off the binnacle and studied him carefully, jaw loose. His eyes squeezed Wade's skin and he rolled his tongue through his cheek.

"So you're in love with a false dream?"

"No," said Wade quickly.

"Mysteries, in the end, never lie against the truth that examines them."

"I want to be the Lighthouse Keeper at Cape Race," he said hurriedly. "Bannock Pierce is going to help me become one. How long until we reach Cape Race?" He felt his strength returning. The waves were less and it wasn't so terrible to have legs.

Captain June kept his eyes trained on him, humbly piercing him. A fresh strength pressed against him, opening his chest. And he struck.

"Your false dream does not exist. You're chewing up the schooner for the unsound. You will suffer for it." And as Wade's countenance fell away from the soft horizon into a swallowing trough, Captain June grounded him further in a deeper darkness. "I'm sorry you have to hear this, Wade. But I have to be honest.... You're not going to survive."

Wade tried to swallow down a thing that was trying to drown him. He felt his chest cave with pressure. His head rung.

"If I had known," Captain June went on, "I never would have challenged you to crew. I am sorry."

His heart hammered. The ringing was louder. "Why did you plant the seed? I thought you knew."

"All I know is that you're a sailor. Anyone can see that. How you sail is up to you. But you're not the Lighthouse Keeper."

"I can be whatever I want to be."

"Honest sailors let life loosen them into something greater than their heart. These are the ones who enter into everlasting grace. Don't think you can be anything if you're lying to yourself."

Captain June did not understand. Jeshurun did not understand. They were shallow men foundering in shoals. They didn't see his heart, his drive, his honesty toward the dream. If they knew that he planned to do only good with his post, they'd endorse him, but they didn't see him. No one saw him. He was alone. If he found Bannock Pierce, he would know. This good man would teach him love, the love of doing good, of helping sailors find their home. Only Bannock Pierce was mysterious enough to understand how honest he was with his heart.

As the wind pushed them along they busied themselves with the care of the vessel. They tidied the bosun's locker and found several mooring lines along with a few heaving lines to anchor the vessel during a storm. Working without shirts under the bare, high sun, Jeshurun and Dion—and Wade with them who refused to go shirtless because he didn't want Jeshurun to discover the apron he was wearing—sanded the extra mast hoops until the grease disappeared, then whipped badly frayed lines and gaskets. Because of fair weather, the off-watch remained on deck enjoying the fresh breeze.

The dark ocean carried the little vessel and they moved in rhythm together beneath the billowing clouds. The crew regarded breathlessly the expanse of sea and sky favoring their passage. Captain June remarked to them that on any other day these same friends might become angry and do to them and their vessel what so many vessels before them had deserved. "Pray we don't deserve our fate," he whispered. "Pray we make it around under their auspice."

Day after day the schooner crawled the ocean. They ventured beyond U.S. waters, past the Tropic of Cancer. The temperature grew hotter and the wind held and soon they found themselves nearing the equator.

One day While Wade sunbathed on the saloon housetop working diligently to sand a mast hoop, Dion approached him holding a strip of rope. He sat between him and Jeshurun manning the helm. "Have you ever tied a bowline?" He held the rope up to him.

Wade's ears tingled. There was something about the rope, something about the name of the knot, that stirred him. He had heard of a bowline before and had always wanted to learn to tie one, but never until now had he been presented with the opportunity. "No," he said.

"I'll show you. Follow me."

Wade got up at once and followed him to the breakbeam where they sat out of view of Jeshurun.

"There are several types of bowlines, but perhaps the easiest is called the fingertip bowline. Learn this before you learn any other knot."

Dion tied a fingertip bowline and handed it to him. Wade studied it and tried to duplicate the steps but his fingers fumbled in the handling. Dion showed him again and a third time until finally he understood and tied the knot.

"Good job." Dion smiled and lowered his eyes vulnerably. "You're learning faster than even me."

Wade folded the rope over and over as if waiting to secure a thing just out of reach, and said, "It's easy, once you get the hang of it." In that brief moment he felt strangely as if he had been a deckhand for the longest time. Surprising himself, he waited eagerly for the next lesson.

"Let me show you a constrictor knot tied in the bight. This one is easy to learn but use it sparingly. It's harder to untie." He tied a constrictor knot by wrapping it around Wade's index finger. Wade tried to pull it off but couldn't. Dion snorted teasingly. "See what I told you? Don't tie it unless you need to secure something for a while." He watched Wade struggle to get the knot off of his finger.

The harder he tried to work it free, the tighter it became. "It's like Chinese handcuffs."

Dion loosened the knot and slipped it off his finger. "Master it, son. It might save your life." Then he showed him several other knots and hitches for practical use. Wade absorbed each one as if they were his tendons. In that single lesson he mastered the fingertip bowline, rolling hitch, clove hitch, running bowline, slipknot bowline, bowline in the bight, carrick bend, single and double sheet bends and the square knot.

He was amazed at how easy it was. In the following days, during his free time, he practiced the knots over and over until he could tie them by instinct with eyes closed. It helped take his mind off the expanse of water surrounding the vessel. Whenever he felt sick or frightened he would take from his pocket the string Dion had given him and practice a knot; or, when possible, he pressed Dion to teach him something new. On his off watch he would step out of the fo'c'sle and press him to help him hone his marlinspike seamanship. Wade digested his knowledge so ravenously Dion dubbed him a junior salt.

As they were making eye splices together one midafternoon on the fo'c'sle, their conversation turned to Cape Race. Wade imagined himself sailing to Newfoundland and finding the Hostel Sound Lighthouse, sailing into the fjord and meeting Bannock Pierce. "Have you ever been to Cape Race?" he said.

"He was not a good man, Wade."

Wade paused from his work, confused.

Dion continued. "There have been other men who have been better. Or healthier. Or who have lived longer. Or who were better known. But he trumps them all with his false dream. He tempts you, son, into becoming the thing that ruins you the easiest. You're not the Lighthouse Keeper. You never will be."

"He's the greatest man I know," he said defensively.

"You've never met him."

"Someday I will."

"He's dead, Wade."

Wade shoved a strand of rope through an opening. "That's not what you said before—the night you told me about the *Vermillion Mourning*."

Dion smiled. "Bannock Pierce does not even exist."

"*What*?" A visible divot plummeted from his chest.

"He doesn't exist. There has never been a Bannock Pierce. There's no such thing as the Hostel Sound Lighthouse."

"Did you lie to me?"

"I wanted you aboard the *Vermillion Mourning*. And I knew I had to say whatever it took to get you here." Dion's tanned pate turned darker. "Was it a mistake?"

"Why are you doing this? You convinced me to go to him." His eyes blurred against the cloud cover.

"You convinced yourself. A liar in love with a lie." He sneered. "I wanted you to come aboard because I wanted the truth of you to become known to yourself. I wanted to make you into a sailor. But you're far too deceived to be one. You'll go to him, and it will be a pathetic waste. A beautiful destruction."

Unconsciously Wade tied a constrictor knot around his finger. He loosened his eyes into the deep rust dripping from the windlass. "… But he's calling me."

"Funny. You can hear a lie. But you can't hear the truth."

After that for several days Wade stopped talking to Dion. Whenever they shared the deck he ignored him out of the corner of his eye. If Dion approached the helm from starboard, he sidestepped quickly to port. Instead of sharing a berth in the fo'c'sle, he occupied one of the smaller Pullman bunks in the saloon.

One night while Dion stood bow watch and Captain June slept in his quarters, Wade joined Jeshurun at the helm. He held a rope and when he sat on the gearbox, he subconsciously began tying all the knots he had learned, one knot after another.

"Can't sleep?" said Jeshurun.

"Still can't get used to the waves." He was thinking of the Hostel Sound Lighthouse and Bannock Pierce.

"You'll get used to it."

"I hope I don't. How fast do you think we're going, right now?" he said.

Jeshurun smelled the wind. "Close to six knots. Maybe."

"But look at the pennant. It's not moving hardly at all."

"That's because the wind is behind us. It's actually blowing hard, but we don't know it because we're moving with the wind. It's the difference between apparent wind and true wind. Apparent wind is what it seems to be blowing; true wind is what is actually blowing. If we were sailing in the opposite direction the true wind would be six knots, but the apparent wind would be much higher because we would be sailing directly into it.... It's the same principle as when you're riding a bicycle. Against the wind, you seem to be crawling and the wind seems to be howling, even though it's not blowing that hard. But with the wind, it feels like you're gliding along with no effort at all, and the atmosphere around you feels like it's motionless. The wind seems like it's disappeared. But the wind is there."

Jeshurun folded his arms steering with his feet.

Captain June, overhearing their conversation, climbed the companionway and joined them at the helm. He snarled like an ancient mariner. "You've no idea how great a wind is until a headwind shrieks through the rigging. Trees fall. Power lines scatter. A house is blown away. But until you've seen wind tear at your ship in the dead of night, a landlubber has no room to talk."

Wade's ears tingled imagining himself at the helm during a gale. He struggled to suppress the thought.

Captain June continued. "On the square-rigger training vessel the *Zephyr* several years ago a studding sail was blown out and we had to furl it, me and two others. We lashed ourselves onto the jackstay with gaskets so we wouldn't fall. As soon as Meuhler stepped onto the yardarm he was blown off. The vessel left him astern. Landin was blown off. The vessel left him astern. I reached out to grab the sail flapping like a rag and was knocked off the footrope. The wind whipped me back and forth, just like the sail. My hand was smashed to pieces." He curled his fingers and bit his tongue.

"Was that around Cape Horn?" said Wade.

"Might have been. Don't remember. I was too delirious. Can't recall where we went. I sailed for a few months on the *Zephyr*. After the ship docked I swore I'd never sail again. But I did, and I have, and I'm lucky. I'm bound to sail the rest of my life."

"But doesn't the wind blow like that around Cape Horn?"

"The wind blows harder, son," he said. He returned to his quarters letting him imagine the ferocity of the grounds they would soon encounter.

Wade made the initial loop of a fingertip bowline and pulled the bitter end up and around the standing part of the line, down through the hole and tight, securing the knot.

"Can you even see what you're doing?" said Jeshurun.

"No. Well, a little. The binnacle helps."

The red light of the binnacle glowed like illumined blood. Wade unfastened the knot and tied another. His hands worked loosely with the rope, intimately fashioning the rope into the shape he imagined. The breeze felt cool and warm coming over the stern.

"Remember Dad teaching you to fly that kite?" said Jeshurun.

Wade reached back to the past and couldn't recall it but then all at once it flooded through him: standing with Abner and Jeshurun atop Strawberry Mountain deathly afraid of handling the kite. "Why do you ask?"

"Just thought it was a good time."

But it wasn't a good time. Abner took the kite and threw it into the clouds and it started to ascend and the higher it flew, the more fearful Wade became because he didn't want to lose the kite. It was his birthday gift given him at the start of his thirteenth year. Abner and Jeshurun had painted on the kite a mosaic of Wade's favorite trips—the Grand Canyon, Niagara Falls, Multnomah Falls, Crater Lake, Old Faithful—places where he had felt most free. Wade was afraid of the kite because he was afraid of the responsibility of handling his freedom. One day he would lose his strength and all would be lost, his dream and everything—floating where he would never ascend, into the heavens. "What's our heading?" he said to change the subject.

Jeshurun smiled. "South."

Wade squeezed the rope. "Are we still headed to the Horn?"

Jeshurun smiled wider, knowing him. "That kite took off and soared like it was bound to nothing. The wind was just right."

"It was bound to me."

Jeshurun focused on the binnacle and adjusted their heading by half a degree. He enjoyed handling the damaged helm, the feel of it, the strange weight of it. It wasn't supposed to be manageable, but he knew it would be right.

"It was bound to me, Jeshurun."

"That kite soared higher than any other kite on Strawberry Mountain that day."

Wade's hands shook. Jeshurun adjusted the helm.

"It went so high I thought the clouds would collapse over it."

He was shaking and his skin felt pale and cold. His fingers tried to handle the rope but they were shaking. In the darkness he tied a double carrick bend and hung it to his wrist.

"You're a kite flyer, Wade. You and I both know you never let go. Amidst the wind that followed, you held onto your birthday present. Remember that."

Soothing comfort rushed through Wade and his lungs thickened. "Why are you telling me this?"

"Because you're going to need a better knot for your kite."

The words hammered him. He felt cool. His chest burned. Ice sprinkled his spine. He sat on the transom and held onto the main sheet. The blocks jostled loosely with the rolling swell. Closing his eyes he felt the easy motion of the schooner and his lungs filling and the thick salty smell of the water.

He recalled his fear of the *Vermillion Mourning* when he first touched her. Now that he was crew he suffered the angst constantly. Yet Jeshurun held the helm powerfully as in command of not only the schooner and their sail but of a deeper dream. He understood their fate and was not afraid. Wade felt Jeshurun's words stroking his spine, the easy words moving into his fear and dismantling it. Even in his angst, a deeper safety gave him rest, and he felt ready to live all at once in the sobriety of the waves.

Jeshurun turned to him and his face was dark against the stars. "But Wade, I have to warn you," he whispered. "Do not go aloft."

Wade raised his eyes to the futtock shrouds shrouded in blackness. He imagined himself moving through them. He imagined a giant wave suddenly smashing over the stern and sweeping him off the shrouds to sea. Overcome with the thought, he fainted over the transom.

CHAPTER SIXTEEN

Jeshurun caught him. But as he left the helm the schooner suddenly lost direction. The main sheet slackened and the boom teetered to port threatening to gibe. He muscled Wade to the deck then rushed to the helm. Just before the boom slammed over, he righted the wheel. The boom swung to starboard and the sail filled, tightening the sheet without loss or damage to the schooner or men.

They carried along gently through the darkness. The warm wind pressed their stern and the bow rose and fell with the swells and the schooner was half-asleep. Wade opened his eyes slowly and above him was the easy riot of the heavens. He studied it for some time with Jeshurun and the quiet calm.

"What happened?"

"You almost fell into the ocean." Jeshurun focused on the binnacle, his hands steady. "You're alive. Be thankful for that. And still a denizen of Springwick Harbor." He sat on the gearbox manning the helm with a hand. As his breathing eased, his heartbeat returned to normal. He would have done anything to save Wade, his adopted brother—even if it meant sacrificing his duty as the Springwick Harbor Lighthouse Keeper. To bring a sailor back from death was more important than the privilege to shine. "Just be thankful for this moment. We're alive."

"What do you think our chances are of making it around Cape Horn?" he said, his voice searching the darkness.

"I think they're good."

"What if we wreck?"

"Captain June knows a thing or two about sailing."

"What if we wreck, though?"

Jeshurun wrapped his arm around his shoulder and squeezed. "Don't worry about it. Even if we do wreck, we won't die."

"But that sounds ludicrous."

"I like to imagine that I know the destiny of Springwick Harbor. So don't worry. About anything."

Suddenly, before they had a moment to brace themselves, a rogue wave flopped over the stern, slamming them against the helm. The water carried Wade down the port side of the saloon all the way to the breakbeam and sucked him through the waterway. Fighting to hold onto the bulwark, he cried out to Dion standing bow watch. The water passed around him as Dion grabbed his armpits and hoisted him back on deck. Jeshurun with his incredible strength held onto the helm, determined to keep the schooner from accidentally gibing. The wave spilled into the saloon and drenched the sole and tables where Captain June was plotting their course.

Dion sat with Wade who was now soaked and clinging to the breakbeam. "Are you hurt?" he said.

"I'm fine.... Just a big bath." The tension in his shoulders and arms ebbed away.

Jeshurun checked the compass in the red light of the binnacle. Still on course.

Captain June rushed to check the holds. The foreward and aft holds were dry, as were the number three, four and five holds in the saloon. He descended the ladder of the generator room, pointed a flashlight toward the sole. Six inches of water covered the planks. The generator, at the base, was submerged.

He plopped into the water, walked fore and aft searching for a hole in the seams of the hull, listening for a gurgling. But the water sloshed back and forth with the gentle pitch and sway of the boat, and he could detect no leak. Dion appeared in the opening.

"I don't know if a rogue wave of such small magnitude could have caused this much water so rapidly," Captain June rasped. "No, I'm sure of it. A rogue wave of that small magnitude could not have caused a wash of this amount of water."

"Maybe there's a leak, Captain. Maybe the ship is not as sound as we hoped."

"We'll have to pump to clear out the bilge. We can't afford to sail with this amount of water." He handed the flashlight to Dion and squatted, pressed his thumb against the switch for the glow plug to start the generator. The glow plug would not heat. With his shirt sleeve he wiped off the water. He checked the wiring, then removed the cage that surrounded the glow plug and checked the glow plug itself. He pressed the switch up and down several times. The switch clinked metallically.

"It's dead," said Dion.

Captain June nodded. "We can't pump. Maybe we can bail by hand. But if the water is coming in.... We need to start bailing right away. We may need to make an emergency stop."

He climbed the ladder, went aft to look at charts. Dion searched for a bucket in the galley, found a salad bowl, and bailed. He scooped water with the bowl, climbed two steps of the ladder, passed the bowl to Wade who dumped the water overboard. The process was futile.

After several hours of bailing the water had not receded. Nor had it gained much. Captain June looked closer in the generator room and found a small leak just above a beam in the aft portion of the room. In the morning the schooner changed course, veering for Rosa Dulce, a gulf in Central America, for repairs.

In the morning of the second day of their sail to Rosa Dulce, Wade spotted the wet, green hills of the coast. The three deck-hands retrieved mooring lines from the bosun's locker and bent heaving lines onto each. Four hours later they sailed into an inner harbor of an inner bay inside the Rosa Dulce. The harbor was small and a village lay along the bight of the shore-line. Around the village, hills climbed into the sky.

Dion and Jeshurun stood at the prow watching to make sure their schooner did not run into the small outriggers and sea kayaks drifting across their bow. The small craft glided alongside them through the clear, emerald water guiding them toward the dock.

"This reminds me of my home in Brazil," said Dion.

Jeshurun was focused on the approaching dock. He said dismissively, "What do you remember about it?"

"It was prettier than this. My home was beautiful." He stepped onto the breasthook. "I remember the smoke and the rain and the rainbow arching over the dead."

Jeshurun said coldly, "Maybe while you're here something will arch over you."

Dion flashed his eyes in fear at the striking water.

The stays'l fluttered in the wind followed by a long still-ness.

Wade came forward and joined them. "Do either of you know what Rosa Dulce means?"

Jeshurun scratched his shaggy hair, glittery like the water. "It means Sweet Rose." He moved close to Wade, out of earshot of Dion, and his tone became confidential. "Do you see how that hill drops out of sight behind that larger hill?"

"Yes."

"There are hills in uncharted waters waiting for you to climb them, Wade. I hope that someday you'll sail with friends to these destinations and discover many sweet roses," he said, his voice hurting with passion for Wade's promising future.

Wade stretched his eyes against the hills, the lush foliage above the men on the beach. Never in his life had he seen a harbor as rich with vegetation. It was almost as beautiful as Springwick Harbor. It rose before him and he longed to drink the rainbow above the waterfall.

The harbor bent sharply from the mouth and widened like a horseshoe to the long, rickety dock protruding from the beachhead. One villager in a yellow straw hat seemed to be organizing the men to receive the *Vermillion Mourning*. The men were crisscrossing each other in chaos and excitement, as if they had never before seen a vessel so large, or grotesque.

As the schooner approached within twenty-five yards, Captain June debated whether the dock was deep or strong enough to support them, but the villagers kept waving them in. Unsure that his crew understood how to prepare the vessel for a mooring, he continued timidly. After the rogue wave had hit he had explained to them in detail how to drop the sails in case a sudden squall or gale came up on them requiring them to heave-to. Either they figure it out now, learning by doing, or suffer a possible bungle that might also terminate their sail. He shouted from the quarterdeck. "Jeshurun! Dion! Ready the headsails!"

Jeshurun and Dion sprang into action removing the necessary lines off their belay pins, taking in all the extra line in the stays'l sheet, clearing a space on the deck to work. Meanwhile

Wade with a sounding line sounded the depth of the water as they neared. He shouted back to Captain June, "Forty-five! … Thirty! … Twenty!"

"Drop the headsails!"

Jeshurun and Dion let go their lines. The headsails plummeted down the stays. Immediately they furled the foresail, then the main. As the *Vermillion Mourning* drifted at barepoles toward the dock, Wade in one fluid motion heaved a mooring line, to which a heaving-line was attached, to a villager nearby standing on the dock.

The toss fell far short. The schooner drifted uncontrollably toward the dock while Jeshurun took over Wade's position and gathered in the loose line to heave it again. But even as he tossed it a second time, and though the toss was expertly placed, it was too late.

The schooner crashed into the rickety dock.

Men fell into the water. Captain June shouted orders to his crew, but to no effect; all three stood aghast at the carnage their vessel had already inflicted on this peaceful village. The men labored to the shoreline shouting in Spanish. In one swift piercing thrust of the bow, the *Vermillion Mourning* had destroyed the dock in which decades of commerce so central to the lifeblood of their village had transferred hands. The little children were shocked, clinging to their mothers' thighs, and the mothers fought to understand why their open hospitality had so abruptly backfired. The dock was in shambles. How would they unload the deep boats?

Captain June, seeing no other option, ordered the anchor dropped where the deck had been.

The man who had lost his yellow straw hat after falling into the harbor swam to the shore. The whole village waited for his barreling voice. He spoke deliberately and solemnly with the weight of the village and their custom heavy on his tongue. "Greetings, señors. My name is Emilio Garza. Welcome to Rosa Dulce. You are in distress."

The whole village sighed relief; they were not, after all, going to kill them.

Captain June, flushed with embarrassment, spoke meekly. "My name is Captain June. This is the sailing vessel *Vermillion Mourning* from Springwick Harbor, Oregon. I am sorry, I am very sorry, for having destroyed your dock. We are sinking. If possible may we make repairs here before we continue with the sail?"

"Where are you bound?"

"Cape Race."

Wade's heart skipped. So it was true—they were bound there after all. His dream would come true. Everything was working out as he had hoped.

"The Canal is not far away," said Emilio. "Then you will turn north. We will help you." The men around him nodded with determination. Emilio smiled and his mustache spread into his cheeks.

Captain June scratched his whiskery chin knowing that once he dug up their true destination the chance of the villagers supporting them might grow tenuous. He guessed that such a leader might know the consequences of venturing for the Horn in a rickety vessel like the *Vermillion Mourning*—as rickety as the dock it had just destroyed. Nonetheless, he had to be honest. "We are sailing for Cape Horn."

"*Cape Horn*?" cried Emilio. "Why *sail* around *Cape Horn*?"

Captain June looked quickly to Jeshurun, who, knowing what he was going to say, nodded approval. "We are retracing the route of the *Vermillion Mourning* when she sailed to Springwick Harbor."

Emilio tucked his thumbs into his pockets, peered at him from under the shade of his straw hat. His soaking white shirt and khaki pants both were streaked with mud and dirt and boat blood—evidence of a seafaring life. Yet by the position of his hands and the tough, still arch of his back, he exuded a presence that easily spanned the village. His eyes looked almost ugly, scowling, as if he seemed to say, I have seen this before. Every season I have seen this. You are fools. Stay here, stay in Rosa Dulce. Do not even abandon the harbor, you headless men. Embrace our hospitality, dock crushers. Do not even go back. I welcomed you here. You may live with us. Many strangers and many of my friends have thought that they could go. Those are the ones we carve into our stools, that we would remember them.

He reached into his pocket and extracted phial, from it a cigar. He chewed off the end and spit it into his palm. The slow crack of a match flared and he brought the flame to the tip and sucked. His cheeks caved and bulged as smoke escaped between the cigar and lips. The smoke hid in his mouth then eased past his nose and he removed the cigar and held it between his fingers like a fine red wine. He breathed deeply.

"This cigar is from the Dominican Republic," he began. "It is one of the finest cigars in the world. Men have been killed over this cigar. It is filling your body with the sweetest leaves of the field. Do you know how it got here?" He squinted at Captain June.

Captain June replied in a joking but somewhat serious tone, "Through the Panama Canal?"

"It was dropped from a plane on accident, a whole cargo load, four feet in front of my porch. The fall startled me and I had done nothing to ask for it. I took every one of the cigars inside. My fathers and brothers have stopped eating or tending their gardens. They have been this way for an entire month.... Señor, you do not need to sail around Cape Horn." He walked away.

That night the crew discussed their plans in the forecastle.

"If we had an iron hull, it *might* be safer," said Jeshurun, settling into a bunk. "But this wood is falling apart. Around the Horn no ship is safe, especially one in this condition. We should scuttle the boat, so close to land. She isn't worth the water she sails over."

Wade spoke somberly still feeling the guilt for having mishandled his bow line. "We've made it this far," he said. "Can't we survive on our booming luck?" Despite his bitter gut, he knew he had to continue to move, had to continue even despite the torture. He hated the water, the salt, the spray, the wind. He would have given anything to be on land, running to Bannock Pierce. Lighthouse keepers do not go out to sea. They stay on land where needed most. But something was drawing him away from the land.

Captain June said soberly, "In summer around the Horn guess how often a gale blows."

None of them answered.

He snapped his teeth. "Almost every day. Now guess how often in winter."

Wade regarded him speechlessly, fear bubbling under lip.

Captain June glared cruelly at them, full of intimidation, and said, "*Every* day."

The men regarded blankly the grave, dampening rot of the sole.

He continued. "The westerlies build for thousands of miles with nothing to impede their strength, no rocks, no beaches, no mountains," he said, scratching his heavy whiskers. "Winds storm into the Horn, terrorizing the sea. Sixty-five knot winds or higher are common. Sixty-five foot waves or higher have devoured entire clipper ships. And the waves are often even higher than that! I'm not sure we're ready for that kind of thing. The Horn is the wet word for death."

"But the *Vermillion Mourning* handled that rogue wave," said Dion.

Captain June placed his hand on his knee and eyed him stupidly. "You really think that rogue wave is what we'll be facing when we round the Horn?"

"Then why round it?" said Jeshurun. "Why not go through the Canal? We'll be safe if we stay here until she's repaired. Even safer for the Atlantic."

Dion laughed. "Jeshurun, you sound like my mother. Are there no sailors in your household? Or are all the sailors in the Springwick Harbor Lighthouse busy darning bonnets?"

Jeshurun lowered his eyes and studied the network of his hands and he breathed evenly and calmly and felt his own strength. His warm, generous face hid the depth of his understanding of both their sail and the men who crewed the *Vermillion Mourning*. He chose not to say anything.

"We need rest," interjected Captain June. "We've been safe so far. If we make good choices, we'll be safe for tomorrow. But right now, we need to recuperate. Our sail has been easy. Pray our luck will continue."

Wade swallowed hard. Fear hollowed him. The farther they sailed toward the equator, the deeper his fear tunneled into him, like a worm hungry for earth, burrowing into his core.

"But why not scuttle the boat?" he said. "Go home to Springwick Harbor?"

He did not understand why he had so hastily jumped for the schooner when she was sailing away, or why even now he felt himself drawn into her charm. The dream to find Bannock Pierce and be the Lighthouse Keeper seemed coldly unreal; he wasn't sure he even wanted it.

Wasn't it enough to simply be alive, able to dream at all? How tempting it was to jump overboard and swim for the beach, live with these peaceful villagers like a castaway and maybe when his legs returned he would venture north over land for Pierce.

But how tempting, how truthfully tempting, it was to stay aboard and rush into the Horn without heed, daring the wind and waves to have their way with them. He felt lost in this power, in this recklessness, unable to grasp what strange, deep elasticity had fastened himself to his end.

"We'll keep sailing," said Captain June, through with his intimidation, meant to test their resolve. "The schooner can take it. Remember the *Timshel Auxiliary*. We may get through the Horn, with help." His eyes lifted Wade. "We'll figure it out together. I do believe there is reason for sailing to the Horn. It's a calling. Something is going to happen there whether good or bad. I'm willing to take the risk to find out."

Dion became mocking and furious. "Where are you from? Who contacted you about the sail? This is preposterous that we would continue."

Captain June's eyes widened as his face filled with anger. "Don't blame me for the condition of this sail. We're all victims aboard a faulty boat. As for me, I answered the call to sail, no matter what. That is faithfulness." He said in vexation to Dion, "That doesn't mean we need to relish in our unhappiness." And then he opened his palm to the crew. "Don't fear. We have grace with us. This is cause for celebration. Now go rest."

Jeshurun squeezed his fists against the rail of the bunk. His anger seethed at the rims of his eyes. He lowered his voice and spoke heatedly, "If we sail to Cape Horn, we die. We'll die before we even get there."

Dion smiled lazily, grotesquely. "*Dulce est desipere in loco.*"

"It is sweet to relax at the proper time," said Jeshurun, glaring at Dion.

Dion laughed.

Captain June, with his hands clasped together, was deep in thought. He clenched his jaw and squinted and his skin turned piebald. "That's it!" he said, leaping to his feet, and continued as if he had forgotten that he had already suggested the idea. "We'll sleep on it. Now get some rest."

He launched up the ladder, out of the companionway, stormed down the deck to his quarters. After his steps receded and silence returned in the forecastle, the three deckhands turned into their bunks without talking. All through the night eddies pulled across Wade's eyelids. He wondered if ever they would set sail again.

The next day the men from the village bailed the generator room. In two hours they had removed the six inches of water from off the sole. This allowed Captain June to take apart the generator and fix it to pump the remaining water from the bilge. He cleaned and dried the wet components, replaced the wires. Disassembling, cleaning and reassembling the generator occupied the rest of the day. Assured that he had done hearty work, he latched the last component in place, then flipped the switch to heat the glow plug. It didn't work.

As he cursed repeatedly under breath, Emilio took over and ordered his score of men to continue bailing. They found the small, dime-sized hole and patched it.

The deckhands joined Captain June around the leak.

"How long will we need to wait to see if the mending will hold?" said Wade.

Captain June snapped the toolbox shut and said without looking up, "We won't need to wait at all. The hold is fine.... Tomorrow we sail for Cape Horn."

"What about ... the Canal?" said Jeshurun. His voice trailed away.

"The *Vermillion Mourning* is fit to sail around the Horn," said Captain June.

"Timshel," chimed Dion quietly.

The generator room was dark and cold and reeked of oakum. Captain June breathed deeply. He stepped toward Wade, the beam of the flashlight musty on the planks, and whispered in the darkness, "With help."

The following day with dawn streaming over the hills men from the village towed the bow of the *Vermillion Mourning* around and came aboard and helped hoist the headsails, weigh anchor, then to complete the revolution, hoist the main and fore. Again, the wind favored them. Leaving the destroyed dock and the hospitality of the village behind, they crawled through the mouth of the harbor, through the bay of Rosa Dulce and out to sea. Captain June ordered the sails trimmed at wing-and-wing. The *Vermillion Mourning* continued running with the wind on her passage south.

CHAPTER SEVENTEEN

They sailed into the doldrums. The already splintered deck curled into slivers of beanstalk. The iron belay pins were so hot they burned a hand. The ropes became warm and soft, almost powdery. The sails sagged. The deck was hot to walk over. The torrent of sunlight sizzled their skin.

Wade wrapped a shirt around his head to protect his shoulders and neck to match the white T-shirt covering his torso. The T-shirt now had a long dark mark across the chest from flaking the anchor chain. Jeshurun untied his long, shaggy hair so that it covered his neck. His clothing had become only more soiled. Captain June donned sunglasses, painted his nose with sunscreen and wore his sou'wester. Dion did nothing except discard his crimson silk shirt and throw it overboard. He looked at the others amusedly knowing he had no need to worry underneath his deep Brazilian tone. But his heart-shaped locket hung from his neck like an anchor.

Wade lay on the housetop sunning his slender runner's legs, practicing his knot-tying. Jeshurun had the helm. Dion reclined on the prow whittling a small sliver of plank with a knife. The swells moved without notice underneath the schooner. The current alone nudged the schooner along.

In the calm, Wade couldn't help but think of the Horn. "What kind of wind will we face?" he said.

Jeshurun shifted his weight wearily and locked his eyes on the brilliant horizon. "You heard Captain June—sixty-five knot winds. Maybe worse."

"Our schooner won't survive that, will it?"

"We're crew now. We don't have a choice. All we can do is hope. It's better to hope for lenience than set your mind on destruction. If you hope, just a little, the sea might listen. A good, wholesome heart is evident to all—even to the wind."

"What wind would you call this?"

The flag was stagnant against the after-leech. The sea looked like a mirror.

"On the Beaufort Scale, a Force Zero."

Wade made a loop for a bowline. "What's Force Two?"

"Wind speed four to six knots. Wavelets. Glassy appearance. Nothing breaking."

"That doesn't seem bad," he said, yawning. "What's Force Five?"

"Moderate waves. Whitecaps. Some spray."

Wade snorted. "I'm so scared," and he made a finishing loop for the bowline.

"You shouldn't be."

"Then what's Force Seven?"

"Here is where the adventure begins. Wind speed 33 knots. Large waves forming. Whitecaps everywhere. Even more spray. At this point, it's time to batten down the hatches."

Wade sniffed. He studied the long arc of the horizon. The sea and sky seemed to have melted into one color. "Force Ten?" he said in a curious tone.

Jeshurun inhaled the salty air, keeping his eyes cool on the binnacle. "If we reach Force Ten, we won't be alive."

Wade slipped the bowline around his finger and pulled until it was tight. "What do you mean?"

"Fifty-five knot winds. Waves over forty feet high. Overhanging crests. The sea is white, foam blowing in dense streaks. The rolling of the vessel is heavy and shocklike. Visibility is strongly reduced. This is categorized as a storm."

"I didn't know you knew so much about wind."

"Abner taught me. The Lighthouse Keeper needs to know the peril of the sea. But I love wind because it hones and smooths the wooden hulls of the ships."

At the mention of the Springwick Harbor Lighthouse, Wade's slender eyes flashed with jealousy, then turned inward and self-indulgent with the thought of becoming the Lighthouse Keeper himself at Hostel Sound. "Why around Springwick Harbor?" he said.

"Not only around Springwick Harbor—but wind of all kinds and everywhere. It's my passion. Winds of all description blow across the seas, native to specific regions."

"Like what kind of wind?"

"Well there's the Chubasco, a violent squall with thunder and lightning off the coast of Central America. We missed that thankfully. There's the Cape Doctor, a strong southeast wind that blows off the South African coast, which some people believe to have medicinal properties. The Santa Ana winds in California."

"I've heard of them."

"There's the Brisote, a northeast trade wind blowing stronger than usual off of Cuba. Then the Borasco, which occurs in the Mediterranean, characterized by thunderstorm or violent squall."

"Are there any special winds off Cape Horn?"

Jeshurun cleared his throat and spoke just above a whisper. "The Williwaws."

"The willy what's?"

"The Williwaws. They blow through the Strait of Magellan destroying sail, even boats, in one powerful, overwhelming blast. I've heard that they can travel at a hundred knots."

"A hundred knots?" said Wade, patting his throat with a limp hand, eyes swollen with sickness. "That's …"

"In *excess* of a hundred knots, Wade—that's forty knots above a Force 11 gale, which blows at around sixty knots. The Beaufort Scale doesn't even have a category for it."

"That's.…" Wade was speechless. "I can't.…"

"There's no warning, no way to prepare for them; they come unexpected, formed from a cold air front slowly building up a mountain then quickly rushing down the eastern side."

Wade, doubled over, clutched his stomach. "But there aren't Williwaws going through the Horn itself?"

"No."

He relaxed, repositioned his back until he felt comfortable. Then he untied the bowline and wrapped it around his tongue. "Good."

"Wade, it's the Horn. I'd rather take my chances and face a surprise attack from a Williwaw in the Strait. The Horn collects aquariums like this one. We won't be safe. But if we sail through the Strait, at least we'll have a fighting chance."

CHAPTER EIGHTEEN

While the weather was still fair Jeshurun showed Wade how to swab the deck. He retrieved two buckets found below, filled one with saltwater, the other with saltwater and Joy. Splashing the deck with the Joy mixture, he scrubbed.

"You scrub as hard as you can, the whole deck. I'll come behind and wash everything out the scuppers."

Wade worked cautiously, fearful that every time he dropped his bucket over the side to collect more water he would be carried overboard. In the distance he thought he saw shark fins. He scrubbed the port foredeck, then the starboard foredeck, moved to amidships. The Joy lathered in the saltwater forming impressive bubbles, which Jeshurun washed away.

"What's the purpose of swabbing the deck?"

"It helps keep the wood from drying out so that it won't leak."

Wade studied the deck with skepticism: already so dry, so warped, it was a miracle water hadn't seeped through. Yet the holds were still relatively dry. Thankfully they had not yet encountered a sea that splashed much more than spray over the bow.

They worked the aft deck to the transom. The sun was oppressively hot. When they finished and Jeshurun gathered both buckets and stowed them below, Wade sat on the gearbox behind the helm to rest. He was weak, sweating profusely, in need of water. Dion stood amusedly over him manning the helm.

"Have you ever been aloft?" he said.

"No … it's not a good idea."

"Of course. There's obviously no reason to go aloft. We don't have a topsail…."

Wade wiped his slim brow that curved into his slender temples and the sweat from his slender jaws.

"It is quite an impressive view of the sea," said Dion. "I was aloft just a bit ago, while you were below. It's amazing. That's all I'm sharing with you."

Wade folded his arms. The flag was idle.

"This may not mean anything to you," went Dion, "but I think the height of the futtock shrouds is about the same height as the lighthouse on Cape Race."

Wade sat up quickly, unfolded his arms. "You're lying."

"I'm sailing."

"You told me before Rosa Dulce that Bannock Pierce was a lie. That the Hostel Sound Lighthouse is a myth."

"Well. I'm not sure. Those things may not exist. But the lighthouse on Cape Race *does*." He pulled from his cargo shorts a faded postcard of the Cape Race Lighthouse. "See this picture?"

Wade slowly read the description: *Cape Race, Newfoundland: First constructed in 1907, the concrete tower stands 95 feet in height with a range of 24 nautical miles.* His smooth, dark face caved around the picture like flame. It was identical to the postcard he had found in the pages of Bowditch during his visit to the Captain's Quarters that lonely moonlit night.

Dion laughed quietly. "I'm just showing you. It's about the same height."

Wade leaned back on his hands like a bohemian, refusing to be bought.

Dion parted his lips into a cold grin, "But I think the Lighthouse at Springwick Harbor is higher."

Wade looked leeringly for his brother who was favored to ascend to higher places aloft. It was enough of that. He sat up. "I think you're right."

"Why don't you go see for yourself? It's not that high at all. I'll keep a lookout for you. Jeshurun would agree to your boldness."

Wade stormed to the shrouds. He climbed hurriedly hand over hand avoiding the broken ratboards. Determined to prove Jeshurun wrong. Higher. Higher still. Thirty … forty … fifty feet … ninety feet. He reached the base of the futtock shrouds.

Suddenly he froze. The height jolted him. Suddenly he remembered his acrophobia. Blood hammered through his chest. His wrists throbbed and his knuckles paled and he felt lightheaded and weak and tried to blink through the dizziness as he clutched the shrouds.

"Are you all right, Wade?" shouted Dion. "Try to climb a little higher if you can. If you get to the crosstree everything will be fine."

He couldn't speak. Breathless. Panicked.

"Come on down, Wade," said Dion in a deflated voice. "It's just one ratboard following another. It's not that hard."

Wade looked into the wide sea. The sharks had swam to the hull.

"You won't fall," said Dion flatly. "You can do it."

He couldn't move.

Jeshurun ascended the companionway. He saw Dion looking up. He followed his eyes to Wade paralyzed aloft, clutching the shrouds. Before any other words or thoughts came to him, he was climbing madly up the ratboards.

Wade felt his grip relaxing as the shrouds vibrated violently. "Stop, Jeshurun! I'm falling!"

Jeshurun paused a third of the way. "Are you hurt?"

"I can't … move…."

"Hold on." He crawled over each healthy ratboard.

Wade clung to the highest ratboard breaking from the stress.

"Wade, just hold on," he said calmly. "Breathe."

Wade peaked at the sharks. It was too much. He started to fall.

Jeshurun rushed the last two rungs and caught him, muscling him against the ratboards.

Wide-eyed and white Wade imagined himself splashing into the water to be torn apart. Jeshurun was close, breathing on Wade's hair, pinning him to the shrouds. "I've got you."

Wade blacked out….

When he awoke in his bunk, Jeshurun was patting his head with a damp cloth. "What happened … I feel like I could eat...."

"The sharks wanted to invite you to dinner," he smiled. "I told them you weren't hungry."

Wade cracked a grin.

"You've been unconscious four hours."

Wade moved his head slightly. It throbbed.

"I spoke to Captain June," said Jeshurun dampening his forehead. "You don't have to go on watch, not until you get better. I'll take your watch, for as long as needed. So rest."

"Did I fall?"

"Well, not exactly ... you sort of quarreled with gravity. And lost."

Wade tried to laugh but grimaced from the pounding headache.

"Your foot got caught in a ratboard. Your entire body went limp and your head slammed into a turnbuckle. I wrestled you to the deck before you became shark bait."

"I hate heights. I'll never adjust to going aloft."

"Maybe not aboard the *Vermillion Mourning*."

Wade studied him introspectively with lazy eyes. "You think I could survive the heights?"

"Not aboard a cursed vessel. And not atop anything on land."

"But maybe on top of the...." He shut his eyes. "The Harb ... I'm go...."

"I know where you're going."

Wade sighed heavily. He scratched the bottom of the bunk above him. "He's alive."

"He's very dead."

"I can *feel* him. I can feel him pulling. I can feel the love of this vessel."

The words sputtered out before he knew what he was saying. He looked at Jeshurun fearfully—this love of an unhealthy boat had already caused too many close calls. Their lives were dangerously close to their bitter end.

"I don't doubt that you harbor a love for a vessel," said Jeshurun. "Every sailor falls in love with his ship. But this vessel doesn't understand you. She'll gorge on your love until her holds fill and you both sink."

Out of the corner of his eye, Wade saw a vein of boat blood trickling down from a bolt on the ceiling, and he scratched it until the tip of his finger was orange.

"You love what this schooner nor any other schooner will never satisfy you with: the lust to be a thing you were never meant to become."

Wade propped himself on his elbow and pointed a finger at his brother. "What makes you the determiner of my destiny?"

Jeshurun placed his hand on his thigh and with the other creased the sheet of Wade's bunk. "You're too ripe for a disaster. You're on the verge of spilling something. Or worse, you're going to get stuck in a tower so high and lonely that you'll never figure out how to come down."

"I'll fall."

"I don't think you'll know how."

Wade felt Jeshurun's strengthening eyes on him and he lowered his chin toward the bunk searching for a spring to plug.

The following afternoon he was clear-headed enough to stand bow watch so that Captain June could be ahelm and smoke his ginger pipe. They both loved the pleasing aroma.

The mainsail was sheeted to starboard and the fore to port, with a preventer bent to the bale, running through the doldrums, making terrible time. Wade daydreamed of what he would do once he reached Cape Race. Would he find him there, hiding in the bilge of a sister ship, atop a tower, strolling with a flashlight in a park?

Jeshurun stepped out of the saloon and walked forward to the bow. In his hand he held a cooling apple pie and glasses of water. Wade's eyes locked on the dessert.

"How did—"

"Lots of apples," said Jeshurun as the water slipped past.

Wade's smooth mouth watered. "I love apple pie."

"I know, Wade."

"Reminds me of home."

"I know," said Jeshurun gently. "Do you want some?"

He nodded and Jeshurun furnished two plates and a small knife. He cut the pie into wedges and lifted a mess onto a plate.

"C'mon, Jesh. Give me more than that."

"How much?"

"I'll tell you when."

Jeshurun piled another heap.

"More."

He laughed. "Well how much more?"

"I want half the pie."

Jeshurun stole a glance over the galley housetop at Captain June, straddled across the helm blowing pipe smoke.

"Well if you get half, I get half."

They stabbed into the pie. Wade snorted. "Guess cavemen are hampered by the modern invention called utensil." He filled his mouth. They ate heartily.

The sun had crested over a cloudless sky and was beginning its descent. It was hot. They were sweating.

"Do you miss home?" said Jeshurun casually.

He adjusted his stance. Drank. "I don't know. Maybe. Why?"

"You're my brother. I have no one else to beat up on."

"I love you too."

Jeshurun licked his fingers. "It's good to be loved by your brother."

Wade imagined a great life given him.

A wind slammed into the sails. The sheets stretched until taut. Captain June struggled to maintain their heading. "It's coming! It's coming!" he shouted. Then as quickly, the wind died.

Wade and Jeshurun turned from him back to the pie and went on. "Abner is poor, Wade. He loves you with nothing less than himself."

"He doesn't understand."

"What doesn't he understand?"

"He doesn't understand how beautiful it is to love someone who wants you to be the best at everything you do, who gives you freedom to be anything and everything you want to be. I didn't have that before."

"You don't think Abner wants you to be free?"

"Abner wants me bound on the island. You know what I mean. I can't do anything there, except watch you become something I'll never become."

Jeshurun laughed. "Your freedom is worth the cost of his life! He's keeping you from the Lighthouse because he has your *freedom* in mind."

Wade shook his head. "That's not what I've seen in the eighteen years I've spent with him. He's the chore I'll never figure out."

Jeshurun squeezed the corner of the gearbox and glared. "What does he do that's so unfair?"

"Besides keeping me from going up? He won't let me leave."

"No, he won't let you leave without a purpose. He kept you on the island so that you can become strong and knowledgeable, to train you."

Wade's eyes widened and his speech slowed. "To be-come … what?"

"What he's always wanted you to be."

"Fettered."

Jeshurun licked his fingers, savoring this rich talk. "You have to discover that for yourself."

Wade snarled, "I already know what I can become." His eyes looked distantly over their port quarter toward the horizon, to the east, to the adventure promised. "That's my direction. That's good enough."

But sharing the apple pie with his older brother, whom he truly loved, pulled his thoughts toward home and to the adventures that they had lived together when they ran through the forests. Those days long ago had seemed like they were teaching Wade the path that he would run on for the rest of his life. He thought back to one particular morning when they ran rushing forward, alive and free.

CHAPTER NINETEEN

A cool day to run. Dawn rose over the eastern hills flaming the thick summer clouds, lifting rain from the grass, warming the heavy forest. Dew pooled on the petals of the yellow evening primrose, the freckled tiger lilies, glistened in the spider webs hanging from the branches of tall Oregon grape. Harbor seals glided offshore near the sea lions while dunlins and whimbrels rummaged in the sand.

"Race you to Strawberry Mountain," said Wade to Jeshurun as they stretched their calf muscles against the Lighthouse. "You won't beat me."

Jeshurun was twice his age and a skilled runner, blessed with stamina and endurance and the knowledge of when to crush. His startling finishes pacified the competition in the town. Having won every local and regional race offered to sailors in Oregon, he led the way for a life of fearless living on land. But Wade didn't know what it meant, truly, to be fearless. He thought fearlessness was a possession you achieved through purity, through life mastery. But Jeshurun kept telling him that true fearlessness comes when you give your life away and all that it possesses.

"I know I can beat you."

Jeshurun stretched his triceps behind his head.

"I know I'll crush you."

"You're a strong runner. But I bet I can make you better." Jeshurun ran his fingers through Wade's coal-dark hair. He pulled his foot to his buttocks stretching his quadriceps without need of balancing himself with a hand on the smooth reddish frustum.

If Wade could just match his stride today he'd witness firsthand the power to crush earth—that's all he wanted. To learn and believe and be guided toward love—that's all he wanted. It wasn't enough to be alive, but to be alive with him and his hope and the peace that gives itself away. The goodness. The therapy of the goodness. The pouring and the peace. Jeshurun ran as one filling the dream of the faith of the people; Wade could only dream of believing in his stride.

They motored to the harbor docking beside the *Vermillion Mourning*, tying the skiff and beginning their conservative jog through town. The trail followed the coastline some distance north to Strawberry Mountain.

Into the forest together. The trail narrowing into riddled roots and creeping groundcover. Wade in the lead, full of grit. Hungry to explore the trail. Working into rhythm. Breathing. Pacing. Thinking. Readying to push the limits. Jeshurun's deep, powerful lungs behind him. His comforting footfalls just behind. Not as fast or full but full of want to prove he shared the skill.

His body relaxing. The working. The perspiring. The cooling. Feeling the rhythm of the footfall. The movement of arms. Soaring into a high where his weakness was fitted with wings.

Suddenly he finds his game. Running faster, faster than ever before. On this twelfth birthday, running without fear of failure, without worry his body will fail him even as he punishes past limits. Breathing harder. Feeling the joy. The élan of life. The greatness. The soaring.

Running now faster through the forest, falling in love with the trail. Brushing manzanita. Passion carrying him. Deft leaping over rock and limb. The striving. The gasping. The hope of the end. Together and painfully moving, Wade painfully moving. The leader of his life with him, the great Jeshurun his adventurer and hero, his runner, his sailor strong and quick and powerful, able to run faster and longer than the little boy searching for a dream.

Remembering running down Main into the Ice Shack to fetch Lady Mint waffle cones, sitting on the rocks overlooking the harbor, Jeshurun making you believe in the greatness of the town and the sailors—boys and girls cradled in Abner's arms.

Remembering finding wild strawberries in the mountains with your hero, listening to his stories of sailors combing the earth for delectable bounty.

Remembering his drive reaching the first green, learning from him your grip, your only grip, that you now love no matter where the ball carries. Jeshurun carrying and using your clubs because he wants you to understand the clubs don't make the player.

Remembering holding that dirty, faded ball too flat to bounce proper, shooting into the darkness with the Red Light plodding the horizon. The court muddy by this morning's rain. Jeshurun taking it. Taking all your shots, the swishes, the missed dreams.

Remembering searching for the Boone and Crocket buck in the cold, thick earth. The last hunt of the season. Your first season and your step into manhood. In the clearing Jeshurun sees one, and you creep. You get to the edge. Urine all over you. The wind in your favor. Jeshurun is there with binoculars and whispers. Go a little farther. Set up on that pine. Be careful. And you feel him behind you, you feel his ribs stirring your neck. And all of it is good. You aim. Shoot. You get the pleasure of gutting it out. Even now you taste the meat.

Remembering crabbing in Netarts Bay. Dropping the pot overboard with half a frozen chicken wired to the frame and waiting twenty minutes before returning, pulling up the line in a fury and finding thirteen feisty crabs all waiting to be cooked. Jeshurun planting in you the miracle of the catch.

Remembering sitting in Jeshurun's twenty-year-old lap as he reads *Cloudy with a Chance of Meatballs* about the quest to sail the sandwich to paradise.

Remembering the four count rhythm and Jeshurun holding your pole too big for you and on the seventeenth cast you catch a big-inch steelhead, Jeshurun reeling it in for you or else you go into the river. The taste of the big one.

Remembering the lights, the lights, the lights of Portland as you canoe together down the Willamette, going into the heart of the city to feed the homeless.

Remembering the constellations atop Strawberry Mountain, humbled to be alive.

"Don't slow. Keep going."

Wade slowing. Falling out of step.

"Keep going. Almost there."

His coolness. His steady coolness. This is running. This hope. This is the vision of the finish.

CHAPTER TWENTY

Clouds bubbled green and purple, towering in the sky. The westerlies blew firmly off their starboard. The schooner was approaching the Roaring Forties. She rolled through the long, arching swells and surged into the troughs. Spume sprayed over her bow. Waves splashed over her caprail. The bronze-green water slid over her deck and down her waterway and out her scuppers, back into the sea.

Jeshurun and Wade sat on the gearbox together, Jeshurun guiding the helm with his toes. Wade made baggywrinkles out of old rope found in the bosun's locker. Dion sat on the transom.

Captain June, wearing a pea-green shirt and matching trousers, roamed the deck and the holds, belay pin in hand, tapping the schooner to test her soundness. He longed for a solid vessel, to be safe on a solid vessel, to sail into troubled waters that otherwise buried careless men. He returned to the quarterdeck.

"We are nearing Cape Horn," he said, peering at the clouds. "I think we're in for a weathering."

Jeshurun felt a drop of rain.

Captain June sat beside him on the gearbox. "I know from deep experience the calamity of a fouled sky and a fouled sea. I know brine and I know gale, and I know the fury of the deep."

Dion smiled to himself from his seat. Jeshurun looked cautiously at Wade.

"Don't be worried, Captain," said Dion. "We'll make it around."

Wade eyed him with skepticism.

Captain June stroked his heavy stubble, squinted at the sea. Squinted at each of them until they returned his gaze. "I've suffered the groaning deep. I've suffered the long, delicate snapping of my bones." He smiled strangely revealing his gap teeth. "Ready yourselves for death."

Wade gulped, eyed the hemp offal before him, stole a glance at Dion then at Jeshurun.

"The color of the sea is changed," said Captain June. "We're close. The Horn is near—the heart of danger. Maintain your heading."

Dion nodded sharply, pointing his chin. He gripped his heart-shaped locket. Captain June turned, faced Wade and Jeshurun. Wade avoided his eyes. Captain June stepped beside him.

"Something wrong?" He moved inches away. "Are you afraid of the Horn?"

Wade weakened on the offal, nervous of his proximity.

"Are you afraid, boy?"

He studied the flag flapping in the wind. Finally he spoke. "I'm afraid I won't make it past Cape Horn."

Captain June paused for a flash then laughed viciously. "That's because you won't. Life after a dashing is a myth. And if you pursue anything more, you'll become a myth, too—when the Horn dashes your teeth."

Wade clenched his jaw, wrestled out his words. "The Horn is a myth."

Captain June laughed harder. "You sound like you've been struggling with that all your life. The Horn is filled with sailors who never believed in truth."

"This vessel is a myth," said Jeshurun.

Captain June hammered his belay pin into his palm. "The *Vermillion Mourning* is a real vessel. She sails with the wind. And she will get us through the Horn if we are humble and do not stir the seas."

"Arrogance is not a myth," said Dion.

Captain June turned. "What is humble is a dead sailor. Dion, you don't have the humility to let yourself die." Dion smarted him quickly with his eyes. Tapped his heart-shaped locket. Captain June laughed, dismissing him, "The sea making you queasy?" He turned to Wade. "Are you bored, boy?"

"No."

"Thinking mermaids?"

Wade grinned with a corner of his mouth. "No."

"I see your eyes, Wade. I know what you're thinking."

"What am I thinking?"

He blew the pleasing pipe smoke across his work. "You want the sea."

"Not true."

"Your eyes are more honest than your mind."

Wade picked up the offal and gave it shape. His T-shirt had become a little dirtier after so many weeks asea. Captain June continued.

"I know what you dream at night. I know the heart of a ship."

"What do you know?"

He laughed. "I see your planking, boy. I see your keel. I see your timbers. Your canvas."

Wade weakened with the struggle to hold firmly to his offal. He said meekly, "You know what I dream. Everyone aboard knows. I dream of the Hostel Sound Lighthouse."

"That's what you think you dream. But a true dream is hidden in the heart. You cannot see what you fail to expose by your courage." He swallowed a heavy pocket of smoke and smacked Wade on the back of the neck, squeezing his spine. "Do you understand what I'm saying?"

"I wasn't born to sail."

"Then why do your eyes light up whenever I send you to bow watch? Why do you long for the bowsprit even in the roughest seas? Why does your ballantine look better than mine? You've learned how to weave a monkey's paw without effort. You coil lines in your spare time. You know the effort of the wind against the sail. You know the direction of true wind and apparent wind. You know when to reef, and you know every knot aboard this vessel. You've learned to take a sextant reading. You have a gift, boy. If you ever have the helm, you'll have her solid."

Wade swallowed hard. The helm, he sensed, was powerful. Too powerful to hold. Even now it functioned despite missing ribs and a full third of its wheel. Even now, even in the roughest seas, it remained true and faithful, determined to carry them to their destination. Yet it felt like he had been the one to dash the helm to pieces by his own fearful incompetency. Overcome by its sobering strength, his eyes weakened. Suddenly he was lost in trance. Oblivious to the vessel or the seas, he felt his ribs and skull to see if a rogue wave had not yet dashed them. He felt his limbs if they were still faithfully carrying him toward his destination—the termination of his dream, Cape Race. He quivered with the wheel guiding him in the gut of his blood, turning slightly east or west by the hand of a cold spirit. He believed there was no sound compass within him to share with the vessel, the helm. He believed he would lead the vessel to the rocks.

A beastly eye came up from the deep groaning, gripping him whispering, Are you afraid to carry in your heart a humble sail? You say you are brave but you cower at me, a little eye who sees only the truth of your heart. You ask for Cape Race. You will find it. God save you. Then it slipped below and vanished into a realm of secret sounds and suffering, battered dreams.

Fear coursed through his body. She was coming, the unconscionable terror. He had stirred an unseen water by his Cape Race desire. He grinned naw, not me. There is nothing wrong with me. Nothing in my conscience that is making me panic now, that bizarre marlinspike pounding through my eye into my brain. What have I done wrong? I am no sailor. I seek the goodness of a man. I'm fighting for a hold. I am not a sailor.

"The hell of it, boy." And Captain June gritted his teeth.

Wade shook his head. He returned to his offal. Out of instinct he was shaping into a monkey's paw. "I hate the sea. I'm afraid of the sea."

Captain June smeared his laughter over the deck.

"Why is that funny?"

Captain June relit his pipe and tossed the match into the water. The *Vermillion Mourning* rolled over swells slipping through the current. The ocean surface swirled flat grey. He spit into the water. Wiped the spit from his chin. Helped them adjust the helm.

Wade went to the bow to suffer the hostile and violent spray. He hated the pitch and yaw of the vessel. He hated the ocean, the fear of drowning, the schooner. He hated Jeshurun.

He hated Captain June. He hated Dion. He hated the fear he felt when he looked at Dion. Dion knew him, his conscience. He knew his ambition, his weakness. He knew his darkness, the fear of the unknown rushing through his eyes. He hated that Dion knew he was not a sailor. The sea meant to destroy him. This Horn.

He wasn't feeling any better when one cool afternoon the wind shifted and Captain June ordered the ship tacked. While Dion and Jeshurun sprang into action at the bow, Wade lay in his bunk in the fo'c'sle refusing to come up.

"Wade, we have to tack," said Jeshurun.

Captain June shouted, "Come about!"

Wade rolled onto his side away from Jeshurun so that he faced the ceiling.

"I'm not interested in tacking right now. We're not going to make it around Cape Horn. It's impossible. We won't survive the fury of the waves or anything in the deep."

"We have to try. It might be the last tack we'll make before the Horn."

"This is the last tack?"

"Perhaps."

"The last until the Horn?"

"Maybe, Wade. I don't know. The wind can do anything."

"I guess I can come up for that."

Wade ascended the ladder and positioned himself on the port jib sheet. Dion and Jeshurun stood at the starboard jib sheet ready to take in the line once the bow of the vessel passed into irons. Wade took the free end of the line off the cleat. Captain June turned the helm and the *Vermillion Mourning* crossed over from her starboard tack. The headsails went into luff from irons and Captain June yelled, "Pass the jib!"

and Wade eased out on the port jib sheet and Dion and Jeshurun took in the slack on the starboard jib sheet, heaving on her until she came taut. Dion made a half-hitch around the end of the cleat to secure the line. Jeshurun checked the half hitch to ensure that it was solidly locked. Wade ran over and sheeted in the stays'l. The *Vermillion Mourning* now sailed on a port tack. The three turned aft to help sheet in the foresail.

Suddenly the line of the jib flung off the cleat. It flapped madly in the wind. Wade started toward the sheet attempting to grab the end of the line that whipped back and forth like a bullwhip. Captain June was shouting for him to stay away, but Wade moved closer. Jeshurun lunged for him, but tripped on Dion's foot, and fell to the ground.

Wade reached for the whipping line.

"Get away! Don't touch it!" Captain June shouted. "Dion, stop him!"

Wade's hand shrunk back. Then he lunged.

The bitter end struck his shoulder. He fell, dazed. Captain June turned the helm so that the vessel went into irons causing the force of the whipping to slacken. Jeshurun grabbed the line and made it fast around the starboard cleat, locked it into place with two half-hitches. Wade lay on the deck stunned, rubbing his shoulder. Dion tended to him.

"You should have made that line secure," said Jeshurun sharply at Dion who frowned in defiance.

"You saw me wrap it around. You checked it. I saw you check it when we turned aft. What do you want me to do?"

"If it had hit his skull it would have killed him," said Jeshurun.

Dion glared at him. "None of us were safe. Let it go."

Captain June, who was more concerned about getting safely to the Horn, turned the helm. "Sheet out on the jib!"

Out of instinct the two rose and sheeted out on the starboard jib sheet. This time Dion made the half-hitch around the end of the cleat. While he walked away Jeshurun made another for safe measure.

Wade whimpered holding his shoulder. “If anything, the force of the wind caused the disaster.”

Jeshurun knelt over him. Examined his shoulder. “You need ice.”

“I need to get off this boat.”

“Plenty of ice near Cape Horn,” chimed Dion.

Jeshurun readied to punch him but considered their greater unity and let his anger subside, turning his attention to Wade. “Go below. I’ll get something cool for you.”

He helped him up, Wade grimacing, then down the ladder of the fo’c’sle. He returned on deck and hunted Dion, who had returned to the helm.

“It’s not my fault,” he said pleading with his hands and shoulders. “You were the one who locked the sheet. Blame yourself if you want to start pointing fingers.”

Captain June stepped between them.

“You’re both at risk. This’ll stop now. Whatever happened, it endangered not just Wade, but the entire crew. From now on, we take responsibility together. Is that clear?”

He fixed his eyes on each of them.

“Yes, Captain,” said Jeshurun.

“Of course,” agreed Dion.

Captain June gave the helm to Jeshurun and went forward to check on Wade.

Jeshurun folded his arms and stood broadly. “When this sail ends, you’ll answer for your treachery.”

Dion laughed. “I didn’t trip you.”

“Just a warning.”

Dion smarted him with his eyes.

Wade could barely lift his arm. Captain June felt around the bone and determined it was just a deep bruise. You're lucky, he was saying, that it only just brushed against you. If it had struck you in full, we would have had to bury you. A few days of rest and he would be back to sailing—just in time for the Horn. Wade wished the bruise had been deeper.

CHAPTER TWENTY-ONE

Three days later having discovered another leak, Captain June came up from the forehold scowling, called the crew together at the gearbox. "The forehold is leaking. Once again, the generator isn't working. It probably never worked." He scratched his lengthening whiskers and stared at a spot of boat blood on the inside of the caprail that seemed to him curiously malformed, and far too large.

Jeshurun laced his fingers together, knowing that this was true, and knowing why. It was due to the true origin of the *Vermillion Mourning*. But he wasn't ready to share his knowledge with anyone yet, foremost Wade. It wasn't time. This voyage was not yet in vain, hopefully. A goodness even now could be unfurled for the eager wind. "Can we hand pump?" he said.

"I thought the forehold was fine," said Dion.

Jeshurun leered at him. "Where did you go last night after you retired for your watch?"

Captain June folded his arms at Dion who widened his eyes in defense. "I went below into the forehold to make sure our ballast hadn't shifted. And she hadn't."

Jeshurun said mockingly, "That's because the water flooding in righted her."

Captain June scratched his whiskers and said matter-of-factly, "We'll have to turn back."

"But we're sailing for the Horn," cried Dion. "If we turn back now it would be disastrous." He folded his arms like Captain June. "I'll fix the leak. I've fixed many leaks in my time. I'm a sailor, Captain June. We were clear on that point from the beginning."

Captain June smiled keenly at him for exposing this hidden thing between them. "I didn't recruit you. I volunteered to be captain of this ship. It's called courage—facing your fears. Licking the thing before you get licked."

"Yes, you arrived in Springwick Harbor so courageously. But I imagine our conversation in the park after you got out of the Roseway Inn wasn't very courageous, eh Captain?" he giggled.

Captain June stared at a spot in the sea for a moment, his mind lost in thought as he calculated what to do. Wade thought he looked panicked.

Dion went on. "You don't have to remember." He motioned to Wade. "Don't worry, son. We just discussed the sunspots. And I'm sorry if it sounds like I'm deceiving you. It's not true. Don't believe it. Let me fix the leak and we'll be on our way."

Captain June blinked himself out of his trance. He stole a glance at Wade and made sure that Dion saw him look that way. Then he and Jeshurun made solid eye contact, sharing an understanding about the sail that was far beyond Dion's scope. Satisfied, he regained his composure. "You were going to say something, Jeshurun?"

Jeshurun nodded to him and then refocused the conversation on the leak. "We can't sail when our ship is leaking."

"But we can't forfeit our sail," whispered Wade, twisting into a ball the front of his soiling T-shirt. "We're so close to the end."

Dion smiled openly and quickly in agreement with the boy. “Wade’s right,” he said. He tapped his heart-shaped locket. “It would be humiliating to return to Springwick Harbor as defeated sailors. I’d rather take our chances against the Horn. We must go forward. We have to go forward to get around Cape Horn so we can arrive in Cape Race.” With calmness he pooled his thoughts at Wade, pulling his eyes up at him.

Wade studied his fingers.

Jeshurun glared at Dion. “You’ve fallen in love with a dangerous myth, Dion.”

“It’s not that dangerous,” said Wade.

“It’s foolish, Wade. You know better,” said Jeshurun.

Dion laughed in a mocking tone at him. “So jump overboard.”

“That’s enough,” said Captain June. “We’re not going to go around accusing each other with false ideas. Last night I went below after Dion had left and found no leak. It’s not his fault. The truth is, our ship is old. We’re lucky to have made it this far.”

“Then why don’t we sail for a safe port?” pressed Jeshurun. “We’re sailing into dangerous waters on a vessel that isn’t worth the planking she was fashioned from.”

Captain June focused his eyes at the mystery of Dion who was smiling nebulously at Wade. “Why don’t we decide as a crew?”

“By democratic vote,” said Wade.

Dion closed his eyes and smiled with his teeth. “Of course by vote.”

“I vote we abandon the sail and head for a safe port before it’s too late,” said Jeshurun. “And then we can mend the schooner, turn north and sail into the deep Pacific without fear of a storm, and Dion….” Dion turned to him. He continued.

"We could find a buried island with treasure. Deep down. In a nest of baby volcanoes. Think of all the gold you could find? Just think, you could drop us off at a reef, take the schooner for yourself. You could go digging in that writhing angry patch."

Dion twitched and sneered, hating that sting, that constant sting from him.

Jeshurun continued. "You'd go free, Dion. And you could dig, dig, dig as long as you'd want, with that locket of yours holding you down."

Dion froze. His trademark wryness was gone from his face, replaced with cold, naked fear. He was speechless and small.

Captain June, who understood Jeshurun's heart, said nothing, knowing that the idea was as good as any, in assessing the true matter of the situation. But he also knew that they had to go forward, for too many reasons to explain; one of them glaringly was his bloodlust for the Horn itself, to conquer it, a notch to impress the mariners below.

Jeshurun put his hand on Wade's knee, who was lost and absorbed in the heavy and painful fid anchored into his chest. "And then one day we could go home," he said to him. "And sail the way we want, the way we were always meant."

"I vote we continue," said Dion, struggling to hide his shakiness. "I have a feeling the *Vermillion Mourning* is stronger than … we think she is."

Captain June rubbed his neck in thought. "I think Dion is right. We'll make it through. I have a hunch."

Jeshurun felt a strain as he regarded Dion, whose smirk had returned, directed now at Wade.

"Well, Wade," he said. "It comes down to you. A tie vote—"

"Means we sleep on it," said Captain June, "and vote again tomorrow."

Jeshurun trailed his voice into Wade's hearing. "Tomorrow may be too late."

Dion snorted. "C'mon, Jeshurun, wouldn't you rather go down together, if we're going down at all?"

Jeshurun folded his powerful forearms. "We can still make it to Chile."

"If I can manage to fix the generator," reasoned Captain June, "we can pump. But there's not much time. The seas are rougher. Soon the westerlies will push us right into the Horn. But if we can make it to the Horn, there's a chance we'll make it through."

Jeshurun stood with both feet planted in front of Wade and tipped his chin toward his ear to wick reason into his hearing. "Cape Horn is the most dangerous sailing grounds in the world, Wade. The odds of surviving on this boat with our undersized crew are impractical."

"But hasn't sunk," chimed Dion. "We're still afloat. Still heading along."

"I think I can fix the generator," said Captain June. "I'm sure I can. Pumping won't be a problem."

"Until something else happens," said Jeshurun. "Look at the foremast—she's ready to topple at any moment. Or the hole in the deck from the topmast. It's a miracle she's still water tight, a miracle one of us hasn't fallen through."

Wade buried his face in his hands.

Jeshurun put his arm around him. "If we sail back to Springwick Harbor, we can rest up for a good adventure. But pass on this one."

"I hate sailing," moaned Wade. He was confused with Dion's behavior who not long ago had cautioned him against the dangers of the Horn, but was now openly supportive of not just a sail into its maw but a bold sail, fearlessly taunting history.

Jeshurun sat on the gearbox and waited for a moment while he crossed his arms. "Then vote we head for Chile. It's not that far. We can probably make it if we change course immediately."

"It's your choice, Wade," said Dion. "But remember, you have to live with your choices no matter what they are, for good or bad."

"I think we'll be safe either way," said Captain June. "I know how to fix the leak. And I know how to fix the generator. Despite what you say, Jeshurun, this vessel is surprising me with her sturdiness."

Jeshurun snorted, his lips derisive. "You know the truth of this schooner, Captain. That's why you volunteered. Don't coolly endear yourself to myths."

Dion rolled his eyes, smirking. "You and your myths, Jeshurun. Your beautiful myths. Tell me, is the wood you're sitting on as mythical?"

Wade dashed his eyes at them. The others fell silent. He inhaled deeply. "It's not a myth. None of it is. We're members of the *Timshel Auxiliary*. We may, with help. We're sailing for the Horn."

Captain June spent the rest of the day in the generator room working tirelessly to fix the generator. It wouldn't start. For a while he stared at the water in the hold, wondering what he should do. He was determined to sail around Cape Horn. It was the one last realm of the world that would prove he had mastered life. He said nothing to the crew of the leak. The *Vermillion Mourning* continued to sail the spine of the Pacific.

CHAPTER TWENTY-TWO

A few days later Wade was sitting on the galley housetop trying to whip an end of a line. His shoulder was still tender from the bruise, and he struggled to push the needle through the strands. Even with the sailor's palm the movement struck a sharp, blasting pain through his muscle forcing him to rest. He gazed up at the main crosstree directly above him, wondering what it would be like aloft—if his shoulder somehow would hurt less.

Dion hopped onto the galley housetop and joined him. Captain June had the helm, and Jeshurun was in the galley cooking stew.

"What are you looking at?" he said.

"Nothing."

"No?"

Wade returned to the whipping and, grimacing, pushed the needle through the tough rope. He looked up again, lost in the heights.

The schooner was rolling along through the cumbersome swells.

Dion folded his legs then tapped on the galley housetop with a drumming finger. Looking aloft with him he said in a sanguine way, "Have you ever climbed a halyard?"

Wade tensed. He pushed the needle deeper into the rope.

"I've climbed in a storm," said Dion. "It was savage."

Wade regarded the throat halyard again. You'd need tremendous strength.

"I can climb hand over hand—without using my legs," said Dion, and tilted his head sideways so faintly at Wade it was dubious whether he was mocking him or simply sincere. "Wanna see?"

"No you can't."

Dion squinted. "Watch this." He rose and spit on his palms, grabbed the throat halyard and climbed fluidly hand over hand. He reached thirty feet and looked down, legs dangling, at Wade. "I can hold this until eight bells."

Wade loosened his grip on the whipping.

He climbed higher. Forty feet … fifty … sixty feet. At ninety feet, just below the futtock shrouds, he paused again.

Wade let go of the whipping entirely.

Dion inverted himself and dangled head-down, legs spread above him like an acrobat. "Come on up. I bet you can't make it half as high."

Wade slid off the galley housetop and reached for the throat halyard but froze just shy of touching it. The line ascended above Dion, wrapping into the block. He knew he shouldn't climb, not with the condition of his shoulder, not from his fear of heights. He knew Jeshurun would keelhaul him if he caught him. But against his better judgment he felt himself being pulled. A tidal strength wanted him higher than his fear, to whisk him to a freedom so expansive and clean it would open his heart forever. It wasn't the Lighthouse calling him but something else, something greater, something deeper. Some part of him wanted him aloft, a hand-over-fist fearlessness waiting to take shape and define the expanse he did not understand. To go high meant he had mastered the fear of ascending, and only the strangely seaworthy understood how to master the heights ... but this was not yet him. Confused, without rhythm, fumbling to hear, against his better judgment he felt the wind urging his journey upward. He heard the wind in himself, the current pulling him aloft, but it was terrifying to think he would somehow learn what it meant to soar.

He started for the halyard, gingerly spitting on his hands. He grabbed the throat and wrenched himself upward. His shoulder filled with sharp pain.

Just then Jeshurun stepped out of the galley to ring the bell for supper. His eyes regarded Wade's foolish ascent and rose to take in Dion's bait. He rushed to him shouting, "Stop! Wait!"

Wade flinched. He let go of the line. Fearfully he looked at him. "But I can climb."

Dion still was suspended above them, clinging to the halyard, legs inverted, like a spider to his silk. "Why not, Jesh? He'll be fine. He doesn't have to climb as high as me."

Jeshurun ignored him and focused only on his brother and said for his sake alone, "You're not strong enough to climb even half as high. You're not whole."

Wade gripped the halyard until his knuckles whitened.

Jeshurun continued, putting a hand above his on the halyard. "If you go aloft right now, Wade, you will fall. You won't have the strength to hold yourself to the halyard. Your shoulder is in no shape to climb. Before you realize it, you'll plummet. And you might injure yourself permanently. You might jeopardize the safety of all of us."

Dion by now had climbed onto the crosstree and was sitting comfortably with one hand on the shroud. Even at almost one hundred feet above them his self-assured eyes shimmered like lures. "Maybe some other time?" he called down. His heart-shaped locket dangled from his neck.

Wade, eyeing Jeshurun with suspicion, let go of the halyard. He returned to the whipping.

Jeshurun put his arm around him and hugged him hard. "Someday you'll be able to climb halyards higher than this one. And then later, once you've mastered the deck, you'll be able to descend or climb—whatever you desire—hand over fist the leech of a skysail. *Several* times. But you have to learn how to do it. And you have to be healthy. It takes courage, stamina, and strength to suspend yourself so far above deck."

Wade gazed at Dion so much higher than the vessel and the sea, suspended in utter freedom, wind fluttering his crimson shirt like a sail.

"Do you understand what I'm saying to you, Wade?"

Wade nodded, gazing upward. He recalled their home in Springwick Harbor when he often stood outside along the base of the Lighthouse and gazed upward at Jeshurun and Abner sharing the view of the Lighthouse together. It seemed to him to be about the same height as the main crosstree, although in truth the Springwick Harbor Lighthouse was more than twice as high.

Wade nodded in agreement, looking at his shoes, promising compliance. Once Jeshurun saw that the danger had been averted, he went hurriedly into the galley to see to the stew, which had caught on fire. Captain June, who had been manning the helm absentmindedly all the while, sipped from his coffee.

But as Jeshurun closed the door behind him, Wade turned again to the halyard and to Dion who still sat in the crosstree looking upon them.

"Wait for some other time," he said, adding smoothly, "when your strength is perfect."

Wade attacked the halyard. Seizing the taut line with both hands, he pulled himself upwards one hold at a time. His shoulder seemed to split open from the pain.

Captain June set his coffee on the saloon housetop. "Wade, be careful," he said, searching the bow for Jeshurun.

Wade climbed higher. Twenty feet … thirty … forty … forty-five … forty-seven. He paused. Just shy of half way. His forearms trembled. His shoulder convulsed.

"Wade, be careful," caution Captain June. "You need to come down. Be a sturdy thing."

Wade's face was as tense as the halyard. His teeth and jaw refused to give. The wind lifted his shirt exposing the apron from the Lighthouse, wrapped so tightly around his midsection that the muscles in his abdomen bulged through it. He climbed higher. Forty-eight. Forty-nine. Paused. The pain in his shoulder was unbearable.

"Wade, come down!"

He smiled to him. "Captain, look at me!"

"Wade, come down from there! It's not safe to be so high! You'll lose your stren—"

Wade slipped.

"Hook the shroud with your foot! Climb onto the shroud!" shouted Captain June.

Wade slipped again. His eyes widened.

"Hook it!" said Captain June. He started for the shrouds to climb but he couldn't leave the helm without risking an accidental gibe. "Dion, help him!" he shouted.

Wade slipped again. He wrapped his legs around the halyard.

"Ease yourself down!"

Wade fell.

Jeshurun, hearing the ruckus from inside the galley, after he finally extinguished the ruined meal, lunged out the door to help. It was too late.

Wade slammed into the galley housetop crumpling his legs, grimacing, clutching his ankle. Jeshurun rushed to him. Dion descended the shrouds and stood over them.

Jeshurun glared in fury at Dion. "I wouldn't have expected anything more."

Dion said in an unassuming tone, "My hand got caught in the futtock shrouds."

Wade clenched his teeth. His ankle was swelling. Jeshurun fetched an instant ice pack from the medicine chest in the saloon, broke it quickly, placed it on his ankle.

Dion scratched his head. "Can you walk? I'm sorry, Wade. I shouldn't have goaded you."

"You didn't goad me. I went on my … ouch! Be careful!" Jeshurun was wrapping tape around the ankle to secure it. "I went on my own will."

Jeshurun helped Wade into the saloon to rest on a bench. "You can't climb the halyards on your own," he was saying. "You need help."

As they were descending through the galley into the saloon, Dion called out, "You were a tiger on that line, Wade."

Captain June was the only one who heard. He shouted to him, "Dion! Come aft!"

Dion strolled with the sway of the vessel to the stern and when he reached Captain June, he spread his legs like an umpire, tipped his chin, blinking.

Captain June barraged him, slewing words: "What were you thinking? Do you realize you might have cost us the sail? Our lives?"

"I'm sorry. I really thought he could climb. He did climb."

"The decent thing to do would be to keelrake you," he fumed.

Dion sized him up. He outweighed Captain June by thirty pounds. "You know you don't have the strength to even drop me in the water."

Captain June returned his gaze without much effort. "I'm surprised no one has yet had the guts to discipline you," he said. "What are they afraid of? It can't be because you're a fine sailor."

"You know I'm a fine sailor, Captain. You promised me the *Vermillion Mourning* once we arrived at our destination. Perhaps we won't wreck and you can give it to me."

Captain June gritted his teeth. "You're desperately ready to die, Dion. Leviathan is bored pursuing you." Before Dion could react, Captain June barreled under him and scooped him up. He took two quick steps to the rail. And dropped him into the shark-infested water.

CHAPTER TWENTY-THREE

Captain June returned quickly to the helm before the vessel lost her point of sail. As the wind strengthened and after the *Vermillion Mourning* gained some distance, he ordered Jeshurun and Wade to the quarterdeck. As they made their way up the companionway, Dion flailed helplessly in their wake. His head, chest and arms bobbed at the crest of each swell, disappearing into the troughs. With ease they were gaining distance from him. Wade propped his foot on the gearbox. Jeshurun sat next to him. Captain June searched their eyes for confidence.

"We have lost a crew member," he said.

"*What*?" said Jeshurun.

Wade searched sullenly for Dion.

Captain June said dismissively, "I threw him overboard. I would have made him walk the plank, but we can't really spare any planks."

"You *threw* Dion overboard?" glared Jeshurun.

"I pitched him. Yep."

"How are we going to sail with only three crew members?"

"How have we been sailing with only four?"

"Captain June," cried Jeshurun, "we can't sail the boat without Dion. We'll die."

"As if we were going to live with him aboard it?" smiled the captain. "He's a bilge rat."

Wade searched the seas and far in the distance, blending with the grey horizon, Dion was waving his hands in desperate plea. He strained his eyes at him and he thought he could hear, just faintly, his distress call.

"But we can't abandon him like this to the sea," urged Jeshurun. "Not when our own lives are at stake. We need him. You know what I'm talking about."

Captain June gathered Jeshurun's eyes in his own and pondered them as he studied the binnacle. The waves sloshed against the hull.

"It'll destroy us," continued Jeshurun, "far sooner than the Horn. We have to go back."

Captain June scratched his whiskers scanning the horizon. "It wouldn't make any difference even if we did," he said. "By the time we come about the sharks will have torn him apart. I'm afraid we'll have to make due. Wade, I'm promoting you in Dion's wake. You are now officially first mate. You deserve it." He laughed again.

"Stop!" shouted Jeshurun. "This is madness! You're gambling with our lives! And with the hopes and dreams of every mariner in Springwick Harbor!"

"At least it's a gamble, son. We don't even have the chance when he's with us. I had to get rid of him."

Jeshurun seethed. "Then we're dead men. Dion gets his wish after all. Is that how you want to be remembered, Captain? That you played into his hands—that you became what he always wanted you to become?"

"I've wanted to become a sailor all my life."

"But that's not what you are with Dion manipulating you. He wanted you to throw him overboard. You lose. And so do we."

Captain June fumbled over this, biting his lower lip. “But I believe we can sail with only three.”

“But like you said—we’re not sailing even with four. We’re exhausted. Our port-and-starboard watches are taking a disastrous toll. In a few days we’ll probably lose another from delirium.”

Wade was still scanning the horizon for him. He could see him.

“What do you propose we do?” said Captain June.

“Vote,” said Wade.

“I vote we pick him up,” said Jeshurun.

“I vote we let the sharks pick him up,” growled Captain June.

They looked at Wade. He was rubbing his ankle. He studied the sails and the topping lifts and baggywrinkles flapping against the sails, the flag fluttering without care, content, for once, to be a part of such an unexpected sail. “I think I’d rather finish the sail together,” he said, peering behind them at the ever shrinking shape of the sailor who had convinced him to sail in the first place. “… wherever that may lead us. But Jeshurun is right. We can’t sail without him. We have to go back.”

Jeshurun’s heart quickened. He knew it was a mistake

.

CHAPTER TWENTY-FOUR

The *Vermillion Mourning* veered for Dion. The horizon was dark from the heavy clouds approaching from the west. Jeshurun and Wade adjusted the sheet of the foresail as Captain June manned the helm and scanned the waters. In the gloaming, they spotted him.

The constant threat of sharks had reduced him to jetsam. After having remained in the water for so long, he was gaunt and terribly cold, suffering from hypothermia. When Wade and Jeshurun hoisted him on deck, his wild sockets still searched for the fins that had been fighting to tear him apart.

He was not the same. Shivering madly, jaw clattering like a telegraph, his body had been reduced to a cool deposit of flesh, submissive to crew. Jeshurun wrapped a heavy wool blanket around him and guided him into the saloon to rest in a cozy Pullman; Dion followed his lead like a child, dependent on the parent stronger than himself. Wade heated water for tea and administered it to him gently, helping him raise the temperature of his core. Slowly Dion regained his strength. But even as he stabilized, there was something different. A coolness. An awareness that man in his deepest strength is desperately abject, at the mercy of the terror of the water. The only strength left in him was to make one desperate lunge to seize all of life all at once, at all cost.

Above deck, at the helm, Captain June was angry for the lost time, for Dion's insolence, for his dishonesty. Once Captain June had arrived in Springwick Harbor with the purpose of sailing the *Vermillion Mourning* out to sea, Dion had come to him as a paper sailor whose resume was impressive: four years of continuous sail with time logged as bosun and first mate on world class vessels; a careful vision for the health of a crew; knowledge of deep anchors. But after talking with Abner and Tobiah and Walter, Captain June was reassured of his true motive for crewing, which was why he had volunteered for the sail in the first place. Dion wanted to frap the boat in elegant sin. Captain June was determined to let him. He was determined to let him spread his strings in whatever direction he wanted while aboard, because he knew it would not alter the bigger picture—the bending of Dion, his limbs whipped in preparation for the deep.

"Dion, I don't know much," he said, "but I know what should happen even when what does happen is not worth remembering. You survived death. You should be thankful."

"I-I am, C-captain. I c-certainly am," he said, his bare chest riddled with goose bumps, his heart-shaped locket shivering along with his skin. "An-nd I'm s-s-orry for h-h-having ever projected an antag...onist...ic at-titude. It's n-n-not fun when death can sss-mell you; it's b-b-better suffering alive, suffering all al-l-larm ... t-than becoming nothing before your t-t-time. I am s-s-sorry."

Captain June appeared pleased. "Will you, then, cooperate? Will you agree to let the sail happen as it is meant to happen? I believe we are destined to sail around the Horn, Dion. But in order for our destiny to happen so healthfully, we need to have all hands in support of the best end. Even one bad thought may destroy us. Is that clear?" He was looking down at Dion as if over the top of a wall.

"Y-y-yes, sir," said Dion, acknowledging his concern. "I'll d-do my best. And I b-b-believe we *will* make it around. R-r-really, I have no choice—if we don't make it around we b-b-become shark bait. It isn't fun to be shark bait," he said, lowering his eyes at Wade as if looking over the top of a wall.

Wade shivered. Dion hadn't been reformed at all. The plunge had only made him sharper and colder.

Yet Dion was powerful. Never had Captain June seen such a display of upper body strength, nor such a resolve to survive for so long in these icy waters. Not even among the crew of the *Zephyr* had he witnessed similar dexterity. But it seemed that Dion had climbed not to display his own strength but to persuade those weaker than himself to discover the limits of their own. If he wanted, he probably could have climbed all the way to the masthead and inverted himself, waiting for those less strong to follow in his path—until they plummeted. He was convinced that the washing would have no effect on him.

Dion, at least visibly, did not share any animosity toward Captain June, nor toward Jeshurun nor Wade. At first he could barely speak, lips blue. But with the medical care—a dry change of clothes, an extra blanket and pillow, tomato soup—the coldness left his body. Wade exchanged encouraging words with him.

"I'm sorry it happened to you," he said.

Dion shrugged weakly. "I had it coming to me." He shivered and pulled the blanket over his shoulder. "Being left for dead, for the sharks, is haunting, Wade."

"It's getting dark."

Dion sipped. "I've been more than combative. I'm sorry for coercing you to climb the halyard."

"I shouldn't have disobeyed Jeshurun."

"Well, from now on, listen to him. He's wise."

"Wiser than Captain June?"

Dion tasted the soup against the roof of his mouth savoring the flavor. "Captain June is very wise. That's what makes him a good sailor. He's one of the best. But sometimes wisdom can work against you. It wasn't wise to pick me up, Wade. You three should have tried to hold your own against the Horn. You should have left me for the sharks."

"*Why*? We need you."

"You need someone who's honest.... I'm not that honest. I'm sorry." He looked up at him with watery eyes. "Sometimes I mean to hurt you."

"It's all right," said Wade with stoicism. "We voted and brought you aboard."

"What did Captain June vote?"

"To leave you behind. But Jeshurun voted to pick you up."

"And that made you the tie breaker."

"I voted you onboard."

Dion's eyes glittered. "That wasn't very wise."

Wade wiped his nose.

"But thank you. I'll get you back."

Eventually his warmth returned. Offering himself as one who from a tough fight had been leveled, he yielded to their instruction and obeyed Captain June with humility. His eyes, however, still shimmered like quicksilver.

CHAPTER TWENTY-FIVE

Meanwhile Wade passed about the boat like a ghost. He feared the expression of his sailing would fail to bring him to his desired end. His hollow veins glowed underneath his skin. He struggled to discover the concreteness in himself or in what he saw and touched. This journey to the Horn and what came after swirled about him like spray. Fearful he was losing whatever hold he thought he had on the destination, he began to loathe the Horn and the crew.

He loathed Jeshurun for his piercing caution, for mothering him with safety. It seemed whenever Wade was on deck Jeshurun was there reminding him to keep himself tethered to the safety rail, refrain from going aloft, keep himself as close as he could to the stern, the safest place to be. Wade tired of his oversight; he wished Jeshurun had not joined him on the passage. In his absence he would pursue his dream of the Hostel Sound Lighthouse without guilt.

He loathed Captain June for his insouciance. He loathed his strange connection with the schooner and his evolving, bizarre relationship to wind and sea. He loathed his strangely personal eyes, in one moment knowing nothing of you nor your skill as a sailor and in the next carving out the rot in your soul so you would sail efficiently. He loathed his dress—pea-green shirts, sou'wester and trousers that made Wade even queasier than the motion of the vessel. Sea legs were no match for an ugly shirt.

He loathed his own heart—so buoyant it would keep afloat any vessel, so weak any water would crush it. He was a burden, a lost cause, to the crew. But in the same he was so in control of the passage and so keen on the relationship of wind and water that it was impossible to criticize him for his skill. In one sense he was a budding plebe; in the next—tasteless salt, waiting to be washed from memory.

He loathed the false harbor, the doomed harbor, he was heading toward. He loathed Cape Horn. He knew there was no harbor there, nothing other than the prosaic rock thrust from sea; Jeshurun had assured him of this. But still, weighted hunger pulled him to it as if destined to become what the Horn wanted him to become—jetsam so terribly hideous that no ship would ever bother salvage it. He loathed the Horn because he didn't understand it. It was too revered, too hallowed, to be regarded by a will of flesh. He simply didn't have the words to describe it, based on the stories Dion and Captain June shared with him. The Horn seemed so deep, so overwhelming, that once he arrived—if he arrived—it would impel him to jump overboard and swim to it, only to be dashed against its cold bluff.

He loathed the wind as it tried to embrace him; whenever free he would stow below and try to ignore the whispering, *Come see the gift I have for you. Do not fear the storm. You will be free. Timshel.* But as he tried to sleep, the violent crash of the bow stirred his unrest and he knew he would not survive the journey. He tossed back and forth against the walls of his bunk, drowned in his piercing conscience, hating the wind because it promised him the Horn.

Eerily, coldly, he loathed Dion's heavy pull, his encouraging words—just the words to soothe him. He loathed his sharp smile and chin and the magical eyes that tried to cleanse him with soap. He loathed his tempting freedom, the professional salt begging him to find harmony with the salt of the sea, free in desire to discover the waters without fear.

In these days Wade felt the wind passing weakly over the schooner as if avoiding the spread of her sickness. It seemed to skip them altogether, mustering courage to push them to some other part of the ocean where they would do no harm.

He tacked without passion. He swabbed without enthusiasm. The vessel held no charm for him. He and they and the schooner all together had been caught in a foolish descent into a maelstrom.

CHAPTER TWENTY-SIX

As they neared the Horn the wind increased. They double-reefed the main and lowered the jib. Yet even with the decrease of canvas they still sailed at over ten knots. Swell after swell rolled under them giantly as if the *Vermillion Mourning* each time caught them at the height of their yawn. They rolled onward for the Horn with the wind that blew unchecked for thousands of nautical miles—a power building all around them, a deep trouble.

The westerlies were hunting vessels to satisfy its anger. It hungered to strip them of their colour and bone. The *Vermillion Mourning* was just that vessel. She sailed with a shambled heart—a reckless will, unprotected; she had not yet submitted to the wind. Wind is jealous for the essence of a vessel, stripping layer after layer until it reclaims the humility of the thing that had not respected its strength. If humbled, the wind carries a vessel into deepest dream—and this is the freedom vessel and wind share together. But any false vessel sailing under false dream with a loose heart is bound to break under the strength of the wind. Bannock Pierce was a foolish myth, a foolish adventure—a false dream, and the *Vermillion Mourning* was destined for the rocks. Soon the wind was going to destroy her and reclaim the heart.

The flag flapped forcibly. Albatross followed them, soaring on motionless wings and asleep. Wind grew to twenty-seven knots and swells increased. The grey clouds bulged. The crew stood present at the helm. Wade's wounds by now had healed, but so had Dion, healed from his false humility toward the crew and the sea.

"Why not sail through the Strait of Magellan? Or the Beagle Channel?" said Jeshurun, trying in a last-ditch effort to persuade the crew and the fate of the vessel to alter its course. "We could survive the Horn if we made it through the Strait. You wouldn't suffer any loss of pride, Captain. The Strait is difficult in its own right. You'll have nothing to hang your head about."

Captain June studied the binnacle sharply, "I will not face the Williwaws."

Wade, heart quickening, rose from the gearbox. He felt an intense knotting at the thought of the Williwaws. Maybe he shouldn't avoid it after all. Maybe his life mattered. Maybe the Strait of Magellan might prove his salvation.

"But the Williwaws are not as dangerous as the Horn," urged Jeshurun.

Captain June spoke coldly just above the wind. "I will not face them."

Wade slumped in his seat. "But Captain, maybe they're not so troubling."

Captain June set his powerful jaw, puffed on his ginger pipe. "You heard Jeshurun. They overwhelm a boat who believes nothing will destroy her. They rush down from mountains at over one hundred knots and destroy in a moment every shred of canvas she's flying. It's not safe. I will not face them."

Jeshurun motioned to the madly flapping flag and the clouds in the horizon and the endless roll of swells and the angry, turbulent graveyard of the sea. And he said, "But the false

Horn, Captain June. We won't make it around. We won't make it past."

Captain June paled. He knew Jeshurun was right. They would not make it around. Even with the favorable westerlies and the hope of avoiding the Horn's insurmountable waves they still faced the hazard of the false Cape Horn. For the last several days they had been sailing under inclement weather, making it impossible to ascertain an accurate sextant reading. If they continued onward, they might easily mistake the false Cape Horn for the real one, as many a vessel had done—and suffer the risk of being dashed into the rocks of Isla Wollaston, east of the false bluff.

His vast experience as captain aboard bulk carriers and private sailing craft would prove fruitless then. And as he handled the helm with blurry eyes, foaming over and over in his mind the incalculable risk in which he had placed himself and his crew, he retreated to the day he had accepted the commission of the *Vermillion Mourning*—and how eagerly he had wanted the challenge.

His original contract stated that he was to passage Dion and the prison crew into the heart of Cape Horn. There, fate would have her way with them. He was prepared to meet his end in the middle of Drake Passage. But now that Wade and Jeshurun were aboard, and now that the prison crew had in wisdom abandoned them, his focus had shifted not only to sailing into the Horn, but around it. And for as long as he could remember, he had wanted to conquer this one personal, this very dangerous ambition of rounding the Horn. Whenever his mood soured considering it, he read *Moby Dick* to refresh his understanding of how a captain ought to behave on a monomaniacal quest.

It was possible that the legendary *Vermillion Mourning* could round the Horn. It *was* possible; although no other captain dared accept the commission, perceiving at once the futility and the purpose of the journey—to supply the Deep with another coffin. Captain June was the only one who had responded. When the parcel arrived and he read over the contract, his lungs filled with assurance. Yet the moment he signed, his body weakened and he felt cold and nauseous. And in that instance he knew that neither himself nor his crew would succeed. After that it became a posture for suicide. A glorious end. An opportunity to count himself lost treasure amidst the Deep.

He didn't care. A calling greater than his understanding had led him to this moment—a strange, jarring comfort telling him, *I will guide you if you trust Me. Sacrifice your life for the bethel. Timshel.* So he agreed heartily to captain the *Vermillion Mourning.* And yet at the moment, all he could see were the ominous clouds and the unfavorable winds looming in his mind. But delivering Wade and Jeshurun mattered more to him than his own weakness; he stormed on, stoically, refusing to give in to fear, pressing on, brazen for the Horn.

No sailing grounds known to man compared to it. Countless captains filled with hubris had been subdued, shipwrecked, and forgotten trying to surmount it. He longed to discover if he could somehow muster the humility, the simple courage, to fight for his life in duress aboard a worthless vessel. His intense struggle to survive had led him to the *Vermillion Mourning* because he knew that if he survived this one epic, dangerous passage aboard her, he would have accomplished all that he had failed to do in his tenure asea.

"We'll sail for the Horn … and survive," he mumbled, a dark weight pulling uncomfortably under his tongue.

They could have sailed through the Canal; they could have taken a westerly course through the Pacific. Guided by destiny, they had chosen the lure of the Horn. From a distance, from a harbor, the Horn had been ink on a chart—something easily conquerable, a rich tavern story. But now their fear consumed them. What they had believed in together—the confidence in themselves, in their ability to push their boat with a grease pencil—now no longer seemed plausible. The Horn was swallowing them. They were not sailors. The albatross knew this.

Captain June drained his coffee. He smacked his lips. Looked at Wade. "We die in the warmth of destiny. We are destined for the Horn."

"And yet … we will not perish," smoothed Dion, eyes smoothly full of silk. He looked into the inward fear of them, their frightening death. "We'll make it around. I am fully confident. There is no jealousy here."

But it felt odd, his words. It sounded like his fingernails had been scraped against a chalkboard. They couldn't tell what he meant, his intention. He was manipulating them, filling them with kindness, as false as the false Cape Horn.

Then he shifted and added glibly, "What of rogue waves? They're troubling in this area of the world."

Captain June hid his swallow.

"The rogue waves are sometimes one hundred feet in height," said Dion.

Wade looked nervously at Captain June but detected only blank introspection.

Dion needled them further. "They might hit us at any moment," he said.

Captain June searched his mug for coffee. He set it down and wiped his lips with his thick, pawlike hand. "I didn't want to say anything about the rogue waves that sometimes frequent this area of the sea, Dion."

"What rogue waves?" said Wade, heart beating. "We've already overcome a rogue wave."

"You're right. They're nothing. Check the holds." Captain June eyed the binnacle.

Dion smiled. Went forward.

Captain June turned to Wade. "Rogue waves come and go and if it is our destiny we are swamped by a rogue wave then let us be swamped." Wade fought to breathe. The Captain added, "Maybe we can find a rogue wave with Dion's name on it."

Jeshurun wrenched his jaws into a toughening smile. Then, subdued, said, "But rogue waves aren't as frequent as you might think?"

Captain June nodded. "Very well."

Wade gazed at the horizon, eyes hollow. Finally he whispered, "Look at the storm."

Captain June raised his binoculars. Jeshurun followed the far off sea.

Hail tore into water. White crests flung away into dark morass. Cumulonimbus clouds shaped like anvils rushed above a layer of those heavy and dull. That layer would be stripped away and those anvils would fall directly on them. Chilling air swirled over skin icing the crew. To the southeast, off their starboard bow, a black mass formed like a giant mountain.

The winds and hail thrashed and ripped at ocean. Captain June wondered how long it would take for the four of them to drift to Chile in a life raft, and how long before they would be rescued. He reasoned how many emergency provisions they would need. Dropping the glasses, he studied the weather pennant bent to the masthead of the main. It was beginning to come around and point toward the bow. The headsails were flapping because the main and foresails absorbed the bulk of the wind.

"All hands. I want the mainsail taken down and the trysail bent on. I want the foresail double-reefed. I want you to sheet out the sails so that we are at a broad reach. There is no time but we must get this done. Do it now."

Wade dashed forward, grabbed a flashlight and descended the foreward hold. The sails lay twisted. He fed them up the companionway to Jeshurun and Dion. They spread them over the deck.

They dropped the mainsail in less than thirty seconds without flaking. Jeshurun lowered away on the throat halyard; Wade lowered away on the peak. Dion sat atop the main boom pulling the after-leech taut as the sail descended. They unbent the sail from the gaff and boom and folded it into the foreward hold, then rigged and hoisted the trysail. With that revolution completed, they lowered and double-reefed the foresail. All of this took less than an hour. Then they dropped the stays'l and unbent it from the stays'l club and forestay. Trimming the sails, they were now at a broad reach.

The torrential black mass hovered over them in the near horizon. Clouds billowed into the hierarchy of the heavens without fear of punishment, their turbulence destroying earth and sky. The dark crystalline anger feuded enraptured, pawing the sea for bait.

"Check one last time if we are leaking," spoke the captain somberly. "Check the generator room. If you see any water trickling, abandon ship while you still can."

Dion checked the foreward hold; Jeshurun checked the aft. Wade checked the three, four and five holds in the saloon. After this they lashed the companionway hatches to the deck. They jockeyed among the planks pounding on them, lashing covers, eyeing the storm. Everything that could not be lashed down they threw into the lazaret. Dion was waiting for them by the time they reached the generator room.

"Did you see any water?" he said to Wade.

"None."

Wade went aft. He stopped near the aft bulkhead.

"Here is water."

A line of water trailed from a bolt halfway up the ceiling. Mixed with rust, it trickled into the bilge. Dion pulled a rag from his pants pocket, tore off the tip and stuffed it in the cavity of the bolt.

"There," he snorted. "Our anxiety can now be dissolved; we are not going to sink rounding the Horn." When he looked at Wade, intense, manipulative, buried hatred bubbled from his lids.

Jeshurun glared at him. "That's not going to hold anything."

"It's not a big leak," explained Dion. "It's residual water trickling from the seam of a bolt. It's nothing."

Jeshurun started for the ladder. "We need to tell him."

"It's been like this since we left Springwick Harbor," said Dion.

"Why didn't you say anything?"

"Why didn't *you* say anything—you're veritable crew. You could have checked the hold as easily as me. But *I* wasn't worried about it. Look—it's barely a line of water at all."

Jeshurun turned back to him. "Something like that may mean much more here."

The generator room was dark and Wade held the flashlight. The sloshing waves gurgled on the exterior of the hull. " Can we caulk it?"

Jeshurun pried the flashlight from him. He felt the trickle. "Do we have any oakum?"

"Some," said Dion. He left and returned with a strip plus a hammer.

He handed the tool and oakum to Jeshurun and he caulked, as best he could, the very small, unobtrusive trickle.

Dion laughed. "But it won't matter, now that the storm is here. The weather will find a way to get inside you and take you down," and against Jeshurun's visible anger he began, "I once read about a boat from Spain that tried to go east around Cape Horn. Just like us. The boat was a seventy-four foot yawl. She was fit-out with airbladders that stretched bow-to-stern in every one of her holds. They were made of an alloy and had only one welded seam. Their stabilizers were meant to provide stability through severe waves."

Wade's boyish optimism, detecting fear, frayed.

"Crossing the Cabo de Hornos," he continued, "they were caught in a simple Cape Horn squall. It lasted twenty minutes at most, and in that time, the ocean pounded their hull until it cracked, along with the bladders. The sloop began to sink and there was nothing the crew could do."

Wade was turning from the conversation with a look of fright. Dion saw this and moved in.

"They abandoned ship for a survival raft, but it leaked. There were six of them. The water poured into their survival suits … and they drowned." He watched Wade crumple; the mounting anger of Jeshurun boiling. In the darkness he laughed.

A quick whack and then a muscled gasp for air. The flash-light crashed into the standing water. Jeshurun grabbed it quickly and trained it on Dion. "Did you bump your head?"

Dion held his forehead, eyes vacant.

"What happened?" said Wade.

Jeshurun sopped up the gash with a handkerchief. "You bumped it on the beam?" he mothered. "Will you be all right?" He touched the low hanging beam. "Maybe you shouldn't get so excited."

Dion remained in the generator room the rest of their journey around the Horn. Too dazed to even move from the immersing bilge water, he adjusted to the life awaiting him.

Back on deck Captain June asked Jeshurun where Dion was.

"He's not feeling well, Captain," said Jeshurun. "Caulking took the best of him. He's down in the generator room bathing in urine."

Captain June laughed, thinking, Maybe we can do it with three after all? And he went on. "Now look. I want you beside me. I don't want anyone on the bow. If you want to sleep, sleep in my quarters."

Clouds and hail approached. The winds stiffened from the west. Waves crested and fell apart as if the ocean had exploded.

"Go below and put on your survival suits. Do it now."

The temperature dropped. They returned.

"I want you in life jackets."

They donned them. The storm formed holes in the crests and tore at the horizon and it vanished as the spray swirled. So far the men and their bunks had been dry, but now they cinched up their survival gear and tucked their hands into pockets as the sea sprayed them. Wade barely managed his zipper. Jeshurun helped him, then looked into his eyes saying, We should have gone through the Canal. Captain June turned to them and said, "It is the worst."

CHAPTER TWENTY-SEVEN

They tied on.

Wind slammed the stern. The storm sails strained. Howling pierced their ears. They grasped for whatever was nearest as waves flung the vessel in tormented anger. The helm, the saloon housetop, the binnacle all became frail guards separating them from the briny deep. Wade watched the card float freely, carelessly, thinking that it might as well have been suspended in a placenta, as clueless as it was of the storm summoned against it; he wished he could float as freely and as safely, back in the cozy, intimate Springwick Harbor. Suddenly a wave buried him.

The vessel lurched up through the water with Captain June stricken at the helm and Wade and Jeshurun holding onto stanchions and cleats. The muscles in their faces and necks were fearsome from the cold as they fought to not drown.

"Jeshurun! Help me!" shouted Captain June, body wrapped around the wheel.

Jeshurun fought the list and took the helm. Together they battled the current and waves, and the rudder beneath. The winds increased in violence.

"Go below!" shouted Captain June. "Get into the saloon! It isn't safe on deck!"

A giant swoosh of water buried the stern. The three men were pushed into the bulwark. Without strong hands to steady it, the helm spun. Quickly the bowsprit spun away from their point of sail. The wind full-force shredded the stays'l. The *Vermillion Mourning* was losing direction. Captain June fought to get his crew below.

Wade felt dazed, one elbow hooked around a loose stanchion. Jeshurun along with Captain June was struggling to get him into the saloon. Captain June yelled something indecipherable at him; he didn't hear: another swoosh of water buried them. The stanchions, their lifeline, their harnesses and themselves all slowly and unavoidably were being pulled into the water and the waves, eager to claim another cache of flesh, crashed over the bow under the clouds that promised to make the sailors ghosts.

"Wade, you fool! Get in the *life* raft!"

Wade, the untested landlubber, froze as the rope he held suffocated in his palm. Any moment he and the crew would be dashed into the Horn's spiny palisade. His vision of being washed asea rounding Cape Horn would become truth. He would not make it past, never sail into his destined harbor. His voyage would end here. His dream, his hope for home, his hope for identity would become flotsam, awash and cold—like spray, utterly forgotten.

And all the while, Dion would sink with the vessel, proud of the ruin he had festered, as the darkness consumed them.

Yet suddenly and mysteriously, at the very height of the storm's fury, giant hands parted the clouds and dug into the heart of their schooner and poured down a blanketing swoosh of sunlight. The foggy cover rolled away. Suddenly the winds ceased. Before they could even lift themselves from the deck, the water had become as agreeable as a strolling lake.

To their amazement before them drawing gasps from Wade was the immense fortress of a rocky island.

"Is that the *Horn*?" he said, eyes glowing and fearful. They were almost upon it.

"Ready about!" shouted Captain June.

Clumsily, hastily, they raised the jib and tacked, bringing the vessel to starboard and away from danger. As they completed the revolution they rested again at the stern and stood in awe of the death they had avoided.

Wade, feeling lost and insecure and unready to move beyond, nonetheless uttered a string of words from his troubled, storm-tossed mind. "Do you think Bannock Pierce … came west?" he said to Captain June. He tried to toughen his eyes against the rockiness. "I … read a quote printed in *The Boston Daily* a long time ago that I thought was about him. It said: 'I will see you all at the end!'"

"Son, live the dream given you," encouraged Captain June. He offered him the helm.

Wade looked nervously at Jeshurun and found confidence in him, and as they left the island to port, he took the helm from Captain June and accepted command of the *Vermillion Mourning*. In that moment a cleansing purging burned through him, tingling through his flesh. His spine rushed into the open air. He forgot, for the moment, of his fruitless quest. And it was right.

Captain June took a sextant reading. "That is the Horn—fifty-five degrees, fifty-nine minutes south latitude; sixty-seven degrees, sixteen minutes west longitude. That is the danger we have been salvaged from."

But even more impressive than the ghostly splendor of the Horn were the clouds above it. The three gazed at the beautiful warm light trailing into the sea.

"Sheet out on the fore. Sheet out on the main."

While Wade continued with the helm, Jeshurun and Captain June sprung forward and carried out the order and now sailed at a broad reach.

The three gazed at the light pushing the storm far ahead of them into the east where a turbulent battle for the soul of the schooner rioted in every wave and flung gory spray into the wind. But the fury no longer swamped their little vessel; they were sailing as if in the harbor, curious to test their happiness against the eager deep.

A soothing change came upon Wade. With the sunlight basking them, his sweeping eyes absorbed the weather, the intense anger of the sea thrashing a part of the sea they no longer needed to worry over. They had discovered a miraculous sanctuary in the heart of that passage. His blood thickened, ebbing his body over the deck. His eyes closed and he raised his hands to feel something, some strange gift given to him not yet named—a rich warmth of movement longing to be with him, light hungering for his chest. The deep dark light devoured him. Suddenly he collapsed and sobbed.

Captain June studied the horizon hungrily. Jeshurun knelt and stroked Wade's head. "Wade, you were born here—rounding Cape Horn," he said.

He knew it. Within the deep current of his blood he had felt the sea and her mysterious weight siring him. But he had not known until now the startling origin of his berthing, this abrupt iciness behind his name. It wasn't a calm harbor or a coral sanctuary, a beach of warm, green waves cresting perfectly in rhythm one after another, the cove of an island pregnant and cool. It was not the glittering horizon filled with joy nor the safety of a place you could get to with a boat and a dream.

These romantic destinations promised the hope of a prosperous life, a glimpse into paradise. And yet to him they felt foreign and sere, impossible to discover. His life struggle had been to find the peace that eluded him, the grace that was nowhere near him—to rush into his natural home and uncover from the deep the true glimpse of his soul. Exhausted by the enormity of this challenge, he foundered in lost direction. Now that he had learned the truth behind his creation, the appalling anger of his being was weighted in the constant fury of unbridled turmoil.

It was the Horn. And he was not safe. Even amidst this temporary sanctuary he knew the clouds and waves were merely resting before they pounced. The savage truth of him rhymed too romantically with the rhythm of this vast, terrible obituary. This drastic climate was the source of his lifeblood, and maybe that was why all his life he had felt the tempest influencing his eyes and ears. All his life he had felt a gory interest in the savage impossible—the beautiful loss.

This was the doom sailors never fall in love with but do. All his life a consuming desire to find his home had led him into a chaos of dead ends, stove dreams. Scouring the earth for lost shelter, for safety, had reduced his heart to a slurry of fitful half-awakenings bound unmoving from a spot in the ground. But to find himself here—soundly alive where the essence of identity demanded the capsizing of one's soul—shocked him, fearfully. It seemed he was not meant to live past this place. He was not meant to endure the great and awesome journey into this water, his water, this brutality of origin expressed by storm.

Where in Cape Horn would he ever find grace? What divine truth would ever bestow on him the favor he so desperately needed—in these waters, in this home? He felt the heavy duty of life and the oppressive weathering bearing down on him, pushing him below the level of the sea, preventing him from becoming the man he was destined to become. He would never discover beautiful form, a beautiful soul here, before the turbulent breath that devoured him.

Had he ever found it? Had he ever discovered the lost gift that allowed him to rest in who he was, and who he was meant to become? Pressed to the deck, no. A man cannot uncover his identity until the free gift of grace opens it for him. He did not understand grace—the freedom for a man to become what he could never have become alone without the wind aiding him. Perhaps this inexpressible feeling of life would yet consume him and change him into an adventurer so that he could search the vast earth by sail and helm, and when the time came, he would understand what it encompassed to explore the heavens.

"You were born on the schooner *Rosewater*," said Jeshurun softly. "Your parents did not survive. You were the only one who made it to Springwick Harbor."

"What happened to the rest of the crew?"

"It was a terrible loss. I am sorry."

It was his destiny, then, that he return to the grounds where no part of his ancestors would ever leave. He wiped his eyes.

The wind shifted tossing the weather pennant toward the bow. Captain June responded at once, barreling, "Sheet out on the fore, rig a preventer."

The wind galloped into the sails and the trysail stretched over the waters and the foresail pressed into the rigging against the port lift, striking a diagonal line head to foot.

"We're running, boys. We're running wing-and-wing! Right past the Horn!"

The rock loomed above the writhing waves. Parallel ridges jutted upward forming the vertebrae of a great beast. Monstro.

Moby Dick. Leviathan. The head half-buried in sea consumed sailors into protein. It licked them out of the storm and rolled them into its dark underworld. No sailor would ever master the Horn. At best he would become only humbled flotsam and now only barely afloat and only still whispering the Horn on icy legs in earshot of the disbelieving. The rock stripped his veins, his poles, and every notion of hubris still lifting him, reducing what once had been hollow iron in his chest into compact bone a child could carve with his finger.

Wade breathed the fear of the Horn, the sick cold weight of it still shocking his soul. Desperate to avoid the inevitable scrimshaw he was becoming, the brutal carving of his joy, he sought death any other way. A beautiful death, any separation of bone and blood—it didn't matter—sufficed compared to what he faced in the Horn.

But even amidst the chaos and the writhing and the torrent of wind and water, he discovered again the change sweeping over him, the cool glory exciting him—deep and resonant peace. Here, strangely, he felt his home haven in Springwick Harbor. He felt the deep dream coming true, a press of the wind rocking him asleep. The everlasting schooner wanted him and sought him here at last, a dream so rich and honest and full of courage that he spread his eyes without fear into the heart of the storm. His spine tingled. It was the depth of his being. Surrendering, finally surrendering, grace sparkled all over his womb and he realized at last the story had been written. He was a sailor.

"We're in Drake Passage," he whispered, remembering the thousands of sailors who had passaged these grounds, remembering their stories, tragic and utterly glorious, whom Abner had read to him at home.

All hands stood watch in view of the ethereal storm clouds. A Jealous Painter tore violent reds and oranges out of their shapes wanting the vessel east. And as He worked in rhythm with the descending sun creating one dramatic seascape after another, He played from his palette a host of pinks and greens, lifting the crescent moon, wicking cool light from the stars. Each of the crew was lost in His artistry. It would be the most beautiful sunset Captain June or the others would ever remember seeing. Then the sun fell from the west and they watched the eerie crimson of the compass and the blackening east horizon. Far ahead of the little vessel the storm raged but they knew they were at last out of danger, feeling the comfort and reassurance of grace that they had all found here, beyond their understanding. For they knew they should not have survived. But with help, they had.

Captain June and Jeshurun in turn rested below, but Wade refused to give up the helm. In the passing of the Horn, in that nursery of gales, he breathed sated by a rose attar. The swirling water along the hull and the timbers moaning and creaking and the soothing movement of the vessel helped him guide the vessel dreaming in dry clothes of rough weather. He dreamt of her breathing, the thick movement of her want, her desire for freedom. He dreamt she had been waiting for his identity to command her. And at last, it had.

Now that he knew he was a sailor, free to shape the unbounded journey before him with the aid of the wind, free to command the helm without fear, at last he had been conquered. Conquered by the Horn. And birthed. From the living graveyard within him arose his everlasting salt, his deepest being. He was free to fall in love with the sea. The freedom to sail had become his palette on which he would colour the earth in grace.

CHAPTER TWENTY-EIGHT

After rounding the Horn they entered the Roaring Forties and beat hard through the wind. Then in the Horse Latitudes they suffered fitful winds, alternating calm days with rough weather. Then one day they had the good fortune of removing the double reefing in the foresail and dropping the trysail, bending on the main. Now they were sailing on a port tack close-hauled. They were making good time toward the doldrums but for the last few hours had been becalmed.

Wade lay in the trysail in the footropes beneath the bowsprit feeling the warm air and easy motion of the water and the starlight. The heavens at play on the surface of the ocean used their vigorous dance to move the vessel homeward toward the comforting harbor, and he touched meteors with his fingers to feel their cool image streak one or two at a time through the sea. By now his pure white T-shirt had several rips in it, several more stains of boat blood and grease.

He longed to sail through the stars with the same victory claimed rounding the Horn. He longed to hoist the dense light of the heavens. The beautiful doom now memory, now a favor, he needed new adventure to fill his heart. He needed something tough, a hurricane panged with hunger, a rush of wind, a nova—to challenge him and his dream.

With the Horn through him, with the passing of the hammering of the waves, he lay warm in the footropes rolling soothingly, dreaming the fill of the sea, his soul aligned in grace. The Horn had pummeled him, weakened his stamina, thinned his vitality. His spirit had been stretched for dead, dead finally, in this adventure. But grace soaked through his skin like rain.

In one fated sail and in just a few hours he had helmed the Horn without fear, with his heartbeat, mastering the movement of the vessel through darkness. It was easy and deep and satisfying to do so, to feel the pleasant obituary behind him, to breathe the smooth sail and the smooth current of the water. It felt good to have the cataclysm washed from memory, his pristine conscience free to roam the boat in the darkening light.

To be birthed, aged and salted by the sea, to be made a sailor, to become one with vessel and crew gave hope of an unbounded life. On nights like these he hungered to spread his nebulous soul farther than the bowsprit and tack into the stars. He longed to discover in himself his mastery of courage reflected in the gentle water and the warm light drifting past. Through the shreds in his shirt the press of canvas tickled his skin. He waited longingly for the moon to rise and challenge him with inevitable promise.

He slept.

Jeshurun on bow watch above him sat on the breasthook listening to the trickling prow and the meteors splashing into ocean, Wade's sonorous breathing against the horizon.

With the passing of the Horn and while the crew rested on their northerly heading toward warmer seas, he was constantly scouring the shadows of the craft for weathering that might press upon their sail. His sharp, clear eyes touched the frayed rigging, the lines, searched the sails for tears. He felt for growing looseness in the spindle casing of the helm and in the rudder. He walked the deck testing her caulking, descended into the holds and examined the water level. Everything seemed fine; the *Vermillion Mourning* was living past her lifespan, past her planned scuttling. She was never meant to have carried the four of them this far. It was a miracle.

His vigilance was to bring Wade back to Springwick Harbor, if he chose—away from this inescapable scuttling. If he continued aboard her it would be a cold, solitary swallowing; she would twist his tender veins until they snapped. Jeshurun knew a better story and he waited patiently to show Wade a helm, a better helm, waiting for him in Springwick Harbor. Dreams unimaginable awaited him there—bold, colorful, fragrant. These and more.

Captain June straddled the spindle casing of the helm, sat on the gearbox and wedged his toes between spokes to feel the subtle vibrations of the rudder. He stretched his arms, squinted at a corner of the saloon housetop, a stanchion, the stars.

Dion sitting on the transom rose from the darkness behind him and lit Captain June's ginger pipe. As the pipe caught flame he fanned the match until it expired. "It's a gift, Captain June. She'll change your life."

"But there's others aboard. It was just us before."

"You're afraid."

"No."

"You're not afraid?"

"You know what'll happen. I can't risk it."

Dion laughed. "It's easier than you think it is. It's a simple turning," he said, jangling his heart-shaped necklace, the weight cumbersome, couched for a descent.

To Captain June it appeared dented or smashed, he wasn't sure—had never seen anything in it besides its charming glitter. He said in a leering drone, "I'm not sure I want that on my conscience."

"You can sail the rest of your life."

Captain June felt a tightening in his chest.

"An everlasting boat, just for you."

His chest clamped and he clutched the helm. "It would be hard to do that, Dion."

Dion scratched his arm. "It's hard any way you look at it. Life is hard."

"Normally I wouldn't let anyone … not me. Not even you."

"Not Dominic? Not the three of us?"

"Dominic is lost. You know that."

"You'd have fun."

Captain June absorbed his mind with the compass card.

"You'd have a lot of fun. Think about it. You can't back out. It'd kill your conscience."

Captain June studied the red card and heard a porpoise surface off their starboard quarter, turned to see the waters circling over its disappearance.

"It isn't safe. Not with these two aboard."

"What *is* safe? We still have time. We can still accomplish it. You have your boat after all."

"Not with these two aboard."

"But the *Vermillion Mourning* will do whatever you tell her."

"I need time."

Dion chuckled. "I thought you'd say so."

"Sleep on it."

"I'm waiting for you."

"I haven't been sleeping much lately."

Dion laughed again.

Captain June swallowed. “Where’s Wade?”

Dion whistled quietly.

“Where is he?”

“I threw him overboard a few hours ago. Didn’t you hear the splash?”

Captain June darted his eyes at the bow, anger seething under tongue.

Dion laughed hungrily, resonantly.

Captain June felt a weight smothering him. He called Jeshurun aft to the helm. Jeshurun made eye contact with Dion who pulled his eyes away into the dark sea. Jeshurun turned his back on him, gripped both hands on the helm. “Thirty?”

“Very well. Where’s Wade?”

“Sleeping in the footropes.”

Captain June went forward. He stepped onto the breasthook, grabbed the stays’l forestay with his right, gingerly lowered himself onto a port whisker stay and inched along, sliding his right foot after his left until next to Wade. He spun and straddled the bowsprit. A breeze stirred Wade and he yawned touching his fingers to his lips.

“Need something to eat?” said Captain June.

“No thanks. Whatever you make tastes like lint.”

Captain June passed his eyes west to Argentina or Brazil out of sight beyond the horizon. He didn’t care what country it was, just that the air was getting warmer and closer to the sun.

He looked dejectedly at Wade, a heavy strain weighing on his brow. “I thought I would become a great man after this. I thought I would find the justice I’d been looking for. But it’s strange. This voyage.”

“It’s a beginning.”

“This Bannock Pierce you’re looking for—you don’t need him.”

Wade swallowed hard. "I'm not anymore."

"No?"

"He was a good man, and I had given my heart over to finding the heart of goodness. But Bannock Pierce is dead to me, a tainted dream I no longer desire. I've found my birth. I've found my life."

He had found a heavy, hammering schooner. A billowing wind. A clean halyard. A bleached canvas. A compass. A deck. A solid keel, tight seams. Pungent oakum. Strong rigging. The helm. His whole identity rested in these, and in the faith of finding grace upon the schooner of his dreams. The terrifying myth of Cape Horn survived in him now as a victory.

"I'm a sailor now. I have the Horn behind me."

"We were lucky. We've been lucky this whole sail. I've never been this lucky in my life. I've never sailed like this."

"But you were in the Navy."

"I worked at a naval shipyard." He pulled from his shorts a metal flask, unscrewed the lid and drank. Silver ice stung his throat and lips.

"But I dreamt that the mariners of Springwick Harbor were saying all around town before we embarked how lucky we were to have you captain this vessel."

Captain June patted his head. "A good dream. But when Abner sent me the contract, I agreed to the sail so I could die. I haven't sailed much. Now that the Horn is past—now that I'm long past death—I have nothing new to live for." His eyes froze and thawed on the breasthook.

"Maybe you have died."

Captain June flinched. "Are you having a good time? You said you loved him."

"I love sailing. It's part of me," he said trembling. "I didn't ask for this."

"You said you loved him more than anything. More than Jeshurun or your father. More than Tobiah."

"I don't really know how I feel. But I don't love Bannock Pierce. And I don't want to be the Lighthouse Keeper." He lifted his eyes. "I want to sail."

Captain June smiled from the corner of his mouth. "Sailing isn't easy."

Wade burned his eyes into Captain June's pupils. "I know. It takes hard work."

"But only with luck. I wanted this schooner dashed on the Horn." He looked cautiously over him then pulled his eyes into the sea.

Wade whispered, "Thou mayest. The *Timshel Auxiliary*."

"We're going to need all the help we can get," he said. He relit his pipe and the soothing glow searched his brow and warmed his mouth and sought his dark sockets. "Know anything about the southern constellations?" he said.

"My Dad made me memorize them."

"Can you find the Southern Cross?"

He pointed.

"Good. The Southern Cross isn't like Polaris, which marks almost precisely the Northern Pole; rather, it indicates an area in the heavens where the Southern...." He went on, giving Wade a long, impromptu conversational lesson in celestial navigation. Wade listened eagerly, applying the celestial education which he had received from Abner, embracing the solid journey into grace which had been prepared for him. They crossed the Tropic of Capricorn and picked up the southeast trade winds, sailed for days without change in wind.

CHAPTER TWENTY-NINE

When they entered the doldrums again the wind stopped and the sun grew hot and the sharks commenced their pursuit. The crew longed to drink but water was low. All four removed their shoes to feel the soothing heat of the deck.

"We need an iceberg," said Wade pouring saltwater over his head.

"There will be no icebergs here," said Dion. "This is the hot weather."

Off their port beam beyond the horizon flowed the mouth of the Amazon River.

Dion gazed into the murky haze, rubbing his palm. "This is near my home," he said. "There was a village up the river, surrounded by dense vegetation. It was destroyed." From his tone it sounded like the storm had been in his keeping and had frowned vigorously from his mouth. "All I have is the *Vermillion Mourning*."

"Is there something that could have been done?" said Wade.

"It was a flood. A terrible flood."

Wade squinted at the dark water and imagined jumping over the caprail into it. "We need a breeze, at least," he said. "Something to cool us off." He dropped the bucket over the side and let it drift with the water. The rope drew taut and the bucket spun and filled. He hoisted it then splashed the deck. The saltwater gurgled to the breakbeam and flushed through the scuppers. He and Jeshurun worked aft scrubbing the deck with Joy. The cool water felt good.

At the helm Captain June sat on the gearbox cushioned by a life vest. He wore a sou'wester to keep the sun off his neck. Since before they had entered the doldrums, he had become increasingly annoyed by the chafing of the mainmast. He called Jeshurun and Wade over to him and told them that he wanted the mainmast slushed. His bewildered eyes stared vacantly at the mirror of sea and the thin line of fins in their wake.

Wade scratched his head at Jeshurun. "What's slushing the mast?"

"You go up in a bosun's chair and grease the mast so it won't chafe."

"Are you sure we need to, Captain?" said Wade. "It isn't moving."

Captain June dismissed his comment, looking ahead, jaw clamped.

"We need to," said Jeshurun quietly. "Captain's orders."

"But it's too hot do anything right now," said Wade.

Dion came aft. "This heat? Tickles the blood, eh?" He yawned.

Jeshurun ignored him. He set his scrubbing brush aside and opened the lazaret. He found turpentine, linseed oil, Vaseline—the three ingredients used for slushing. He mixed two parts Vaseline, two parts linseed oil and three parts turpentine in a bucket to create the deep ochre hue. At the mainmast he rigged the bosun's chair onto the hill rope, a line on the portside main shrouds used for such a task as slushing the mainmast, using a double sheetbend.

Dion dipped his hands into the slush and squeezed it through his fingers wiping the excess slush onto his cut-off shorts then readying the hill rope. "Who's going up?" he said to Wade.

Wade turned quickly to Jeshurun.

"I'm the heaviest," said Dion. "It can't be me. I'm also the strongest. One of you should go. I can support either of you."

"Let's do pushups," said Wade.

"OK Wade. Let us do pushups. The most in a minute."

They took a space on the deck.

Wade gave the signal to start and he moved up, down, up—his sharp shoulder blades protruding from his underneath his white T-shirt, which reeked with sweat stains. Dion pushed up, then down, then up, easily. At the end of a minute he had doubled Wade's set of twenty-five. Wade collapsed exhausted. Dion rolled onto his side.

"I win. You're up."

"I'm going up," said Jeshurun, bored with Dion and his conniving.

"But I'm not afraid of heights anymore," interjected Wade. "I know I can slush the mast."

Jeshurun glared at him. "Is that so?"

He nodded defiantly.

"On the next sail you can slush to your heart's content. But I'm going up. You'd fall if something got out of hand."

Captain June called out from the helm, "Jeshurun, why don't you go up? You're a sport. You'll have a lot of fun."

"I think the heat's affecting him," whispered Wade.

"The heat is not affecting me," said Captain June. "He *will* have fun."

"Captain June does not know where we are," whispered Dion in confidence. "He lost the charts for this area. He doesn't know what longitude we're at. He doesn't know how far we are from Brazil. He's going mad. He's our special captain."

The smell of the slush lingered around them and the imposing mainmast.

"Captain June needs rest," continued Dion. "Maybe we can persuade him to sail to Brazil for repairs. It's not far."

He let go of the chair and it swung freely. The hill rope was rove through a single block, which meant Dion would support Jeshurun's weight directly. In all, he would be holding up one hundred and ninety-five pounds—Jeshurun's body, the chair, the bucket, the slush and the three-inch brush. They bent the slush bucket onto the line so that the bucket would hang level with Jeshurun's waist sitting in the chair.

A cold pressure whispered through the crew. Jeshurun gave a brave nod to Wade and said confidently to Dion, "Timshel." He braced his shoulders against the triangle of the ropes fastened to the four ends of the plank comprising the chair.

Dion raised his eyebrows in an arrogant manner and blinked to himself. "Don't worry, Jeshurun. I have never dropped anything in my life."

Wade was thinking, Dion should make two turns around the belay pin in case the line slipped; that way he would be able to stop the rope with his hands because the belay pin would take up the force of the weight. But should he hold the line freely, unbelayed, and if the chair and Jeshurun began to fall together, there would be no way he would be able stop them with his grip alone without tearing off the flesh on his palms. Yet he held the line free.

"Belay the line, Dion," said Jeshurun, "or June will fish you to the sharks."

He smirked obligingly. "Okay, But I assure you, you will not fall." He wound the line only around the underside of the belay pin where it butted against the pin rail, and held the end of the line in his hands. “It will be more difficult for me to hoist you this way; I don’t know if I can hoist you at all. The friction of the belay pin will take momentum from me.”

“I can belay the line,” said Wade.

Dion studied him with an obtuse look. “With your shoulder? You wouldn’t hoist cheese.”

“My shoulder’s fine,” he said with little confidence. “And you know it.”

Dion hauled away with his powerful arms making the reel in the block squeak. As soon as the chair climbed he let the line slide off the belay pin, hauling Jeshurun hand-over-hand to the top.

Wade noticed the dangling line and grabbed it quickly making two turns around the belay pin. Dion smirked at him.

“I’m not a loose cannon, Wade. You really think that’s necessary?”

Wade trembled. Dion looked at him coolly.

“I’m very strong. I can handle the weight.”

“But it’s Jeshurun.”

“You don’t think he’ll fall, do you?”

Aloft, Jeshurun dipped his brush deep into the bucket and smeared the mixture over the mast. He worked slowly downward, coating the circumference of the mast to keep it lubricated for the twisting mast hoops. The slush spread onto his fingers, rope and chair. He leaned out to smear the aft of the mast.

Suddenly he fell.

His feet hit a mast hoop. He grabbed the hoop above and held on with the tips of his fingers. His cheek rested against the wood, and the smell of turpentine and linseed oil was strong. The bosun’s chair and bucket tapped him on the curve of his back.

"Are you OK?" shouted Dion far below.

Jeshurun looked like a squirrel huddled against a trunk. The angle of the sun cast his legs and feet in shadow. Dion squinted to see him.

"Are you able to climb down!" shouted Wade.

"I'm all right…."

His coated, greasy fingers gripped the mast hoop. He held his body erect. His heart pounded against the slush and mast. His feet wedged between the mast hoop and the mast securely. The paintbrush, which he had let go of when he fell, teetered on the edge of the seat. Suddenly it jarred loose and fell off the plank and landed on the rim of the swinging bucket. His fingers started to slide off the mast hoop. He squeezed it harder. His feet slid away following the curve of the mast.

Captain June could see the mast and the empty bosun's chair swinging back and forth. He saw that Dion was braced, holding the line, staring upward, face contorted and Wade grasping the line, stricken. Then Jeshurun's toes became visible as they slid around the mast hoop. But he refused to leave the helm of the *Vermillion Mourning*; the schooner might accidentally gibe, flinging Jeshurun to his death.

"Can you climb back on the chair?" shouted Dion.

"Climb down the mast hoops!" cried Wade.

Jeshurun lost his grip. His body fell in a soft, gentle arc through the sky and his arms flung backward.

But thankfully he hit the bosun's chair. His right arm curled around the line. His feet slid off the mast hoop. Suddenly his entire body hung freely in the air wiggling, like a squirrel dangling from a limb.

Dion smirked calmly at Wade. "So you think your turns on the belay pin will hold him if I let go?"

Wade felt flashing fear.

"If I just let go, he won't fall?"

"Don't do it, please," said Wade. "Please."

Suddenly Dion sneezed, letting go of the line. The force of Jeshurun's weight pulled on Wade's end and his legs slammed into the pin rail.

"Lower away!" shouted Jeshurun. "Lower away!"

"Lower away, Wade," said Dion in a cold tone.

Wade struggled to hold on, teeth grimacing. Dion grabbed the halyard and lowered away until Jeshurun touched both feet to the deck. He collapsed from the adrenaline draining from him. His thighs and forearms and hands shook violently. The bosun's chair lay limp on the deck like discarded lumber. The brush still lay on the rim of the bucket.

"You looked like a swaying monkey. I wish I would have been up that high…." said Dion.

"Are you hurt anywhere?" said Captain June.

"He came down very hard," said Dion.

"But is he hurt?"

"No," said Jeshurun, looking wearied, too wearied to retaliate, yet. "Everything's fine."

"That's a sailor," said Captain June.

Wade's face turned ashen studying the height of the futtock shrouds. He feared falling from them into the ocean abyss with the sharks. As they continued in the doldrums the sun pressed the *Vermillion Mourning* through veiled skies.

CHAPTER THIRTY

A fog enveloped the vessel preventing the crew from seeing bow to stern. When Captain June discovered that the fog horn was inoperable, he worked vigorously to repair it while at the same time ordering a bow watch. After lingering listlessly for days without a break in the oppressive haze, he found his mind shattered and cold.

"How long before we reach the States?" said Wade.

"I don't know … the doldrums … we could be listless for…." His voice trailed away.

"We crossed the doldrums when we came south. They didn't slow us much then."

"I don't know how long."

"Do you know where we are, Captain June?"

He thought for a moment, then looked at them with the guilty eyes of a dog who had just been caught. "Not far from the equator?"

"When was the last time you took a sextant reading?"

"Yesterday noon."

"In the fog?"

"I'm practiced."

"Do you know our latitude?"

"Two degrees, south."

"The longitude?"

"I lost my pocket watch. I think we're at thirty degrees west."

"Do you know how far off the coast of South America?"

Captain June smiled and his beard revealed his gapped yellow teeth. "… haven't looked at any charts for this area.… So I don't know.… But I'm hungering for a shark, all right. So come on. I need a lure. Go fetch your Lighthouse key. Who needs a Lighthouse key?"

Wade fetched it from below, handed it over without reservation. Captain June gave him the helm with instruction to shout if he saw anything coming their way. Then he found a long, skinny boat hook to serve as a pole. Using seine twine he bent a curved needle to the end and attached as a lure Wade's Lighthouse key. Standing amidships he cast and the key plopped into the blue water, disappearing into the fog. He hummed off key "The Battle Hymn of the Republic," tapping out of rhythm.

Suddenly a mackerel struck at the bait fighting to rid himself of the lure. Captain June fought to bring him on deck and after a terrific battle heaved it over the transom, onto the deck. In several minutes he had caught enough mackerel to mash into bait, to catch the sharks.

Jeshurun came aft and, witnessing the mess, scratched his temple. "Are you sure you want to try and catch a shark, Captain?"

"Can't you see I'm hungry, man! I'm tired of eating my stew!"

"Why don't you let Wade cook. He doesn't know how, just like you, so he can't mess up any more than you already have."

Captain June stood spread-eagle on the transom with his pea-green shirt off throwing the chum in high, lazy arcs to the hungry sharks. They thrashed mercilessly, snarling with their pointed teeth for the mackerel. Captain June spotted a shark nearby, lifted the harpoonlike boathook to his ear and threw. It splashed in the water aimlessly and sunk. He retreated to the gearbox brooding, studying the compass, listening to the pursuing sharks, then dumped the bucket of chum into the water. The sharks closed in.

Dion appeared in the companionway. "Captain, you won't believe this. The holding tank is leaking."

Captain June followed him into the generator room. He checked the valves and discovered the truth. The holding tank was leaking profusely and would cause further damage to the schooner if not repaired. He was convinced of this.

"Must be a big hole," said Dion.

"Someone has to mend it from the inside."

At the helm Captain June raised the dilemma to the crew.

"I'll go in," said Wade.

Captain June studied him profoundly. "You don't want that."

"It's really nasty," said Dion, wrinkling his nose.

Even Jeshurun understood the appalling ghastliness of such a chore. He folded his arms and said matter-of-factly, "It's not the best side of sailing, Wade. You're surrounded by feces. Are you sure you want that?"

Captain June laced his fingers together and said, "Jeshurun, I want you to man the helm. Dion, bow watch. I'll go down."

Wade thrust his chin. "I'll do it."

"You've never imagined something so gross," said Captain June, suddenly lucid.

Wade glared into his eyes, mouth firm, arms akimbo.

Captain June realized that he wasn't going to back down. They all realized it. This was a baptism for Wade, one of many to come. Captain June nodded confidently. "All right. You get your wish." He turned to Jeshurun. "You have the helm."

Dion went forward whistling.

Captain June took Wade below to the generator room to purge the holding tank by running saltwater through it. He fitted Wade with gloves, goggles, sou'wester and mask. When he unbolted a panel of the aft holding tank, a rancid stench flooded the generator room. He covered his nose with a handkerchief then hosed out the tank thoroughly.

Before Wade climbed in, he turned to Captain June and asked him to not seal him in. Captain June snorted. He fetched a light to illuminate the dark tank.

Using a sturdy chisel Wade scraped away the layers of feces. Five hours later without a break he found the hole—smaller than the edge of a quarter. Guided by Captain June's coaching, he patched it up with solder and soldering iron then climbed out of the holding tank a sweaty mess and pried off the mask, breathing heavily.

Captain June was smiling.

Wade set his jaw. His T-shirt was riddled with stains and ripe with a stench. He had torn it on the steel hatch. "More so than ever, Captain June. I'll slush the mast with the stuff if I have to."

Captain June assured him that probably he wouldn't have to.

When Captain June returned to the quarterdeck, he was shocked by Jeshurun's words.

"Captain, I can't turn the helm."

"*What*?"

"It's stuck."

"How long has it been this way?"

"I just noticed it."

"Is it the sharks?" said Wade.

They listened together for the sharks. Dion appeared through the fog.

"The rudder isn't turning," said Jeshurun.

"We have to fix it," said Dion.

Captain June squinted at this stupid observation. "You're right, Dion. Maybe we should call Triple AAA." He stood wide legged whispering to himself, "We might as well sink."

"No, I mean, we really have to fix it."

Suddenly from far away a deep, barreling horn blew through the fog.

Wild-eyed, Captain June seized the helm and tried to turn it. It wouldn't budge. He cried for help to free it. He, Jeshurun and Wade yanked as hard as they could. It was to no avail.

"I'll go in," said Dion.

"No you won't. Not with sharks in the water. They'll tear you apart." Captain June tried harder to jerk the helm free.

"Sir, I've done this before," said Dion.

"Maybe you have. But I imagine not with sharks in the water."

Dion rolled his eyes and caught a glimpse of Wade and Jeshurun who were both locked with Captain June in trying to free the helm.

"Listen, I'm expendable. I'll go in. You've wanted me off the boat anyway. Here's your chance."

Captain June stopped and regarded him briskly. "All right. Pointed thought. Couldn't have said it better. We're not moving anywhere. If you want to go in, go in."

"I need your knife."

"I'm not giving you my knife."

The fog horn blew again, closer.

Captain June was on the verge of panic.

"I can fix it with your knife. I'm swift."

Wade shook his head at Captain June, who remained transfixed on Dion, who had folded his arms.

"You have to trust me."

Captain June tapped his foot.

"I know how to fix it."

Jeshurun was using his weight to pry the helm loose. It still wouldn't budge.

"Then I'll use a wrench and we'll perish." He started forward.

"Wait," said the captain, drawing the knife and handing it to him. "Be careful."

Dion took it, looked at the crew.

Captain June realized he might have just made a rather futile mistake.

Jeshurun stopped tugging on the helm.

Wade braced himself for an attack.

But then Dion removed his crimson shirt, kissed his heart-shaped locket, jumped off the transom into the shark-infested water.

"Jeshurun, Wade—fix the horn!"

They leapt forward for tools in the bosun's locker. Captain June wrenched to free the helm. A tremendous horn blasted through the fog. Suddenly the lights of an enormous oil tanker appeared heading for their bow.

Captain June screamed. He wrenched hard to starboard. Suddenly the helm jarred loose.

Although they had little momentum in the otherwise becalmed seas, there was just enough wind to turn the bow. The oil tanker brushed their starboard bow jolting them, rocking the helpless vessel, moving past them like Titanic. And then it was gone, leaving the *Vermillion Mourning* rocking in her wake. The next time they heard its fog horn it was an afterthought.

Captain June heard a dull, tinny voice coming from somewhere out of sight. It was Dion, crying for them to help him up. Wade and Jeshurun returned to the helm and pressed the button to activate the fog horn; it beeped like a broken baby toy.

Captain June, still numb, muttered numbly that Dion had saved them and their vessel.

Wade looked over the transom. Dion was treading water slowly, ever so slowly, losing ground to the *Vermillion Mourning*.

"Water water everywhere, and not a drop to drink, eh Dion?" joked Wade.

"I slit my ankle! Throw me a rope!"

"You're a good swimmer," said Wade. "Swim alongside. We're not getting anywhere soon."

Curiously the fog lifted just then. In the background, closing too rapidly, was a school of sharks.

Jeshurun rushed forward to the bosun's locker to fetch a mooring line. Wade offered his hand over the rail. It wasn't long enough. Jeshurun heaved the line. Dion caught the bitter end. Captain June wrapped the standing part of the line around the sternpost. The three of them heaved in desperation lifting Dion out of the water just as the nearest shark rose for his heel. The shark gnashed its teeth and broke his skin. The three grabbed his arms and shoulders, hoisted him onto the deck. Blood flowed profusely from the gash.

"Where's the knife?" said Jeshurun.

Dion was breathing heavily examining his heel. “It dropped out of my hands. Thank you for saving me. Thank you. Thank all of you. You protected my life.”

Captain June slumped to the deck, adrenaline spent.

CHAPTER THIRTY-ONE

They rounded the Ponta de Calcanhar between Brazil and the Arquipélago Fernando de Noronha and veered toward Cape Race. High, whispery clouds seemed to wrap themselves into the eastern ocean. The salty wind stirred up the waves and jostled the schooner and the men.

"In a few hours we'll be in sight of Barbados," said Captain June. "The food is low. If we anchor there we can restock and make repairs, and rest." He sipped from his empty coffee cup and continued. "However, I have never been in more favorable conditions as on this boat, on this voyage. We could ride our luck into Cape Race. Who knows, a fruit tree may sprout in our bilge. As was our decision rounding Cape Horn, we choose together."

"Whatever it is you want to do," said Dion.

"Sail. At all cost," said Wade.

"We could remove the barnacles off the hull," said Captain June. "That'd make us faster. We could also dust. We haven't done that yet, not since that rogue wave."

"I think we should fish," said Dion.

Captain June snapped at him. "We're running out of keys."

"What about water?" said Jeshurun. "The foreward tank is empty. The aft tank is empty. Only the day tank is left, which holds less than twenty-nine gallons. Under normal conditions that wouldn't last a week. We don't have enough to last."

"We'll flag down a ship," said Captain June.

"Have we seen a ship?" glared Jeshurun at the three.

Dion smirked. "Sure, we just need to get into fog."

"You're right," said Captain June softly. "We'll sail to Barbados."

Dion rose onto the saloon housetop. "I'm not sailing to Barbados.... Their maggots don't taste any better even when you let them rot in the sill."

Wade's eyes flickered. Jeshurun clenched his teeth.

"Now look," said Captain June. "I've thought about it. The attraction of a prisoner in a Barbados prison is not very attractive. I wasn't born to waste away with maggots. Come on—none of us were. We're sailing for Cape Race."

The schooner passed so near to Barbados that the island seemed visible over the dark sea. At noon they crossed the Tropic of Cancer. From one current to another averaging over seven knots they pressed on for Cape Race.

Their clothing turned to shreds. The meat drifted from their bones.

Wade lay in the footropes beneath the bowsprit craving water. His tongue cleaved to his mouth as he tried to lick his salty skin. The burning dryness in his throat prevented him from talking. It wouldn't have mattered even if he could talk; the only need on his mind was to cool his parched throat. Better to waste away silently, feel the ocean silently, dreaming of tears. Captain June hungered for meat, thirsted for water, weakening. Dion rolled his eyes trying to lick the blood in his skull. Jeshurun withered inside his sere skin. The schooner felt powdery and soft under the burning sun.

As Wade lay motionless in the footropes, his mind jostling as if in storm, he recalled the poster of the *Peking* that Abner had given him to hang in his room back in Springwick Harbor. The memory of the vessel gave him comfort; his room was filled with posters of sailing and sailing ships, but the *Peking* stood out above the others. She had made it around the Horn intact, more than once, and was now docked at South Street Seaport. In the picture her four masts towered above the dock, stretching to blend with the Manhattan skyscrapers. Her shipshape bare poles beamed in sunlight. Nautical flags spanned her shrouds to the skysail masthead. An enormous crowd stood on the dock listening to a man read an account of the vessel around the Horn. He was in awe of her. His eyes rolled and he remembered breakfast with Abner and the conversations he had about sailing.

"Wade, breakfast. I have fresh squeezed orange juice," called Abner warmly.

He jumped, startled from his trance. "Coming. I'll be right there."

In the kitchen he rubbed his eyes with the heel of his palms, exhaling heavily.

Abner was at the griddle cooking. "Did you sleep?"

"Yes I did." He gulped down the orange juice. "Thank you."

"You look tired."

He raised his eyes slowly to Abner's chin and stopped. Swallowed. "I got up to take in water."

Abner slid two pancakes onto his plate. "I see. Do you have any plans?"

"Just running with Jeshurun." He cut off a wedge forgetting to moisten it with syrup and Abner watched him fold the wedge into his mouth. "Do you?"

"Oh, no," said Abner, returning to the griddle, hiding his amusement.

Abner dropped two dollops of batter to make cakes for Jeshurun. The wet batter sizzled as it spread over the iron. Wade tapped his fork nervously against the plate.

"You make the best pancakes, Abner," he said, again meeting the chin.

"Do you want more?"

"No thank you."

"You usually eat more."

"I guess I'm just not hungry tonight—*today*, I mean. This … what is it, morning?"

Abner laughed politely. "I think it's bedtime for you. Watching for ships is a tiring enterprise."

Wade toyed with his food. Gulls cried outside soaring in the gentle wind. The chimes outside the kitchen window clanged with the softening wind. "Have you ever gone sailing, Abner?"

With a casual motion Abner flipped the pancakes. "Sometimes."

"Why do you always give me sailing things?"

Abner appeared surprised. "Who, me?"

"Yes."

"What sailing things?"

"The posters."

"Oh … yes. Those." His brow deepened. "Do you like them?"

"No."

"Neither do I."

"Then why'd you give them to me?"

"Because there wasn't anywhere else to put them. Jeshurun's room was already full of pictures of lighthouses."

Wade fought to hide his flash of anger. He thudded the fork against the uneaten pancake.

"But we can take them down if you like."

"No. . . ."

"No?"

"No."

"Not so, huh?"

"Abner, understand me. Right now I'm a pancake eater. In a few minutes I'll be a hair washer, then a trail runner. This afternoon, a horizon watcher, searching the curve of the earth for distressed ships. But that's all."

"What if you became an island tamer?"

"I'm adopted jetsam."

"And I'm glad you are."

Wade blinked. "Abner, I get seasick when I wash dishes."

The salt and the light and the heat were churning through him now. This withering—was this the life of a sailor? Was this the life he wanted to adopt as his new dream? Crewing with his adoptive brother who seemed to have his own knowledge of the sea that he wasn't willing to share? Crewing with a brutal, bald beast who wanted a sample of his blood? Crewing with a captain who had lost his sanity, who seemed to be suffering scurvy, who might as well have been eating the paper charts, as useful as they were for him and the rest? Was sailing nothing more than an island of patchwork wood waiting to sink in the sun, waiting to send itself down to rest on a cool bed? What about the provisions, the scarcity of food and water? Was sailing by design the conflict of a thirsting man with the water he could never foolishly drink? Was it a ripe lesson on wasting away? Was sailing the story of a man who must give up every hope of a sound current, the dream of an adventure, of a tale survivable enough to take back home to Springwick Harbor, and scrawl it on the bar for his tavern mates? Sailing was nothing like dreaming. Sailing was what happens to a man when the land spits him into the one cold womb no sane explorer dares conquer—the Abyss.

He writhed, eyes rolling, remembering the days of his youth when he went running with Jeshurun after breakfast.

Heading uphill to summit Strawberry with Jeshurun pushing your limit. The running, man. The hot path. The joy. The heavy freedom under sun. Getting moving now. Breaking into clouds. Fast dreams. Slippery laughter all around you. You ease into the memories given you in the hope they'll be true and you ease into the music of better dreams. That's the hope you live for. To be humbled. To hit that stride.

The theme of life. Goodness bathing you. Persevering in the goodness in Jeshurun, in Abner, in Tobiah, in Walter and others. Determined to uncover the heart of man. That lion in the forest, that brother who knows how to carve a path. Determined to feel him running alongside you and gain his blessing. Determined to let him carry you to the finish. Running on and on and madly, madly in love with the life ahead.

The summit coming. Jeshurun coming abreast. Perspiring. Legs slippery. Falling behind. Come on, son. Come on. A little farther. Come on, son. Come on. Weak knees. Failing. The suffering, the brutal suffering—light frozen and unmoving in your blood. At all cost the suffering. Come on. Come on. The hate in yourself. Enveloped in the struggle to outdistance the myth. Come on, Wade. Keep going. The pain in the flesh. Determined to endure the crucible. Come on, come on, Wade. Determined to smear your lungs. Determined to be snapped. Come on. Don't give up. Come on, boy. You were never meant to die. But you're dying. The falling. The fear of falling short. Jeshurun just ahead, just a little in your lead, bounding, seeming to tease you with being just ahead, just pulling you along, potent with his finishing kick. Your poor stamina. You can't go. Can't do it. But his nearness, his faithfulness, pushing you, stretching you. You're not a runner. But you're running. You're surpassing any run you've ever imagined enduring, because he's with you.

The running seemed silly now, wasting away on the high seas. What good was sailing if you couldn't run free? He climbed out of the footropes and stumbled aft to the quarterdeck, met the crew, blinking woozily. They watched him, wondering if he was going to fall.

"I've been a beast to you … to all of you. I took this sail for the wrong reason. I'm sorry for hurting you, and for thinking vain things…." He collapsed.

Jeshurun rushed to his side, took him below, used the rest of the water in the day tank to cool him.

The long keel and the planks of the *Vermillion Mourning* shrunk and her seams stretched open tingling with the heat.

"Listen," mumbled Captain June, sounding his voice at the helm, "We have no way of telling how long it would take. It could take much longer…. Maybe three more months. Dion, if I were you, I would prepare for three more months…. That's what an able-bodied seaman would do…. Three more months. Hope for three more…."

Dion went below to check on Wade, who was mumbling incoherently. "… have back lighter … found my home … found my compass … just want to sail … been a long … just want to share this sail with my *Vermillion Mourning*. By the way, did you know your lighter doesn't work? It doesn't work. I'm so sorry, so sorry."

Dion's eyes widened in fear, reminded of the lighter, which he had given away as a curse. He backed into the corner of the fo'c'sle trying to claw his way through the double hull.

CHAPTER THIRTY-TWO

From the south a purplish mass of clouds rushed at them in tremendous fury. They were smothering and ripping the waves. Captain June manning the helm shouted out, "I want the main and the fore double-reefed *now*!"

Jeshurun's heart thumped racing to reef the fore. Wade stumbled on deck and joined him and together they brought down the fore.

"It doesn't have to look good!" shouted Captain June. This storm could be a bad one, he thought. It could be over quickly. Let it be over quickly.

Jeshurun worked furiously tying reefing knots. "Don't overdo yourself," he said to Wade.

"I'm not.... I'll be fine," he said, exhausted.

The white wall approached with fury.

Dion rose leisurely from the fo'c'sle and stretched, insouciant to the chaos.

"You've got to help, Dion!" shouted Captain June.

He ignored him. Watched the storm with one hand supported on the foreboom. His smooth, Brazilian, bald head seemed laughing in the burning fury of the coming storm.

At the quarterdeck Captain June trimmed the mainsheet so that the main boom came directly over him, taut. He secured the boom with tackles. Wade stationed himself at the throat halyard.

Meanwhile Dion climbed the foreshroud and watched the storm from the crosstree.

Captain June shouted at him. "Dion you bitch! Get the hell down here and help furl! What are you looking at—pantyhose!"

He seemed not to hear. He seemed in a trance, as if the halyard of his intestines was being hauled away by clouds of the coming storm. He seemed to be communicating with the thunder and lighting and he closed his eyes and lifted his palm to feel the air.

Captain June shouted again. "Dion! Get the fid out of your eye and get down here now! I swear I'll throw you overboard and we won't come back!"

Dion probed the low pressure of air with his slender tongue. His cold skin moved off the crosstree and descended the ratboards. He stationed himself at the peak halyard.

"Jeshurun, you cowboy!" shouted Captain June, and Jeshurun swung himself onto the end of the boom and straddled the boom so that he would be able to grab the after-leech as it came down, because the sail was going to come down in a hurry.

The storm was imminent.

"Lower away the halyards!" shouted Captain June.

They lowered away. Jeshurun pulled in the after-leech. At the second reefing point Dion and Wade stopped and made fast the halyards on their belay pins, using two figure-eight turns and a locking half-hitch. They jumped onto the saloon housetop and tied the reefing lines together, below the boom. The knot they used was a combination of a bowline, a sheet bend and a fisherman's knot, which Captain June had taught on their way to the Horn; not until now had they used it. Jeshurun, still atop the boom, yanked on the reefing cringle to stretch the sail out along the boom. Then he and Captain June found a hawser from the lazaret and rove it through the cringle, then through the bale of the boom. They drew the sail taut. The main was double-reefed.

The strength of the speed of the storm approached unabated, rumbling, raging.

"I want the stays'l dropped! You've got to get that thing down, *now*!"

Dion walked forward to the bow and cast the stays'l downhaul off its belay pin on the breasthook, outboard of the bowsprit. He tossed the coil aft so that the line was straight and loose and the bitter end was aft of the foremast, free and ready for hauling. Wade trimmed in the stays'l until the sheet was taut. Jeshurun cast off the stays'l halyard from its belay pin, saving one turn around the bottom. Wade and Dion manned the downhaul. Captain June ran back to the helm and rammed the helm hard to port to face the storm.

"Strike the stays'l!" he shouted.

Jeshurun let go of the halyard. It whipped up through the gasket, running free. Dion and Wade at the same instant hauled in on the downhaul, and the line gathered in coils behind them. Dion refused, but Wade hauled. The stays'l slid down the forestay like a lead sinker and he hauled in with all his strength. Jeshurun rushed up to the stays'l club outhaul, which was rove through a block at the base of the breasthook and made fast to the port side of the anchor windlass. He cast off the line and tried to slide the club forward but the club did not move. Cursing, he remembered that he had to release the tension on the stays'l sheet first before the club could move forward; he released the sheet then hauled on the stays'l outhaul and the club slid all the way up to the turnbuckle.

Wade, meanwhile, made two figure-eight turns on the belay pin using the now-spent downhaul and proceeded to furl the stays'l atop the club with the line, using a daisychain. In five minutes, from the time Captain June had shouted the command, to the last rolling hitch on the daisychain, the stays'l was furled. The schooner had not quite changed direction although Captain June still held the helm hard over.

The rain hit them with the force of a monsoon. White hot water riddled the soft wood. The deck rolled under the deluge. The scuppers shot foam. The force of the rain pinned them, numbed them on the deck. They could not lift their heads or arms; all they could do was close their eyes and hope their schooner would stay afloat and keep them safe from being swept asea. The pounding and rushing drowned out their voices and thoughts; couldn't hear themselves think. Captain June had to drop his arms from the handles from the force of the water. He tried to look forward to see where his crew was, to see if they were gone, but couldn't see past the saloon housetop. He closed his eyes again letting his skull take on the blunt of the squall.

As soon it began it ended—sweeping over their deck port to starboard then away, followed by warm tropical rain and heavy sun. Wade and Jeshurun and Dion donned their jackets and sou'westers and now felt slick as ice. The water spewed off their brims, shoulders and arms. The rain fell steadily gently firmly. The rain dropped onto the deck everywhere. Sunrays burst through and splashed against the inside curve of the foresail, against the deep cherry-blushing, slush-stained foremast. Rays and rain poured into the deck.

Wade and Jeshurun placed on deck the two five-gallon buckets which they had used for washing it down. As the rain filled them, the crew poured the water into the tanks. The steadiness of the rain warmed and cleansed them. Their shredded clothing. Matted hair. Salty skin.

Wade dropped his shoulders and sighed in relief. "Jeshurun, go figure. Just when we needed it, it came. It hasn't rained like this the entire voyage."

Jeshurun smiled and his golden whiskers surrounded his bright teeth and he dumped the bucket over his head. Water swooshed over his face and shoulders and down his throat. "Timshel, Wade. It isn't possible without help. This sail isn't possible. But we're sailing. Aren't you and I glad that we're crew in the *Timshel Auxiliary*?"

CHAPTER THIRTY-THREE

They found life in the northeast trade winds. On the sixth day after sailing past Barbados and on the second day after crossing the Tropic of Cancer, one morning while Captain June struggled through his exhaustion to hold the helm of the *Vermillion Mourning,* and as Jeshurun sat on the main crosstree fighting to keep from falling in his famished condition, watching the dark sea for vessels, a little rogue wave rolled over the fo'c'sle. Water rumbled down her deck and flowed through her scuppers into the sea. The schooner rolled to port then righted herself.

Dion had been conserving his strength in the fo'c'sle with the hatch open to let the wind drift in when the ocean poured down over him. After the water left through the scuppers and the deck was clear and sparkling, Jeshurun shouted for Dion. All at once he launched up the ladder yelling, bald head glistening. "Come look!"

Jeshurun descended the shrouds. Wade, who had been sleeping in the saloon when he felt the rogue wave, weakly appeared on deck, struggling to stand upright from malnourishment. Dion pointed into the forecastle.

"Look!" he said.

A blue fin tuna half the size of a man lay on the sole of the fo'c'sle, wedged between bunks. The tuna thrashed in water. The big, dumb head slammed against planks.

Jeshurun snorted.

"Nice catch. Whaddya use?"

"It hit me on the head."

They laughed.

Jeshurun grabbed a belay pin off the pin rail and descended into the fo'c'sle, slipped, dashed his head against a bunk. When he regained his balance, he clubbed the tuna with short, stubby swings. Blood flowed from the brain. The tuna hung limp. He and Dion hauled it up the ladder, slipped it over the coming.

Captain June came trotting up behind them. He peered into the fo'c'sle, at the tuna, at Jeshurun and Dion, threw his hands into the air and shouted something in Irish, took out his spare knife and stuck it into the fish. He tore off a chunk of meat and crammed it into his mouth. The others followed. After several weeks they finally feasted on protein.

For the next hour they salted the tuna on deck. The sun's heat beat the schooner through the afternoon, curing the tuna. They left the meat out through the evening and into the night.

Leaving Bermuda to port they closed in on the main channel of the Gulf Stream. Gradually the schooner increased in speed. In the fo'c'sle where Wade tried to rest, the bow struck the water hard. With each wave he slammed against the headboard in his bunk. His eyes stayed open and he remained awake. Jeshurun stood on deck, helm in hand. The oncoming waves and tailing wind slapped together. High, choppy crests collided in the moonlight. He struggled to keep the bow straight. The next day Captain June noticed the color of the water had changed.

"We are now in the center of the Gulf Stream, heading into northeastern waters—toward the Labrador Current—its extension. The westerlies are taking us, sailor," he said. "Cape Hatteras should be off our port beam."

He gave command of the helm to Jeshurun then climbed aloft. Wade stepped out of the saloon. Seeing Captain June so elevated, so free, he burned to join him. Looking sidelong at Jeshurun, he snuck onto the shrouds and crept aloft.

"Wade, be wise!" said Jeshurun.

But he climbed higher, joining Captain June. Sunlight soaked their bones, warmed their hair, pulled on their desire to be free.

"You climbed up here against Jeshurun's wishes?"

Wade studied the bright, golden clouds towering above the ocean. The light rushed through them. The surface of the water sparkled.

"I remember your first day out from Springwick Harbor—you were scared to lift your tongue off the deck." He laughed.

Wade stuck his tongue out a little in a playful gesture.

"You're a different person."

"Aye."

"A natural sailor."

"I wouldn't say that. I've got a lot to learn."

"You seem guided by a deeper calling."

"I don't know. I feel humbled."

"I feel that too."

"None of us known what we're doing."

They were running wing and wing with the wind at their backs carrying gently through their hair.

"This vessel is a tomb, Wade. I knew that from the beginning. I'm surprised it's lasted this long."

"Then why did you sign on?"

"That's why I came to Springwick Harbor in the first place—I volunteered for this adventure. But unexpected things happened, things no one was planning on."

"What things?"

Captain June's calming eyes soothed him. "It was originally designed that Dion and I and the prison crew take the *Vermillion Mourning* out to sea. But when you came aboard, and Jeshurun to help you, I had to change plans."

"What were your original plans?"

"To take the *Vermillion Mourning* to Cape Horn and let the storms have their way with her, for better or worse." He pulled on his grizzled beard and rubbed his watery eyes. "The plan was to scuttle her. With all of us aboard."

"But she's saving our lives."

"I don't think she is. I think grace is saving our lives. The *Vermillion Mourning* is driftwood. She's not saving anything."

"But she's a strong ship. She endured the Horn."

"I think the Horn endured her."

"But she's beautiful."

Captain June inhaled, exhaled. "There's another vessel, Wade."

"You mean a sister ship."

"I mean a vessel made of stones. Golden masts. Diamond sails. Sapphire shrouds. An emerald hull. Amethyst keel. Spars of midnight jasper. Beryl belay pins and a heavy carnelian anchor. Coral ballast in her bilge. Her lines are twisted pearl and they never foul. Her ruby binnacle houses a topaz compass and she is never lost. Her wind pennant is pink hyacinth to guard against tempests. She sails at your wish and never is without wind. She has your name and my name written on her helm and we steer her together, and she steers herself. We ride with her into lands of rain and rainbows. She is alive. Her name is written in the clouds, and she wants you to sail aboard her."

Wade felt like he had discovered the deep secret of the sea. "I'm not sure I know how to find her."

"You've already found her. You've had your Horn, you're lucky. Accept your grace. Ready yourself for the day you come aboard."

He put his arm around the glowing rainbow of Wade. Believing and hoping in him, he knew they would one day sail together upon the ship prepared for them. He thought of his own youth and the day he fell in love with sailing.

Storm clouds moved fast toward *Maypole*. Peter June and his father rapidly reefed the sail of their sloop. They were in the middle of Penobscot Bay and would not make it to Castine in time. The clouds were carrying heavy slashing rain and wind capable of destroying their sails.

Peter's bewildered eyes locked on the water rapidly bursting before him as the clouds moved closer. It looked like the sea was walking into the sky.

"Brace yourself!" said the father. "Tighten your life jacket!"

Peter quickly tightened it, but before he could position himself below, the fury struck. The sloop rolled. The father fell overboard. The storm pushed the vessel toward the shore. He lost sight of his father, closing on the rocks. Peter had never navigated the *Maypole* himself. Quickly he worked the helm and brought her into the storm, then started the motor, but the motor proved ineffective. The rocks loomed but strangely he didn't become fearful; in that moment a tremendous peace swept into him and he knew everything would be all right. He would save his father and the two would be in Castine by the end of the day. He threw out the storm anchor and kept the bow pointed into the storm.

Miraculously, just before he was dashed, the storm passed. Peter spotted his father with binoculars, hoisted the storm anchor, and sailed to him as if he was a veteran sailor. He threw him a safety ring, helped him onboard. That afternoon they enjoyed hot chocolate in Castine. He fell in love with the power and beauty of the sport and in its redemptive end. From then on, he knew he would be ready for whatever challenge came his away on the high seas.

Dion appeared out of one of the holds. In his hand he held a knife; in the other, a flare gun.

CHAPTER THIRTY-FOUR

"**You two can stay up there for a while now,** Captain June. You don't need to come down. Not right now."

The back of Captain June's neck stood on end. Wade shook himself out of his daydreaming when he saw the seriousness on Captain June's face. Jeshurun flooded with wrath, but he couldn't rush him without losing their point of sail and causing an accidental gibe, which would fling Captain June and Wade off the crosstree to their death.

"You all are good just where you are."

"What are you doing, Dion?" said Captain June.

"I'm doing what you're incapable of doing. I'm taking over this ship."

"We had an agreement. I deliver you to New York so you can see Dominic."

"That was before these two little sweet peas came aboard. It's different now."

"What's in New York?" whispered Wade to Captain June.

"His beginning."

"Oh don't worry," said Dion. "We're still sailing to New York. Forget about Cape Race for the moment, Wade. Yes, we're still bound for New York. But I don't think you three are going to get there under our current order of things. It's the way of the sea, Wade. I'm sorry. I'm so very sorry."

He grabbed a belay pin off the pin rail and threw it at him. It struck the mast and ricocheted into the water.

"I'm to inform you that I've punctured several holes in the foreward holds with an augur—a *sea* augur, Wade. A real honest to goodness *sea* augur. A *sailor's* augur." He laughed. "Your kind of augur."

"If you stop now it'll go easier for you," said Jeshurun.

"But I don't want to stop now, Jeshurun." He laughed again. "I want to go to New York. I want to fa la la la la in New York. Wanna come?"

"But you saved us when you fixed the rudder," said Wade.

Dion frowned. "I know, son. I'm not all bad. I just taste things better when I am."

Captain June seemed distracted looking over the sizeable waves at the horizon. "What do you want us to do?"

"It's simple, thank you. You three are to remain where you are while I get rescued in the life raft. Try not to move, because if you do try to move, I'll shoot you with this flare. I'm really good at shooting flares. Or I'll stab you silly with our captain's knife. It won't be long before you sink, so pucker up. Death is hard any way you look at it."

"Where's the augur?" said Jeshurun.

"Don't worry about it. I threw it overboard."

Captain June continued to gaze at the horizon.

"So stay where you are while I toss the raft."

He tucked the flare gun and knife in his belt and jumped onto the saloon housetop to unfasten the plastic container which contained the raft. He heaved it onto the deck.

Captain June began to creep off the crosstree by placing one foot then another onto the futtock shrouds. Slowly he crept down the starboard shrouds.

Jeshurun was watching him. Dion looked at Jeshurun, darted his eyes at Captain June, pulled out his flare gun and shot.

The bright flare hit the shroud beneath Captain June and ricocheted into the water. Captain June paused, waiting for Dion to reload. Dion shot again. The flare went between a pair of ratboards and rocketed into the air, fully maturing in arc before bursting beautifully.

Captain June raced down the shroud. Wade had never seen a man move so rapidly. Dion loaded quickly and raised the gun. Before Captain June could reach the deck, Dion pulled the trigger.

The flare shot into his gut. The impact flung him off the shrouds. His momentum carried him onto the deck. He lay writhing, the flare burning his abdominal muscles.

Wade started to dash down the shrouds screaming. Dion reloaded and pointed the gun.

"Wade, stay where you are!" shouted Jeshurun.

Dion turned aft to Jeshurun. "I'll save you if you help me get the life raft overboard."

Jeshurun suddenly caught a glimpse of the horizon. "Okay. Whatever you want. But spare Wade."

"I'm not going to spare Wade. Sailors die asea. You know that."

"What has Wade ever done to you?"

"It's not what he's done to *me*, but what he shouldn't do for all of you. He deserves to be the Lighthouse Keeper. You know he's not born to sail."

"He was never born to be the Lighthouse Keeper."

"I suppose you think he can become what you want him to be? He doesn't have the courage. The rocks'd tear him alive. He wouldn't last an outing."

"I'm not sure you understand the strength of a sailor," said Jeshurun.

"You mean like Captain June? The man destined to take the *Vermillion Mourning* out to sea and scuttle her? With *me* aboard? What a mistake in judgment, Jeshurun. Who engineered this trip—Abner? You thought an inexperienced sailor like him could overcome the rocks and scuttle this vessel? She's mine! I scuttle her when I choose! Guess you underestimated my strength, ahoy? Guess you underestimated the weakness of Captain June."

A powerful horn blew.

Dion turned to see that Captain June was no longer lying on the deck but standing at the bow waving his work shirt at the barge muscling toward them. Dion soiled himself.

The engine of the tug whined. The bow rocked from the waves that sloshed against the outside of the hull.

"The *Pine Tar*," whispered Wade.

Dion realized that his power had been lost.

Wade flung himself down the shrouds to see to Captain June.

"I'm fine," he said. "Check the leak."

Wade went below into the foreward holds.

The seawater was coming in fast.

The tug came alongside pushing wave after wave into the small schooner rocking it back and forth, then moving ahead of the schooner's bow. The engine hummed and lurched and bubbled in the froth of the waves.

A man at the stern cupped his hands around his mouth but Captain June couldn't hear him. The man turned and motioned to someone inside the wheelhouse. The sound of the engine vanished. His puny voice echoed over the waters.

"What channel are you on?"

"We have no radio," said Captain June in his weakening voice.

The man upon the bridge remained motionless. Then he went inside the wheelhouse and came back out, holding a bullhorn, raised it to his mouth.

"WHAT IS YOUR CONDITION?"

"We are the sailing vessel *Vermillion Mourning*, and are sinking!"

"PLEASE REPEAT," said the bullhorn.

Captain June limped to his quarters to retrieve the bullhorn that he had stashed away for the rescue after he would have scuttled the vessel.

"PLEASE REPEAT."

Dion stepped in front of him.

"DO YOU NEED TO ABANDON SHIP?"

One moment later Dion was knocked out on the ground from Captain June's quick uppercut.

"Yes!"

"PLEASE REPEAT."

"Yes!"

Captain June raised the bullhorn. "THIS IS THE SAILING VESSEL *VERMILLION MOURNING*. WE ARE TAKING ON WATER."

"DO YOU NEED TO ABANDON SHIP?"

Wade shot through the companionway and shouted. "Captain June, I plugged the leaks!"

"DO YOU NEED TO ABANDON SHIP?" said the man on the *Pine Tar*.

"NEGATIVE.... CAN YOU TOW US IN?"

"AFFIRMATIVE.... THIS IS THE *PINE TAR*. WE HAVE RESPONDED TO YOUR DISTRESS CALL. WE CAN ASSIST YOU TO NEW YORK."

Captain June slumped to the deck.

Wade rushed to his aid. He wrapped his gory side with his shirt.

"You and Jeshurun need to furl the sails. I can't help you."

The *Pine Tar* threw over a hawser and Wade made it fast to the bollard. As the hawser came taut and the vessel started to follow the tug, Wade and Jeshurun furled the four sails as best they could. Wade had a sinking feeling he would never see those sails flying again.

When they finished they prepared the schooner for docking. In the bosun's locker they found the mooring lines—a bow line, stern line and two spring lines—deployed them along the port side of the vessel. They coiled and readied the lines, then washed the deck with saltwater and suds.

Jeshurun looked around. He shouted to Captain June, who was using up the last of his energy in caring for the helm. "Captain June, where's Dion?"

"Find him now," said Captain June, his voice trembling.

Jeshurun darted to the generator room. Wade checked the fore and aft holds. They didn't find him.

Jeshurun ran to the forecastle.

Dion was below, lying propped on a bunk. "I'm watching the leak, Jeshurun. I'm saving the boat."

Jeshurun squeezed his fists. "I want you on deck."

"Then move me."

"Okay."

Jeshurun clubbed him on the head, muscled his limp body up the ladder, pushed him through the companionway onto the deck. Using a constrictor knot he tied his wrists to the windlass. Captain June laughed.

The three sat on the saloon housetop on the quarterdeck inhaling the brisk air. Sunlight shone soft over the deck. Jeshurun and Captain June talked back and forth. Every once in a while they would look at Wade. He said nothing, wondering what he would do once he arrived in New York.

Four hours later the *Pine Tar* towed them through the Narrows marking the passage into the anchorage channel of the upper bay of New York. New Jersey lay on their left; New York on their right. The surface of the sea changed from large to smaller and calmer ripples.

As they passed under the Verranzo-Narrows Bridge, a plane streaked overhead. The shadow swept over the deck then merged with the distant waves, banking to the northeast. Wade wished he could be that plane, soaring in freedom over the seas.

"Do you like to fly?" said Dion drowsily, disoriented. "I wonder where it's going? To Bannock Pierce?" He tried to scratch his eyebrow but couldn't.

"That's over with," Wade said with assurance. He went below to fetch the postcard he had found so long ago before the journey had begun. The entire voyage he had kept the postcard in a plastic sack. Only once had taken it out to look at it—the night the rogue wave hit. Miraculously the water did not wash the postcard off the deck.

"What's that?" said Jeshurun.

"Just a postcard." He stepped to the caprail and tossed it into the sea. The postcard landed on the water and was folded into the rhythm of the waves.

They passed through the Narrows and into the outer harbor of New York, chugging around tankers. The passengers of a yacht looked at them curiously then returned to their cocktails. One onlooker snapped pictures. In the calm outer harbor small sailboats sailed leisurely, gibing or close-hauled. A little girl steered from her father's lap, waving to the *Vermillion Mourning*.

Having never sailed in these grounds before, Captain June watched the panorama through binoculars, toughened from his abdominal wound. This was the resting spot of the *Peking*, the vessel that had survived the truly violent Horn too many times to count.

The thick clouds parted and light splashed on the Statue of Liberty. Overwhelmed by her presence, Wade, Jeshurun and Captain June fell silent. They passed by bell buoy thirty-one, veered toward the East River. The gongs and hums in the city sounded over the waters. Captain June spun to his crew, his teeth savage from the pain.

"Now look. Jeshurun, you take the bowline. Wade, you take the number two line. I will take the number three line and the stern. This isn't like casting off. You have to hit your mark the first time. If you don't, the boat could swing out or surge forward and crash into something. Or someone. Hopefully we've learned since Rosa Dulce. If we mess up, you'll find out just how rich these people are."

They spread along the port side and manned their lines. Jeshurun stood by the anchor chain favoring his right foot, holding the coil of the bow line in his left. The tips of his right fingers traced the top of the anchor chain and the shackle and the pin and the hawser. He watched the boardwalk. In the backdrop the buildings of Manhattan leaned into the sky. Sunlight glinted off the tops of the skyscrapers and they seemed without care for what was happening in the city.

Jeshurun and Wade released the hawser. The *Pine Tar* peeled away to starboard and the dock behind it came into view off their port. Men were strewn along it. One man at the end was shouting commands. The schooner crept toward the dock. Jeshurun and Wade hurried to transfer their mooring lines from port to starboard. Wade rove his line in panic around a kevel cleat then through a hawse hole. Jeshurun needed only to switch sides since his bow line was made fast to the bollard. He felt the weight of the heaving line and readied to toss it but noticed that Wade was eying him soberly.

"Think you can get her onto the dock?" he said.

Wade nodded. "Yes. I know I can." He still felt grieved for having missed the toss during their approach to the village in Rosa Dulce. "I can do it, Jeshurun. Give me another chance."

They switched positions. Jeshurun took the foreward spring line and Wade took command of the bow line, the most important line of the four mooring lines because it was the first to be thrown and without it, none of the others would follow.

Captain June turned the wheel hard to starboard and the schooner veered toward the end of the dock, the same dock where the *Peking* and her masts and bare yardarms towered. The men on the pier prepared to catch the lines.

"Get your lines over! Make sure of it this time! We can't afford to be wrong here!" yelled Captain June. He held the wheel hard over. She came in at a steep angle. The bow swung around in a heavy, lazy arc.

The man on the pier yelled to the other men in harm's way of the bowsprit, "Get away from there!" It glanced off the pier and the schooner righted itself, coming parallel.

"Throw your lines! Now! *Now*!"

Wade threw his heaving line in loosening coils through the air and it landed expertly across a man's shoulder who made it fast around a cleat.

"Nice shot, Wade," said Dion. "In my book, your arm will live forever."

Jeshurun next flung his heaving line and it too landed beautifully in the hands of a man on the dock.

The bow drifted away and the bowsprit readied to scrape against the transom of the *Peking* foreward of it alongside the dock. The bow line stretched so tight it almost snapped. Captain June flung his stern line and a man made it fast around a cleat.

"All fast!" said Wade.

Suddenly Captain June collapsed, clutching his gut, trying to acknowledge from their vessel that they too were all fast. But his words sputtered.

Wade and Jeshurun rushed to him. His body, unable to repair the mortal wound, succumbed to shock. As they cried for help, Captain June turned his eyes softly toward the horizon, toward a sailing ship striking water and sky with diamond sails and golden masts and a deep and solid emerald hull—glittering, all of her, sparkling like water. He stretched his fingers. Called for her. His cheek struck the deck. With his will expired, his eyelids lifted if only a fraction. In the distance the vessel of his dreams had tacked for him.

CHAPTER THIRTY-FIVE

An ambulance transported Captain June's lifeless body to the hospital. People gathered around and in the commotion, Dion slipped away into Manhattan. Jeshurun and Wade stood on the bow at dusk waiting for the port authorities.

"I was watching him," said Wade to Jeshurun, his mind distracted by the loss of their captain.

"He wasn't supposed to come to New York," said Jeshurun bitterly. "Captain June volunteered to sail the *Vermillion Mourning* with him and Dion aboard under the pretense that they would sail to New York, but the real plan was to take her out to sea, to Cape Horn, and scuttle her—with Dion aboard."

"That's what Captain June told me. But what about Captain June? What about the prisoners?"

Jeshurun put his hands in his pockets.

"He wasn't going to die," said Wade fretfully.

"He made that choice, Wade. He's not a perfect man, the kind of trouble he got in with the Navy. But whatever shortcomings he struggled with in the past, he made up for when he agreed to captain the *Vermillion Mourning*."

"What did he do?"

"He scuttled a few Navy-issue lifeboats."

"That sounds odd."

"Maybe. But he had been practicing for this sail for some time now. He was willing to do whatever it took to scuttle the

Vermillion Mourning—even if it cost him his career in the Navy."

"But what about the prisoners?"

"What prisoners?"

"What do you mean? The ones that were going to sail aboard her."

"You mean, the ones who are safe, and alive, in their prison cells? Those prisoners? The ones who couldn't handle the *Vermillion Mourning*? The ones who were never meant to sail her in the first place? Those decoys for Dion?"

Wade whistled coolly. "I see what you're saying. She's bent. The penal salts long for something a little more diluted."

"That's right."

"So the story about Bannock Pierce creating the *Vermillion Mourning* out of flotsam and sailing around Cape Horn …?"

"Is false. There's no such thing as Bannock Pierce. Dion fed that myth to you to get you aboard."

Wade hardened his eyes. Some myth. Some dense tongue.

"He wants to destroy you. He hates you."

"Then where did the *Vermillion Mourning* come from?"

"From Abner."

"*What*?"

"He built it for the purpose of attracting Dion so the doomed man and the doomed vessel would bond asea, and sink."

"Why didn't he build it faster?"

Jeshurun squeezed his chin and his eyes shone brightly against the Manhattan skyline. "That's what everybody in Springwick Harbor was thinking. But he couldn't. He could only build a little at a time, only when another boat crashed against the rocks. Countless ships failing to make it into the harbor have gone into fashioning that vessel. Abner knew he had to build it with the planking made from destroyed ships—to create a destroyer for the destroyer.

"As Tobiah hauled the dashed components to the shipyard to shape into reality the *Vermillion Mourning*, Abner helped the dashed salts find safety in a Springwick Harbor home. Once they fled indoors, they refused to come out, their eyes weak and diluted. A cold horror touched the town. Men and women cut out their hearts and threw them back into the sea.

"But as the vessel took shape, a goodness happened: it became a fly trap. Dion took residence below, savoring her until she was complete. And Dion took the bait, just as Abner had anticipated: he became obsessed with the vessel, burning with the notion to take her to sea as a false pilot boat so he could steer every vessel bound for Springwick Harbor into the Northern Point."

"He doesn't belong in Springwick Harbor."

"He doesn't belong on the sea, either. He's an imposter."

"How did he ever come to the harbor?"

"Over land. From Brazil."

"You mean he's not a sailor?"

"No. He once was supposed to be Second Assistant to the Keeper. But when he tried to take over the Lighthouse, Abner kicked him out. He hates you with a passion. He lusts to destroy you. But he hates Abner, Tobiah and me more. He's been trying to get back at us ever since—by destroying the livelihood of those in town and those still asea who believe in the bloody light that the Lighthouse creates."

"How does he cause the ships to wreck?"

"By intimidating all the sailors in Springwick Harbor from going out to help the distressed incomers. Sailors are fearful of becoming who they are born to be when an ugly plank is all they see between them and their calling. But Captain June answered the call. He vied for the inner harbor during storm, a most severe storm. Abner salvaged him and also the finishing component that the *Vermillion Mourning* needed to make her seaworthy."

"The helm," said Wade, recalling how he held it soberly rounding the Horn.

"Once Abner fitted the helm, Captain June was set to deliver the vessel with Dion aboard. He was going to take her to Cape Horn and scuttle her, and risk perishing. But you disrupted our plan when you dove for the vessel," smiled Jeshurun kindly. "I had to save you, Wade. The only way I could was by bringing you aboard. Thus, we two have ventured together along with Captain June and Dion like two stowaways on a journey we both were never meant to embark upon." And then Jeshurun whispered, "*But we were.*"

Wade rubbed his palm. "Go on."

"You and this vessel are strangely fated to suffer a testing, Wade. The *Vermillion Mourning* has become something she was not intended to be."

"What's that?"

"Your coffin."

He stammered, "Well uh … we're in … New York … sail's over … glad I passed it…."

Jeshurun swallowed hard. He gathered himself, let the comment pass, and continued with their conversation. "By the time we had reached Rosa Dulce, Captain June realized he had to change his plans. So he destined the vessel for Cape Race—to make you believe in the validity of the journey so that you would embrace your calling, which you have, albeit before you were meant to. You're a sailor."

Wade nodded with a heaviness on his shoulders and closed his eyes and felt something deep inside him holding up his pride.

"But to deceive Dion, he had to give the impression to him that we were secretly sailing for New York so he would willingly crew, all the while thinking nothing of Dion's longevity but only of preserving our three lives. Unfortunately, now that we're here, Dion's wishes have materialized. We're in New York, facing the worst. He's loose in this city, eager to bind sailors to the earth."

"What about the life raft?"

"It doesn't work. Abner ordered it from a catalogue."

"Oh. Well I guess that makes sense."

Lamenting the injured Captain June, angry from the mutiny of Dion, thankful for their survival around Cape Horn, weak in his craving for the Lighthouse, fearfully eased for having lost Bannock Pierce, despondent for being so far away from Springwick Harbor, elated for having found the city, fidgeting because he was not yet settled—he wondered if he should stay aboard the *Vermillion Mourning* and wait for another sail, or return with Jeshurun to Springwick Harbor. Neither seemed right. The port authorities had not arrived.

Night had fallen and the lights were in the streets. Caribbean reggae with stranger rhythms all floated over the dock. He tapped his fingers, stirring. His eyes thrived. His eyes danced. He wanted to feel the light, the supple bending of the heat. "Jeshurun. Run with me."

"You won't find him."

"I'm not looking for him."

"What are you looking for?"

"Come with me."

"We have to notify the port authorities, identify Captain June's body."

"We'll look around. We'll find something."

"Forget him, Wade."

His eyes pulled into the beehive. "It's here. I feel it. I feel something I've never felt before." He hopped onto the dock. "Come on."

They passed under a freeway. An energy clipped into Wade's step. He quickened his pace. Easing. Striding. The warm city lay on his skin. The big, round, smiley shoulders of Jeshurun falling into rhythm. Faster. Faster past pedestrians. Falafel, the aroma of seasoned lamb. The quickening throng. Heading deeper. Skyscrapers packing the skyline. Guitars on corners. Thin violins. Piccolos and six string steel guitars. Saxophones. Steel drums. The aura. The sea. The meat of the eyes feasting on the life of the light of the city, the music of the night.

He rushed for the heart. A gritty runner finding his stride. His jaw finding joy, a deft percussion off the buildings. Jeshurun following. Faster. Streetlights made green.

A flash! A marquee glowing in the dark. The brilliant glow. The brilliant sprint. His legs kicking his buttocks. His finishing kick. Blazing down Broadway. The stop lights falling behind them like channel buoys. Weaving among taxis and crowded sidewalks. Horns honking wildly behind. Not caring that they're honking. Something burning in him, a desire to see something. His thighs burning. His side aching. He ran hard, desperate for a flush.

What cannot come true, he hoped in. What is impossible, he believed. This sweet journey given him, this sprint into the heart of the city, into Times Square, where the lights—the lights! the lights!—overwhelmed him, this cool rush of illumination from the faces of the buildings that poured into the streets—as if the town, the nation at its most foreward point, brightened the intersection of its people. Any dream was possible.

Jeshurun followed him panting, stood beside him in the street. "Wade, come home. You don't want what you want. It's not good for you."

"I'm finding something, Jesh."

"He doesn't exist," he said breathlessly.

"I'm not looking for him."

Bitter that his maiden sail had ended prematurely, his wobbly sea legs tenderly were adjusting to the overflowing life of the city. Barely upright from exhaustion, he felt his soul coming to life in this better harbor, this humming awakening, this birthing.

The steady hum of traffic, the skyscrapers, marquees lit in cool heat, the rising warmth of the pavement, people moving together. The feeling of radiance burrowed into his chest. What had he just left? ... Oh, that schooner? His identity had been rooted in her for as long as he could remember. But the city had taken her place and had given him something new to cling to. He forgot everything under the freedom of what he saw.

The illumined eyes. The faces. The brilliant bodies. Radiant souls. The people. All at once, the people. And every hope in them the people. And hearts made alive in the people. The freedom of the people. The beautiful hearts.

Individuals bound for better life. Bound to discover sailing, the adventure of the Keep. The storm called them. The humility of the Horn longed to sire them. Life wanting them bathed them in the sobering deep. This was the hive. The harbor for the moving. The pounding expression of humanity.

Compassion surged through him dreaming in them the dream—helming the hope, the glory, in pursuit of a horizon, bowsprit cutting through storm, through the Horn and its crushing birth and the fear to embrace the chaos of water and the movement of a conquered sailor, of a soul who cannot be defeated when conquered by love.

He collapsed, realizing that this city was filled with sailors waiting to helm the light. The people. The people. The opening people. Salted and alive. Never before had he seen or believed in the people—not like this, not with this will. They reminded him of the sailors in Springwick Harbor. The beautiful sailors, anchored in truth, their hope waiting to be unfurled. Their brave dreams, waiting to be carried by the wind. Joy coursed through him, filling his eyes with tears. In the city in the heart of the city, sailors filled this city of heart with light.

CHAPTER THIRTY-SIX

Jeshurun rubbed his sweaty neck. The race to the Square had made him glistening. His shorts pulled on his skin. "You're not ready to be here, Wade. He baited you."

"Then where is he?"

"In an alleyway. Shedding skin."

"I think I'm okay," he said, voice mixed with assurance and apprehension.

"Come back to the schooner until we figure out—"

"I think I'm figuring it out."

Wade's slender eyes dismissed Jeshurun as he scrutinized the Square. "I feel the sailors," he said, studying the sidewalks and taxis teeming with the outward bound.

Jeshurun's heart melted for him, this eager care for the sailors, this concern for their welfare, this heart. It was not a waste to have come this far around the Horn with Captain June. It wasn't supposed to have happened this way but he saw the good in being here. It was good. It was always good. Every bad thing turned into good. But he had to get him home. "You need to eat."

"I'm not hungry."

"Really, Wade?"

Wade rolled his eyes as his stomach growled.

On a dim block away from the main current they halted before a hamburger parlor filled with neon pink and powder blue booths. A round, red awning hung over the door with the name of the restaurant in the rectangular window: *The Sweet Meet*. Wade's mouth watered.

They jogged in long, loping strides to the door and grabbed the handle. Went in. Small. Checkered floor varied pink and blue. Grilled chicken and vanilla and strawberry milkshakes and thick fries and ketchup and sautéed onions and mushrooms and American cheese and cola and melted hamburger wafting with the draft.

The old-fashioned diner hummed with Oldies filtering from speakers. They sat at the counter where it turned to the wall. The counter was empty but they heard two voices behind the kitchen door. In the back left corner against the window an intimate couple occupied a booth.

They studied the menu written in white chalk behind the counter above the ice cream machine. The smell of ice cream and fries. The couple halfway done with their burgers. The pattering rain starting to strike the windows.

"It's starting to rain," said Jeshurun.

Wade looked. The drops were starting to roll and merge together, like sailors carried into the same current. He turned from the window to the menu saying, "I thought I might try a Doub—" when his speech cut off. For through the swinging door a young waitress stole his breath. Her light, smooth eyes regarded fully the boy at the counter. She walked to him and placed a spoon and fork onto a napkin and slid the napkin to within inches of his hand. She smelled like fresh apples.

He removed his hands from the counter and placed them underneath his thighs so that they wouldn't tremble in front of her. He looked agonizingly at Jeshurun. She adjusted the silverware on the napkin. Her fingers were bare.

"We'll that's good," he said awkwardly.

"Excuse me?"

"What?"

"Did I say something?"

"Oh, no. I was just wondering what's good to eat here." He looked blindly at the menu.

"Oh!" she gasped. "Our hamburgers." She didn't mind that they were both the most ragged men whom she had served. She sort of liked their rustic appearance.

The smiling Jeshurun made her blush.

"What's in the Double Trouble?" said Wade. His T-shirt, though not as ragged or as soiled as Jeshurun's, was riddled with holes. Most of the letters of the BORN TO RUN stenciling on the back had been shredded.

"Oh, goodness. It's a big one," she went on. "Two patties. Two slices of ham. Two slices of bacon. Two eggs. Two onions. Two slices of tomato. Two pickles. Two slices of Amer … no, pepperjack cheese. And two buns. It's really big. You'll never finish it."

He was caught in the fullness and the warmth and the beauty of her eyes.

"I think so," he said.

"What? I'm sorry—"

"Nothing. I thought—do you have any …" he fixed his eyes determinedly, "… hamburgers?"

She squeaked laughter. "Our hamburgers are *very* good."

Jeshurun bit his lip to keep from laughing.

"Well I'm hungry for a hamburger," said Wade.

"Would you like to try the Wednesday special? The All-American burger? It's good."

Her heart beat uncontrollably. She thought she might faint. She squeezed the pen in her fingers. This boy, she thought.

"Yes. The All-American burger."

She met his eyes. Dropped her pen. Isabella was a strong girl. She had lived in New York all her life without seeing the soul of a boy. This was the boy she was going to marry. "I'll bring you your order." She went into the kitchen.

Wade half-groaned, half-sighed. Picked up a spoon and tapped, then faster.

Jeshurun was brimming.

"What's so funny?"

"Keep tapping."

"Stop smiling."

"I'm not smiling. I'm resting my frown."

"Stop it."

Jeshurun laughed.

"Have you ever been to New York before?" said Wade.

"When I was your age."

"What do you remember?"

"The people tapping."

The burger tasted delicious, spices and seasonings like cilantro and oregano, red pepper and thyme. He ate the last of the thick cut fries, licked the splattered condiments on the plate then his fingers. He wasn't full.

Isabella came out from the kitchen carrying a cloth and wiped the counter and tables. "How was your meal?"

"That was the best hamburger."

"Would you like dessert?"

"What do you have?"

"Ice cream. Vanilla ice cream. It's good—better than our milkshakes."

"What else?"

"Apple pie. But it's not as good as our ice cream. They send us the milk from Oregon."

"The ice cream?"

"The milk for the ice cream."

"From Oregon?"

"It's from a town on the coast. It's called Tillee—oh I forgot the name."

"Tillamook."

"That's it."

"They make cheese in Tillamook, and milk." He shrugged his shoulders thinking, What can you do? You try to leave Oregon but you can't get away from it. "Yes, I'll have some of your vanilla ice cream. Want any, Jeshurun?"

He shrugged okay.

"Are you from Oregon?" said Isabella.

"Yes."

"Where in Oregon? Are you from Portland?"

"I'm from a little town called Springwick Harbor. It's on the coast."

"I *love* Oregon."

"Very well."

"I've been there."

"You have."

"Yes. I've been to Portland. I flew there on a business trip with my father. Portland is beautiful."

"Portland is beautiful, yes."

"If you like cities.... I like cities."

"I do, too."

"I'll get your ice cream."

She placed a napkin in front of him that said, Open Me.

He opened it. It said, Please call me, Isabella; with two exclamation points, a smiley face, and her phone number in dark, bold letters.

Tingles surged up his neck. He glanced at the grinning Jeshurun for approval, then at Isabella. They laughed together.

"Hi, Isabella."

"Hi."

"You have a pretty name."

She blushed. "Thank you…. What's yours?"

"Mine? Oh, Wade. This is Jeshurun."

"You have a pretty name too."

They blushed again.

The couple who had been sitting in the back corner got up and the man withdrew his wallet and plopped a few dollars on the table. Then he pulled several more dollars out and plopped them in the center of the table and set the saltshaker on top of them. He had a large, square face with creases halfway up his jaw. His face matched his square hat and coat, which he put on. The woman had a round, olive-like complexion and wore high, thin heels. They were both smiling as if in after-thought of a joke that they had just shared between them. They were both inaudible and he took her coat in his hands and helped her into it. They made the long walk out of the diner together, hand-in-hand.

As the woman walked out, Isabella noticed the ring on the woman's finger. She spun around and faced Wade with a new freshness in her eyes.

Wade had no idea what she was thinking. But he knew. And he trembled. "Well, thank you for the meal," he said.

"You're very welcome."

"Well."

"Are you a sailor, Wade?" she said.

He caught her eyes, held them for a moment, wanting to ask how she knew.

She explained. "A sailor knows a sailor. It's written in your eyes." She took off one of her rose-shaped earrings and laid it in his palm. "But you lack a dream."

"I don't have a vessel."

"Make this vessel your dream."

They discussed wind, the tingles in the chest as a sail dips through the water, the swell, the gentle list to leeward, the true compass, home in sight, a safe bay, a harbor mooring, anchor lanterns sharing the moonlight, the joy of sailing. She longed to sail with someone who owned a schooner to take her into the Atlantic on holidays. She wanted Wade to come out with her and her father.

"Can I ask you a question?" said Wade.

"Sure."

"Don't you have about a million boyfriends chasing you in this city?"

"Oh no," she said, shaking her head. "All the boys are too silly in this town."

The distant hum of the city smothered by rainfall drew their eyes into the warmth of each other.

"Do you think somewhere in the world there's someone waiting just for you?" she said.

Wade slipped his eyes into hers giving her tingles. "I don't believe in that sort of thing. But I think … well I think she's not waiting anymore."

She smiled desperately and kissed him on the cheek.

"We have to go," said Jeshurun. "We have an appointment."

They got up to leave.

"Will I ever see you again?" he said.

"Build a boat. I'll be waiting."

They went to the door.

"Oh, dear," she spurted out.

They turned.

She looked stricken, but said, "You still need to pay for the meal."

Jeshurun regarded Wade with a conspiratorial look on his face, as if he knew this was coming and had wanted it. What are we going to do? he was saying.

Wade squinted at the wall, thinking of something clever. He pulled out a short strip of seine twine. He took Isabella's trembling hand. He tied a constrictor knot on her ring finger.

She gasped.

He held her small hand in his palm. "Consider it a down payment."

Her shoulders dropped. Her chest heaved. Her eyelids drifted to the table. She was hoping he would kiss her.

Wade suddenly lost his strength. He started to fall backward. Jeshurun caught him, laughing. He righted him and patted him on the shoulder. Come on, boy. We need to fix your list. Wade staggered behind him as they left *A Sweet Meet* and carried down the street, rain falling on the pavement and awnings. The rain fell through the yellow lights and landed in the puddles. A saxophonist under a street lamp was playing to a mallard and her brood of ducklings, quacking obnoxiously and waddling away. Wade glowed thinking of her.

"We have to get you home," said Jeshurun.

"I don't want to go home. How are we going to get home anyway? We have no money."

"We can sail home."

"On what? What's our appointment?"

"I know a man who once lived in Springwick Harbor. He was a good captain but he made a foolish choice once. He's a lost, fragile soul. If we can find him, we can get home. But we have to find him before Dion does."

CHAPTER THIRTY-SEVEN

The terrible burden weighing on Captain West rounded his shoulders, smashed his will. He was tired. He hated the body given him, this sponge condensed into a searing, painful point. His dream had been to lead them safely into the outer harbor, away from the Northern Point, a pilot boat captain. He now lived with the loss of it.

Roaming the island, tired of fighting the streets, the suffering cold, the impoverished struggle to believe in a better life, he knew he would never find another harbor. He walked barefoot. His old-hand leather Australian duster too large for him drug on the pavement. His nose ran through his beard. His shattered glasses hung loosely from his ears. His torn wool sweater hung from his breast. It was going to be a harsh winter. He missed Abner. He missed him terribly.

Limping through Central Park beneath the yellowing leaves, he drug his leg like a kedge anchor, arms low. He found a team of ducks waddling near the water and sat to feed them. In Springwick Harbor he remembered embracing this time of year—the cooling harvest, the canning, the hope of being warm with family, the warm laughter in the evening after a sobering journey over water. But now his struggle was for survival—a one-time water king rummaging for a next meal. He had eaten better as a sailor dining on hardtack than he did here.

From a plastic bag filled with rotten apples and other waste, he extracted bits of soggy bread and tossed them to the ducks. They waddled curiously to his feet and took the morsels in their beaks then quacked into the water. His goofy smile came out. The longing to one day again be as carefree as these, waddling in his own way into the water, made his eyes wet.

But he felt the punishment in him, the sobering death claiming and keeping what he wanted most. Something cold and smooth kept his eyes in the earth. He wanted to kiss people but he couldn't because he was no longer a sailor. He writhed in the history of himself, in the old tyrannical garb wrapped in everything he saw, so heavy and so wrathfully wrong. He hated himself. He hated the sea. He wanted someone to see him to a slaughter.

"Hello, Captain."

He spun. Gazed upon a man shredded in pants and sleeves, whiskers long but eyes a brilliant, eager hunger. His tongue scrolled down his cheek as if tasting the cannibal want of his own flesh. He looked like a castaway, an imposing castaway—marooned in New York City.

"Do you remember me?"

Captain West tore off another piece and handfed a quacking duck who waddled into the water joining the team.

"Do you remember who I am, Captain West?"

Captain West speechlessly turned his mind toward the ducks.

Dion had swallowed his anchor, and then had disappeared into the alleyways, into shadowy trash, waiting to destroy the homeless. He preyed on their blood and will. Spread lies in their dreams about the sea. Flooded them with fear. The sailors hid their eyes in the pavement, grappling for a foothold, for safety. He overwhelmed them and drowned them in his ruinous wake. The Port Authority police had dredged the darkness to find him but surfaced only whispers and anguished screams. Finally they had endured enough and closed his file playing down the wild, fearful eyes. He became a myth.

"Do you remember the *Peking*?"

He felt his capillaries curl. "No."

"You don't remember the *Peking*? I'm here, Captain. I'm in New York. A pleasant journey to get here."

"I don't want to sail."

He sat on the bench next to him. "I know you don't. I didn't come here for that. I want you to be free." Placed a hand on a knee. Turned. "Do you miss your home?"

"I'll never round the Horn."

He fought to remember his greatest triumph asea, when he had sailed in inclement weather, just as terrible as the Horn, to rescue Bethlem, adrift for weeks in a life raft....

The 70 foot fiberglass ketch dropped into a trough. Captain West lost site of the yellow raft. The bow of the ketch crashed into the next crest sending water over the vessel. He held his breath, holding onto the helm, as the water swamped him. Riding the crest he saw the yellow raft again, this time farther away than he had thought. He could barely hold the helm, suffering from exhaustion, malnutrition and blistered skin. This was the 88th day of his search, and by now he had strayed over two thousand nautical miles off course, drifting toward New Zealand. The ketch pushed through crest after crest until it reached the raft. Bethlem lay in the rain-soaked bottom, so exhausted that he could barely open his eyes. Captain West managed to hoist him aboard. When he sailed him home, the town celebrated as it hadn't in years, dubbing Captain West its pilot boat captain—a dream come true. He beamed knowing he would willingly brave the heart of storm time and again to guide sailors safely into the harbor….

He tried to remember the long years when he served Springwick Harbor and its sailors with alacrity, joy and vigilant pluck. No one else in the Northwest possessed comparable skill. Even in his budding career he had carved into the sea an impressive wake. Sailorfolk shared with him the bullion they had found on their voyages as a thank you for guiding them safely home.

But at his zenith a man whom he had never seen approached him with bullion so savory he could not take his eyes off it—against his better judgment. There was a storm brewing and in that storm, an inbound wayward vessel, and in the hold of that vessel, a child. It was rumored by this foreign stranger that the child was destined to become the pilot boat captain of Springwick Harbor. Captain West's heart sunk.

Although a strong sailor, he feared losing the bounteous life given him, feared losing his grace. With Dion's succulent eyes dangling over him, he determined that no sailor was going to threaten his comfortable hold on the helm of all helms. He would take Dion with him and the two would venture into the heart of the storm and guide that vessel and her crew into the clutches of the Northern Point.

"Come around the Horn," said Dion. "Come back to Springwick Harbor. We'll sail together. Wasn't that our pact?"

He had striven all these years to forget it.

"He was just a child. He didn't deserve to suffer."

Dion turned on him with vitality, whispering into his ear, "The boy aboard that vessel is still alive, and still destined to sail as pilot boat captain of Springwick Harbor. Your reputation is waiting to be tarnished when this boy grows into the pilot boat captain you'll never become. Destroy him now while you're still safe. Guide his vessel into the rocky Newfoundland shore of Cape Race. After that, you and I can captain the pilot boat together."

Captain West first felt shock at the proposal. His stomach churned. But he knew it was true—his job *would* be taken away from him, this imminent eternity. Though he had long ago believed whole-hearted in the boy's arrival and in the arrival of sailors from all over, he had agreed with Dion to destroy Wade Burns.

"He's not *just* a child anymore—he's a sailor now," said Dion. "We have work to do."

"I can't begin another adventure, I'm too thirsty. There's no water on this island."

Dion breathed unhurried through his nostrils. "You're too thirsty in this city, Captain West. You shouldn't sail."

"What blood is on your hands? He's just a bo—"

"Then let him take your schooner."

Captain West was breathless. "What?"

"Abner gave him the *Vermillion Mourning*. It's not yours anymore."

"It was never mine."

"It was going to be yours. Until you ran."

A flame waned in Captain West's eyes—a memory of a warm past, a passionate life long ago fed with hunger and desire and ambition. Dion had convinced him that a schooner called the *Vermillion Mourning* was going to be built for Captain West alone, as a gift for succeeding at such a difficult task. But the schooner didn't matter to him anymore.

Dion crossed his legs leisurely, and as a mallard and her ducklings waddled past, he kicked at a straggling duckling, and continued. "I need you to sail the *Peking* back to Springwick Harbor."

"I'm not bound to that sea anymore."

"You're not bound to my pact? Our gentleman's agreement? C'mon, we tore up some country together. I remember you loved to hunt."

"Stop, please."

"We're just going to go out there, Dominic. We'll play around a little and experiment. I'll even hoist the sails. All I need is for you to steer."

Captain West felt hollowed and vacant and his eyes passed over the cute waddling ducks and the pond and trees and his eyes burned dryly.

"All I need is for you to helm the schooner of your dreams."

"You're cold. You're starving."

"I found you."

"But you're starving."

"I just want a rich life, Dominic. You know I've always wanted to share my vision with you. We go wayyyy back."

A couple walking the pathway laughed to themselves. Captain West lost his daze and fixed his angry eyes on the waddling ducklings. He clung to them passionately.

"Then what do you want?"

"I need you to drum up some of your city buddies. You must have buddies on this island. We'll round the Horn together, back around, *back* to our *duty* as pilot boat captain of Springwick Harbor. You see, we've got to get back there and keep on pressing with the purpose of the sail."

"I'm weak," he mumbled.

"Well, that's because you're not sea hardened. A few months on the waves will button you up just a bit. It'll be good for you. You're born to suck water."

"I'm not born to destroy sailors."

"You *told* me Springwick Harbor needs to remain a place of purity. We can't just let any fool sail into the harbor, can we? Dogs and cats living together? Boats stacked so deeply you'd have to move ten just to get one out to sea? What kind of life is that? It would be chaos. Springwick Harbor isn't meant for clutter. It isn't meant to be dirtied. You have to select the sailors, Captain. You know that. You know we've talked about it. We've talked it over too many times to count—and don't lie to me. You know that's your heart. You want the town as pure as I do. If we go out there, we can choose who to let in. That's some pretty weight, Mr. Kidslap. That's power. It'd be good for your bones. But I need you to sail. Because I'm a sailor. And I want us sailing together."

Captain West was beginning to remember his life as a sailor before he had the life of Bethlem. He was terrible. Rash. Greedy. Arrogant. Impatient. He had tried to master the waves. He had wrecked too many vessels to count and had been rescued off the coast of Springwick Harbor by other mariners. He burned to find the glory of the horizon at the expense of vessel and crew, but more often he found the bluffs of the Northern Point. He could count on both hands the number of times Abner had rescued him from its clutches.

But when his conscience sobered and he discovered the beauty of humbly sharing the waves with the sailors, he found an inner strength far greater than the horizon he was longing to discover. He found a horizon within him so vast, so unyieldingly good, he gave up his life as buccaneer and settled down into a good sail and a good life. That was when he found the courage to rescue Bethlem; and shortly after, when he was awarded the sobering duty of officially guiding mariners away from the Northern Point, which he knew too well as a dangerous end; the ideal man for the job for that reason alone.

But then Dion had visited him at just the wrong time with the promise of a permanent vessel and a permanent dream—in just the wrong wind—if he in turn would promise to take him when he sailed. Unable to fight off the slick that ran up his spine, he swore an oath with him, bound in blood.

But on his maiden voyage as pilot boat captain, when he guided that first vessel into the Northern Point, with Wade aboard, he fled Springwick Harbor running east, hiding from the oath that had sealed his heart to a landlubber. Dion had finally come for his reckoning.

He wanted nothing to do with him. He wanted to wallow in his own demise as a man lost of sea legs and not worthy to gargle saltwater. Too many times he had stumbled in his own bitter wind and knew he deserved this pungent existence with trash.

Yet having Dion here created jealous urgings all over again, greedy want, terrible lust. He hated the dark world he lived in—the only darkness in which he felt comfortable. Every day ended in exhaustion. Exhaustion from the cold. From lack of sleep. Poor nutrition. No nutrition. Poor hygiene. Poor medical care. Numb legs. Heat exhaustion. Harassment. Theft. Lack of friendship. Lack of rest. Pain. Tremendous physical pain. If he only could find rest. He craved a comforting bed. Clean sheets. Running water. A hot shower.

"You can rest on the *Peking*."

"What do you want me to do?"

"The boy is here, marooned like you on the island. Jeshurun is with him."

"What do you want me to do?"

"I want you to drum up some of your buddies and let Jeshurun come to you. Bring him and all the other mariners with you onto the *Peking*. Wait for me there. Don't worry about the boy. I'm going to help him sail to Cape Race on that pine drape, anchored to a nightmare," he said. His voice was frigid, recalling the nights he had spent in terror aboard *Vermillion Mourning*, feeling her weight cracking him open. He continued. "It's where he's always wanted to go. It's his dream, Captain West. Well, I'm going to help him sail his dream in a keen way. We'll sack a city to celebrate."

Captain West felt heavy at heart over what he knew he had to do. Dion was his best friend asea. And after all these years, they were still so close, even now. "That will take some time," he said.

Dion nodded, leaned over and Captain West kissed his heart-shaped locket. The trap for the false sailor had been set.

CHAPTER THIRTY-EIGHT

As fall turned to winter, Jeshurun and Wade searched the streets for Captain West, who lay among his brethren suffering the brutal, lonely weathering. They scoured the heart of the city—the homelessness and the poverty. Dead end alleyways. Underground passages. Dark, cavernous spaces. Combed the grid for the unrecognized, those not given a name—to inspire them with the hope of a ship. Like sailors shipwrecked and cast asea, these homeless were most hungry for a home—most hungry to be rescued, most aware of their foundering among the sharks. Jeshurun knew their vulnerable hope. The battle for the heart of the city lay in the heart of the marooned.

Wade, rather than becoming soft on land, grew in his hardened seaworthiness. His stomach grew lean, clothing sagged, cheeks caved as if pressed by wind. His eyes widened with hunger. His hands and feet dried and cracked until calloused and raw. Yet as his body deteriorated, his spirit surged with life as he explored his character as sailor—a character anchored and toughened by the sea. As a sailor he fought to endure the harsh winter as if pitched about in the fury and brutality of an icy storm. Entrenched and deep, he believed in the harbor ahead.

The streets flowed alive and turbulent with sailors wandering the streets without shelter, food or clothing, in search of grace. Mariners in turmoil with their calling. Sailors grappling with the unbounded freedom of the water. Their adventure just over the horizon promised to soothe damages they had accrued in their lifetime bound by land. Clinging to a hope they did not fully understand, they starved themselves with wind, trimmed their soul, suffered the wait for the everlasting vessel. The deep truth of Springwick Harbor was a powerful gift for the hungry sailor. The best life for the everlasting being.

Several months had passed since their arrival in New York City and it had yet proven fruitless. They still did not know where Captain West lay, if he lay at all. Every homeless man or woman they accosted had never heard of the man. It was a foolish quest. Did he even live? They searched into the heavy months of winter, starving, emaciated, sickly. Finally they plopped into the dead end of an alleyway and Wade waited for the garbage men to scoop them away.

The icy January wind rushed down the alley like a Williwaw. Gust after gust tore their flimsy cardboard coverings into the waves of traffic. Sleeting rain stabbed at their bodies and burned and numbed their hands and feet. Their wet, ragged clothing dangled from their limbs like shredded canvas now worthless in the overpowering wind. In their delirium, in the cold sway of the alley, they suffered weakness and poverty and the devouring mass of the storm. Foundering against a building devoid of warmth and shelter, they fought to make themselves fast to life.

"I can't do this, Jeshurun," gritted Wade. He meant he couldn't do his job, stick with Jeshurun, believe in Springwick Harbor. Was the harbor even real? It maybe wasn't real. Maybe Jeshurun wasn't real. Maybe the sea wasn't real. He missed Abner and Tobiah and Walter and his crew and the dense vegetation of Springwick Harbor, the bungalows holding dreaming sailors. He missed the Lighthouse and was sorry he had so greedily desired Jeshurun's destiny as Keeper. It was a terrible mistake. He wasn't the Keeper and never would be.

But even in the storm of this city, this hive, his role as sailor was developing new dimensions, deep passions, powerful love. The people held the map to his dream.

"We'll do it together. Come close to me."

Wade shivered madly.

"W-w-why are we doing this?"

He knew why. At the back of the alley against fencing a homeless man lay exposed to the winter. His bare feet and hands suffered frostbite. A flimsy strip of cardboard covered his torso. Suddenly a gust flung his covering down the alley. The man did nothing. He seemed immune to the elements, near death.

Jeshurun at last recognized him, his hulking, powerful shape, crawled to him whispering, "It's just a little longer before a pint of Nog, Captain. Hang on."

The man was lifeless.

Jeshurun laid over him a dirty blanket he had found in the dumpster and tucked his extremities.

"… Who are you?" he said. But he knew. He recognized the voice. But he wouldn't believe it. Dion was right. "What are you doing here so far from Springwick Harbor?"

"I've come to bring you home."

"But I'm destined for trash. I forfeited Springwick Harbor when I came east."

Tormented by the loss of Wade and the vessel that had carried him, he forsook his destiny as an honest sailor and went east to pirate the Caribbean, burning supplies, marooning crew. He boasted a score of tankers ransacked and scuttled—but nothing made up for the guilt suffered from the loss of that vessel. He ended up in New York City where the streets masked his identity, clouded his will, made him fruitless.

"We need mariners," said Jeshurun. "This is forgiveness."

"But I'm doomed."

The sleeting rain tore at his skin.

"Everyone at some point feels like they're doomed," said Jeshurun. "And in your words, 'Sail out of it. Hit the storm when it's hardest. Hit the storm now while she's young and lacking confidence. All will be well. You'll survive on the waters. You'll find the harbor. You'll not suffer forever.'"

"What do you want?"

"Come sail the *Peking*."

"I can't sail the *Peking*."

"Come gather a crew and we'll sail the *Peking* back to Springwick Harbor."

"But then who are you?"

"I'm a marooned bum just like you. And we're here, alive together. We have the grace. The *Peking* is waiting for you. All this time."

"She's rotting."

"She's docked at South Street Seaport—waiting."

Captain West rolled onto his side to regard him who was standing up to his words and the wind and the sleet and the brutal cold. "Who are you, Jeshurun?" he said openly. "You don't want me."

Jeshurun wrapped his hand around his broad back and said, "I do. I want you, and all the other marooned sailors on this island. I'm going to take you home."

The name moved slowly in him until it was confirmed, and his face changed from hollow confusion to bristling steel. "Our Lighthouse Keeper?"

Jeshurun nodded against the sleet.

"You were just a teenager when I left, when I aban … when I departed from Springwick Harbor. Why aren't you manning your Lighthouse?"

"You disappeared into the forest and no one ever found you. Some thought of the wolves."

"How is Ab … "

"He's doing well. When I return he will give me command of the Lighthouse."

"… Jesh … Jeshur-un … our Light? Our Keeper?"

Jeshurun nodded and squeezed him hard on the shoulder. "Good to see you again, Captain West."

The storm howled. Snow blanketed the alley. Jeshurun and Wade lifted Captain West through a doorway into a vacant room where they started a fire out of newspaper and broken boxes. As the night continued the snow piled on the sill but they at last were out of the elements. Captain West shivered uncontrollably until Wade found a twin mattress that covered only a portion of his body. Then he fetched snow and melted it in a cup to warm him. Captain West took the hot beverage slowly, lips burned from the severe cold.

"Than-k … than-k … you…."

"Welcome."

Wade found another blanket in another vacant room upstairs and covered him. His warmth returned and his mind cleared a little and he felt the sharp lucidity that had defined his life asea. "What is it you want?"

"I need you to sail the *Peking*."

"I'm not sailing anything. I tried. I'm cursed."

"You need the right vessel."

"She doesn't exist. You came all the way from Springwick Harbor to drag me back to Springwick Harbor to sail a boat that doesn't *exist*? Mad."

Jeshurun warmed his hands to the fire. "Tobiah can build you a boat."

Captain West widened his face at this expansive possibility.

Jeshurun laughed. "This passage to New York was not planned, but nonetheless we're here. We need you to captain the *Peking*, along with your friends, so we can sail home."

"Who brought you here?"

"Captain June, who died. Wade and I sailed with him. And Dion."

Captain West noticed Wade for the first time. "Who is this with you?"

"This is Wade. This is the boy. He survived."

He seemed not to hear.

"You didn't kill him, Dominic. He's very much alive. Feel him. Hold his hand."

He was looking at a ghost.

"Touch him."

He extended his hand gingerly and felt Wade's cheek. "You're not … dead?" The cold fingers sent chills through Wade's neck, electrifying him. "Oh salt, you're alive. You're well. Your dreams, your heavy dreams—the dreams of the town—are alive!" He barreled laughter deep from within his lungs and it made the corners of the room bow. He grabbed Wade and embraced him, strangling him out of joy. "You're alive, son! Wholly alive!"

Jeshurun said to Wade, "This was the man who tried to end your life. He guided your vessel with your parents into the Northern Point. You are the only one who survived."

Anger flashed through Wade.

Captain West's eyes flooded with tears and he stretched his arms around him and said with ingenuousness, forgetting for the moment Dion's plan, "Boy, I'm sorry. I'm so sorry."

But as swiftly as Wade's anger arose it ebbed away and was replaced by an absorbing toughness. As Captain West deepened his hold around him, he realized he felt no animosity toward the man; he would have made the same mistake, in his own hubris. Sailors are faulty, he knew.

"I've had a good life. Abner has been a good father. I miss him."

Suddenly Captain West could not control the emotions that were flooding through him. He wept. The death of this boy had been the weight bearing upon him all these years, the fear of having destroyed him and the dreams of the town. How could he live with himself after slaughtering the hope of an entire people? But now the burden snapped off his shoulders, replaced with soothing, relentless joy. He laughed.

Springwick Harbor was a tough harbor, an ancient harbor, filled with the light of a Lighthouse refusing even in despair to keep from shining.

Captain West leaped to his feet and danced like a child, lifted Wade and danced around him knowing that Springwick Harbor and her people were still alive with hope. Not even he himself, such a faulty sailor, had led to its demise.

"We have to get you home, Wade, at once, before...." He peeked over the window for Dion but saw only a flurry of snow. "We all of us need to sail home."

CHAPTER THIRTY-NINE

Late spring arrived with rain on the city. It fell under the glow of the streetlamps, glistened on stone and grass. The pavement shined. The light warmed the neighborhoods. It was a beautiful time, a passionate time, brilliant and full, a mosaic of color illuminating the thoughts and prayers of a people. While Jeshurun and Captain West searched for mariners among the homeless, Wade strolled through Central Park.

He paused at Huddlestone Arch to admire the yellow forsythia. Resting on the immense uncut boulders, his mind wandered back to Springwick Harbor, the sun setting behind the Lighthouse. He wondered what lay beyond the horizon, beyond the south seas? What sunrise might overtake him if he sailed far into the west? He dreamed heavily, envisioning washing a schooner with Joy, adventuring across the seas to find the unbounded freedom of life.

He heard music drifting through the American Elm. The leaves rolled and swayed. The beautiful leaves rose and dropped. It unfurled him. A deep anchor weighted him. The music surged through his bones. A harbor and a people. A sound schooner. A secret dream. A new adventure. An ablution. A healing.

A musician was speaking. "It's been tough. It's been rough. You're tired. We barely move. Barely hear anymore. The sounds are everywhere but we fear to be opened. We're all touched, all broken, by this heavy harm. But there's healing.

There's healing. There's wonder in healing. So let's roll, let's roll. Let's let our bones riot and flow. This is the Healing Bones Tour. And this is our song."

An alto saxophone broke out in painful, solemn measure, cool anger on the grass. Then a quartet of strings worked in behind her in rhythm, raising from the earth the wearied. A trio of acoustic guitars began to strum, soothing and resonant. A trumpeter joined in blowing sharp, powerful notes that snapped the trees. Heavy rumbling followed from a drummer. Finally a tenor in hot, melodic joy lifted the eyes of a people refusing to be silenced or crushed. A healing harmony.

Wade stood on the fringes in awe of the people. A mother feeding her child in her lap. A man resting his cane against a trunk. A teen and his brother lying patiently on the grass while their parents swung their toddler between them. A youth in dreadlocks with eyes closed in the rhythm. A pale girl adorned with piercings folding her arms self-consciously. A circle of smokers passing a hacky sack. An elderly married couple in thin bifocals reading by booklight with blanket draped over their legs. Sisters with foreheads touching and tears streaming together.

The music opened them. Their bones. Their blood. Their harmony. Hurt passed. The dark anxiety bled into the ground. And in rhythm they came together, sharing their hands with those around them, free from fear. Finally free. Free to let the sun lift them away.

His bones flooded. He longed to be carried with them to an everlasting light. What vessel did they sail? Where were they going? What were their dreams? What joy, what grace, awaited them? He longed to be touched by tenderness and compassion and strength in their heart. Longed to see them sail their own vessel, their own adventure, discover their dignity, their deep courage. His bones cried for a blessing, a renewal, a swift catharsis ending an agony. He stepped closer, neck crooning to feel the music and the people.

It was dark. The park was lit by lamp. The rain glistened through the light.

"Hello Wade," he said.

Wade froze. The healing music cut off abruptly; he couldn't hear it. There was a crowd before the stage enmeshed and moving. But his mind had been shocked out of the music that unified them.

"How are you getting along as a marooned salt?"

The words were grating. Powerful, shrill metal. A train tugging him back to the dark.

"Do you need any encouragement?"

Wade spun into a swollen tongue and eyes so vacant they looked like shells of glass. He gasped. An eerie tingling coursed through him. He wasn't sure he liked the vinegar honey flowing from those lips. He had given up Cape Race and all its luster for life in Springwick Harbor. But his words were rekindling the latent desire that was burning fast and nervous. The inferno he feared had come at last.

The months spent looking for Captain West and these frigid winter months in the city should have frozen forever that latent desire. But the thawing. The struggling urging in rebirth. He fought to suppress it, to be forever cold. But it surfaced in him and bulged in the blood beneath his skin. And his veins flushed with the opening.

"Come to my boat."

"What boat? Where's your boat?"

"Come to my schooner. The *Vermillion Mourning*. You've forgotten. Oh dear."

He thought he had forgotten. In the months since arriving in New York he had struggled with the harsh life of a homeless landlubber, marooned on an island without hope of rescue. But had he forgotten her form? The intense push of her line? Had he forgotten the terror of being aboard her as she sought his doom? He had embraced the island with a gusto, but now that he thought about it, every one of his footfalls on this solid rock had made the thorn of the schooner wedge deeper.

"I can't go with you," he said weakly.

"Then I'll go with you. Where do you want to go?"

It was too much. The powerful intimidation was too much. He wasn't ready for it. He wanted to be safe and free from intimidation, free from the spell, from temptation. But the tempting was turning his heart and bending it until he saw life upside down.

"I want to go to the schooner."

"I knew it. Come on, old boy. We'll go."

But he couldn't go, not now. Not when he was sharing music with people—the evening healing. He felt sorrow for his past, and he longed to be touched and grown again. "I can't go with you. I have to stay here."

"It's good music."

Wade's eyes glazed over hearing this false interest jar against his own sincere intensity. He *wanted* to be with the people. He wanted their goodness to become a real dream. He believed a man discovering his vessel is the highest joy given by the mercy of grace.

"It's good sound, Wade. It moves you. Look at them."

But the pulling. The twisting. The jarring viscosity.

"There's an endless oil just for you, waiting at the Sound. They'll come. Because you'll be there, waiting."

But the painful rending. The agony of doing what wasn't right.

"I'll even show you how to cast off. It's up there, Wade. The whole thing."

The darkness. The heart trapped in cement.

"I can't go—I mean I can't go with—" but he couldn't say it, because he didn't mean it. The powerful tongue of Dion was too much, overpowering him, emasculating his conscience.

"Am I supposed to know who you are?"

"*Know* me? Son, you're living me." He laughed brutally, his heavy neck full of grit and strain. Then he turned with a cutting grin. "We sailed together. Remember? Aboard that boat?"

The thorn was thick.

But the island had withered him—not just his limbs but his vitality and the life he had lived before the island. In fact, being marooned in this heavy block of earth had consumed his deepest awareness. There were too many mysteries here needing to be answered by right, if not strange, questions. For example, how was he going to get all these castaways off the island? But his life before landing here had been washed away; there was no earth outside this block of rock and steel.

"Remember? We sailed for Bannock Pierce? For the Hostel Sound Lighthouse?" He slapped him on the shoulder. "Hey it's me. It's your Dion. The old lissome, nimble, strong-chested, smooth-armed, powerful-legged boy of yore. I've come for you, buddy. You're gonna sail. Because *you're* a sailor."

Wade's chest deflated, revealing his weariness. This rectangular island had become his home. He was a bum now. Stranded now. He was as impressive as sewer, adjusting to the horror. And the people. He couldn't leave these other sailors stranded on the island with no means of rescue.

Dion smiled. "Come on now. She's real. She's truly real. She's been here the whole time. Could've sailed off the island the whole time. Could've been safe."

Wade's mind bogged in the swamp. His muscles slowed. His nerves missed altogether and it felt like someone was spooning Jell-O into his cavernous middle.

"Wanna dance? She's a marvelous, savory, seaworthy thing."

"I don't want to dance," he said numbly.

"I don't want to dance either."

"I want to go home."

"Do you really want to go home, Wade?"

"I wan—"

"Think about it. What do you really want to do? If you could do anything?"

"I want to be home."

"I thought so. The Hostel Sound Lighthouse is waiting for you."

"That's not my home."

"Remember? You don't have a home. You're homeless. You're stranded. You need a vessel. The only one here is her and she's going one direction. Yep—to Bannock Pierce. Now you can choose to die alone in this city, or, if you're brave, you can man the helm and get into the sea where you're meant to be. Now think."

"But I want to be with the peo—"

"Uh huh. Think good thoughts. Intelligent thoughts. This is how the old men discovered Spanish cheese."

Wade closed his eyes and his dark thoughts spun out of control. He felt creamy and just the right temperature. "Where did you say she's going?"

"She's going to your home. To your Bannock Pierce. To your Hostel Sound Lighthouse. When you get there you can ditch the boat—I don't care. Do what you want. But for the rest of your days you can climb that tower to your heart's content. It's worth it."

"You're a strange man."

"I'm an awfully strange man."

Wade laughed.

"Wanna go?"

"How will I get there?"

"Now I know for sure you're a silly goose. You're going to sail. It's going to be a brilliant endeavor. You'll tell stories to the children."

"What about the people? The sailors? What about Jeshurun?"

"I know. The whole island is begging for a show. Not everyone is fit to sail, Wade. Not everyone can fit aboard the *Vermillion Mourning*. Let the people make their choices. You're lucky to have a way off the island."

Wade laughed half-hearted. "You can't sail a boat like that with only one person."

"Oh, ha ha and la la la. But you can. I had a buddy haul her out and stick a screw on her. She's a motorboat now. You don't even have to hoist a sail—even though I had those silly boys bend on fresh tanbark sails. No halyards to haul on. Nothing to trim. No worries about wind or apparent wind or fetching the wind. It's just you and a boat and the sea and nothing else. It's gruntwork. And you should be damn proud you're a grunt with a set of fingers."

"She's not seaworthy."

"She *is* seaworthy. We sandblasted the barnacles, tore out the worm rot, replaced the planking, recaulked the seams. Replaced the standing rigging. The running rigging. Bent on new canvas. Made the deck watertight. Painted her Bloody Water. Rove her with fresh hemp—if you care. She's what everyone thinks of as a phosphorescent animal. She's a new vessel, Wade. She's just for you."

"Who did this?"

"A low key lot of landlubbers. People who aren't assuming anything. They worked hard."

"I don't want to go aboard."

"Go aboard. You don't have to. But don't worry about the Horn. You conquered it. You're totally at ease. A real master of the sea, and you need a new adventure. Let's go fight the way a boy is supposed to."

"What do you want me to do?"

He laughed heartily. "Run, boy! *Run*! Run to the *Vermillion Mourning*!"

Before he realized what he was doing, he was running madly, against his conscience, to the *Vermillion Mourning*. Running madly down the streets, blazing blindly through cross traffic without bothering to stop, darting in front of cars who screeched to a stop, honking, pushing past pedestrians, clipping them and knocking them down.

He ran with a vicious sorrow, a brutal self-love, a possessiveness. All the people on the island didn't matter at all to him compared to his glory as the Keeper of the Hostel Sound Lighthouse. He would give them up, he would sacrifice them—just to be fed in the light, no matter how dark in the light.

He reached South Street Seaport, gasping, hurling. The *Vermillion Mourning* rested against the dock, just behind the *Peking*. He stepped aboard. The heavy hammering in his heart returned. He saw stars. He plopped onto the deck too dizzy to move. His mind spun out of control and he felt himself drowning in a rush of starlight. "I don't want to be at the Lighthouse.... I want to round the Horn." But he rose and readied the ship for sail.

"Where's Wade?" said Captain West, standing with Jeshurun at the edge of the crowd in Central Park. When they realized he had strayed off, they came searching for him and found The Healing Bones Tour and guessed he might be here with the people. They searched the crowd, moved through them.

In the middle of it, Jeshurun spotted him, standing on the fringe talking with Dion. He shouted to him but the people were too numerous, their voices too overwhelming, the music so sweetly alive. Then he saw Wade turn and run away from the concert toward South Manhattan—for the schooner. Without hesitation Jeshurun barreled through the crowd, knocking people down to get to him. Captain West followed hobbling in his wake.

Dion stood at the fringe smirking, his face torn upward in merciless contempt, knowing that he had finally ruined Wade. The boy would reach the vessel and cast off and motor—just as he had hoped, having conspired with a few other financially-endowed lubbers to fit the schooner with a screw so one person could by himself power it without need of hoisting a sail—to Cape Race, where he would be dashed against at the rocks. And when he died, he himself would be ready to crush the town with all its hopes and dreams. It would be easy to manipulate Captain West into pirating the *Peking*, the old half-salt. He wasn't worth anything. Too weak. Too weak physically. They were odd friends. It was funny.

Jeshurun barreled into him like a linebacker. He hit him with such force Dion's head snapped back and he bit off the tip of his tongue. He went through him, leaving him in his wake, continuing through Manhattan. All he cared for was Wade.

As he lay stunned, half conscious, Captain West came limping past him, saying, "What's that from your tongue, Dion? Losing your words prematurely?" And he followed Jeshurun in pursuit. He understood where they were headed. He knew the way to the *Vermillion Mourning* because it was next to the *Peking*. He was never going to compact with Dion, he knew in himself, not ever in his life. He had made mistakes, too many mistakes, for which he was sorry. But now he felt new life, new breath. At whatever the cost, he was going to do in his power everything to make a wrong disappear and see first-hand a right.

He ran hard, determined to catch Wade before he left. And then something miraculous: Just as he felt his body was going to give out, he found in him a Williwaw. It was as if a blast suddenly pushed into his clothing propelling him across the island—far faster than he could have ever run otherwise. A surge of adrenaline rushed through him. The wind picked up his feet. He felt so light and free that the years on his body mattered nothing to him in this gorgeous moment.

Wade didn't know how to start the motor. He had cast off, but the *Vermillion Mourning* rested against the dock, still, as if nervous about going into the water with this new screw from her stern. He fumbled with the buttons but the engine wouldn't ignite.

Dion came out of his stupor slowly. Blood poured from his mouth. The children around him shied away in fright and the mothers shielded them, ushering them quickly away. He looked like a half-eaten zombie, stumbling across the grass. He had to catch them. He couldn't let Captain West sail on the *Vermillion Mourning*—that ship was Wade's destiny, not anyone else's. He had to get him on the *Peking*. They had to sail back to Springwick Harbor and fulfill his dream. He knew how to keep his dream alive, it was familiar to him, he understood himself in its construct. Captain West would help him. That's all he wanted from him. He ran drunkenly through the park in pursuit.

"Wade! Wade, stop!" shouted Jeshurun, arriving at the dock.

Wade spun with a vicious self-protection in his eyes. "I have to do this."

"I know you do."

"You can't stop me. I'm going."

As if he hadn't heard, Jeshurun said again, "I know you do, Wade. Take me with you."

"I won't survive."

"I'm not asking you to survive."

Wade lost his words before they left his throat. "Then why would you come?"

"Because I don't want to be anywhere else. Because I'm willing to bring you home—no matter what becomes of you. I'm your brother. I love you."

Wade stood solidly on the deck, looking at him disapprovingly. It wasn't Jeshurun's business to come. "Well, then show me how to start this thing."

From a stationary position, Jeshurun leaped over the caprail and the stanchion onto the quarterdeck, spanning three feet of water plus a change in height. He studied the console. "See this button here, where it says START? You push that." He pushed it. It started.

"Oh."

While they were busying with the throttle, Captain West came limping onto the dock. Perceiving that the gap between the vessel and the dock was too much to stride over, he barreled, "Throw me a line!"

Wade quickly fetched a hawser from the lazaret and heaved its end to the waiting hands of Captain West. "Make yours fast around the sternpost!" he said. Wade complied. Captain West braced his feet against a cleat, then with his powerful torso, he pulled slowly, then with momentum, the entire vessel back to the dock, and strode aboard. "You and your silly foo-foo jumping, Jeshurun. You step aboard a boat like a man or not at all."

Jeshurun laughed.

Wade milked the throttle. The *Vermillion Mourning* started to pull away. But before it managed much distance, Dion came sprinting, zigzagging, into the water, chasing them.

"What's this?" said Captain West. "Jetsam?"

Dion fumbled to speak, blood gurgling out of his mouth. He snapped into a tone of conciliation. "I'm sorry. Throw me a line. I'm sorry for hurting you. Please throw me a line."

The *Vermillion Mourning* was starting to pull away from him.

"Throw me a line! I'm sorry! Captain West, I'm sorry!"

"You should bite your tongue more often, Dion. I like hearing what you have to say. It's an improvement," barreled Captain West.

Jeshurun looked consolingly at Captain West. "Maybe we should throw him a line."

Captain West gasped. "Jeshurun, I can't believe what you just said. But maybe we should."

"I'm sorry! I want to come with you! I don't want to be on this island forever! I'm sorry!"

"I think he's sorry, Jeshurun," said Captain West.

"I think you're right. Let's throw him a line."

Captain West coiled the hawser with his shoulders and in one powerful, fluid stroke, heaved it so the line smacked Dion in the face. "Hold on. We'll get you."

Dion swayed, then regained his bearing slightly, fumbled with the line.

"Hold on to it, Dion."

Dion was fumbling with the handling.

"You've got to grasp it," said Captain West. "If you can't grasp it, we won't help you up."

The schooner was pulling farther away.

Dion gripped the line savagely, a bloody fierceness in his teeth.

Captain West hauled on the line until Dion was aboard. He lay on the quarterdeck panting, Captain West and Jeshurun standing over him, Wade steering the vessel through the Narrows.

Dion looked up at them in conciliation. "Thank you."

Captain West and Jeshurun exchanged glances. They smiled silently to each other.

"What?" said Dion. "I'm done with my ways. I'm changing my ways."

They exchanged looks again and stood akimbo, their sailor legs spread far apart feeling the muscular roll of the schooner.

Dion felt a gnawing pit eat through his stomach. "What?" he said weakly, then passed out like a drunkard.

Jeshurun inhaled deeply feeling the painful destiny of the schooner and its men knowing that at last, the trap for Dion had been set.

CHAPTER FORTY

Off the coast of Newfoundland the storm struck. The thunderous water ripped up the sea. Waves slapped over the bow and swamped the deck, flooding the holds. Heavy wind shredded the sails hurtling the schooner forward out of control. Swells crashed over the stern one after another, swamping Wade, Jeshurun and Captain West.

A wave crashed over the bow smothering the forecastle. The schooner moaned, hesitated, then pushed the water through the scuppers and reemerged. Another wave smacked into the binnacle, shattering the dome. The card spun randomly with the schooner as she tossed to port or starboard.

Though they had hoisted the sails with aid of the windlass, the schooner still behaved like a wayward raft. The foremast wobbled incessantly, waiting to topple. The life raft, which Abner had purchased from a catalogue, had been washed away. The motor rumbled, the propeller churned, the schooner plodded. But in the blinding storm there was no direction.

The three huddled together at the helm with Wade steering and unable to use the smashed compass in the binnacle. Why be here? Why drag these two with him? Why not sail for home, forget the deprivation? But he couldn't. He didn't have the power to say no. He felt himself being propelled toward the rocks—an inglorious end. Without hope he moved forward, resigned to suffer his fate and drag down these two who were with him. But he was willing to end his life as it had begun, as flotsam.

Jeshurun served as Keeper, Wade knew that now; Jeshurun alone kept the light of the hearts of men in his blood. And he kept their light alive in the grace of his hope and will. But Wade also knew that Jeshurun did not keep the premature end anywhere in him, and that was why he did not jerk the helm away from Wade and steer them home. This was Wade's own fateful adventure, his personal discovery. If he did not risk all and discover himself now, he never would. He knew that Jeshurun's free will wanted Wade's full life—and any life worth living in full must first before it find its death.

Dion lay shackled in the forehold. When they had first left the Narrows, he had fainted fearing Jeshurun's strength. Wade had determined that he himself was going to dash the vessel against the rocks of Cape Race and be done with him forever.

It's a storm, said Captain West to the group. Jeshurun clenched his teeth.

Wade felt the storm in himself. He could end Dion's life. It was a struggle. Even though he knew that Dion was ill, and that he would rend Wade sideways through a hawse hole for the thrill of it, he felt regret, even now, for letting him suffer his fate along with the fate of the schooner. They were all destined for the same inglorious end. But he couldn't let him meet that end bound in a dark, smothering hold. He couldn't let him go, not this man who had inspired him to take up his maiden voyage asea, whatever the impetus behind it. Some thing in his heart was made fast to him—an unmistakable thump that pushed and pulled him to himself. He felt him in his blood.

Giving Captain West the helm, he went forward pretending to use the head foreward of the galley. But when he was out of sight behind the galley housetop, he dipped below into the forehold to be with him.

It was dark. Wade found the flashlight dangling loosely next to the ladder. He used it to scan the musty hold until it found the prisoner. He looked cold, weak, emaciated in the sloshing water. His eyes flickered weakly with the pale heat of the flashlight. They had been motor-sailing for over two weeks without food for Dion and little more for the others.

"Do you see her?" said Dion.

Wade crouched at his feet in the water.

Dion coughed. "They might wreck us," he said.

"It looks ominous," said Wade. "The clouds look ominous."

Dion tipped his head back against the post to which his wrists were tied by a constrictor knot. He eyed him through heavy lids as though asleep. "This is where you become a sailor. Here is the test. Behind those clouds is the Keeper you've craved your entire life…." He swallowed.

The sound of the twin motors made the 250 ton schooner vibrated as it chugged through water. Thunder and lightning struck the sea.

"I'm sorry this is happening," said Wade. "You know I have the power to wreck you."

Dion tried to scratch his chin with his shoulder. He laughed flaccidly. "That's what I want. All of you aboard, like this. All of you dashed against the rocks. I have no life, I never had life. I'm just here to take yours. And Jeshurun's, and Captain West's. Your selfish ambition is going to cost you and your town quite a bit of damage. Anguish. Suffering. Hopelessness. Despair." He coughed violently. "I'm sorry for you, I am. It's quite a load on one's conscience. But don't worry, I've got you." His eyes glistened with pride.

In his insolence, Wade writhed to feel compassion for him. The planking, timbers and beams moaned against themselves through the water begging to break apart.

"One hand for the ship, the other for yourself," said Dion. "Save yourself while you can."

Suddenly a tremendous wave rolled the vessel. Wade tumbled in the hold, crashed into the portside ceiling and timbers, into the underside of the decking, then fell to the sole again as the schooner righted herself. Blood gushed from a gash on his forehead. Dion lay unconscious, his shoulder grotesquely out of joint.

Even though he felt remorse for doing so, Wade fetched two belay pins and twine and tied them to Dion's ankles using constrictor knots. And he thought to himself, finally, Let him sink. He's not you. He staggered up the companionway to join the others.

"Jeshurun! Captain We—" he wanted to tell them that it was a ruse, this whole sail. It was a bait pulling them down. But he couldn't. He was too appalled at the horror of their condition—that they really were going to die, and it was because he had been too selfish and blind to realize it. The two were clinging to the helm, alive and alert, soaking wet. "We've got to go home!" he shouted, limping aft. "We can't continue! We'll be dashed to pieces!"

"I'm afraid it's too late for that, son!" said Captain West through the wind. "We're low on fuel and our sails are shredded! We have to go forward!"

Sickening fear punched him in the gut and he hurled. "Then let me steer! Let me get us out of this!"

"You can't! We're bound together!"

"Then lash me to the helm! Save yourself!"

Jeshurun calmingly settled his eyes into the scattering fear of him. "We're bound together," he said. "Our fate is whatever it will be, together. This is the best end."

Dion wrenched his body out of the hold, laboring up the companionway bearing the blocky weights of the belay pins, holding a strange new boathook, grotesquely flared, which he had stocked before the sail, and he came grueling at Wade. "It's time for you to know the truth of who you are, Wade. Don't worry, you'll sing down the stars after I tell you this." He glared murderously from Jeshurun to Wade. "Did Jeshurun ever tell you the little scandalous story involving your past?"

Wade braced himself. "Tell me what?"

Dion sneered through the overpowering wind. "Hasn't Jeshurun told you who we are?"

Wade searched the coldness of him and turned to see consolation visible on Jeshurun's face. Jeshurun squeezed his shoulder. "What do you mean, Dion? I'm a sailor. You're a bilge rat. Isn't that clear?" He searched Jeshurun for a confirmation of humor, but found none. "What's going on?"

"He didn't tell you about our relation?" said Dion.

Wade felt like his thoughts were sinking into the deck. "What …?"

Dion's jowls looked as savage as a canine's. "That we have the same mother?"

Wade backed away toward the transom. His hamstrings touched the caprail. One more step and he would fall overboard. "It's not true."

"Believe what you want. You'll die just the same. In fact we're about to die together. At last. I can finally exhale."

Wade turned to Jeshurun. "You told me he came to Springwick Harbor on foot."

"And you came via boat," said Dion. "Our mother had me and she didn't like the thing in me, so a few years later she had you. She didn't like me because I wasn't a sailor." He grimaced with the shoulder. "So here we are, asea. And I'm ripe to witness how your destiny as a sailor ends you."

Wade plopped down on the caprail. A large swell splashed his back. "How can you be so much older than me?"

Jeshurun jerked him off the caprail until they were seated on the gearbox aft of the helm. "Wade, listen...."

Wade pleaded with his hands, "But he's *older* than me!"

"I'm not that old, Wade," said Dion.

"Snakes sometimes aren't that old," said Captain West.

Dion curled his lips and thrust out his tongue.

Wade braced himself for Dion's attack.

A giant wave swamped the bow, sending water aft, knocking Dion to the deck.

Dion seethed in his bitter gale. "It was by design that this happen. I've trapped you. You won't survive this sail. None of us will survive."

Wade crumpled with the sinister gravity bearing down upon him. He scattered his eyes at the chaos of the sea for escape. He gripped the helm feeling the silvery hatred of his brother in him. Was this the blood he felt in himself? Was he as him? Had his heart faltered, from the beginning?

Dion turned to him. "You're sailing for the wrong reasons," he continued. "You're just like me, a quack. Imagine any other end but it won't matter; you're going down with me. We're going down together."

The punishing wind flung the vessel forward, heeling her over. It took all of Wade's strength to cling to the helm and keep himself from hurling into the sea.

Jeshurun's cool ears had listened to enough squawking. "You two came from the same womb," he began, holding Wade close. "But his heart in its goodness is as foreign to yours as wet from dry. Our Father, Abner, has permanently adopted Wade. We are sealed now, forever, in a brotherhood, deeper than the physical sea. He now lives in the family he was destined for, a homeless seafaring clan thankful for the harbor given it." He turned vengeful at Dion, heavily bent on ending his life. "So step away from him, Dion. It will go easier for you."

"But I need to free him from his helm. He'll die unless I unhelm him. He has to be freed from the *Vermillion Mourning*."

Jeshurun moved over the slanting deck toward him.

"Okay. I'll step away." He backed off. "But can I come at you? Do you mind if I share my boathook with you? That's not in the script but I really like the sound of it." Dion minced toward him, boathook in hand.

As the schooner rolled heavily, Jeshurun backed down the companionway into the saloon. Dion, baited by bloodlust, followed. The vessel rocked with the waves and as each wave splashed over the transom, water splashed into the saloon. The next wave was so large that when it splashed down the companionway it knocked Jeshurun over. Dion charged at him.

He rammed the flared edge deep into Jeshurun's side. Jeshurun fell against a table onto the sole. He lay in shock, punched open, coughing. His face was long and pale.

"Think you can stop me?" said Dion. "I'm stronger than you. I always will be."

He pushed the boathook deeper. Jeshurun felt it grinding into him. The pain was unbearable.

"Think you have any power at all? I just speared you, my Moby Dick. Ha, I got you at last. I speared the pasteboard mask and what's behind it, in one deft thrust!" He pushed it farther. Jeshurun grimaced, in shock, hands quivering. "How does it feel to feel your universe closing in around you? To feel your sea couched to swallow its ruler? From my angle, this is where your sea ends, and mine begins. I'll just wait till your lungs fill with blood and then sell the oil that's left of you to your Dad. Doesn't that feel right?"

He pushed it farther and touched bone. Jeshurun's face caved inward. Dion twisted the point. "You goon," he said. "You monomaniacal goon." And he twisted harder. "Risking your harbor for one boy. Such a lost hope. The boy and you and the harbor are perishing, with me. Just remember that after I pull this out and you start bleeding everywhere, when you have an oblivion of regret, remember one thing—that your little Wade, who was meant for so much in your sailing community, is sealed in my blood. I'm taking him with me to our destiny. The rocks. We'll be dashed together. A sweet salty lick."

Jeshurun grabbed the boathook with both hands and, eyes locked on him, pulled it slowly out of himself. Blood spurted from his ribs. And walloped, he stood. Trying to pin the blood to his body with his palm, he leaned to the quaking false sailor. And he whispered in his ear, "Come aloft, Dion.... *Dare* ye." He staggered up the three steps into the galley, out the foreward doorway to amidships, slipping over a stream of blood. He flung the boathook into the ocean.

Numbed, Dion followed him through the galley and met him, at the breakbeam. He felt powerless. He felt his body being pulled down by the angst of the Keep. Jeshurun, haggard, climbed the starboard foreshrouds, slowly, deliberately. Dion followed, like a clueless orc, laboring up the ratboards, the clunky belay pins taxing his effort.

"Are you scared of a landlubber?" he tried to jeer, his words shallow. "You, of all people? You're the Chosen Keeper, a landlubber like myself. You're not destined for the sea. You're not destined to be here. This isn't in the script, either. So why are you here? Isn't this my dream? Didn't you promise me I could have my dream? My dream is to be you. To be the Keeper. You're endangering yourself by being here." As he spoke, his words seemed to wane as Jeshurun's resilience waxed, blood and water was flowing from his side.

While they climbed, Captain West held onto the helm with all his strength. The storm punished the vessel in the grey blackness of the clouds. He knew any moment the vessel would crash into the rocks, but with Wade aboard he had to keep him alive as long as he could. He had to guide them into the safe narrow inlet.

The waves flooded over the deck. The vessel rocked bearing the full strength of the storm. She heeled to leeward severely and they had to hold onto the gearbox for support, to keep from being swept into the sea.

Jeshurun reached the futtock shrouds and climbed onto the crosstree. Dion followed clumsily. They were over one hundred feet above deck. A fall to the deck would kill them. If they fell into the ocean they would eventually perish from the frigid cold. Jeshurun hooked around the foremast to the portside crosstree and waited, crouching, clutching his side.

Dion reached the starboard futtock shrouds, climbed onto the crosstree. He peaked around the mast at Jeshurun and laughed. "You're smart to take my boathook. That was a strategic move on your part. Job well done," he said, trying to convince himself with his own words. "You didn't see my fid?" From his trousers he pulled a long, slender, pointed fid, capable of impaling him.

Jeshurun was gurgling with every breath, wheezing from the climb. But he was crouched and calculating, waiting, for one hope. He moved to the end of the crosstree.

"Abner's not going to rescue you, Jeshurun. He's not going to save you the way he saves all those shipwrecked mariners."

Dion climbed around the mast, the belay pins weighting his every movement, joining Jeshurun on the portside crosstree. "You don't have enough blood in you to be the Lighthouse Keeper forever. Today is the day I tapped you at last. The Lighthouse will go dark. How does it feel to know all your mariners are entering into an age of darkness?"

"It's not what I want. It's what Abner commands. And I'm willing."

"You like letting blood, your own precious blood—everyday, to fuel the lamp?"

"I like it and everything more, when mariners find the safe harbor to rest."

Dion crept closer.

"I like it when sailors enjoy the freedom and safety of the seas."

"I like that too. I like that you're letting blood. So why are we fighting?"

Jeshurun climbed onto the upper portion of the futtock shrouds and made the short distance to the masthead. Letting go of his side, he grabbed the mainstay with his bloody fingers and climbed hand over hand across. He stopped midway between the mainmast and foremast.

Dion laughed nervously. "You made a mistake," he said, the terrible angst pulling him down. ".... I'm born to reach the heights."

Jeshurun inched a little aft and waited. From the blood, he looked like a channel nun.

On deck Captain West was steering with all the life in him to make it to the small inlet that might, if everything went right, provide safety for the battered vessel and crew. It was tenuous. In this storm with visibility so reduced it would be a miracle to find the small fjord and sail in. But he had to try.

"Can't we drop anchor?" said Wade, peering aloft into the darkness for Jeshurun and Dion.

"It's too deep. But try. Do you know how?"

"Yes."

"Do it fast!"

Wade sprung forward, fighting the heel, until he reached the anchor. He unlashed the five hundred pound anchor from the caprail and strained with everything in him to push it overboard. Captain West was shouting from the quarterdeck to guide him but Wade couldn't hear. He strained and pushed underneath the fury of wind howling through the rigging. For one brief moment it relented and he suddenly heard Captain West screaming. He looked up at him who was pointing madly ahead of the bow. Wade turned.

Aloft, Dion sat on the crosstree and waited, refusing to follow Jeshurun onto the wire. His necklace dangled from his neck, weighted like a plumb line. He threw the fid as hard as he could and it struck him in the abdomen but failed to impale. It fell to the deck. Dion flung himself onto the wire in pursuit. Though he had run him through, his wild hatred had failed to pierce Jeshurun's cool reserve. Midway, he stopped. The burden of the belay pins, made of solid iron, progressively taxed his stamina. He realized he didn't have the strength he needed to make it off the mainstay. Intense fear coursed through him. Jeshurun climbed the rest of the way to the main crosstree and, clutching his side, now waited for Dion to move. But he couldn't, so weighted, so paralyzed.

"Don't let the heights fool you, Dion. It's a long way down."

The chaos of the waves flung him to and fro on the wire. He felt his grip loosening.

Jeshurun shouted at Captain West, who turned the helm hard. The great boom gathered momentum and swung heavily over, slamming into the portside rigging, jolting the vessel to the keel from an accidental gibe. The mainmast cracked. Dion lost his grip and fell ten stories, slamming into the deck. His bones cracked like the thin shell of a crab. His heart-shaped necklace shattered between the deck and his skull. A wave crashed over the railing, swept it to sea.

Wade's full, wild eyes took in the rocks looming only moments away from the bow—but he couldn't move, paralyzed. Terror cemented him to the deck.

Captain West was shouting, "Wade, get away from the bow! Come aft!" He put the helm hard over to reach the safety of the fjord but suddenly a heavy sea overwhelmed the deck. Before anyone could react, the vessel struck the rocks at the entrance of the fjord.

The sea pounded the vessel, dashing it against the rocks. The masts toppled, sending Jeshurun into the sea. Captain West stayed with vessel as long as he could but uselessly; a wave swept him overboard. Wade was cast with the wood against the rocks and lost consciousness. And the cold night passed as the lonely sea drank her dead.

CHAPTER FORTY-ONE

Lying face down in the sand and rock with dawn rising over the waters, Wade regained consciousness. Cold and numb, he blinked from the sand in his eyes as the tide came in. His head spun, couldn't move from the rocks, couldn't remember why he was there, turned achingly to regard the surf. Flotsam of the shipwrecked *Vermillion Mourning* lay floating in the surf, nothing larger than a plank or two. The whole vessel had been destroyed, purged against the rocks. Wade felt an aching hollowness in his stomach. All had been lost. Jeshurun and Captain West were nowhere, but Dion's body lay face down, lifeless, in the surf.

A breaker pushed him forward. He stumbled and fell down and landed on his arm—and something either broke in his shoulder or his shoulder popped. The pain was so horrible he choked and felt the wind knocked out of him. A breaker crashed over him and pushed him forward over sand and rock. His ragged shorts and shirt were torn in the thighs and hips and back. He used his right arm trying to stand up. A breaker crashed at his calves and he stood up. Stumbled out of the water.

"Jeshurun ...?" he tried to call, but weakly, his voice drowned in the waves. Jeshurun was nowhere in sight. He was alone. And he felt empty and hollow, like the shell of a discarded crab.

When he sat upright his abdomen throbbed from a deep purplish bruise the size of a cantaloupe. The tide was rising and he had to move and he slowly, painfully rose to his feet from the wreckage, crawled through grass and rock to the top of the beachhead, a steep grassy knoll, collapsed.

His head spun and he saw stars and vomited. They might be inland but he couldn't move. He was disoriented and dizzy. An hour later he had advanced less than a yard. They had to be around. He couldn't be alone. He needed care. He passed out.

When he awoke the sun had nearly set. Shivering violently he tried to rub his arms for warmth but his arms were too numb and he knew that if he didn't find shelter soon he'd go into shock.

A towering shape caught his attention and he looked at it upside down: a little farther inland was a lighthouse. His heart sputtered. Writhing, gnashing, he rolled onto his stomach.

He looked back toward the sea, and could see, faintly, a white splash churning violently through the waves. A shark, he thought. A school of sharks. There was a great thrashing of water, and he turned, against his will, to the lighthouse.

"Bannock ...?"

Was it the Hostel Sound Lighthouse?

"Mr. Pierce ...?"

Grimacing until the muscles in his face ached he rose to his feet and drug his foot for the lighthouse, breaking into a limping run. His ankles felt broken and he fell several times. Tears rushed down his face—this was the thing he had wanted for so long, finally coming true. It felt strange, unreal. It wasn't supposed to feel as hollow as this. Did a dream always feel this thin when it came true?

He reached the workroom. The sun was flaming pink and orange and yet the lighthouse wasn't lit. He had to light the lighthouse. He had to be the one to guide the mariners. Finally, he had to fulfill his duty.

But the door would not open. He tried to bash it in. The sun was about to dip and he had to get inside because a ship was approaching on the horizon—he could see her with her sparkling lights. His heart pounded fearfully—afraid of failing the duty given him, afraid of failing as the Lighthouse Keeper.

Frantically he searched around the outside of the workroom and he found a metal pipe. With several wild, desperate whacks he broke the padlock. But when he pushed the door open, it fell off its rusted hinges. He went inside.

Fighting the horrible musty smell he searched the wall for the stairwell and limped upward, upward in the darkness on the shaky wooden steps.

"Mr. Pierce …?" His words sounded hollow in the cold frustum. "Mr. Bannock Pierce …? Mr. hello …?"

He climbed higher, and as he climbed higher, the natural light pouring through the lantern filtered down through the dark frustum. The splintery rail stabbed his palm and he jerked his hand back. Then he reached the lantern. The breathless afterglow of the sunset. The vessel approaching Cape Race.

He pulled off his shirt and trousers revealing the linen apron he had stolen from Abner which he had worn hidden underneath his clothing throughout the voyage. Also in his possession was the windproof lighter given him by Dion, which he had snatched off the branch and taken with him the day when the *Vermillion Mourning* had departed. Eagerly he focused on the lantern. His heart pounded against the dying sun. Was his dream coming true? The vessel was approaching and all he needed to do was light the lantern and save the ship from the rocks.

But strangely an oddness crept at him. There was no oil in the lantern and no wick and no lens at all but only the rusted lantern surrounded by numerous shattered glass panels and baseball-sized rocks lying on the walkway.

The wind cooled his wet apron which now felt uncomfortable and restrictive. He wanted not to wear it anymore, but out of desperation and lust he fumbled with the lighter. It sparked. Sparked again.

But before he could light it, the gnawing awareness crept into him again. He felt uncomfortable truth pressing against his being with the irrationality of this lighthouse and his arrival. Cool, unnatural pain touched his nerves. For the first time in this journey to the easternmost reaches of his life he saw a vague, goring anxiety of what he had done. Three sailors dead—his brother dead among them. His father dead, from hopelessness. His thoughts, once before concealed and bound tightly in a complex history packed by want, now tore into the open without concern for his pain. Perhaps he had been wrong after all in his quest to become the Keeper. Truly wrong.

Overwhelming confusion burst from him. He lost trust in himself. A hand gripped the trash in his heart and ripped it out of his body, the sharp gutting wound. The hand hacked out of his fragile skin his fears and doubts to get at the yoke, and the hand pierced the yoke and the yoke ran free and well, bleeding into the lantern, into the light. Out of a desperate flooding the end came, and the end came and he let the end take him down.

He surrendered to his shame and guilt and they flooded in, this brutal self-destruction. As he lay pinned to the lantern, he shook as he reflected on his history, and it hurt being shaken because his history had been shameful, a terrible hurt, a history without promise. In his dark humiliation a deafening explosion beyond all comprehension struck him. The awareness of his fall, which he had not realized until now, at this moment, came fully upon him and he realized now fully what he had done with his dream of loving: he had massacred the people whom he loved most. Jeshurun was lost. Captain West, lost. Captain June, lost. Abner, lost. Tobiah and Walter and Bethlem and Hank and Abigail and Springwick Harbor, all lost.

He wept.

Bannock Pierce did not exist. The Hostel Sound Lighthouse did not exist.

Springwick Harbor met him then in his nude shame. He did not love. What he loved, had no substance. He loved the vain beauty of lust. He loved frayed cloth. He loved brittle skeletons. He loved thin shells in light. He loved withered membranes, as useless to him as his own skin. He hated what loved him, and loved what hated him. He wept.

A purging gushed from him.

Am I Bannock Pierce? Am I a man I want others to worship?

Oh help me.

Bannock Pierce does not exist!

He wept, and the hand clawed him. The fingers squeezed his nerve. He wept in denial. In fear—afraid of the finality of the hand upon him. His tears dripped onto the empty lantern of the lighthouse. A shell.

As he lay dying, feeling like he was passing into forgotten land, a grief like rain washed the dryness in his limbs, pounded the deep coast on his bones, filled and pounded his lungs and chest and replenished lost feeling, and the waters flooded upon him a foreign and strange and absurd and rude forgiveness, and it hurt and it cleansed him and he strove to undue the struggle of his life. Writhing, establishing the great sculpture of torment destined to scar his life, he still breathed, still sought the freshest air. His breathing thickened amid the flood, and death and life all at once consumed his being so that he neither moved nor wanted, but existed by the sheer weight of grace.

Let me pass into the abyss. Wrath dismembers me. I am sorry.

Love crushed him.

He died.

Bannock Pierce no longer existed.

For a long time he lay on the walkway of the abandoned lantern unable to move, toying with the lighter. The storm had passed and the darkening purple sky blew through the holes in the glass. The wind toyed with his hair, lifting it, stroking it. The lighter caught.

Come home, Wade.

He sprung to his feet. Looked at the ship closer on the horizon.

Abandoning his dream of being the Lighthouse Keeper, he dropped the lighter through the aperture beneath the lantern. It flew, still lit, to the bottom of the frustum. When it landed the entire base of the frustum suddenly exploded in flame. The fire crept quickly up the conical structure.

His movements slowed to a crawl. There was no way down. The thought of jumping into the flames flashed in his mind. Suddenly a shape burst through the glass. Jeshurun, bloody and mangled from his fight to reach the shore, grabbed him, shouting, "Wade, outside! Come outside! I found a ladder!" Wade did not respond, dazed by the speed of the rising flames. Jeshurun ripped him from his crouch. They went through a shattered panel, hurried down the ladder.

When Wade touched the ground, he collapsed, his body exhausted and surging with adrenaline. Jeshurun knelt, clutching his side. He was gaunt. Expired. He took his elbow and led him away as the Cape Race lighthouse burst into an inferno. With Jeshurun's help, Wade started to limp back to Springwick Harbor.

"Where did you go?" said Wade shamefully, keeping his eyes from his injured brother.

"Captain West and I were washed out to sea. I swam against the current, fighting sharks, until I made it ashore. I don't know where Captain West is."

Wade trembled fearing the loss of his brother.

The large, three-masted square rigger arrived and dropped anchor. A skiff came ashore. Abner stepped through the surf and came on land carrying a medical bag, eyes hunting for Wade. When at first Wade saw him, he flinched, thinking of the stolen apron and his flight from Springwick Harbor. But as his father approached, his face illuminated by the inferno of the lighthouse, Wade saw not anger nor hatred nor wrath—but compassion. He felt his eyes screaming for him, *You're alive! You're alive! Alive!*

Suddenly his heart gave way. He broke free from Jeshurun's guided hand and ran, limping, into his father's arms. His father ran to him and embraced him, pulled him to his body. And he kissed him and kissed him, burying his son into his chest, and he closed his eyes and rested.

"You're home," he said. "You're home. I've been waiting."

His deepest hope for his son had come true, at last: he was home, a rich celebration. "Thank you for the fading light," he said. "We knew where you were."

The blazing lighthouse licked at the towering sky. Already it had begun to collapse into itself. By morning it would be a heap of ash.

"Dad …?"

"Son."

"Dad.…" He burrowed his face into his father's broad chest, shivering uncontrollably. "It was wrong for me to pursue the Lighthouse Keeper.… I'm sorry. I'm sorry for straying. Jeshurun, I'm sorry. I'm so sorry.…"

The glass of the lighthouse burst from the intense heat.

"I just wanted … I didn't mean.… Please let me come back."

Abner pulled him closer. "I have some borscht waiting for you," he said.

Wade's shoulders dropped. He felt dizzy. His father held him even closer.

"But aren't you supposed to be manning the.…"

"Tobiah is serving as Keeper."

Wade's tears stained his father's chest as he became aware, for the first time, of the mutilation of Jeshurun's body. The aftermath of his fight with Dion, the fight with the school of sharks, the fight with the rocks had coated skin with blood. Blood flowed from gashes on his head and shoulders and back and legs. The wound on his side was appallingly butchered. He looked like a red nun … like the Springwick Harbor Lighthouse itself.

"I caused Captain West's death," said Wade, fingers quivering.

"We picked him up," said his father. "He's aboard *Roseway* right now, safe and warm and enjoying hot soup, which you're about to enjoy."

"I'm so sorry…." he wept. "Dad, please take me back to Springwick Harbor. I'm not worthy to be a sailor. I'm not worthy to be your son."

"I forgive you," said his father.

Jeshurun dropped like an anchor to the ground, having finished his run. Blood spurted from his side. His eyes closed. This victory.

Wade hurriedly untied the linen apron now damaged from the journey and stopped the wound. Jeshurun was shivering violently. Abner knelt. Felt his weak pulse. And he said, "He's not going to make it."

"*No*! Don't let him die! Don't let him die!" cried Wade.

"He needs blood. He's not going to make it to the vessel."

Wade wept. "Please don't do this. Please get him home. Please get him home, Dad."

Abner unzipped the medical bag. "We will. But I need your arm."

He offered it.

"I'm going to transfer your blood into his," he said. "A great deal of it. It's the only way he's going to live. It will work because you both have Type O blood."

Wade lay next to his brother. Jeshurun felt him and instinctually opened his arm. Wade lay his head on his chest as if a young boy again, suffering another nightmare, when Jeshurun would come into his room and lay on his bed, and Wade would lay his cheek on his heart and hear the *thump thump … thump thump* of his life that would send him into a deep slumber. He could hear his life now, sputtering and weak. *Thump… thump …… thump … thump….* Wade took his hand.

Abner commenced. He cleaned off their arms—Jeshurun's riddled arm and Wade's—and inserted the needles and began to fill a bag with Wade's blood. As the blood transferred into Jeshurun, Wade could hear slowly the strengthening *thump thump ... thump thump* of the life of Jeshurun returning, and his own heart beating harder.

"Jeshurun.... Can you hear me ...?" said Wade.

"I hear you," he said woozily.

"You know something? You're something else."

Jeshurun smiled. Laughed a little. "You know something? So are you."

Wade fell asleep on his brother's chest.

While the blood was being transferred, Abner applied a more permanent bandage to Jeshurun's side, then the same to the cuts and gashes. After some time, both were ready to be transported to the anchored vessel. While they were motoring, Abner draped a blanket around them.

Wade clung to him. His father stroked his head and said, "All of Springwick Harbor is awaiting your return. All this time we've been planning to celebrate your new life on the seas, when Jeshurun becomes the Keeper. You'll see when we arrive."

The terror passed out of him, the fear of the open water, the fear of falling, of wrecking, ending as one destroyed, dashed against the rocks, crushed by water. That terrible wreck now lay permanently within him.

CHAPTER FORTY-TWO

Fall in Springwick Harbor is beautiful. The maple trees yellow and the blossoms flame orange and fall to the ground like fragile sunsets. Families rake their yards and jump into the piles then go indoors for cider and split pea soup. Homes warm with fire, chimneys smoking. And then the families share the wealth of Thanksgiving: turkey and stuffing and stories and games and rumors of undiscovered lands. The town waits for winter and the carols and the promising rain of the spring and summer and the hope of setting sail. This was the season when Wade Burns returned.

With Abner, Jeshurun, Captain West and the crew of *Roseway*, he sailed into Springwick Harbor and docked where the *Vermillion Mourning* had once but no longer thorned the village. The memory of her doom had vanished and now the town felt full of life. The sailorfolk gathered around *Roseway* and once the mooring lines had been made fast, Wade, wearing navy blue trousers and matching work shirt, stepped onto the wooden platform to a shout of hoorahs. Abner followed him.

When Jeshurun stepped onto the dock, the town hushed. His gruesomeness. His bright eyes. His limp. His scars. His joy. No one spoke for a long time. It was a beautiful sunny day, and the light was glowing over the entire harbor. He patted his brother on the back and said, "Welcome back, Wade."

The sailors cheered after him. "Welcome back! Welcome back!"

"We knew you could do it!" said Walter, who along with his crew from the grocery stood brimming with happiness.

"I've got a roast beef sandwich for you when you're hungry for it," said Bethlem.

The olive-faced Abigail stepped forward from her sandy-haired boys. "And I baked apple turnovers, warmed a mug of Sailor's Nog." She smoothed out his shirt. "You look handsome."

Wade cast his eyes from Abigail to the crowd. Next to her and Bethlem was Hank and Thaddeus and Walter—all of them shining bright.

And next to them was Clement Oakes, the captain of *Weathering Peace*: For too long now he had struggled with the fear of losing his vessel to rot. But now that he knew she was safe, his sharp facial features had softened.

Then there was Mariana Thrush, long boned and reddish, the keeper of the Lantern Fish. She had dreamt night and day of seeing her tavern filled with hearty sailors back from a fresh sea run. She was a first-rate mariner herself, having sailed throughout French Polynesia. She longed to sail there again and rekindle the friendships from her past after the long, terrible years.

And beside her were the Honeycutt twins, Gail and Grace, blond and freckled, too young to remember when Springwick Harbor was a bustling port to another world. In the attic of their father's abandoned sail making shop they had been secretly stitching their own sails in the hope that one day Tobiah would build them a craft. (In time, all vessels would be built.)

Next to them was the oldest salt in town, Mastiff Hood. Sunken eyes. Sunken ribs. Sunken knees. The joy of sailing in and out of the harbor had been a distant memory. But over two years ago one morning when Wade had run down the barren streets of the town to visit the *Vermillion Mourning*, he had spied on him from behind his curtain, hoping against hope in an impossible miracle. He had been the first mariner in town to donate to the piñata his most treasured bounty: his gold ring, which he had been pierced with when he crossed the equator on his maiden voyage around the world.

These sailors and more—men and women of varying complexions and compositions and voices—all were gathered that day to welcome back Wade and Jeshurun and Abner and Captain West.

Wade took them in. The gleaming teeth. The sparkling eyes. The handshakes. The embracing. All of them waiting to discover the *Timshel Auxiliary*. And he said to them, rather sheepishly, rather humbly, "I'm glad to be here."

Walter hooked his thumbs around his belt loops. "That piñata in my shop is waiting, son."

Wade's eyebrows raised out of a feeling of modesty. "But you said it was for a sailor."

Walter nodded and his cheeks widened into a smile. He folded his arms. The harbor town stood behind him. "That's what I said, for a sailor—especially for a sailor who runs well. It's filled with goodies."

Wade dropped his eyes. Drug his foot along the dock. Grabbed his arm. Said just above a whisper, "Then it goes to Captain West, who deserves it after his return."

Captain West appeared from below. He followed the rest of the crew over the caprail onto the dock. When the crowd saw him, a vibrancy electrified them. Bethlem stepped forward. "You're back," he said in his humble baritone.

Captain West nodded.

"I knew you'd return."

"It would have been impossible without Jeshurun or Abner."

"That's why I knew you would."

"I'm sorry to have strayed."

Bethlem looked at the others in the crowd, at Jeshurun and Abner and Tobiah. He clenched his fists as if ready to punch someone. Bursting open he shouted, "My hero's returned. I can go sailing again!"

Abigail and the rest of the town laughed.

"How does it feel to be home, Wade?" said Tobiah in his large white overalls.

Wade dropped his eyes again out of shame. "Suppose my pedigree isn't all that admirable." The smiles went away. "So I'm brother to a bilge rat? How did that happen?"

Abner put his arm around him. "You're not him."

"But how were we related?"

"You had the same mother."

"Was she bad?"

"No."

"Was my father bad?"

"Your father was a beloved captain. He was good."

"Dion's …?"

"He was a longshoreman. Hated the sea. He didn't have the courage to explore it. For that reason, he hated the people who did. When Dion was born, he bled his hatred into him. Raised him to destroy things. By the time Dion was in his teens, the whole coastal town where your mother and soon-to-be father lived had virtually been abandoned, like a ship on the verge of sinking."

By Wade's expression, he looked like he was on the verge of dropping over an edge. Abner held him closer.

"The father died. Your mother remarried. You were conceived. When Dion found out about it, he set fire to the town. Your father and mother—and you inside her—escaped on the last vessel to leave that port—the *Rosewater*. They were bound for Springwick Harbor, because they wanted you to be safe.

"But Dion arrived here first, determined, out of jealousy, to destroy you and the town. That was why he tried to become the Keeper—so he could fill up the sky with a false light and guide you and every other inbound mariner into the Northern Point.

"When I banished him from the Lighthouse, he swayed Captain West into piloting you into that terrible cauldron. The storm destroyed your vessel. But I salvaged you. And Tobiah salvaged the first component that would become the *Vermillion Mourning*: the mainstay.

"That vessel fulfilled what she had been created to do—destroy the destroyer." He squeezed him gently. "But that story is over now, Wade. Let's embrace what waits for us on the horizon: It's time for a new chapter." He hugged him, and Wade's trepidation ebbed.

"I'm just glad I'm here," said Wade, "with all of you. I'm glad we're together at last."

"Well. What do you want to do now?" said Tobiah.

He studied the faces of the salts, all energized, eager with the true thing that had enveloped Wade. He could not sense what they were looking at. "I don't know, Tobiah. Drink Nog?"

Tobiah patted him on the shoulder. "Why not sail? There's a schooner waiting for you. Look across the harbor."

Wade studied him with reservation.

"Go on. Look." He pointed across the harbor to his shipyard where a vessel stood waiting to be launched into the water. She was beautiful. Wade gasped. He felt an electric current rip him to her.

"*What*?"

"This is the vessel I built for you," said Tobiah. "This is your birthday present—celebrating your birth in the Horn."

Wade thought back to the knoll with him over two years ago. "Does she have a name?"

"Not yet."

His heart leapt. He tried to swallow. He stood in disbelief of her shape, a schooner waiting for the sea, waiting just for him, waiting to make adventure together, falling in love with her long, smooth, graceful sheer and solid prow and her sloping transom that took his breath away.

He jogged around the curve of the harbor to the 42 foot schooner, placed his hand on her smooth and sturdy teak hull. He felt her solid planking made smooth by careful artistry, her slender and powerful curves and the line of her breast and beam. Tobiah, Abner, Jeshurun and the crowd followed.

"Can you hoist me?" he said to Jeshurun.

Tobiah laughed at his malapropism. "We have to launch her first. But before that you have to give her a name. And christen her."

Wade's heart pounded.

"Can I make a suggestion?" said Tobiah.

Wade swallowed and nodded and braced himself for the name. Tobiah made such beautiful things with his hands, such beautiful words with his heart.

"Call her the *Vellamina Dream*."

The name seemed to spread like a wind through the harbor.

"She's longing to write the journey of you and your friends into a neverending story."

The name deepened and strengthened him.

Thaddeus handed him the sailing ship piñata from the grocery. Wade took it out of surprise. "But this is for a sailor," he said again, bewildered.

"It's for the captain of the *Vellamina Dream*," said Tobiah.

The piñata was heavy.

"Go on," said Thaddeus. "Christen her."

Wade stumbled to the bow. "What's in this thing?"

Walter winked to Abigail, Bethlem, the others. All of them knew what was coming.

He reared back. "I christen this vessel the *Vellamina Dream*." He whacked the bow. The piñata burst into a rainbow of rubies, sapphires, emeralds and gold—gemstones of every kind and color—spilling to the ground, an iridescent deluge of treasure.

"All the sailors in town gathered their most prized bounty from their favorite sails and have given them to you, Wade," said Walter. "We dream for you to hide them again, so we can sail out for them and live new adventures."

He blinked not realizing the full weight of the gift given him—his duty as sailor to carry the dreams of the town. Weak and gracious, he thanked them for this life.

And yet something distracted him. He gazed at Jeshurun in disbelief, fumbling over words for a thing that had troubled him the entire passage home. "The lantern is lit from your *blood*?"

The crowd fell still.

Jeshurun cupped his hands together in a humble gesture. "That's what makes my Springwick Harbor Lighthouse unique."

"But your *blood* …? How does that burn?"

"With courage. Because our community is thirsty for a pyrrhic illumination. It's what I want. Sailors see the light and know it's the bloody Lighthouse guiding them. They see the light filtered through the blood-stained panes and know they're almost home. At rest in this cozy haven we are free to drink the life that shines upon us. If you go deep enough, my blood is like a spring for the wick of our harbor."

The red glow was personal and knowing—pulling at the blood in a sailor's limbs. It made sense. The holocaust daily of Jeshurun's life made sense.

He robed himself in the now permanently damaged apron, forever in his Keep, a memento of the journey to Cape Race. The sailorfolk fell silent gazing at him and the Springwick Harbor Lighthouse so imposing and sound.

Overcome by the immensity of Jeshurun's sacrifice, Wade fell to his knee. He swallowed hard. That explained the gross metallic smell emanating from the empty casks and the coolness of the oil room. He stared at him in shock. "But I don't under … you light the Lighthouse with your …?"

Jeshurun hugged him hard. He enveloped him. "I love you," he said. And wept.

And Wade wept. "I love you…. Thank you for not giving up on me."

A resonant silence—sailors wrapped together, at rest from their long journey home.

"Sail, Wade," said Jeshurun. "See the Lighthouse for yourself." He drew his attention to the *Vellamina Dream.*

Wade flushed. Regained his composure. He inhaled, exhaled. "So I get to hide our dreams?"

"These dreams and more," smiled Tobiah, tapping the hull of the *Vellamina Dream*. "We're all eager to get underway. So you better get going."

Wade pushed the prow. The *Vellamina Dream*, fully rigged, slid into the water. It rocked gently then settled. Longshoremen pulled her to the dock.

As he took the teak helm, tingles surged through him as he imagined this schooner carrying him under stormy clouds, amazed that at the core of him was the deepness of her hull and helm, this oneness in spirit. Now that he was aboard, he had found his true home, the reassurance of a new identity. He had become the sailor he was destined to be, never in his dreams imagining a blessing so honest. It was a pleasure now to be lost and unknown under the heavens.

"Sail her, Wade. Take her to sea!" shouted Walter.

"Go on!" shouted Thaddeus.

"What about Captain West? Shouldn't he be given a second chance too?"

"Captain West is going to serve as our pilot boat captain," said Tobiah, "to guide you and other mariners safely into the harbor. But your freedom is to carry our dreams." He gathered the bullion into a teak chest and handed it to Wade.

Wade's trembling hands stowed it below. Then he glanced into Tobiah's content, flooding eyes. "Will you help me raise the sails?"

He nodded eagerly. "We'll all help."

Walt's crew and the others stepped onboard and helped raise the main, fore, jib and stays'l. They embraced him and returned to the dock and helped untie the mooring lines. Wade turned to Jeshurun. "Wanna come?"

"I'm now the Keeper. I'll be waiting for your return."

Wade turned to Abner.

"I'm staying here with my son," he said.

"Tobiah?"

His barrel chest shook with laughter. "Of course! I've been longing to sail her for some time now! We have to test out that little vessel!" causing the sailors lining the dock to laugh. He hopped aboard and helped Wade cast off.

Sailing through the channel of the inner harbor, they crept through the outer harbor and out to sea, the town waving bon voyage.

"We can go anywhere," encouraged Tobiah. "Where do you want to go?"

Wade removed from his pocket the first bullion given him, the rose earring of Isabella. "We need to hide this first on an uncharted island, then sail for New York.—I'm hungry to find marooned sailors."

He noticed embedded into the planks of the pine deck flat glass hexagons so numerous he could not count them all, stretching bow to stern. Less than three inches in diameter, they varied in color. Most of them were clear, but some were tinted red or blue and seemed to be arranged in patterns. "What are these?"

Tobiah stroked his beard. "I handmade them. They're deck prisms. They bring light below. They're unique. Long after the sun has set, they're able to shine into the night. Like stars."

Wade imagined what it would be like anchored in a cove, lying in a hammock below, looking up at the glowing deck prisms. It would feel like an illumined womb. The stars blanketing his body. The sea and the heavens warming his blood.

What was this divine grace? His journey had been wrong, but now by no effort of his own, these radiant gifts, one after another, crashed over him like wave after wave over the bow. He told Tobiah he hadn't imagined life could be so good, now that he was asea.

"It gets better," said Tobiah.

"Can it get better?"

"It gets better. And better."

"Can it, though? Better than this?"

"It gets better, Wade. It's better enough to be the best."

"But how?"

"I've in me some ships. I'm going to sound each mariner and study the sheer of his soul. Build him the vessel that will reveal his depth. Each vessel created to be the outward character of her Captain. Each one with her own journey written in her beam, in her hold, under her keel. The vessel's form asea will reveal the true gift of each salt. They'll be the best ships—better than … well … they'll be the vessels that shine through the storm."

"Isn't the *Vellamina Dream* such a vessel?"

"Aye," he nodded. "Hold fast. She is. And these vessels, too. They will have their own story, their own dream. Vessels who will go where no other boat dared ever to imagine."

"Those sound like stories waiting to be written about."

Tobiah laughed. Rain washed the deck, the rigging, the sails, the helm. They trimmed the sails and ran down the Oregon coastline awhile then veered for Hawaii on their way across the Pacific for New York. Tobiah shared with him all the good things Abner had planned for the sailorfolk of Springwick Harbor and they talked night and day of ways to bring their dreams to the town, to the *Timshel Auxiliary*. The deep, nourishing sea flooded them. Enjoying the sea, the sail, the hope—the vision of forgiveness and love—they basked in everlasting freedom, the everlasting grace, the everlasting gift of the unending joy of a deep and wet, endless embrace.

THE END

EPILOGUE

Sailing is the journey into grace. If he is lucky, a man born of the earth takes to the sea and discovers the adventure he is destined to live. Aboard his vessel, his past is forgiven. He sails out of joy. His dream is found on the mercy of the sea, and he lives because the waters pour their mercy into him. They flood him with the sail he does not deserve, the one that never ends. By grace, he sails into paradise.

Fitted with courage, he sails into danger in love with the life given him, challenged to bend his spirit to his dream, braving the current and the storm. He risks all for the one journey in search of the eternal, where dream and storm share the same rain. The hope of unfurling his strength drives him into the ocean, and at last he is flooded with his calling—a helmsman entrusted with the bounty of grace.

Once upon a time, Wade Burns had never been to sea, had never let anything master him. He was too afraid to be conquered, too in love with the weak things in life. He believed life was best lived fully alive, not yet understanding how death alone brings a man the peace he seeks. Afraid of grace, he sought what it was not: the lust for power and wealth, the lust to master love. He was not a sailor.

But a finished sailor is saved on the waters, made fast to the favor of the sea. His grace is thick from the overwhelming wind. He makes passage with friends, and they sail together into his dream. As he weighs anchor and the sails fill, he grips the helm and guides the bow into the deep waters; the deep, heavy waters—the everlasting sound. In his most precious journey, the unthinkable storm is his. Trough and crest drench him and he becomes humble in search of the deep. The beauty of death changes him, and he sails onward made alive by the mercy of the sea. By death he navigates his vessel into the welcomed harbor. In his courage he rests. He is free to be the sailor he is called to be.

If he is genuine in his surrender to his sail and his craft, the waters open around him. He is free to brave the wind, free to bear the heart of the storm, free to suffer the brutal cold until lost in the abyss. In the darkness, grace calls him by his new name, touches the hidden Keep within him, whispers into him a strength stronger than the death of the sea, and returns him to the sky. The hidden deep is full of men lost in want of life, but the sailor and his craft by grace are destined to sail into the light together, stronger now—stronger than death—cool and new, their risen life testimony to the power of their bond.

In the end, Wade discovered that when a man born to sail surrenders to his heart and lets the floodwaters drown him savagely, he becomes part of a world much larger than his own. He loses his life under the ocean, but gains a heaven far more real and overwhelming. And in this heaven he is free to make passage at his heart's desire, upon his most intimate vessel, fully alive with the courage to be brave at any watch, in any storm. That is the course Wade now sails—aboard the *Vellamina Dream*, chosen to run in the fresh wind free.

GLOSSARY OF NAUTICAL TERMINOLOGY

aft	situated in or toward the stern of a vessel.
after-leech	the aftermost side of a fore-and-aft sail.
aloft (to go)	to ascend a shroud for the purpose of work on any one of the lines or crosstrees, furling a sail, etc.
anchor lantern	a white lantern displayed when a vessel is at anchor.
apparent wind	the seeming speed of the wind in relation to the speed of the vessel.
baggywrinkle	the frayed ends of discarded rope used to prevent chaffing between lines and sails or other areas aboard a vessel.
bale	the tip of a boom, encased in metal, to which various lines and sails are secured.
ballantine coil	a way of coiling a line using alternating large and small circles to prevent a halyard from fouling when used again.
ballast	any number of heavy objects placed in the bilge or keel of a vessel to counteract the forces pushing against it, to provide stability and to prevent capsizing.
batten the hatch	to lash a hatch down so that water will not penetrate the holds.
beat	to sail into the wind, such as at close-haul.
Beaufort Scale	a scale referenced by mariners to ascertain the degree or severity of the wind asea. It ranges from a windless sea (Force 0, wind

	speed less than one knot) to gale-force winds (Force 11, wind speed 56-63 knots)
belay pin	a heavy, iron-made tool, shaped roughly like a tapered club, used to make fast halyards and various lines around the caprail.
bend	to lash or secure something such as a line to another.
bilge	the lowermost area of a vessel, directly above the keel.
binnacle	the brass-encased apparatus that contains the ship's compass.
bitter end	the working end of a rope used to tie a knot, etc.
block	part of a pulley system through which a line is reeved to move a sail, lift a bosun's chair, etc.
boathook	a long, spearlike tool with a hook on the end used to raise or lower an anchor or craft from the deck; also called a boatfall.
Borasco	A thunderstorm or violent squall, especially in the Mediterranean.
bosun's chair	a small chair suspended from a block by which a mariner is raised to attend to an upper portion of a mast.
bosun's locker	a small storeroom on the deck of a vessel located on the forecastle.
Bowditch	or; *The American Practical Navigator*, by Nathaniel Bowditch (1773-1838). Born in Salem, Massachusetts, the author was a mathematician known for his brilliance in ocean navigation. His tome includes information on piloting, celestial navigation,

	navigational mathematics, etc., and is widely referenced in modern day maritime communities.
bowline	a loop knot prized for its sturdiness and workability; various types of bowlines include the fingertip bowline, slipknot bowline, bowline in the bight, and running bowline.
bowsprit	the spar extending foreward from the prow, to which the forestay, jib, staysail, etc. are connected.
breakbeam	a small step in the deck located amidships that prevents water from traveling along the entire length of the vessel.
breast line	a mooring line extending from the bow of a vessel.
breasthook	a horizontal timber fitted in the bows of a vessel to add strength and to connect the sides to the stem.
Brisote	The northeast trade wind when it is blowing stronger than usual on Cuba.
broad reach	a point of sail slightly away from the wind, where the wind arrives from either the port or starboard quarter; between a beam reach and running. On many vessels, this is the fastest point of sail.
bulwark	the exterior portion of the hull that extends above deck, providing protection for the crew and a place to work lines, sheets, etc.
Cape Doctor	The strong southeast wind which blows on the South African coast. Also called DOCTOR.

Cape Horn	an unadorned rock at the southern tip of South America forming the northern boundary of Drake Passage; the area surrounding it, often regarded as the most dangerous sailing ground in the world.
caprail	a rail stretching around the deck, above the pin rail, wide enough to use as a seat.
carrick bend	a type of knot used to bend two lines together, suited for large-diameter rope.
catadioptric	pertaining to or produced by both reflection and refraction.
center of effort	the point on the sail on which the greatest force of the wind acts.
chainplate	a metal plate secured to the hull of a vessel to hold shrouds in place at the lower end.
chronometer	a timepiece used for determining a vessel's longitude.
Chubasco	a violent squall with thunder and lightning, encountered during the rainy season along the west coast of Central America.
cleat	a wood or metal object with one or two projecting horns to which ropes may be belayed, located either aboard a vessel or on a dock.
clew	the aft lower corner of a fore-and-aft sail.
close haul	a point of sail where the bow of the vessel is trimmed as far into the wind as possible without sailing into irons; also called beating.
clove hitch	a simple and well-known hitch, but not a secure one.

constrictor knot	a binding knot effective in its ability to hold things together, but extremely difficult to remove once tied.
cowboy	during the revolution of furling a sail, to sit atop the bale of a boom and flake the sail as it comes down.
cringle	located at the clew of a sail, used to stretch the sail taut.
crosstree	timbers located at the masthead, used, in conjunction with futtock shrouds, to provide support for the topmast.
day tank	on the *Vermillion Mourning*, the smallest of the three tanks (incl. fore and aft tanks) used for storing water.
deck prism	a conical piece of glass inserted into the deck in order to bring natural light into the compartments below.
dioptric	pertaining to refracted light.
doldrums	an area of ocean at the equator known for its lack of wind. Ships have lain idle for weeks at a time before passing through.
double sheet bend	a bend used to join stiff, slick or synthetic line, or to be extra safe when joining two lines together.
downhaul	a line and tackled located at the foremost end of a boom to tighten the luff of a sail.
draft	the measurement of a vessel from its waterline to the keel.
fairlead a line	to belay a line around a pin or a cleat, etc. so as to ensure that the line will not foul or cause difficulty when taking it up again.

fender	an object such as a tire or rubber bladder suspended from the deck in order to prevent chaffing while the vessel is dockside.
fid	a tapered hardwood pin used to open the strands of a rope in order to splice; a marlinspike.
fife rail	a rail around the mainmast of a sailing ship, holding belay pins and coiled lines.
figurehead	a carving set at the prow of an old-fashioned sailing ship.
flake	to guide a chain or sail, etc. by hand as it accumulates (as in the revolution of weighing anchor or furling) so that it folds over itself evenly, preventing it from fouling when the vessel again drops anchor or raises sail.
flotsam	the wreckage of a sunken ship floating on the sea.
fo'c'sle	an area of the deck located at the bow of a vessel, traditionally the sailors' living quarters (abbr. of forecastle).
foot	the lower edge of a quadrilateral sail.
foremast	on a two-masted schooner, the one foremost on the vessel, carrying the foresail and if needed, a topsail.
foresail	the sail hoisted from the foremast, foreward of the mainmast.
forestay	a line of standing rigging used to support the foremast, foresail and jib.
Fresnel lens	a type of lens designed with large apertures and short focal lengths, invented by

	French physicist Augustin Jean Fresnel and first used in 1823.
frustum	in terms of a lighthouse, the conical base leading up to the lantern.
Furious Fifties	the area of sea in the Southern Hemisphere located below 50 degrees.
furl	to gather in a sail and secure it, as with gaskets, so as to prevent the wind from influencing it, when at harbor or in a storm.
futtock shroud	a shroud located above and below the crosstree on a mast.
gale	a very strong wind (32-63 miles per hour).
gasket	a short rope used to secure a coiled line or sail.
gearbox	a compartment visible above deck which shields the axel of the helm from seawater.
gibe	a possibly disastrous occurrence when the vessel travels off course, changing its point-of-sail so that the wind forces the mainsail to shift violently from one tack to another. Rigging a preventer, as the name implies, prevents this from happening. (also gybe).
grace	undeserved favor; for a sailor, this means the freedom to sail into the setting sun while helming a sound vessel.
green can	in conjunction with a red nun, a channel marker used to guide a vessel safely into a harbor. A mariner keeps the green can off its port side.

gunwales	the upper edge of the side or bulwark of a vessel (sometimes pronounced [*gun*-nhl]).
halyard	a line used to hoist or lower sails.
hank	a small metal hoop around a stay used to attach a sail so that it will slide when furling or unfurling.
hatch	an opening in the deck that leads below.
hawser	a large rope or cable used for mooring or towing a vessel.
head	the upper edge of a quadrilateral sail.
heave-to	to come to a stop, especially by turning across the wind, leaving the headsail backed.
heaving line	a thin line used when a vessel is docking. It is bent onto a mooring line and then thrown to someone dockside, who then reels it in so that he can secure the heavier mooring line to a cleat.
heel	the sideward lean of a vessel due to the force of wind or wave.
helm	the steering wheel of a vessel.
holding tank	a small metal compartment used for temporarily storing human waste until it is purged into the sea.
Horse latitudes	a belt of calm air and sea located about 30 degrees north and south of the equator, between the trade winds and the westerlies.
hull	the exterior of a vessel, including the area that is submerged.
inclinometer	a device used to measure the angle of a vessel with the horizontal.

irons	a point of sail when the wind arrives directly over the bow, rendering the sails useless.
jetsam	goods jettisoned in an effort to delay a sinking ship.
jib	along with the staysail and flying jib, a headsail used to provide direction for a vessel. Sometimes in rough weather the jib is the only headsail used.
kedge anchor	an anchor with a stock crossways to its shank, ending in a crown whose arms extends to a fluke (with a bill and a palm) on either side.
keel	the central fore-and-aft line of timber running from the sternpost to the stem, located at the lowermost portion of the hull.
keelrake	to bind a sailor with rope and drag him under water against a barnacle-infested hull.
kevel cleat	a type of cleat fastened to the inside of the timber posts on deck. Mooring lines and preventers are often made fast to them.
knot	a unit of speed equal to one nautical mile (about 1.15 statute miles per hour).
landlubber	an inexperienced, earthbound person unfamiliar with the sea.
lanyard	a small line used for light duty.
lazaret	a small storeroom on the deck of a vessel located at the extreme stern; a glory hole.
leeward	the direction downwind from the point of reference (often pronounced [*loo*-erd]).

lift	a line used to raise or lower a spar (e.g. on a schooner, a gaff).
log ship	along with a reel and glass, an archaic mode of determining a ship's speed by counting the knots paid out in a given time.
luff	(of a sail) to hang limply as the vessel passes through irons during a tack; also, the foreward edge of a sail.
mainsail	the sail hoisted from the mainmast; usually the largest sail onboard.
mainstay	a support wire running from the masthead of the foremast to the masthead of the mainmast.
make fast	to secure a line, etc. so that it will not unloosen.
marlinspike	a pointed implement, made either of wood or metal, used in separating the strands of rope in splicing, marling, etc.
mast hoop	a hoop used to secure a sail to a mast.
mast	an upright spar used to hold sails, rigging, booms, signals, etc.
monkey's paw	in marlinspike seamanship, a piece of rope woven into an unsolid ball.
oakum	loose fiber obtained by untwisting and picking apart old ropes, used for caulking the seams of ships.
outhaul	a line that adjusts outward tension along the foot of a sail along the boom.
peak	the aft-most upper corner of a quadrilateral fore-and-aft sail; it is extended by a gaff.

pin rail	a rail with several slots for belay pins, where lines are made fast. Beneath the caprail.
port tack	a point of sail when the wind arrives at the vessel from across the port side; as opposed to a starboard tack.
port	facing foreward, the left side of a vessel.
port-and-starboard	a type of watch where hands alternate time above and below deck, without the benefit of a third watch to relieve the two.
porthole	a circular window set in the hull of a vessel.
pram	a small, flat-bottomed boat.
preventer	a line made fast to a boom and a cleat to keep the boom from an accidental gibe.
prow	the bow of a vessel.
Pullman	a uniform bunk located below deck where a sailor rests when off watch.
quarterdeck	the aftermost deck on a vessel.
ratboards	slats of wood in a shroud serving as a ladder, by which a mariner ascends or descends when going aloft; similar to ratlines, which are made of rope.
ready about	a command issued by the captain to position the crew at the appropriate sheets and lines for a tack. ("Ready about!")
red nun	in conjunction with a green can, a channel marker used to guide a vessel safely into a harbor. A mariner points the bow so that the red nun will pass by its starboard side ("Red Right Returning"). Also referred to as a channel nun.

reef	to partially lower a sail in order to reduce the area affected by the wind; as such, a safety measure during violent seas.
reeve	to pass a line through a block.
Roaring Forties	the strong westerly winds found in the Southern Hemisphere, generally between the latitudes of 40 and 50 degrees.
rogue wave	an unannounced wave which is sometimes high and powerful enough to swamp a vessel.
rolling hitch	a hitch noted for its trustworthiness and simplicity.
running rigging	rigging such as halyards, sails, buntlines, used for handling sails and spars (contrasted with Standing Rigging).
safety rail	a thin metal rail above the caprail to which mariners secure themselves by a lanyard to prevent themselves from being washed overboard.
saloon	a room below deck furnished with tables, providing a space for dining and various activities.
Salt	an aged sailor, possessing a wealth of nautical wisdom.
Santa Ana	A strong, hot dry wind blowing out into San Pedro channel from the southern California desert through Santa Ana Pass.
schooner	a vessel with at least two masts (fore and main) or more, the mainmast taller than any other.

scupper	an opening in the bulwark allowing seawater to flow from the deck, back into the sea.
scuttle; scuttling	to intentionally sink a ship for an advantageous end.
seize (a line)	a component of marlinspike seamanship where a sailor uses thread to wrap and secure a line so that it will not loosen.
sextant	a tool used at sea for determining latitude and longitude by measuring angular distances, especially the altitudes of sun, moon and stars.
sheer	the fore-and-aft disposition of a vessel, evaluated in terms of beauty and form.
sheet in/sheet out	to adjust the sheet so that the vessel will utilize more wind. ("Sheet in the fore!")
sheet	a line and tackle system used for trimming a sail.
shroud	standing rigging comprised of chainplates, turnbuckles, ropes or wires, ratboards (or ratlines), etc. that support the masts and spars.
single sheet bend	see double sheet bend.
skiff	a small motorized craft powered with an outboard engine, used for transporting people or supplies short distances.
slush	to lubricate the mast so that the mast hoops will not chafe. The mixture consists of turpentine, linseed oil and Vaseline.
sole	on a ship, referring to the floor of a compartment or hold.

sou'wester	a type of hat with a long, wide back and folded front, affording a mariner visibility and a dry neck.
spoon	a large wooden concave apparatus used to help position an anchor to the deck after weighing.
spring line	a mooring line extending from amidships.
stanchion	a metal post inserted into the perimeter of the deck as part of a rail.
standing rigging	rigging such as ratboards (ratlines), turn-buckles, chainplates, etc. that are fixed permanently on a vessel, offering support to spars, shrouds, stays (contrasted with running rigging).
starboard tack	a point of sail when the wind arrives at the vessel from across the starboard side; as opposed to a port tack.
starboard	facing foreward, the right side of a vessel.
staysail	a sail located at the bow; on a two-masted schooner, this sail flies from the forestay, beneath the jib, and its sheet is controlled foreward of the foremast. (abbr. stays'l).
step the mast	to position a spar in its slot so as to raise the sail.
stern line	a mooring line extending from the stern of a vessel.
stern	the back end of a vessel, where the quar-terdeck is located.
swab the deck	to wash the deck with saltwater for the purpose of preserving it, keeping it her-metic so that water does not penetrate the lower decks. Combined with Joy (the only

	cleaning agent that suds in saltwater), swabbing also purges any impurities soiling it.
tack	to change the point of sail by turning the helm and subsequently adjusting the sheets.
the sun … yardarm	an expression of optimism.
throat	the foremost upper corner of a quadrilateral fore-and-aft sail.
thwart	a seat on a smaller vessel.
tiller	on a smaller vessel, the helm.
topmast	a spar extending upward from the cross-tree of a mainmast, etc.
trade winds	relatively permanent winds on each side of the equatorial doldrums, blowing from the northeast in the Northern Hemisphere and from the southeast in the Southern Hemisphere (Bowditch).
transom	the aftermost area of the stern, above the water line.
trim	to adjust the angle of a sail according to a change in the direction of the vessel or the wind.
true wind	the speed of the wind independent of the speed of the vessel.
trysail	a triangular sail hoisted from the mainmast instead of the mainsail for the purpose of reducing sail area in stormy seas.
turnbuckle	a tool with left and right hand-threaded screws that is used to adjust the tension in standing rigging.

walk the plank	the path that all Oregon State Beaver fans encounter at the start of a football season.
waveson	goods which, after a shipwreck, appear floating on the sea.
weather bomb	an explosive development of weather.
whip (a line)	a component of marlinspike seamanship where a sailor threads a needle through the end of a line so that it will not fray.
Williwaw	A sudden blast of wind descending from a mountainous coast to the sea, in the Strait of Magellan or the Aleutian Islands.
windward	the direction upwind from the point of reference.
yardarm	aboard a square-rigger, a horizontal spar hanging perpendicular to a mast.

A Note of Thanks

Christie (I four cheese you!) My parents. Steve Sauter. Tim Baker. Brad Kleiner. Jason, Luke and Anna. Jane Freund. Alyssa Cooper. Thom Hollis. Grandma and Grandpa Cronin. The Cramers, Lendermans, and Cronins. Harry and Kay Krussman. Andy Carmichael. Jackson and Jeanne, Joel and Melinda and my Bible study friends. My teachers and coaches who have shaped my character and development as a person and as a writer: Mrs. Sasser, Carl Lino, Mrs. Deroy, Mrs. Nodine. Al Olson, Art Thunell, Max Goin, Matt Jones, Larry Matthews, Coach Flippence, Bill Robertson, Mr. Ediger, Mrs. Reynolds, Mr. Jones, Mr. Kimball, Mr. Echanis, Colette Tennet, Jennifer Cornell, Christian Winn. Thanks to my friends at Barnes & Noble: Barry Hunt, Sarah Jenks, Kelly, Sue, Tamara, Steve, Josh, Katie, Jared, Lynn, Nancy, Laura, Carlie, Michael, Jeremy. Thanks to my friends at Captain's Nautical Supply: Lance, Drew, Betsy, Mark D. Mark A, Mark G., Bob, Matt, Jon, John Chase, Nancy, Catherine and Chris. Thanks to my friends at Capital: Steve, Cathy, Kathy, Bret, Mary. My friends on Schooner *Roseway*: Michael Tolley, Marco Miller, Kyle Sundet, Kate & Jen, Rick, Anne, Lisa, Captain Sloane. Special thanks to Matt Molnar, my brother in the trenches. Thanks to Jesus Christ! And thanks last to the reader for your time and interest. God bless!

About the Author

In the summer of 1999 Samuel sailed as a deckhand aboard the schooner *Roseway* out of Camden, Maine. Working seven days a week, he helped sail passengers around the islands of Penobscot Bay on three or four day cruises.

A typical day would begin promptly at sunrise, first squeegeeing off the caprail and hatch covers so that the passengers could eat their breakfast without getting soaked with dew. Following breakfast, the vessel would weigh anchor, employing the passengers to help raise the fore and mainsails, the latter of which weighed about two tons. Depending on the route and the weather, *Roseway* would beat into the wind or sail at a broad reach, etc., tacking when needed, resting on the saloon housetop or deck in between tacks.

More experienced sailors warned the novice at the beginning of the season, when *Roseway* was being fitted out—and before any sail—that the yogurt and pastry he was eating for breakfast would not be enough calories to sustain him, which the novice scoffed at. He remembers one sail in late July when for dinner he ate seven whole chicken breasts, plus three or four bars of caramel brownies for dessert, neither of which tied him over for long.

One of the pleasures of the summer was when the crew would ferry the passengers on the accompanying skiff to an island to bake fresh lobster, often purchased from the lobster fisherman as he was catching them. For an entire summer, twice a week the landlubber ate perfectly cooked lobster in seaweed and saltwater, and it baffled him that the owner of the vessel, who had been sailing for his entire life, was so tired of the fare that he made sure the crew cooked a hotdog for him.

At night after the sails had been furled and the awning erected, and the passengers enjoying their aperitifs, the crew took turns serving a two hour anchor watch. One night, unbeknownst to all aboard, the *Roseway* lost her anchor off an island, right before the morning winds started to blow. It was an unforgettable summer.

Samuel is the author of *Warm Gold*, a historical novel set in Eastern Oregon during the 1890s, where impoverished miners must face their fears inside a dark, unholy mine to find gold—long after the gold is gone—in the impossible hope of discovering the Motherlode.

In 2016 look for *A Season for the Blessed*—a novel set on the golf course where a woman, serving as caddy to her husband, commits a rule breach that ends his dream of playing on the PGA Tour. In his anger he fires her, not caring that she suffered a miscarriage during the competition. After a long depression, she takes up golf to heal. Surprisingly, she qualifies for LPGA Tour. He agrees to caddy for her.

Also look for *Hope of Home*—a novel about a grandfather who is so frustrated by the materialistic traditions of Christmas that he shuns his role as Santa Claus, thus abandoning his family—only to lose them in a Christmas Eve tornado. To cope with his loss, he opens their presents.

Made in the USA
Charleston, SC
25 November 2015